Carey, have you ever made love before?"
He shook his head, afraid to speak.

"Don't you think this is all a little too much?"
Ikbal said. "I mean given your age, mine?"

He could not look at her anymore but had to
stare out over the blurred fields, back to the
tower. If he only knew what to do or say. Her
hand touched his chin and turned his face to
her.

"Don't look so sad. You must talk to me now."

"I love you," was all he could say.

---

"THIS IS THE KIND OF NOVEL
WHICH . . . REQUIRES A DELICATE SENSIBIL-
ITY, A POET'S SCENE-PAINTING, AND A
WORLDLY UNDERSTANDING OF THE MANY
FORMS OF LOVE. BROUGHTON POSSESSES
THESE GIFTS IN RICH MEASURE AND HIS
NOVEL IS PROOF OF IT."

—*John Barkham Reviews*

Fawcett Crest Books
by T. Alan Broughton:

A FAMILY GATHERING   23965   $1.95

WINTER JOURNEY   24369   $2.95

# Winter Journey

## T. Alan Broughton

FAWCETT CREST • NEW YORK

*WINTER JOURNEY*

THIS BOOK CONTAINS THE COMPLETE TEXT OF THE
ORIGINAL HARDCOVER EDITION.

Published by Fawcett Crest Books, a unit of CBS Publica-
tions, the Consumer Publishing Division of CBS Inc., by arrangement with E.P. Dutton, a division of Elsevier-Dutton
Publishing Company, Inc.

ISBN: 0-449-24369-9

Work on this novel was assisted during 1977 by a grant from
the National Endowment for the Arts.

Printed in the United States of America

First Fawcett Crest printing: February 1981

10  9  8  7  6  5  4  3  2  1

In Memory of Henry Robbins

... whose advice, encouragement, and friendship
have made a lasting imprint on this book
and on my life.

# PART ONE

# *Prelude and Fugue*

# 1

"You could have been more gentle, Frank. That's all." Nancy looked at him across the kitchen table and tried to ignore the bottle between them. "He's going to keep it all inside now, like he usually does."

"Wrong. Carey and I discussed it before we came home. I stopped the car and we sat by the side of the road and talked and he knows there's nothing to say. If he brought it up again, it was just sympathy he was after—yours, I mean."

"And why shouldn't he have it?"

His eyes were blurred, hair more disheveled than usual, and his mouth had that slight downward turn it slipped into when he was drinking heavily, the face of someone partially paralyzed. That made her even angrier, as if he were doing it purposely to remind her of her father, still sitting around years after his stroke, that same look on his face, but wordless, listening to the radio all day.

"You're too easy on him, Nancy. I tell you this was something between the two of us. I can see when he's acting phony. It was real out there. For both of us. I've never hit anything that big. Rabbits, squirrels. But a dog. Jesus, what an awful sound, and then the howling afterward." He was not looking at her, drank quickly, brushed one hand across the tabletop. "But anyway, tonight when he started choking up before he went to bed, that wasn't real. That was acting."

"And you know all about that. The acting."

The top of the bottle lay on its side near her, looking as if it might roll. She wanted to screw it back on the bottle, tight.

"I can tell when someone's acting."

"In others." She did reach out, but only to take the top and bring it back to her, holding it between her palms in her lap.

"What does that mean?"

"You see it so well in other people. In your students. But not yourself."

He took the bottle by the neck, and for a second she thought he would throw it, the way he had that glass two years ago, breaking the window over the sink. He often ended arguments that way, a foot through the panel of a door, fist pounding on the plaster until his knuckles were raw, like some struggling beast wound round and round in ropes. But the ropes were not hers. They were always there, mostly of his making, and even the glass was hurled against his own image he had seen in the dark window over her shoulder.

"What has that got to do with anything?" He did not throw but tilted it deliberately, filling the tumbler again with bourbon.

"Never mind. How did we get started on this anyway?" But she remembered her son's face as he turned to go up the stairs, that scorched look as if no one in this house could help him, as if being sixteen were the loneliest age of all. "I just think we let him down tonight."

"Speak for yourself. We were doing fine until you got all mushy about the poor little animals and mean human creatures and all that Walt Disney crap."

That was an argument as old as his duck hunting, which had not been resolved at all by the selling of his guns and the refusal to join his buddies again in their annual trip to Maryland. It never had been the ducks she cared about, even if they argued on those terms. What she envied was the time, all that anticipation and energy and so much she could not share. He sold the guns the same way he might throw a bottle—a quick angry trip to Philadelphia, the money flung on their bed, a petulance for weeks afterward that still surfaced when a flock went over in late fall or when Jerry teased them if he and Marianne came to dinner. He had given her nothing when he gave up the hunting.

"I didn't mean it that way, and you know it. I only said it didn't *have* to happen. You probably could have swerved and missed the dog."

He snorted, lips set firm. "Sure. And if it hadn't been afternoon and we hadn't been driving but were walking instead, and if the dog was a bird instead of a dog, nothing would have happened." For a moment she thought he was going to be amused, but he was frowning. "All that guff is just another form of sentimentality. We were there, and the dog was, and it had to happen and there was nothing that could be done about all that. Nothing."

"Fate," she said in a mock-oratorical tone.

But she wanted to move backward, slowly, gently. There had to be some way. He would make one of those gestures displayed to her but turned against himself, and then there would be days of silence, nights of lying there hearing him breathe, knowing by the sound that he could not be sleeping. He could go far inside himself, be obdurately distant, and even if she came to him, touching his body until he rose at last, he would not really hold her or look her in the eyes but would only plunge into her quickly while she would murmur, "Please, please," all the while knowing he was somehow punishing himself much more than her.

"You keep on thinking it was a matter of choice, then." He looked at her again, eyes half closed. "You know, we had a good time until that damn mutt decided to cross the road. I think you're jealous, mostly. You were when we left and you did your best to spoil it, not coming, prune-pussing us. And now you're trying to blame it all on me."

"You know you drive too fast."

He glared at her a moment before he slapped his palm on the table.

"Dammit, I wish you'd have a drink. Why the hell do I always have to be the only one drunk?"

She put the cap back flatly beside the bottle.

"All right. If that's what you really want."

She took the glass from his loosely curled hand. She could smell the mash, her stomach lurched, then she lifted it, choked, held it down, swallowed rapidly until it was gone. She coughed. Blurry-eyed, gasping, she realized he was laughing, not meanly but the way he would when they were in bed and he read something he liked; he would startle her, laughter boiling up, and his book would fall away laxly.

He was standing beside her and his hand pulled her head against his belly, palm on her cheek, and she could have pushed back, a fury in her for that burning where the liquor made its way. He stooped, face to her face.

"You dummy," and even though that was the voice of the director who knew all the parts by heart, she let him coach her and held still as his hands wandered, untucking her shirt, cold on her bare back, the other riding up the skirt. He was wholly, drunkenly absorbed in what his hands found—her breast, her cleft moistening to his fingers—and she wanted the bourbon to take her mind away, numb the uneasy sense that the struck dog, Frank's dulling face, were some awful pattern she could not understand.

She stood, not letting go of him, steering them up the dark stairs as if he were some lumbering piece of the night, his breathing so heavy beside her, her shoulder jamming against the wall. They did not turn on the lights, had their clothes off and were in bed quickly, and as if he were a toppled wave, he was on her with all his weight for a moment so that she could not even move her legs apart, and then he rose slightly on his elbows. She groped for his mouth, his tongue, trying to open her body to every hook and curve of him.

When she had come back from the bathroom, her eyes adjusting to the dark, she pulled the covers over them both and lay beside him. She thought he was asleep but his head turned quickly and his voice, very awake and low, said, "I couldn't explain it to him, the fact that there weren't any answers."

"Did he want any?"

"That's what he wants all the time now. And he thinks when we can't, that we're only concealing the answer. Oh, Lord, don't you remember how awful it was to be sixteen? All the time you're younger you think you'll get to a certain age and everything will be clear. You think people our age understand and just aren't telling. But what we're not telling is that we often don't understand."

It was true. Even when Carey did not ask for explanations, she could see the hesitation in which he expected answers to be given.

"What did you tell him?"

He described running over the dog again, and she closed her eyes, giving herself up to the images he raised, annoyed when he reported their long talk afterward, the car pulled over into a field somewhere near Valley Forge, Carey furious that there was nothing they could have done, as if he were experiencing the word "accident" for the first time, and Frank, of course, flatly, almost brutally trying to explain that some things had no explanations, were random and meaningless. The dog had crossed the road, as it often did—this time at the wrong time.

But she had never accepted his view of that blankness behind everything. How often they would end bitterly at odds, she asserting that if he was willing to settle for that fixed sense of the zero point behind anything, he would never get beyond it—the way he *thought* would shape the way it was. But he would always laugh, calling her a lapsed Catholic drifting into Christian Science, naïve to think that the mind was such a shaper of realities; her view of a freer will was only an illusion by which she preserved herself from seeing what he saw. And it had culminated in that awful year after her father's stroke, a date she could not forget because it coincided with Frank's rejection by the army just after Pearl Harbor. For days afterward Frank had seemed as paralyzed as her father, sitting blankly here and there in the house or talking disconnectedly to anyone who stopped by. She had insisted with a daughter's hopefulness that the lack of recuperation over the following months, John Shannon's lapse into greater silence with fits of petulance, were only the working out of his relationship with her mother and their world, of his way of seeing things. Frank had laughed a little meanly, as if to say, "At last you see," and when she had said, "What was that for?" he replied, "It's not just your mother, it's the pattern of his life and he's living it out to the end, just slipping along those old fixed rails." She felt trapped, said, "But don't you see, Frank, he doesn't have to, he can change all that. Patterns can be changed." They had ended in bitter abstractions far from any discussion of Pop or her mother, but she had wept, angry at her own weakness in doing so. Time had not silenced the argument. Her father had not risen triumphantly from his swollen chair and endless radio or altered the brief dragging progress between bed, bathroom, chair, doctor's office, even though her mother had left him more and more to the busy patter of nurses. "That proves nothing," she would say. "It *means* nothing," he would reply. All she knew was it did not seem possible to live, to get through, thinking the way Frank did about things. Even when he was happy, even their best moments were for him acted out in front of a dimensionless, colorless backdrop.

"Then what is it Carey wants to know?" she murmured. "What is he testing?"

But he did not answer. She would see if Carey wanted to talk tomorrow about the dog. She would avoid any sentimentality. Frank was right about that. She did not want to argue anymore, so she turned on her side, putting her cheek on his shoulder.

"Will it be all right, the play?"

— 12 —

"We'll see. Honestly, I think I have the worst bunch of students I've ever had. I tore them to bits today."

Somewhere beyond the drowsy wave beginning to take her, uneasiness remained. Something was going on in him that she wanted to know more about. She would try harder to find out. "Goodnight," she thought she heard herself saying and then lapsed into a dream that began with her slow, floating descent of the porch stairs into a soft rain. The tree was laden with birds, as if they were fruit, and when she tried to gather them with her hands, all she held was light. But the dream sheared away from any portion of her mind that could remember, so when she woke in the middle of the night, curled close to the edge of the bed, she thought she had recently finished talking with Frank but could not recall what else she had wanted to say. She went to the bathroom, certain that the bourbon waked her since she rarely had trouble sleeping, paused for a moment by Carey's shut door but heard nothing, then went back to bed, where Frank muttered in his sleep and turned.

With shocked clarity she remembered they had forgotten to go to the Dean's reception for a new member of Frank's department, and wondered if she should wake Frank to share her irritation, but decided it could wait. She had forgotten to put it on the calendar in the kitchen, and Frank was never any good at noting things down. No, that was not quite right. His memory for trivia was poor so he made endless notes, but they fell around him like leaves off a tree, randomly accumulating where he dropped them—his study, the telephone table at home, or by the bedroom extension. And his study was a hopeless place to find anything: books stacked on chairs, wigs and masks and photographs of old productions scattered in shelves and boxes, and a desk that surely he could not work on without first using a shovel. But tomorrow he would be irritated at her, not himself, even though he would pretend to think it fine that they had not gone. He kept up an appearance of disregard for institutional functions, and yet went to them—perhaps a little late, or not dressed quite right, or drinking too much of the booze on parents' day. Although, thank God, Frank was not political. She never was a good "faculty wife."

She had been a fine executive secretary for a law firm when she and Frank had met in Philadelphia and early in their marriage, but she was not willing yet to risk letting the firm know she wanted to work again. They might turn her down. With the war over for five years, the city growing in unexpected ways, Carey out of the house almost all the time, and too often only the distant yells of the hockey team being whistled through some drill, the clack-clack of their sticks gusting randomly through the kitchen window, she missed those early walks to the station, that sense of being surrounded every morning by such a different world: dapper yet severely dressed men of law and business who read the papers as they moved securely down the rails from Main Line homes to work. Now she was not only enclosed by the mock-medieval architecture of the campus, the literal facing inward of all its buildings ringing the acres of grass and trees like gray walls, but also by the minds turned steadily toward things she could not care much about, and the endless circulating crop of women from eighteen to twenty-two, the rituals of bonfires and lanterns and maypoles that they filed through so earnestly. Even if Frank mocked them also, he drew out of those young women amazing voices and gestures and appearances. She was a mere observer.

It was late fall and soon the groundsmen would be stacking lumber in the middle of the hockey field into a huge cone, then wetting down the field in a circle unless there was an early snow. That night the seniors would light the fire, join hands in a circle and dance around it, singing some song until, high up on the bank across the field, the juniors would appear, torches in hand, and they would swoop down, screaming, a crazy pattern of fiery slashes, to break through the circle, to chant their own song by the surging cone of fire, sparks crackling up into a black sky. There would be a charred smell the next morning, minor burns reported, a few turned ankles from the pell-mell descent, and for Nancy, a queer sense of unreality, as if surely this could not be anything she would ever see again. Frank viewed it as just another form of dramatic production, only anxious lest his lead part be one of the injured, but for her those gatherings of women performing so intensely such shallow rituals were frightening; energy was in their harmonized voices, their rapt eyes, but terribly misplaced.

The neighbor's dog barked furiously on the lawn and then settled to an occasional yap at some distant, answering mutt. Not really a neighbor, not their lawn. They did not own the house, the college did, and even if Frank was tenured, she knew he could at any moment give all that up in anger, in restlessness, in unaccountable despair. But those moods had nothing to do with this place. Was it Frank's youth in Ohio, a world so different, that made all this of no real concern to him, something he could angrily deride or obliviously walk through, but never have to face in her state of ambivalent and paralyzed seething?

Sometimes while she was growing up in Philadelphia her family would fill the car and drive out into this lush countryside in midsummer, usually with a picnic lunch and the expectation of a cool ramble through the hills and fields of Valley Forge, and even then it was a wholly different country, something she might see in *The Illustrated London News* that her mother bought at Christmas, one of those established, ancient lands of hedges and lawns and manors. For Shannons like herself, living on the edge of a less than genteel section of South Philadelphia but at least in their own home, attending church in a parish that all too clearly had its divisions between those who had scrambled out and those who could not, the Main Line was as deeply fixed and remote as some of its trees, spreading oaks and maples surrounded by perfectly tended lawns. But after she had journeyed back and forth each day to attend the junior college for women set down in the very middle of that world, after she had graduated and gone to work in the city for the people who lived out there, she came to see how much of it was veneer, only the purchased images of age and stability. The trees were carefully maintained as objects that their various owners could possess for the moment, but the families came and went, no less restless and pushed in their own polished ways than the people she had grown up with. And left. Which made Frank wrong again, because she had chosen to do that, had willed to work her way out of the city, and that was no simple matter of "fate."

He jerked abruptly as if trying to kick his feet loose, and muttered as he rolled away, taking most of the covers with him. He would twist soon toward her and the loosened sheets would be flung back. She had become accustomed to this tidal flux of bedclothes. He was always a restless sleeper at best, and yet never knew it, would insist he had slept quietly—except when he could not sleep at all, and would stalk downstairs heavily, treating Carey and her the next day as if it were obscurely their fault that his mind had not let him alone. She tried now to close her eyes and keep them closed, but they shifted back and forth, the muscles in her lids straining. Sleep, sleep, she kept saying to herself.

He turned and the covers bunched between them. She quietly groped a loose end and pulled it around her, being careful to secure one flap under her hip. Again, she felt the uneasiness that had been with her all evening, as if the vaguely imagined figure of the stretched and battered dog were worse than actually having seen it, and then she recalled standing in the kitchen that morning before Carey and Frank left for their drive. Carey was practicing a Bach prelude, the one she had come to love so much. She was used to hearing small phrases played over and over, and did not mind, although sometimes she wondered at how he could sit there for four, even five hours working on a sonata or an étude. She was leafing through the cookbook, not reading the pages carefully anymore, so she looked out the window to the back lawn covered again with leaves, the car hunched outside the garage. A rabbit cautiously slipped out from the hedge onto the broad border of grass by the road, not hopping but stretching its hind legs along slowly, and then for a moment it sat there, bunched tightly, nose and ears twitching—a small, mottled hump of fur in the fading green. The music paused. She put her hand to her throat, against its soft pulse. For no reason she could understand, in contradiction to what her eyes told her, Nancy suddenly had felt she knew nothing she could see or touch.

Frank's bare knee rested against her thigh, the dog was silent, the house cracked once deep under them in some wall adjusting to the cold. She gently grazed his cheek with her palm. There was nothing as mysteriously peaceful and whole for her as these moments when he lay like that, so calmly breathing, close enough to touch without his knowing. Her eyes closed, she tucked that hand beneath her own cheek and slept.

# 2

"You'll kill yourself that way, Carey." Nancy's voice floated up from a dormered window toward the ground. "Come down."

Down was up and up was down. He was swinging by his legs from the branch of the maple. The last leaves shivered and hissed around him, his hands hung into air, swelling with blood. On the yard the rake was sitting where he had abandoned it, and the porch pushed out at him like an opened drawer.

"I mean it."

She meant it. Her voice stiffened. One leaf floated, a lazy back and forth past his hands.

"I want you to finish that lawn before your lesson. Now act your age."

He could never resist the maple.

"Carey."

Last warning. The hammock, his father's favorite place in summer, was swinging in a wind as if Frank had left his ghost that morning when he went to work.

"I'm coming."

The voice was deadened by his swollen head. She had left the window. A squirrel was on the roof, scolding. What if suddenly gravity pulled outward, into that mottled sky? clinging to treetops, leaves stripping through his hands, the squirrel toppling up, Nancy, who now pushed the screen door out, stretching her hands for something to hold onto.

Her hands clapped together. The world had not come loose. He started to pull up, the branch biting into the backs of his legs. The ground was six feet past his fingers. He had been clinging too long, and his stomach muscles refused. He swung out full length again, wondering if his legs would hold. Why did she have to be watching? He would catch himself with his hands before his head hit. Tuck and roll. His mother took a step out onto the porch, looked hard beyond him.

Hands were on his arms.

"Need help?" His father's voice from behind.

Two hands on his waist. He let go, slid down, heard a grunt. They staggered, he kept on sliding down, then they were tilting over, his blood rushed sideways, and they were heaped, tangled, laughing under an upright tree. Even though Nancy's voice was saying, "For heaven's sake, you two," she was laughing also.

Silence. His world spun, house and mother a wheel of gray November light, and he leaned on an elbow, Frank's legs sprawled across him, arm over his neck. He looked down to steady his eyes, staring at Frank's hand. The fingers were splayed out, grass rising between them. That puffed and mottled skin was the earliest of memories, from a time when his own fist could be folded into the palm. The ground steadied under them as if the hand were keeping it in place.

"That's like trying to carry myself," the voice said in his ear, still a little breathless.

It was lunchtime and Frank went into the house with Nancy. Carey made a few passes with the rake. But raking leaves, the final jumping into piles, did not interest him anymore. He had waked late and was not hungry, and besides he did not want to sit there while they talked or argued about Frank's morning or, worse still, they might bring up the accident, and he never wanted to think of that dog again, the misshapen body, tongue lolling and legs scrabbling at air as if it could still escape. They did not seem to believe he knew there was nothing more to explain, and such conversations quickly became their argument, not his.

A yellowish shell of a locust clung to the trunk of the maple; he found three or four, dried as fingernails, split in the back where the live insect had escaped. When he was young he had always collected them in a bag. Their perfect shapes of eyes, legs, body slightly curled with tension, were a transparent version of the creature, as if it had faded away leaving this fossil imprint as a final, smoky gesture before it changed. The sharp claws stuck to his shirt.

He finished raking one pile together. He had a lesson that afternoon, and then Stafford and his wife Alice were going to take him to a concert in town. He knew that if he began practicing, his parents would not send him back to the leaves. Frank had wandered upstairs, Nancy was in the kitchen, and his music was spread out on the rack: Bach, and the Mozart sonata that he had started work on two weeks ago. From the piano he could see the slope down to the hockey field and far off on the distant rise were the roofs and turrets of the upper campus. He never understood the resistance, the silence before the first notes when his hands would seem so heavy and he would stare around as if he wanted to do anything but this. The prelude was open, but he turned away from the page to imagine himself walking up through that patch of woods and vines to the distant spire of the auditorium where Frank had his office and where three years ago he had learned how to sneak in through an opened window during vacation. He had wandered through the huge building alone, as if he were the prince in a deserted castle, went under the stage where all the dusty sets were stored, climbed far up into the balcony to look back at the wide, motionless curtains, finally found his way up into the tower by some tightly winding stairs and looked out through slits on a world he had seen only from the ground. He was dizzy with the height, but excited to be in control of the whole stretch of paths and trees and buildings whose roofs he had never seen.

He heard Nancy moving out of the kitchen and, not wanting to have her ask him what he was thinking, he let one hand begin, then lifted the other and played some scales. How he had hated scales at first. When he had switched to Stafford Newfane last fall because old Mrs. Horner was getting senile, they were the first thing he made Carey do—major, minor, chromatic. Because Stafford had seemed imposing, a big-boned but slightly overweight body always propped up in vests or scarves, with a way of raising one hand, looking down his nose at Carey and saying "Aha" with a cruel smile, Carey did them grudgingly, even crying sometimes in frustration when his fingers slipped awkwardly on the upper intervals of a b-minor scale. But there had come a point when he could do them all, rapidly, smoothly, and they were such a clean, clear way to begin, to let that instrument become some part of him again instead of the dark brown, heavy bulk of indifference he pulled the bench toward.

Up and down, up and down, then hands in opposition, meeting, flying apart again, and he leaned into it. He paused, looked hard at the notes, still recent and strange, and tried the last passage he had been working on. Nancy crossed the other end of the room, something moved quickly through the air beyond the window, bird? squirrel in a leap? and then he was narrowed down to the page, the keyboard, a coming and going of notes in his head, and nothing else.

But he never seemed to get this prelude quite right, at least to Stafford's satisfaction, and although he went to his lesson certain that this time he would hear nothing but praise, Stafford said, "That's Mitchell, not Bach."

Newfane stood at the window with his back to Carey, staring as if he saw something very interesting out there, but it was dark, so Carey knew he could see nothing, except perhaps his own reflection. The man's hands were clasped behind his back, held there in a loose knot. He turned from the window and went over to the fireplace to poke at some logs that were steaming.

"Except the last measures. That crescendo. That was better."

He stood, leaned the poker against the wall, and rubbed his hands together. He was dressed in his best "English squire" manner, the tweedy coat, the ascot with its stick pin; but too aware of its being there, he would pull in his chin against the puffing silk. He looked at his watch. "Once again. Then I suspect Alice will want us at the table. We mustn't be late for the concert."

"Where shall I start?"

"The last page. All of it." Again, the hands clasped behind him, and facing Carey he stood in front of the fireplace where small blue flames began to pipe up.

Carey looked at his own hands, the keyboard, smelling the dinner Alice was cooking beyond the door to the kitchen. He was very tired for a moment, resisted lifting his arms, and a wedge of time came between his present motions and Stafford's last words. He had been totally absorbed in playing the prelude only a moment ago. Now it seemed impossible ever to play it again, as if he had dropped its notes one by one, stones into clear water. But he lifted his hands, remembered the measure, and began.

For a number of bars he heard only the music, then Stafford was giving advice and he simply allowed his hands to become an extension of the man's voice, so that when he came to the passage in question his hands no longer played it as they had for the last two weeks. Carey had learned this did not matter; it imposed nothing on him. If Stafford's way did not feel right, he would never be able to accept it anyway. This time he knew Stafford was right.

A knock on the door to the kitchen, the latch rattling, Alice's square, heavy face looking in with her bowed eyebrows raised. "Since you're both just staring off into space, why don't we have some dinner?"

Carey stood, folding down the cover, and Stafford waited for him at the door. Alice had already started serving on to their plates, and Stafford worked quickly on the drink she had made for him. Carey thought he liked her. She was peculiarly shy, hiding behind the solidity of her square, heavy-boned body, the firm way she drew in her chin before she spoke, moving her lips only slightly as if the real speaker, some ventriloquist, were talking above and behind her. But in spite of her heaviness of body, she had a sense of humor that Carey liked, especially in its tendency to punctuate the self-seriousness that Stafford often assumed in talking about politics, or the world of music or, as it was tonight and often, the misery of families.

Both Stafford and Alice claimed unhappy childhoods, parents who subjected them to situation after situation in which a child's feelings were not taken into account. Why they felt obliged to tell him all this, Carey could not understand, but they unleashed anecdotes and afterward they would be silent as if expecting him to present some woe of his own, and he would try, but his stories were pale compared to the things they told him. In fact, Carey realized he and they were talking about two different things. After all, his parents might be terrible to each other at times, but they were not cruel to him. Stafford had even said one evening when Carey had stayed for supper, the third whiskey sour drained to its ice, "This is nothing I would want you to repeat, you understand, and yet everyone knew it at the time so it doesn't matter, I suppose, just old family history, but my mother, at the age of forty, when we were just teenagers, about your age, had an affair with the concertmaster of the Philadelphia Orchestra, famous man, won't tell you his name, but very famous, and my father knew but did nothing about it. She would go in every Friday to the concert and sit up there in her box and then not come home until Saturday afternoon, and everyone knew. Imagine. And I was just a teenager, hearing all this gossip. It was very embarrassing. And it says something about my father, too..." and on he went, his chin trembling slightly when he paused, and Alice's eyes, her stone face, were fixed in an expression of indignation.

So he was not surprised that they returned to the subject of families, although tonight the various explosions from Stafford, the sharp flicks of wit from Alice, were more general, less related to personal history. Until dessert. Carey said something about his grandparents that Stafford listened to very closely, glancing significantly at Alice, until finally he could not contain himself and said, "Aha, you see?" Carey stopped. He was not sure he did. He had been talking about how Pop once said to Gramma, just after Carey was born, that the only good thing about having children was grandchildren. He could not remember why he had told it. He thought it connected to something Alice said. The wine was confusing him. His mother would be annoyed to know they gave him any, but it was only a glass or two, and the Newfanes insisted it was better for him to learn how to deal with alcohol early.

Alice nodded. "It does seem a long time to wait. A whole generation."

Stafford laughed once, bitterly. "Exactly. I'll tell you what we are coming to, Carey. Some day there won't be all this pressure to have brats. You can't believe, I'm sure, how much pressure there is. Now, look at Alice and me. We have no children."

"Thank God," she said solidly and Stafford nodded approval, continuing quickly. "But you can't imagine how everyone treats us like freaks or cripples. 'A childless couple.' As if we were missing something. Well, let us tell you something, Carey, and it's exactly what I tell my friends. We simply decided not to have children, that's all."

Carey did not know what to say. He watched them as they looked at each other, but somehow he felt, as he often did, that by telling something personal about his own family, he had betrayed them. That same story was told as a joke by his mother, something she would say when talking affectionately about Pop's eccentricities.

"We can't have children," Alice said, as if laying another brick on a sturdy wall she and Stafford were building together.

"By choice, though," and Stafford held up his finger. "We made the decision. Simple operation. Right here at the hospital. Alice had it done. Does that shock you?"

Carey shook his head. But it did. What had they done to

her? He thought of her body as strangely mutilated. What if his own parents had been like them? He wouldn't be sitting at the table thinking about not sitting at the table, and he might have been someone else's son, but no, that would be different because his parents would not be the same, and suddenly he was dizzy and worried that it might be the wine and he would show it.

"I mean, given our childhoods, can you imagine what kind of parents we would make?" Stafford said, and they went on, sharing reasons back and forth for how wise they had been: the interruptions children would make in their lives, the expense, the need to move to a larger house, tying Alice down so she would have to give up her job. But toward the end only Stafford was interested in the points, and her face went blank, she sipped at her coffee, then said with a flip of her wrist, "Oh, my, how late it's getting," and they all rose quickly.

"Well," Stafford said quietly to Carey as they walked out to the car together and they could hear Alice closing the door, then her heels on the flagstones, "I hope we haven't shocked you with all this, Carey. But I wish," and he paused, then took a hand from his coat pocket to toss and jingle the keys, "I wish adults had been more frank with me when I was your age." She caught up with them and Carey stooped into the back seat, glad for the darkness that left his face to himself.

They parked the car and reached the Academy of Music in time to find their seats high in the balcony. Carey's face was chafed by the cold, damp wind followed by the heat inside, and he barely glanced at the program before the lights began to dim. Everyone was applauding and a small man with tightly curled hair piling back from a high forehead was bowing, then he sat abruptly. Carey had only seen pictures of Arthur Rubinstein, and for a moment he seemed too small for the black spread of the piano. He adjusted the seat, head held slightly back as if listening for some signal, and then sat perfectly still while the hall quieted. When he raised his hands and began to play, Carey realized he had been holding his breath. Those three firmly falling notes, the rise ending in a trill and pause of the "Appassionata" took him simply and clearly into the music and for a while he kept his eyes open, watching the stiff back that bowed and swayed, the face often turned up toward the dark vault of the stage. He closed his eyes, followed nothing but the pure sound that was unraveling from the core of his own mind as much as entering his ears from the outside. Finally his breathing and pulse were governed by the music's sense of time, his body was the instrument the piece flowed through, and he did not know if he was playing, or Rubinstein, or if the music itself was playing all of them. In the pauses between movements the hall returned to him—the slight shiftings of Stafford and Alice on each side, someone coughing, a chair back slapping, and then with a tug, it would begin again. When the sonata was over he could not applaud at first; his hands were heavy, his body exhausted. Then he did, not even hearing his own hands beating because of the others and the voices yelling "bravo" at the man whose face seemed paralyzed, whose stiff bows could not stop the ovation. Stafford was saying something to him about a passage that had interested him, but Carey could only nod, and when Alice began talking across him to Stafford, he pretended to be reading his program.

But he was not. He wanted to shout. He wanted to stand with both of his hands on the railing and scream something wordless at that high and gaudy vault of gold and chandeliers. He knew, he knew. Oh, he might never play that well, but that was his world. That was where he belonged, it possessed him—not just the outer circle of quiet people listening, their faces turned inward, the dim sweep of tiers, but even beyond his own hands moving where they had learned to go—to the last core where the notes rose out of a silence as full as the deepest sleep. He shared that with the man who had just taken him there, and that place would be where he would want to go for the rest of his life. But all he could do was sit quietly, perched high on the edge, his eyes fixed on the words of a page he did not bother to assemble, and Stafford nudged him saying, "Sleepy? Want to walk around a bit?" and he could only turn to say, "No, thanks, I'm fine," surprised to be speaking so clearly in his own voice.

Rubinstein returned and sat down quickly after only one short bow as if he were eager to go on and tired of applause. It was Chopin, a ballade, one of Carey's favorites that he had begun working on and had not played for Stafford yet; but he could not concentrate anymore. He tried closing his eyes again, even tried to cut out the sound of his own breathing, but his mind was determined to wander now and so he gave up, disappointed that he could not go back to that lifted mood. At least he would listen to the technique, would try to understand how this man played. But his mind, as if muddied by the stirring of something passing on its bottom, would not even permit that, and as always when it wandered now, he thought of his father with a jab that almost left him breathless. He did not know if he was lonely or feeling what he sensed to be his father's loneliness or whether it was only a vacancy that belonged to his father, maybe his mother, himself, and even at times to the people he knew like Stafford and Alice when their eyes would wander in mid-conversation, as if they were listening to something no one could quite hear. But that frightened him, like that nightmare he had often now; he would hear a clear and perfect tone, a sustained pitch like the ringing of fine glassware when rubbed by a finger, and the tone would be so perfect that a dread would build the longer it was sustained because it had to break, it had to wobble like a slowing top into dissonance, and then it would, descending to noise. But at least he knew that racket had to modulate back to the clear, tuned pitch again, producing a state of relief as intense as the breaking. And this rhythm of clear tone and noise would alternate until he would wake sweating, his own voice moaning like some wintry wind. He told no one of this dream, not even his mother when one night she woke him saying she had heard him from the next room. And why thinking of his father should hurt him in this way, he could not tell.

Stafford leaned into him. "There, that retard, that makes sense of it," he whispered, and Carey nodded, having missed it completely.

He tried to rise with that deep-breathing melody unraveling over the arpeggios of the bass, but failed, still feeling Stafford's elbow on his arm, thinking of how sometimes when he was alone at home and practicing he could feel the music gathering as if in his back and shoulders, a sense of the room and all the individual separate notes receding, blurring— then a clarity, his mind floating out into the sounds themselves, and the music would become the thing holding everything else in place: the stool he sat on, the window with its cross-hatched pattern of light, the tree beyond it, the vague spread of carpet, a fireplace and mantel—a sense that the whole house and street and all he knew of the small geography he walked through every day were held in what he played. No words could possibly carry that scorching shiver in his back, so he had no way to tell anyone about this after it happened. He had thought it was some strangeness in himself until one time he had come early to Stafford's house on a summer evening. The front door was split, with old, wide, strap hinges, and that evening the upper half was open. As he walked up the flagstones, Carey began to hear music. It was almost dark. The bats were fluttering high over the stretch of lawn, quick motes of dark squeaking against a purpled sky, and the Chopin ballade was only a turmoil of notes, then a small dying down, and by the time Carey was at the door, a melody gathered, clear, borne along by the reaching, steady folds of the left hand, one of those melodies that seemed to stretch toward breaking, tightening Carey's breathing as if the long pull of the phrase must collapse, could not sustain itself, and yet it did to the last note. He stood there in the square of light from the half-door, unable to knock or interrupt, his body abruptly cut off into darkness from the waist down, and he could see the small room clearly: the way the huge concert grand pushed the other furniture— a couch, table, some chairs—into whatever space was left, the great wagon wheel with bulbs that hung from the ceiling as a chandelier, the almost life-sized portrait of Stafford as a college student that hung over the fireplace, a young pale face, already very self-absorbed, not too much older than Carey, dressed in costume for a ball, a hussar with a sword to rest one hand on. Feeling as if he should not be looking on, he saw Stafford, eyes closed, mouth partly open, a look on his face like a man asleep or a little in pain, and his voice was not singing but moaning from time to time. Then he realized that Stafford was only experiencing what he had, and for a moment, even though he did not like the man as a person, he loved him in some very simple way beyond all those quirks and costumes. He backed away out of the light and went across the wet grass to an old arbor with some iron chairs. He sat with the cold steel against him, letting the whole piece be played out. The sky became black, there were no more bats, and Carey had been very peaceful, glad to know that he was not alone in feeling what he did, and that he did not have to try to explain it anymore.

"Bravo, bravo," Stafford's voice was saying, hands beating again; they were standing and Carey stood too, dizzied by the surge of lights in the auditorium that fully revealed the drop from balcony to the distant seats below.

In the narrow, carpeted hallway during intermission, Stafford bought them some orangeade, and they stood in the gathering cigarette smoke while he talked about the performance or stiffly greeted people he knew, that vaguely remote smile on his face and back straight as if to remind them that he was holding audience and they, whoever they were, had come to say, "Good evening." They retreated from the smoke and chattering that had become so loud they could not hear each other, and sat for a while in their seats while Stafford remembered other concerts he had seen there and the performances of some yearly college review when he was at Princeton, which was always followed by a masked ball. Alice could even remember what they had worn for disguises.

He listened more closely in the second half, many of Chopin's preludes tumbled out one by one, and only once toward the end did he find himself daydreaming, hovering in some long room full of light, swept clean, a little like the assembly hall at school with its stage at one end but without any chairs, and someone was whispering his name.

When they reached the street they found it was snowing, the first of the year and early, but Carey was excited as he always was. They had to drive slowly through the thick fall of large wet flakes, Stafford holding tightly to the wheel with both hands and leaning forward. The trees bent in at them on the last streets near home, white above the glistening black road, and they were silent as if the moths floating at them, swept away by the arc of wipers, were another kind of music. He thanked them, they leaned into the dashboard lights and smiled back, both seeming a little embarrassed, and he watched the car drive off. Left to a muffled world, snow drifting into his face, brushing his bare hands, he wondered if he was in some odd way their child, even thought of the queer possibility that his own parents might not be truly his. Maybe he was anyone's, belonged to any couple who wanted him. They were leaving him late at night on someone else's doorstep.

# 3

"Frank?"

She stood at the bottom of the stairs. The afternoon sun struck fully through the window on the landing and she had to look away.

"Are you there?"

No answer. The car was in the driveway. But he did less and less of his work at home now. Until two years ago he had spent as little time as possible in his office or at the theater—would read, mark papers, walk around in the small room upstairs that was part of a converted attic, and when he emerged, an opaque wall of smoky air would tumble out behind him. Now he would even go sometimes in the evening, driving the short distance because he said that after reading papers or doing a small scene over and over, he needed to drive around, going as far as Valley Forge "to unwind," maybe stopping at a bar or two on the pike. On those nights he would come to bed where she might be reading or lying half asleep, and he would smell of bourbon and toothpaste. This year his restlessness had started so much earlier, and finally he had snapped at her, "Nothing's wrong, for God's sake, now leave it alone."

She could hear the voice of Miss Smedley, the hockey coach, her whistle, the beating of wooden sticks, and she went to the dining room doors to lean, looking out the porch, down the long slope to where they were running around in green and blue tunics. The early snow had quickly melted, and now they churned the dead grass into the earth. For a moment they grouped so that she could not see contact made between ball and stick, and it seemed to squirt around on its own, drawing their pumping legs, their eager shouts. The ball broke suddenly away from them all, a solid thwack came up through the air, and it streaked all the way over the ditch and into a heavy clump of vines and sumac. Nancy watched them mill around, stooping in and out of the bare bushes, and if it had been Carey she would have been yelling from the porch. A patch of poison ivy there had once attacked him so badly that he had spent two weeks with both hands tied in paper bags to keep him from scratching arms and legs and spreading it further. The whistle blew them out. A new ball was rolled to them from Miss Smedley's equipment bag.

She went back to the kitchen, thought of making some tea, but was still full from lunch. Carey would be home soon and she checked to be certain there was enough milk, some cookies. She went to the closet for the vacuum, imagined picking up a book instead, but made herself clasp its handle, draping the tube over her neck, and she lugged it up the stairs. She would clean the third floor, Frank's office, the room where Carey had his old trains and books—the rest tomorrow. She paused in the close air under the sloping roof. There was a thump far below, the paper being delivered, and she decided to start with Carey's room, the noise whining up out of the motor, the long tube hissing.

She had spent part of the afternoon with her mother, who had driven out to pick her up and take her back to Germantown, where she and Pop lived now, in much better surroundings than they ever had when Nancy was a child. Her father's business had done well, a wholesale electrical supply company that he and his partner, Bill Slocum, had set up together before the war, and Pop had luckily sold out his share of the company before his stroke. A premonition? Nancy's mother publicly promoted the idea of Pop as a masterful businessman, but Slocum had been the one who had made all the right moves, often against Pop's advice, and Nancy had too often heard her mother chide or even ridicule her father's ineptitude. Her mother used those extreme images to rub up a constant flame of bitterness, comparing her ideal conception of Pop as strong and wily manipulator, the image she used in conversation with others even in front of him, to the more truthful but still exaggerated figure of failure she would raise privately for him at home. Pop knew the public description was the person her mother wished him to be. Frank was partly right in saying Pop's collapse, his total dependence on her mother, was a form of vengeance, a way of saying, "To hell with your image of strength and manly wiles, see how you like dealing with this," a gesture ironically strong in its desperation. But Nancy also rejected that theory; it was the way anyone outside a family saw only the broadest motions of give and take. She had been told that many stroke victims fell into that pattern of petulant dependence, that it could be purely physical, like the symptom of a disease, and she also saw other things in Pop that she hoped could change all that—like his quiet sense of humor that had often turned her mother's anger into affectionate bickering.

She unplugged the cleaner, dragged it thumping along the hallway to Frank's study. Stalemate, she thought. And even if she insisted—opening the door, smelling the old cigarettes in the stuffed ashtrays, almost as if arguing now with Frank's presence in the room—that both her mother and father had the freedom to change, get out of this pattern that seemed so suffocating to her, she had to admit that what was almost the same as Frank's determinism was the way that people *chose* to be bound, refused to think beyond the lines of the magic circle they had drawn around themselves.

She moved carefully, trying not to dislodge any of the casually piled books, the stacks of papers. The ceiling sloped sharply and when she pushed into the corners she had to be careful not to hit her head. From the small dormer window the hill dropped away much more steeply than in the same view from the porch, and from this height she could see much more of the upper campus, the tower of Tyler Hall with its clock. She stooped to ram the sweeper under the battered easy chair, swung back too quickly and knocked some things off the desk. She did not bother to turn off the cleaner but lifted the stuffed envelopes from the floor where they had scattered. There were four, with the college monogram, and they were so filled that they barely closed, but oddly enough there was nothing on the outside of them. They had not been sent or received, but their contents were securely sealed in. She shrugged, stacked them again where she thought they had been, but they slid. She picked them up, and when she slapped them down, the breeze she made fluttered a piece of paper over onto the floor. She said, "Dammit," caught her foot on the hose and stood up straight, knocking her head on a rafter.

Cleaning his study was always like this, and often she would proclaim he could vacuum it from now on if he couldn't make it more cleanable—but that never worked because then it would simply never be done. She picked up the piece of paper, saw Frank's signature, just his first name, the type from his machine at the office. She began reading, wanted to stop after the first sentence, was sliding, wanting to go backward, out of the room, out of this bad dream, and then was simply reading, shocked.

*Well, Andrea, now you're back. Come see me. I want you to tell me what you want—whether you want things to go on as they were last semester or whether you want to chuck it all. And telling me you don't know isn't any good. I can't go on this way, living as I have this summer, in a stupid imagination, on drinks and long drives without you. And my letters—why didn't you answer?*

*Now you've got to tell me what you want. I can't stand not knowing really what you are doing. Tell me that coming back here is coming back to me, that it's not just the plays, the acting.*

                              *Frank*

*P.S. You were fine in rehearsal last night. I can't say that in front of the others. All of you are one cast, a whole, and if this thing is to work I have to praise or blame you as a unit. But you were not just "one of them" to me.*

She held on to the page, sat in the chair, closed her eyes but opened them quickly to reread it. It was dated four days ago. He had not sent it. But no, there were crossed-out places. He had probably recopied it. She reached down and yanked the vacuum cord. The silence was as if the house were sealing itself off floor by floor. She stooped, was on her knees and plugged the machine in again. Then she put her hands to her face and wept.

The longer Nancy waited to ask Frank for the truth, or to tell him she was planning to leave since she was certain she knew the truth already, the more silence surrounded her. In the middle of a conversation she would look up, find that Carey or Frank or her mother had asked her something and would realize she had heard nothing for a few minutes. Every day moved deliberately. She watched the bedroom float up out of the dark, watched the evening trees sink back into it. When he turned to her at night to make love, she tried desperately to forget. His hands numbed her. When he entered her a cold, firm voice rehearsed what she could say to him, her heart pounded, and she was certain that in a few minutes, when he was done, she would ask him blankly. She groaned, and he mistook that as an expression of her pleasure.

She tried to tell herself that what Frank had done was not unusual, recalling a very feverish year when she was fifteen and Pop had been accused of having an affair with a secretary he had fired, a mess that was public enough to make things hard for her with friends at school. But Pop had scoffed at it—the woman was known to be cheap and vindictive—and her mother never wavered in defending him. At least outwardly. But one evening when Nancy stayed up late reading, she went down the hall to the bathroom and the doorway to her parents' bedroom was open. Pop was in his bathrobe, sitting on the edge of the bed, his back slumped and forehead held on the heels of his hands, and her mother was a few feet away with arms crossed, face puffed with weeping and mouth in a furiously tense line. Neither of them was speaking and Nancy had moved away as quickly as possible but with that tableau of doubt fixed in her mind.

Some mornings she woke perfectly calm, certain that all this was only a moment. He had not left her and was only infatuated. She could change her own mind about leaving. Then she would decide again to go. Wouldn't she be free of all this worrying? Wouldn't all kinds of things become possible? But the door slammed. She turned to the kitchen window to see him, books in hand, go slowly out the driveway, walking with Carey, and the house grew absolutely blank as if he sucked everything with him. She avoided his study, told him angrily one day that it was too messy to clean and heard him barging around that afternoon with the vacuum cleaner. But all day when he was gone the room in the attic perched over her as if Frank and that girl were there together, hiding.

She looked a bit frazzled, Sally Mance remarked—Sally who was always perfectly dressed as if ready to go to a meeting, who answered the phone with a tone of dead calm, whose house with it cases of ancestral bric-a-brac and darkly veneered furniture was faultlessly dusted. Nancy looked across the oval tea table at her smile as composed as the cookies sprinkled with colored sequins that had been produced when she arrived without calling, and envied her for a moment. Surely Sally's life never fell into this kind of torment. She had hoped to talk with her, but found that as impossible as saying anything to Frank. Sally's cool grace was overbearingly discrete, and Nancy feared her measured compassion, that slight withdrawal when they discussed anything emotional or difficult. And this was the best friend she had here, who went with her often to concerts or museums or sometimes driving out to one of the old houses open for a tour.

She left abruptly, not wanting to change her mind and blurt something out, and walked along the boarded path by the row of faculty houses, started to turn up the stairs to her own, but veered down through the trees by the side of "The Farm," a small house and barn where cows still grazed in one field and the chickens provided most of the eggs for the campus dining hall. She liked the smell of the manure heaped outside the barn door, the cackling and crowing, and a cow wandered through the muddy yard to the fence, staring out over the wires, jaw working. Through the screen of trees and bushes she saw the pile of wood on the hockey field, heard men slapping the bonfire into place. She looked down for a moment at the little stream that sluiced under the path, still clear enough to grow its beds of watercress farther up. In the distance the men were laughing.

She would talk to him as soon as possible. Tonight. Because if she did not she would be eaten up. And there was no one but Frank to talk to, no one could help. She started to make up how she would say it, but if she did that she might get stuck again. No, it would just have to happen with whatever words were there.

As if to prevent her, he went to rehearsal after a supper during which no one had much to say. Carey ate as fast as he could since he wanted to finish his homework in time to watch the fire from the hillside, and Frank was preoccupied, even short-tempered. He took the car with him when he left.

First, she smelled the fire, and having forgotten for a moment, she breathed deeply, fearing it might be somewhere in the house; she heard the distant snapping of sparks and went to the dark dining room to look out on the cone of flames, the black silhouettes of circling people.

"I'm going now."

Carey had come in quietly, was tying his shoelaces in the doorway. The car slid to a stop on the gravel of the driveway.

"You be careful."

"Pete's coming too. He's going to meet me."

He was still groping into his jacket as he went out. She closed the door to the porch and stood there for a while. His figure grew smaller as he walked down in front of the fire, then he moved to one side and disappeared into the dark. On the top of the opposite hillside bright sparkles of light began to wink and swirl as they lit the torches.

Frank did not come in for so long that she wondered whether he had gone around the house and out into the field to watch also. But the door opened, was held that way until a small snaking of cold air brushed her legs, then it slammed. He thumped something down—books, maybe his shoes. A few voices began singing by the bonfire, a small cheer was yelled from the hilltop, its chanted words unclear.

"Nancy?"

She turned reluctantly, already a little breathless. Standing in the lighted hallway in his sock feet, he leaned with one hand against the wall, the other in his pocket.

"I'm in here."

He lurched, bumping the hall table slightly.

"Where's Carey?"

"Watching the bonfire."

He squinted past her shoulder. "So it is."

"I want to talk with you, Frank." She was glad to be in the dark room.

"That's odd. I want to talk to you too. 'Fraid I'm a little tanked up, though."

"Obviously."

He peered at her as if deciding whether to be insulted.

"What is it?" she said.

"Not here. C'mon," and he turned, hair tufted in every direction, his shoulders slumped as always when he was drunk. He used the banister heavily as he walked ahead of her. "I want to talk to you alone."

They went up to the bedroom. He turned on the overhead light, flicked it off, and found the switch for the bedside lamp. "Too bright." He pointed at the ceiling and sat heavily on the end of the bed.

Nancy moved to the chair near the dresser, stood for a moment with her back to him, then turned and sat. He was not looking at her but at the toes of his socks. The singing was louder and the fire was a burning spot in the middle of the window.

"You go first," he said. "Because what I have to say might take time. Complicated."

Suddenly she did not want to say anything. She did not want him drunk. Or else she yearned to be drunk herself, envied that release and numbness. But he glanced up at her from under his bushed eyebrows, mouth slightly turned down, and she was certain by the look in those eyes, frightened and belligerently defensive, that they were going to talk about the same thing.

"I think I know what you have to say."

"You know?"

"About her. Is that it?"

His hand shot up from the mattress, scrubbed at his cheek. "How did you find out?"

"A letter. I was cleaning."

He nodded. "All of them?"

"What?"

"All the letters?"

"Just one."

"Too bad. Always kept them in my office, locked in the desk. I had them home that week because they were painting. Afraid the workers would break in and get them. They're always thieving."

She could not speak for a moment, taunted by those concrete facts of an established conspiracy. He was smiling oddly.

"You can't imagine how queer it's been. You get to thinking everyone's watching you. Been going on for two years."

"Who is she?"

He shook his head. "Worse than that. Them."

"What do you mean?"

"Not just one. Who was it you saw?"

"Andrea."

He laughed abruptly. She thought she must be insane and then, far more terrifying, she suspected he was, and wondered if she knew him in any way.

"I'm sorry, Nancy. I am. I don't know what to believe anymore. I'll try to tell you, all at once. In some ways it's not nearly as bad as you think, and sometimes it's even funny, but then at others," and he rubbed his fists together at the knuckles, his face looking at her numbly, "it's crazy. I'll show you the letters. Saved them all. I don't know why. Most of them, you see, weren't even sent. I'd write them. then revise, put them in an envelope, and I'd get to the mailbox but take them away, unmailed. Once I had to wait for the mailman, told him I wanted it back, wrong address, but he wouldn't, said I had to get an okay from the postmaster. I let that one go. Wait."

He stood unsteadily, walked out and down the stairs. She did not move. A heavy shout went up and from the black top of the window a cascade of blinking spots flowed down toward the bright eye of the bonfire. She could see a transparent version of her own face in the glass. He shuffled back in, handed her three typed sheets.

"Read it. Please. This one."

"Do I have to?"

"It's the best way for me to explain."

She tried to pay attention to the words. There was a date, actually a year ago in October, but closely written across the top of the page was an afterthought that read, "I'm not afraid to talk. You know that. And I'd much rather talk than write you. But it's hard to find a place when and where people aren't around."

Reading the letter while he was there watching her face was obscene. She listened for a moment to the distant howling.

"I can't." She handed it to him. "If I have to know, you read it to me."

He took the pages, was silent, and then began.

"'Dear Miriam...'"

"Who?"

He did not lift his face.

"Miriam."

"I thought it was Andrea."

"That's different."

"But when..."

He shook his head. "That's part of what I'm trying to tell you. There's also Antonia, and Paula. Names."

She held perfectly still.

"'Why should I trust you with this letter? Hell, I don't know. At least go someplace where you can read it in private, and I mean private: read it a number of times. Slowly. Then let's talk. You've done about everything you could do to give me the message—that it was fun for a while, but you've had your kicks with me and it's so long, buddy. Well, I'm not up for that. About all I can do is be here at the office as much as possible, but you'll come when you damned well feel like it, I know that. I've been here all morning, all afternoon, and will come back tonight. Christ, I'm a fool.'"

He was reading in a slurred monotone, and now he paused, breathing deeply.

"'You know damned well that for me to write you a word is a terrible risk, that if something happens with these letters I'll lose my job.'"

She was dizzy, thought she might be sick. But when he began again she listened if only to have something to hold onto.

"'And I kept on going back to the sexual relationship thing, that you wouldn't have gone for those drives if you didn't care. Now you've come back, stranger, taking my words in one hand, saying goodbye with the other. "Let's be good friends?" You played with me. Even if nothing very real did happen in those drives. But you made it seem possible. What a way to spend the summer, like a damn kid in his room conjuring up scenes with a young girl...'"

"Stop it," She stood. "What the hell are you reading this awful thing to me for?" She reached out, took the letter, half-balled it up, then tore at it. She let go of the pieces and sat down quickly, bending her face to her knees.

"I wouldn't want anyone else to tell you any of this."

"Who else?" She sat up again, trying to be calm.

"Oh, Nancy. It's all so screwed up. I'm so screwed up. For two years. Like being a kid again, you know? Like when you had your first big crush. I pick out a girl, usually in one of my classes, or she's in a play, and my mind fastens on, won't let go. Then I start it. We talk a lot. They're usually in need, somehow—of a comforter. First thing I know, I'm writing letters, and if I send them, they sometimes write back. Letters, secrets. Maybe we go for a drive after a rehearsal. We sit in the car, talk. Flirt. And sometimes I don't even think they understand. I go kind of crazy. I can't get them out of my mind. That letter," and he pointed at the scattered shreds, "that was last fall. Now it's Andrea. But it's all the same. And they say 'no' at some point, because it starts to get crazy, my wanting and not wanting at the same time. It's almost like I want them to say no. So then I can write them about the hurt. How it's their fault."

His face looked so wildly confused, his words were so nonsensical to her, that she feared he might be uncontrollable. But he must have seen her expression, and shook his head.

"I'm sorry. I've actually been too good at hiding it all, haven't I?"

— 37 —

She nodded.

"Except now *they* know about it."

"They?"

"The Dean."

"Oh, Lord."

"It had to happen, you know. They're little bitches. That's what I must like in them. Someone ratted on me. The Dean won't say who. She had a pile of letters. There are probably little stacks all over the campus." He smiled ruefully. "Words. Words. They hardly ever wrote to me. But I kept copies of all my letters, the rough drafts. It's queer. I guess very soon I got the idea I was writing to myself as much as to them."

"What will they do?"

"The Dean?" He shook his head. "Maybe get rid of me. Probably not. She seemed to understand it was my head. Wants me to see the school shrink. Says I might need a rest, a little leave. You see, Nancy, it's something they're afraid of. And firing me, they'd have to let it all out, wouldn't they? Not good for the image."

"I don't believe it, any of it."

"I guess I'm not well," he said quietly. "But it's a relief somehow, to have it out. To say that."

She was crying, racked as if someone were holding her over the chair and shaking her body roughly, and even his hand on her shoulder could not hold her still. She let her head fall against him, but not for comfort. There was no place to find that, certainly not from this total stranger who was saying something over and over to her that she could not hear clearly. She stopped only when he left her and stood with his back turned, looking out the window. She wiped her face with the palms of her hands. Crying always did some good. This did not.

He spun around, and suddenly he was smiling broadly. "I'm sorry. But I just remembered. You know the way the door to the car doesn't shut right?"

She nodded.

"It was this summer. I went to mail a letter. To Andrea. I used to drive all the way to Rosemont to mail letters, usually at night. I was that furtive, as if anyone who knew me would know what I was doing. I went to that box on the corner by the post office. It was closed, Saturday night. I got out the passenger side of the car, was about to mail the letter when I saw the Mances' car coming. Panic. I mean, why would I be mailing a letter with my getaway car running like that, without there being something sneaky? So I dropped the letter in, dove into the car, jammed into reverse, and I'd forgotten to close the car door. It caught the box, almost ripped the hinges off, but instead the whole mailbox toppled over. Jesus, what a racket, and out of the corner of my eye I saw the Mances' car go by and two faces staring like white blobs, but I ducked and I don't think they knew because they never said anything. I sat there for a moment, then went out and stood the box up and started laughing my head off. Crazy fool."

He was laughing again, and she could not help it either, moved by the vision of him as he was now, hands out, tired face grinning so lackadaisically, and for an instant she wondered if all of it, everything that had happened this evening, were something not at all grim or sad, but a farce.

"Oh, Frank," she said, but hearing her voice and his name sucked that mood away and everything was strange again. She listened as if the house itself might tell her what to do next. The voices outside had settled into one song, no more competing, and soon they would be breaking up, Carey would be home.

"What now?"

"Who else knows, Frank?"

"Couldn't tell you. Surely a number of the students must. The Dean."

"What did she say?"

She thought of Dean Wilkins, her sternly braided hair gathered like a perfect basket inverted on her head, her slowly enunciated sentences, always complete. That must have been a strange meeting.

"Not quite what you would expect. Of course, the usual repugnance, the Moses-like protector of her people's virtue. But then she turned motherly on me, started talking about tensions, working too hard, what the war has done to us all. And she meant it. No, not motherly, I guess. More like I was her kid brother. Of course she was relieved to know it was my head."

He gave a sharp laugh that made her look up. She thought she heard Carey on the porch, and immediately she wanted to go downstairs, to shut Frank away someplace and keep Carey from all this incomprehensible information. But she heard no doors opening.

"He'll be home soon."

"Who?"

"Carey."

"So?"

"I don't want him to know any of this. He doesn't have to."

"Why? It's..."

"No." She stood.

"All right. All right. Sit down."

"I think I'll go downstairs now."

"But we need to talk."

She looked at him, the door, the fire in the window reduced now to a red mound.

"There's nothing to say."

She moved to the door, his hand came toward her, and she shrank away, taking her body to the other side of the threshold.

"You can't just leave me with this. Say something, Nance."

That was when her feelings gathered into one clear emotion that made her hands start shaking as she held them tightly clasped. Anger. She could have kicked, bitten, scratched him like a child.

"Go to hell," she said, and did not wait to listen to what he was starting to say as he stood. But at the doorway she half turned and without looking at his face she said, "We're leaving. Carey and I. As soon as it can be arranged." The door slammed below, she whirled, was halfway down the stairs when Carey and Frank both called at once, an overlapping of "Nancy?" from above and "Mother?" from the dark stairwell below. The tone of voice above her was peremptory, but did not repeat. Carey's voice said, "Mother?" again, and she was ready by then to say "Yes?" to him. A light went on below, and his face was turned up to her, hand on the newel post.

"Someone broke a leg coming down the hill. They had to get a stretcher and they didn't know she'd done it until they heard her yelling after the others were all the way down."

"For heaven's sake, why do you watch those idiots?" Her voice was too angry. "I mean, it's too bad, but they certainly ask for it."

"Nancy." Her name was almost bleated, and she watched Carey peer up with a frown, then back at her.

"Your father," she said slowly, "is angry because he lost some papers." She yelled up, "Frank, I'll be along in a while. Why don't you look for them yourself?"

A pause. "For what?"

She put her hand on Carey's shoulder, started guiding him

— 40 —

toward the kitchen where the light was still on. "It's one of those nights," she murmured; "a piece of cake?" He nodded, and she did not remove her hand until they were close to the refrigerator, as if she were blindly pulling herself along from one familiar object to another.

He hunched over his cake, chocolate with white icing, and watched her pour the milk, but her hand was trembling and sloshed some onto the table. He figured they were having one of their bad nights again, and that would mean he would go to bed, they would resume in some way, loud voices, perhaps something broken. He did not like it, but had learned not to fear; when he was little he was sure he would wake in the morning to an absolutely empty house, a gray light like the first morning of snow, no parents anymore. If his father's voice sounded unusual tonight, if his mother, walking back to the sink to get a dishcloth and lean there for a moment with her back to him, seemed ragged, still he would rise in the morning and they would be there, probably more close and friendly than they had been in weeks. Besides, he liked chocolate cake.

"Pete and I watched with Mr. Mance. He said they were going to quit doing the bonfire next year. Too many people get hurt."

"Oh?" She swiped the rag around in front of him. "I'm not surprised. Now, when you've finished that, go on up to bed. And don't bother your dad. He's in a bad mood."

"I know, I know," he said, to signal how bored he was. She was putting on a coat. "Where're you going?"

"Just for a short walk."

He pushed his fork into the back side, heavy with icing, that he had saved for the end. But he was angry. He wanted to talk with someone about the bonfire, about the men with the stretcher and the girl screaming at them from the dark side of the hill. "Mom, can't you guys quit it?"

He did not go on when she turned in the doorway, her face exactly the way that girl's had looked as they carried her past to the waiting ambulance, her eyes not seeing them, wide face turned to the bonfire. How could someone who had been crying out in such pain a few moments before look so blank, daydreaming, almost like the faces of the people in the crowd around him who were staring back—eyes, noses, straight mouths underlined into masks by the flames.

"Quit it? Yes, Carey, soon I hope." Then she was gone.

He stared at the door for a moment, shrugged, and drank some milk, saving a gulp or two for the last bite. At least they weren't yelling this time. Last spring Carey had heard arguments downstairs at night that were sharp, things were broken, and in the summer he and his mother had gone without Frank for two weeks to Avalon. Frank never liked the seashore much anyway because his skin burned easily. But he appeared one afternoon, and luckily there was a double room available in the boarding-house where they were staying. During the day he would go down with them to the beach and take long walks up or down the shoreline, and Carey would look along the sand where he was lying in the wash of waves to see his father, a slightly curved stick far off in the haze, standing on air that shimmered, looking out to sea.

Damn, adults were weird sometimes. What did they always find to argue about? He wouldn't, he was sure of that. If he were living with a woman, and he imagined with a flush a few of the girls he knew at school, especially Lisa or the older ones who never deigned to talk to him, they would never argue. But maybe women were just that way. He and Pete did not argue much, except about little things like whether Pete had really touched Carey before he crossed the goal line. But Lisa wanted to disagree with almost everything, and even if she did not say it, she had a way of pouting. Like the first time he kissed her in the school basement. He had said he was sorry, and she had blurted, why, wasn't she any good? and he'd said yes, she was the best, which was a lie only because he had hardly ever kissed a girl before, and so she had said, then why are you sorry, silly? and he'd done it again three or four times until the bell rang. Recently her lips opened up a little, and once, day before yesterday, he had touched the tip of his tongue to hers and she had not pulled away as he expected, but pushed harder against him so his tongue actually touched her teeth. The next time her tongue was there too, but he had needed to stand back and pretend he heard someone on the stairs because of the hard-on he did not want her to feel.

Which he began to get now, just thinking about her. He took the last bite and swished it around with the milk and put both glass and plate in the sink. Upstairs he could tell by the light that his father was still on the third floor, so he went straight to his room and undressed fast, touching himself lightly to keep hard, and with the lights out and his door closed, he stood by the window, looking down to the mound of coals and few dark figures that stood there, starting to hose down the embers.

He closed his eyes. The women were dancing around and around, hands clasped, and the inner circle went one way, the outer, singing their own song, went the other. Their faces were full of the singing against each other, concentrated and hard; their bodies pranced, long legs flashing under the tossing skirts and smocks. Women. He could smell their bodies, the perfumes, the musks of their hair, their sweat; the same ones he would watch in groups pass laughing, their books clutched to breasts. Women. They were all naked, dancing around that fire, dizzily wheeling in opposite ways, his body joining theirs, fierce faces leaning to him, voices singing in his ears, the fire hot and cracking high over them.

He opened his eyes and went to his bed to lie on his back, trying to imagine what it must be like to thrust into another body, trying to think it was not his own hand but Lisa doing something he did not fully understand.

# 4

Frank turned the glass on the desk top, lifted it, and took a sip. Step one, two, three. He did it again, registering each action separately. The bourbon needed ice, but he did not want to go downstairs until he was certain Nancy was in bed. Oh, hell, that wasn't quite the truth. He snorted at himself, lips moving as he talked silently, staring at the glass. No, he really wanted to see if she would come back. On her own. Talk things out. He hadn't explained. She didn't understand, maybe couldn't. Problem was, explaining wasn't all that easy. Very complex, and obviously so far he'd botched it. Talking about those students, the letters. That was only part of it, the easiest to deal with. Maybe not for her, though. Other *women*. That sounded bad.

He lifted the bottle from the floor, filled the glass and put the bottle down between his feet as if trying to hold it steady. "No, don't touch me," she'd said, Andrea, her cheek leaning against the back of the seat, her legs drawn up under her so that she faced him. They shared the bottle, and her hand brushed his as he passed it to her. The light of the dashboard showed her white knees and shins, the long-fingered hand. The fires of the forge below the bluff at Conshohocken kept pulsing up in a glow that pushed against the windows of the car. He was turned to her awkwardly, his own legs pressing the lower rim of the steering wheel, the gearshift rising between them. "You little bitch," he said, "you fox," and she tilted back her head and laughed the stagiest of her laughs. "Oh, Frank, I love it when you curse me out," and as always the sound of his first name on a student's lips shocked him, agreeably. "I want to touch you, I need to," he said. She sipped her bourbon, swallowed, leaned her head back again, then reached out to take his hand and hold it to her breast, but as soon as his fingers moved, she thrust it away. "Naughty, naughty." "I could have you, now, right here, you know. No one would help you." But she did not look frightened. "Yes, Frank. You certainly could."

The only gesture she made in response to his staring at her was a small flick of fingers on the hem of her skirt, tugging it slightly down on her knees. "I tell you what, Frank, why don't you write me a letter about it?" Silence again for the briefest moment in which they stared at each other, enjoying the sense that anything could happen, extraordinary things, performances they never knew they had in them, and then they began to laugh and he muttered, "Oh, Jesus," as he wiped his eyes; and after he had started the car and backed out onto the road, pulling away with a swerving squeal, she leaned her head on his shoulder and stroked the inside of his thigh while he muttered, "You bitch, you bitch," all the way back along the familiar roads to the campus and her dorm.

Andrea, Paula, Miriam, others too. Some of them he had been wrong about. He hated the ones who were so eager, willing, leapt at him when he touched them in his office, did not understand when he ignored them immediately afterward. But the best, like Andrea, had an instinct for it, knew exactly how to circle the fire with him, always keeping the flames between them, their faces lit up, laughing at each other. Inevitably they were the best of his students, the ones who sensed in themselves the ability to be anyone he wanted, and loved touching that possibility. But the holding back was what made it possible, what made them richer than any real touch or tumbling could—then the letters, his words, their responses, the way the best ones keyed to his long and detailed assumption of this emotion or that.

Lord, it was like some astounding performance by Fred Astaire and a long-legged woman, he tuxedoed, she wrapped in filmy silk, gestures in air that hinted more than any real clasp could give. Nancy could never understand that. There was none of that in their lives. Their bed was as real as the boy who slept below him now, a body and its own mind grown from their tumbling and moaning. He choked down a larger sip of bourbon to catch himself up. He loved her, loved Carey. That wasn't the problem. Couldn't explain it all, that need for everything—for her and her real touch and understanding, but also for all the awareness of what he might be that the others gave him.

One small spot of light in the center of the windowpane was left and he stared at it, losing the space between his face and that dying bonfire. The window turned his reflected room into broken highlights: the bent head of the lamp, a corner of his desk, the cut-glass tumbler rippling light back as he turned it, his shoulder and a hand, and that faint dot in the field—all in one space, the dark drop of hillside erased. At moments like this he felt as unmoving and unchanged as any star. Nothing made sense and everything did—a simple opposition of two forces that held still. There was no way to explain what was happening to him, or to change any of it. He could see each thought, each motion, in a flashing prevision. He would now reach his hand to the glass, and he did, he would put it to his lips, and he did, he would think of his mother, who was buried in Columbus, and he did. The thought and action were not simultaneous; always the thought preceded, mind hovering over the body, all things already known. He was drunk now, but liquor had no effect on this condition. Other people, like Nancy, would become so spontaneous, her gestures, the pure energy of her life outracing the sleepy mind; for him it all became worse, the gap wider and wider, time slowed to an echoing pulse. At the worst, as he suspected it would be tonight when the bottle was almost finished, there would be such a gap of sheer emptiness between the thought and the motion that he would lurch into the same paralyzed fear that he always experienced when looking down from a high place, like the tower at Valley Forge that Carey always insisted they climb. At the top, the wind streaming up over the clumps of trees, the wide fields with their miniature cannons pointing here and there, he would stand without speaking, one hand on the rail, holding back the thought that could not be prevented from rising, hurling his imagination out into space where his body like a pitched dummy spraddled in plummet—"Jump, jump."

The fire was dead and the truck began to wind up across the field, its lights showing hummock and bush as it made seemingly random twists, a mechanical animal nosing some quarry. The other night when he had dreamed of his mother, she advanced toward him with that same fixed but uncertain motion, standing like the statue of a Roman matron, stiff, her dress severely pleated, eyes staring wherever the dolly she stood on rotated. It moved on its own across the long parqueted floor of a hall with elegant, dormered windows. He was sitting in a chair, something very antique and brocaded, with a page in his lap that he had to memorize before she reached him, and yet he could not turn his eyes to the words, stared at her as she came, zigzagging in sudden starts and stops, and although her eyes were open, she could not move her head, so whenever the dolly turned her away, her voice said plaintively, "Frank, Frank," as if telling the hidden wheels of the machine to redirect her. She held up something in her hand, a packet of papers. He forced his head down; "read, read," he said, and it was all the parts he had ever learned, jumbled in one mass of tangled print, a hundred voices speaking without order. If only he could find one clear enough to begin with, but the sound of the casters on wood drew nearer and nearer, her voice was that thin, complaining one he remembered from her dying in the hospital. The dolly stopped. Her eyes stared over the top of his head. "Frank, Frank," she whined. The envelopes were letters from a girl, he could not remember her name, the first girl he had made love to. "Where did you get those?" "Frank, Frank." He could not stand that voice. "What? Stop it." The book slipped off his lap. "Promise me, promise me. This must never happen again. Never again," she hissed. He put his hands over his ears. He caught the strand of a speech and recited as loudly as he could, voice bursting in his ears, "You have won a happy victory to Rome; but for your son,—believe it, O, believe it, most dangerously you have with him prevailed, if not most mortal to him. But, let it come, but let it, but let it..." He had waked mumbling incoherently in the dark bedroom.

Even that dream figure announced itself as something blurred, some larger presence in the disguise of his mother's flesh. Dreams, women, what was the strange power they possessed? He pushed the glass aside with the back of his hand, took the bottle by its neck and drank, then cradled it in his lap. When Nancy was angry and held herself apart from him, or even more powerfully when he came into the house and she did not hear him and from two rooms away he could see her standing, arms folded, half-turned face absorbed in her own thoughts, she would have a presence he had never seen or known. He would hold still, paralyzed by longing and fear. She would hear him, turn, her eyes focus on him and face assume some expression, depending on how they had last left each other, and that power would withdraw, dispersing into the light that filled the window or into the sound of falling rain. Women had always been that way for him since his earliest memories, possessing a power he wanted to flash through him, yet which he needed to hold back and away as if at the moment he let it take him, he would no longer have anything of himself.

He heard a door shutting under him. Carey would have gone to sleep. That would be Nancy closing the door to their bedroom. They had never been through anything as severe as this. Bitter arguments, the unyielding anger at his drinking and emotional binges, at his inability to endure her family, but never such clear infidelity. Often enough in the past she had threatened to leave, but that summer she had tried he had followed her and talked her out of it. Surely he could again.

The bottle was almost empty. His vision blurred and circled when he tilted back his head. He thought of the house empty, only himself to come and go in it, and there was something comfortable in that—a secret solitude like the times after his father died and he was seven, when his mother would leave the house and he would be alone, wandering from room to room. The house was strange and new and his for whatever he wanted. Which was actually never more than that, just indulging in the potentiality surrounding each unoccupied bed or chair or table held in the morning's light. Andrea could come cook a dinner for him. Or someone else. But he imagined her taunting laugh, how they would chase and tease each other from room to room, blocked as if a clear pane of glass slipped always between their reach.

He put the bottle quietly into the trash basket by the edge of the desk, stood, steadying himself for a moment by keeping one hand on the back of the chair. Everything was sloping, the curved neck of the lamp, the tilted books, his own flesh pulling out over the belt of his sagging pants, and as though his face were a mask, it too seemed to drag down—all subject to gravity, a name for some force not entirely physical since his mind was in that same slow descent. Toward what? He shivered, tugged at the belt of his pants, pulling them up sharply to his crotch as if he could lift himself against whatever force it was. A place full of the worst images his life had known, but not really those specific memories—more likely some whirling core they all came from, separated and discordant—might be waiting for him. But if he was lucky he would fall into a drunken unconsciousness before it all accelerated, before he scrambled desperately against the glass-smooth sides like a cat trying to run on marble. His face in the window was split into four segments and the light from beneath puffed out the nose, his cheeks, puckered like yellow blobs. He reached for the switch, the light toppled away from the awkward thrust of his hand, he caught it, and flicked the room into darkness. He stood, hearing his breathing. In, out, in, out, heavy as a sleeper.

He walked down very carefully to the second floor and stood in the hallway. The dim nightlight near the bathroom floor cast a bluish stain on the carpeting. With a distant shudder and heave the furnace began to push heat out toward the radiators. He listened to it climbing toward him, the clack-clack of cooled pipes adjusting to the new flow of steam. To the right was Carey's room, to the left, theirs. Silence in both. It would be cold out tonight and clear, not freezing but close to it, the kind of cold that always reminded him of Halloween even though that date was long past—the world of houses hunched under streetlights seen through the awkward slits of the face of cat or gnome or monster, his mother's hand helping him along when the hem of sheet or ill-fitting pants threatened to throw him to the pavement between the doors that always opened to bell or knock, beyond which were too sweetly smiling men or women who stooped to drop something into his bag or let his hand grasp into a bowl, all the good things slipping back through his fingers. The smell was of burned leaves or acrid mixture of muslin and paste in his mask, and the warm house he returned to was full of his father's cigar smoke. He would spill the gatherings on his bed, throwing aside the brown paper sack with its wrung neck, to sort the old popcorn and crumbled cookies from the neatly wrapped chocolate bars, the taffies and hardballs. Then he would go to bed and the trees still clattered in some wind, his mother's hand lifting him out over the rooftops in ragged flight, his mouth open, stuffed with dark air.

He wobbled back slightly and leaned against the banister. He could go to bed. But he was too drunk now, would wake in an hour or two with heart pounding, unable to sleep. There they both were, wife and child, each in their honeyed chambers, doors closed to him. He wondered if his waking presence, poised like some wizard or predatory bird between them, sent a puzzling ripple across their landscapes, someone shaking the screen in a movie. But she might not be sleeping at all, might be listening to his breathing. In, out, in, out. Maybe he had even been muttering to himself. Their doors, their rooms, their minds. Closed. Of course they did not sense him.

Apart from them. Never really understood. Nor did he want them to. How awful if she could know this swamp of his mind, this slow beating of time as he turned now, caught his balance, walked downstairs, sagged for a moment against the wall by the closet as he groped to be certain he had the keys to the car, then blindly grabbed for some jacket or coat, hearing the hangers ring and scatter onto the floor—fortunately *his* coat, shrugged on, buttoned unevenly—and the next thing he was distinctly aware of was staring at the dials that blinked on, pushing at the dashboard with a key that would not find the hole. Easy. No need to blare into motion waking the neighbors. He shivered. Should have brought gloves. The motor coughed, groaned, ripped finally into a steady chugging. He waited a moment, moved the shift smoothly around in its channels, settled on reverse and crackled over the pebbles; first gear, lights on fully, the driveway ending, no need to look for traffic at this hour, out on the road. Away.

Speed, the antidote. The world rushing at his lights, his body hurled past trees that snatched at his bright circumference but could not snag him, houses in their own darkness thrown up for a moment into the landscape by his passing like great lumps of snow before a plow. The road at the crest of the hill ahead seemed to end, he accelerated for the pure ecstasy of that one moment when the car spun over the top and space without gravity rushed up out of the ground—then the snug tuck of his wheels to the road spinning down, down into the gulf, toward the crossroad, no need to stop, slowing, a slight drift on gravel as he turned, wheels catching just in time and then the long road out toward Valley Forge, Lancaster, anywhere he wanted.

He loved this little Plymouth, nursed through the war, round and ugly as the humped carapace of some ill-proportioned scarab. There were cars now in underwater shapes made to look as if they were speeding even when parked, but he did not need that—only this wheel he knew so well, the smell of the rotting cushions and grease, stale cigarettes in an always unemptied ashtray. Lights ahead, a car, a rip of passage by his side, come and gone even before either of them could blink down. The wall of an estate spun by him, there was the old duckpond and the phony mill, and his eyes lost the two bright spots from the long-passed car. Here everything went fast, fast. No danger of that awful cessation of motion and the gaps.

Only voices moved with deliberation in him, and then he

would sing or recite out loud. He was warm again. The bourbon could do that, burning back against the cold air, flame taking a draft of pure oxygen. Frank, Frank, his mother would say, why do you always have to go somewhere else with them, where do you go? Why can't you just bring them home? I'd like to meet them too, you know. Are you ashamed? Is that it? Ashamed of your own mother? Surely they can't like that awful car better than the living room. Or are they that kind of girl?

He laughed, started singing, "I've got a girl, just like the girl who...," crested the long hill down toward the stream, the hanging rock. No need to coast anymore. No rationing. They used to go this way when they were off to the mountains for a week, Nancy and Carey and himself, singing those same songs together, games, collecting license plates, how many states have you seen? And always coasting the hills, engine off, silence, slowing, the pop of exhaust as he turned the key again. Sometimes his mother would be there in the back seat too, visiting, her shiny black hat pinned tightly to the blue-gray hair, her face sternly piking up into his rear-view mirror. Mother, can't you move to one side a little? I really can't see the traffic; then sullenness, at the door of her cabin when they stopped for the night a terse, "I never want you to speak to me like that again in front of Nancy and Carey, especially Carey. It is no example for a young boy of how to honor your mother."

Uneasily he glanced up at the rear-view mirror, but there was only the faint rush of his lights along the road. Honor your mother. Forget your father. The intersection gathered form, floating toward him with its scattering of warnings, names, directions; he spun under the jut of stone, swept along by the stream, its dark cleft to his side. How far he would go would depend on how the whiskey held. He needed enough to get back on, a small reserve to take to bed, to droop with into sleep, not waking fully to the sounds of their rising in the morning as Carey went off to school. Energy. Controlling it, using it. That was the key. Hemingway understood that. The wonderful bastard. How did he get so much done? All that writing and still he did those other things he wanted to do, just doing them whether anyone wanted him to or not.

Something was wrong. He had lost track of where he was for a second, had not anticipated the curve beneath the trestle. Here already? his mind said, and some spurt of fear beat up in him as the car, bewildered by the jerk of the wheel, drifted sideways. For a moment there was no speed at all, only the huge stone blocks of the trestle looming obliquely, the curve of windshield, the lights trying to hold onto some surface—no speed, no motion, the pure gap of his worst dreams, and silence flooding it all.

Some catch in the road, a crumble or abrasion, gave the tires a hold, the car lurched and sped back into the center, and the wide hedges on both sides were flowing smoothly again. He laughed, or tried to, but the sound caught in his throat like phlegm. His hands were so tight on the wheel that his fingers were stiff with pain when he let go. What took him now was not fear of any accident or physical pain, but that image of speed with all its motion sucked out, the absolute lack of motion at the very center of this wild rush. What if the center of everything was a long wave eternally gathering, gathering water up its slick and streaked inner side, combing but never falling, held forever in endless breathing in.

He stopped by the side of the road. His hands were trembling, wet. He rubbed them along his trousers. A wind across the briars and bushes moaned in his partly opened window. For the first time that night he saw the sharp, clear points of stars. He swallowed, wondered if he would weep or vomit, but nothing happened. He heard again the slight rusty complaint of block and tackle as they lowered her long box into its earth. The highly polished marble of the gravestone, purple on one side, was carved and dated, but the figures seemed unintelligibly random.

He put his hands on the wheel and turned across the road, driving toward home, past the trestle and overhanging rock, dead tired, with just the right amount of energy left to get him up those stairs, into bed, driving still, tires humming in his blood.

# 5

"I've lived here for eighteen years," Nancy said.

She sat on the edge of the trunk in the morning light. The walls and floors joined starkly now that her things and Carey's were packed and lumped together throughout the house. They were waiting for the van which she and Frank had decided would be necessary because of the piano. Or she had, since Frank had become incapable of deciding anything, as if by not taking part he could ignore it out of existence. Only by pleading had she been able to get him up early that morning and away to his office so that he would not be there. Facing the curiosity of the moving men, knowing that the neighbors on each side could see it all, would be hard enough. She had decided not to go outside that morning until she could take Carey's arm and get into the taxi. "Please, Frank, for Carey's sake." He had gone, already nipping at a pint that he pushed sloppily into the side pocket of his jacket.

Now Carey, almost as if imitating his father's attitude, would not talk, would hardly look at her. In tensely self-conscious sessions the past few nights they had sat Carey down between them at the kitchen table and tried to explain it all—how couples sometimes do this for a while because they need a sort of vacation from each other ("Carey, remember Harriet Winslow and her husband Tom? No? They lived in Low Buildings? Oh, you must, they had a girl, Judy, almost your age. Well, anyway, they did and...") and of course Carey would still see Frank, just as much as he wanted, both places would be his homes, and well, it was a little hard right now to be more specific, but they weren't getting along very well. She and Frank had both decided not to mention the students, the letters.

Frank was sober the first night. Carey had become quieter
— 53 —

the more his questions went unanswered, and the second night Frank was drinking and started saying Carey might as well know he didn't want this at all, it was Nancy's idea and he didn't think it would do any good, and what the hell was she doing breaking them up like this, they could work it out together like they always had. But Nancy had surprised herself, keeping calm although a hard rage knotted her shoulders, and she had said, "We never worked out anything together, Frank," and they both held perfectly still when Carey's voice said firmly, "That's for sure." They had all left the table as if they were mediators for separate countries, going off to rooms alone.

The spaces where furniture had been moved were taking the sun as if hungry for something to fill them and the bare floors looked brittle. She slithered down the edge of the trunk to sit with her legs folded, the full, pleated skirt tucked over her knees, and she leaned back.

"Carey, dear, I hope I know what I'm doing."

Was that the wrong thing to say? Even the little book she had found, *When Families Break Their Ties,* warned against showing indecision. But what had all the careful explanations accomplished? They were false. She was constantly pushed back and forth—not about going, she knew that had to be, but about whether it was right or not—and she had finally decided to try to say what she felt, not to censor or translate it for Carey. Maybe he would understand better than she did if he could see it. But she had already discovered at breakfast that simple directness was the hardest way of all.

Her hand probed nervously at the tight bun of her hair for any stray locks. He looked at her this time, and behind the truculence, the stubborn will to be excluded from their argument, she saw a pained bewilderment that made her want to cry out because there was no way to reach the place that look came from. He turned back to the window where he had been watching for the van.

"I've lived here for sixteen."

So he was claiming his own rights. He had them, and she wanted to acknowledge that somehow.

"You still do."

But he did not answer, and they heard the sound of tires on the driveway. He lifted the curtain slightly to one side.

"The van?"

"No. Dad," he said blankly.

— 54 —

She stood quickly, her first instinct being to hide. He was not supposed to be coming back; he had promised to let them get out. The front door swung open, cracked back against the wall.

"Sorry," he muttered, reaching out to hold the knob as if to keep the door from slamming again. He lurched in and closed it carefully. "Not here yet, are they?"

"No."

"Good. Listen, Nance." He stepped fully into the room and for the first time saw Carey by the window, still looking out with the curtain pushed aside on the back of his hand. "Hello, Carey. Maybe you'd better wait outside a minute."

Carey crossed quickly and the latch snicked behind him.

"Frank, for God's sake."

He stepped forward, hand already raised slightly to make some point, his pocket empty, but she could tell that the contents were long gone. She moved back, letting the edge of the steamer trunk come between them.

"Look. How're we ever going to work this out with you living somewhere the other side of town? How'm I ever going to show you things are changing?"

"We've been through all this, Frank. I..."

"No. Now let me finish. I've been in touch with Dr. Townsend. School psychiatrist. You know him. Nice guy. Absolutely discreet. Had a chat. I'm going to start seeing him. Regular basis. Work some of this out. You see? I understand now, Nancy, at least I see it's all a kind of sick pattern, the letters, students, the booze..." and he stopped with hand in midair, that waving, gallant flag of a hand she had seen him saw and rant with so often, and she suddenly saw his hands as the puppets of his layered emotions, his many selves living in the space between himself and the people they sometimes touched.

They both stood looking at the hand for only a second, and then it balled up as if badly burned and he drew it close to his gut.

"Christ," he muttered. "I know, here I am zonked at ten A.M. and talking about the booze, but it will take time."

She was still staring at his hand.

"Stop it, will you? Say something."

"There's nothing to say, Frank. I hope you're right. I hope he can help. I'm not leaving for good. We will stay in touch. But I need to be alone. Space, I need."

"You need, you need, what about me?"

She was about to laugh bitterly for his needs, his needs—but he was coming toward her now. She moved farther behind the trunk, held up a hand, bumped back against the bookcase, when the front door was pounded by some fist heavy as a ram. He stopped, both hands toward her.

"They're here," she said quickly, and he looked back over his shoulder as if someone were coming to arrest him, turned once more to her, and his face assumed a look she had not seen for years, guileless, unmuddied by the cross-currents of his growing confusions, a simple undivided gaze that she had seen from time to time on the faces of people she loved, Carey, her parents, only when they were alone and did not know anyone was looking at them. She put a hand to her throat as he turned silently and went out the back door without looking at her again.

Whenever she stepped outside as the men hefted boxes and crates, Nancy could see Carey sitting under the maple tree, his back to its trunk, as if he could care less about the whole process, but when it came time for them to move the piano, he walked back into the house and stood as close as he could, watching them so grimly and silently that the men kept glancing over at him. She sensed he had placed all his hopes on the piano, as if it were the center of his life they were heaving with small words of encouragement, or perhaps the household gods themselves. When they were closing up the van, she called the taxi and told the men she would meet the truck at the apartment, Ithan Avenue, ground floor, yes, the big old house across the street from Canolli's, the Italian food store; and when they had climbed into the taxi Carey did not look back once but kept his face straight forward.

The piano filled much of the living room, but they each had their own bedroom, and the kitchen was large. She gave up trying to tell the men where various boxes belonged, so they stacked them in what was left of the living room, took her check, thanked her, and the foreman said please to be sure to call if they moved again, and Nancy wanted to say that was none of his business but realized he was only looking for clients. Carey had started to put his bed together, and she sat on the edge of the trunk, hearing the slats being dropped in, his tussle with the springs. "Need help?" she called, his voice said, "Nope," and when she looked up, a birdlike woman with a shocking frizz of white hair and dressed in a black smock was standing in the doorway.

"Good morning," she said with a slight accent that Nancy could not identify at first. "Okay I come in?"

Nancy did not want to talk to anyone now, especially a stranger, but saw the woman was wearing big floppy slippers so she had to be the woman who lived upstairs.

"My name is Magnarella. Mrs. Magnarella. Anna. You can call me either. Most people in this country say Magnarella," she pronounced the "g" heavily and shrugged, "but our people don't. Magnarella, see? Almost like you are trying to swallow it."

She was in the room now, the slight limp in one of her skinny legs making her seem even more like a small bird hopping. "I'm upstairs. Over your head. But quiet. I don't have no husband, just grown boys who come see me, and they don't make much noise except the days they bring their kids and wives and we drink a lot of wine. But you'll like them. They're good kids. Most of them."

She stopped and turned to Carey, who had come into the room.

"This is my son, Carey. And I'm Nancy Mitchell."

"Yes. I seen by the name the landlord put up on the door. Sol is okay, but like all the Jews, don't cross him up on money. How much he charge you?"

Nancy hesitated, then decided she might as well say, but the woman had already waved a hand. "Never mind. Better you don't say. Better we don't get into that. Just pay on time, he won't bother you. I been here twenty years now, you guess how old I am?"

She was looking at Carey.

"Come on. You guess. It's okay. Can't insult an old lady like me. Then I'll guess your age."

Nancy saw him smile, the first time in days, grudging as it was.

"Sixty."

She laughed, a high warble that snagged somewhere in the back of her throat.

"Oh, I like you. Sixty. I seen sixty go by so long ago I can't remember it. You know what? I'm seventy-seven."

She turned to Nancy. "Five boys I have and brought up and did all the cooking and work, and I'm seventy-seven, nothing wrong except bum knees, arthritis, and my husband dead for ten years now."

"I'm sorry."

"No matter. Toward the end, he wasn't much fun. You

know what I mean? I still had plenty of fun left in me. Your husband dead?"

"No," and Nancy could not keep her eyes from glancing away. But Anna pointed a very lean and bony forefinger at Carey.

"You're eighteen."

Carey blushed, his hands in his back pockets, and shook his head.

"Seventeen?"

"Sixteen."

"I don't understand how come they grow so big in this country. Must be vitamins. You feed him vitamins?"

Nancy laughed.

"You play that?" she said to Nancy, pointing at the piano.

"Carey does. I hope it won't bother you. He practices five hours a day sometimes."

She shook her head. "Listen. Music is what I love. I play the radio, I have a record player my son Luigi gave me five years ago, I love music. You know Verdi?"

Carey shook his head.

"Well, you come up sometime, we listen to Verdi together. I got his operas on records. You like music, you got to like Verdi." As quickly as she entered, she turned and limped to the door. "I'm going now. You want something, you call." She turned in the doorway. "Listen, you both call me Anna, okay? We're all Italians around here, some better than others. Watch out for the Sardinians. The Simonettis. Two doors down. Bad blood. Most of the rest of us, we're okay. Especially the Abruzzesi." She was gone, her footsteps so light that they could barely hear them on the stairs.

Nancy went to the door and shut it quietly. When she turned, Carey was still standing there, staring at the piano.

"Maybe you'd better check it out."

"What?"

"The piano. Make sure it's not damaged."

He started to cross toward it, skirting a crate near her, and those big, gangling limbs knocked off a smaller box. It tumbled, the top opening, assorted kitchen utensils clanging out on the floor. He started to stoop, saying something she could not quite hear, but instead he veered aside, she put a hand on his neck and he let his head rest for a moment on her although he was taller than she was now, while she tried to say, "It's all right, it will be all right," through a throat tightening toward tears, and then they both stooped and clattered the tin cups and spatulas back into the box.

She woke slowly to the sound of the piano playing. Eyes still closed, she listened, letting herself be carried along in a state close to dreaming by the rush of notes, a piece her waking mind tried to name, then gave up. But they were not at the house and she sat up to look at the clock. He must not start practicing too early. It was eight-thirty, late enough, and she lay down again, heart settling its pace, eyes closing. He stopped, went back a few bars, began again.

Saturday. She could sleep if she wanted, but nowadays when she woke, even in the middle of the night, she would not fall easily to sleep again. She needed to be very tired, and whatever sleep first came would either carry her through to morning or would take off the edge of weariness and leave her lying on her back, eyes wide open, but afraid to check the time. She was learning not to insist on sleep, satisfied if her mind would not harass her, letting her lie and watch as the occasional passage of car lights through the slit of the shade veered across the ceiling. Now that she had a job again, the weekdays were easier; she could concentrate in that office, come home tired, even bring work for the evening. The weekends were difficult. Especially the ones when Carey left to stay overnight with Frank. She had to eat alone and face the empty apartment in the evening or the sound of Anna's slow walking overhead, her voice on the telephone.

She was frightened sometimes to think how much she had come to depend on Carey in the brief months they had been living together. She tried to treat him as she always had, but that was impossible if only because they were so close together in the small apartment. She could not help wanting him to talk to her at breakfast and dinner, or she would try to tell him about her job, the people there, why she wanted to work. He held back somewhere. She would find herself describing complex emotions that knotted in her when she had talked to her mother or Frank. His comments at first seemed naïve, then afterward struck her as right. But she seemed to be doing so little for him.

He began the slow middle section again. She listened more carefully this time. He practiced all the time now, and occasionally she had to ask him to stop, not for her need of silence—she had discovered a tolerance for his practicing as great as his need to do it—but out of fear that Anna would not be able to stand it, that he would never do his homework or go outside. Practicing might be partly a compensation for the confusions of their new life, an absorption with a known and safe thing, but she could tell by his face when he played and she pretended to be reading, or by the thoughtful way he would sit and look silently at a page of music spread out on the kitchen table, a pencil in hand, that the music was not devouring him as much as it was growing out, taking him along. She talked to Stafford Newfane about it on the phone; that pompous tone he usually took with her was suddenly shucked off, and a very personal voice talked to her with pride, as though Carey were his son, and when she said that sometimes the practicing worried her, he reacted with a bristling defensiveness. "You sound as if there were something wrong with it," and he bluntly told her not to intervene. She had not meant to imply it was wrong, but perhaps a little obsessive? There had been a silence, then, "He will need that, to persist."

Although the snow had stopped falling, the sky was still gray. Through the slightly raised shade she saw a few limbs, an edge of lawn and street, all heavily lumped, and she let herself succumb to that euphoria that always accompanied a snowfall, receding into a childhood that had never really existed, something to do with imagining a forest of covered limbs, a cabin with lit window and smoke from the chimney, as if she were looking forever and peacefully at a picture of someone looking at a picture of snow and forest and nighttime coming.

When Frank came at noon everything was ready. She had kept an eye on the street and wanted to pass Carey on quickly, giving Frank no chance to talk. Not invited in, he poised awkwardly on the threshold, looking around nervously at the room as if he could not help it, his eyes settling on her the way they would when he was full of something to say. But she kept Carey between them, moved with him toward the door, making Frank back out onto the porch so there was no way he could say to Carey, "You go on to the car, I'll be right there," as he had last time when they had launched into one of those futile conversations about how insane it was for her to be still here when she could come home, and Carey too; wasn't she thinking about how awful it must be for him? She gripped Carey's shoulder and said, "Then I'll see you late Sunday afternoon?" and Carey nodded back at her.

She watched them walking down the path, Frank carrying some of Carey's schoolbooks, his galoshes widely unbuckled, that old tweed coat tight now to his thickening waist, and the roll of his shoulders more pronounced by the shuffling pace his boots made him take. The pang she felt was not for him at all, but for Carey. How was he going to deal with both of them, handed back and forth, a hostage? She saw Frank not as her husband but Carey's father, and in the same moment twisted back to see herself, equally fallible and incapable of bringing Carey through it all with understanding. Frank touched his son's head playfully but also leaning for a second. They were both doing that, holding on to him as the only clear point of reference.

At first, through habit, Nancy wandered from room to room putting things in place, making Carey's bed, hanging his strewn clothes, cleaning up the kitchen, but that was all done quickly. She could not learn to stretch out what few chores there were, and she moved through them with the same efficiency she had learned in a house with three floors, three people, sometimes guests. She wondered which was worse, days or nights. She tried not to take pills. But there was nothing to keep her from all her thoughts. She would leave her bedroom door ajar in case Carey needed her, but he never did. She would watch the lights of a passing car move the crack between shade and window slowly across the ceiling and down the far wall, and sometimes if the car came from the other direction the light rose from the floor and curved back again to its crack.

Often what struck her was the absolute waste of it all. Why had they ever met, ever married, lived those years together, had a son, to arrive at this point—their bodies turned to stone, hers lying restlessly in a bed watching a light come and go. The anger she had located in Frank for a while bled out into everything, paling, becoming a total lack of emotion. His absence had made a hole in all the fabric around them, but now it enlarged, sucked her out and beyond into a blank space. She loved him, then she did not love him, but sometimes she thought that she did love him, even if she could never live with him. Having a point of reference was what mattered. Even if they lived apart, she wanted them to be *living* apart, not caught in a ghostly obsession with each other. What if the act of leaving him had only been to circle back, either to live together differently than they had or to know each other differently? Those same bodies might change, be ready to try again.

At such times she saw her own thoughts as small, ugly creatures rising to pain her. What was she doing to herself? Why didn't the mind leave one alone? She would breathe deeply, think of the pills, grope over the bedside table with one hand, then draw back. No. Let it go now. And quickly her mind would refuse that whole last series of thoughts. She was not doing this for Frank. There was the possibility of their returning to each other, but to say that was the purpose gave her actions more direction than they had. What if, finally, there was no more direction in any of it than that illusion of light on her wall, the seeming purposefulness with which it grew out of its crack, arched to the corner and sometimes returned, so fixed and directed, but only the pattern of random passage guided by the chance positioning of a screen, a window, walls.

Last night she had thrown back the covers, gone to yank the cord and let the shade rattle up. A dog trotted loose-limbed down the center of the street, veered to sniff at a snowbank, then sidled off. So this was that gray and motionless state that she always said was his excuse to do only what he wanted, to evade. And which she had evaded. But still, there was something he was not right about. She was there now, but he had always talked about the loneliness. She could not call it that. She was not alone. What she was feeling now had no sense of a being that could be called herself, so that she could not say she was alone. She was not even afraid. She closed her eyes and heard two words that she had listened to since childhood and had thought were magic because of their strange syllables: *Kyrie Eleison.*

She had gone back to her bed and said the words out loud, then to herself again. For the first time she did not hear them as ritual in a church, as priestly terms. They were simple words, ones that anyone had a right to say, especially in the space she had touched. She did not think of them as Greek. They were sounds, and all the words of other languages, like her own, could sprout from them. She recalled the music she had heard them sung to, had even sung part of when she had tried joining the college chorus. Bach. A Mass. She would have to listen to that again, and she had fallen asleep saying the syllables until they were nonsense, until they were steps leading up or down without a railing on either side of them and she did not want to fall.

She found herself sitting at the kitchen table, sipping at the warmed-over dregs of tea, and for a moment she mocked herself, tried to laugh, thinking, so this is your new freedom, all the time in the world—for nothing. But thinking. And she was tired of that because her mind would only circle back inevitably to the same things, and there was nothing new to think about them now. How imbecilic if that were to prevail, and she panicked under the thought that maybe when two people separated they stepped outside of time into a place where nothing moved and changed, or into an eddy, as if they had become so dependent on defining where they were by the other person that they even continued to invent them in the mind. She closed her eyes. No. They both lived in a larger world than that. That would only happen if she let it, and even as she said that to herself, she recognized she was talking inside as if to him, as if they were once again preparing to reword their argument about the will.

Out. For a walk. She stood, looked out the window by the front door. The sun had begun to shine, great chunks of snow were thumping down from the roof and already the street was mostly clear or roiled into slush. It would all melt quickly. She decided to investigate the neighborhood or walk downtown. What she needed was a good book, something to sink into, a long slow novel. She would go to the bookstore.

She walked the long way around through small streets she had never looked at carefully before, then up the pike past stores where she paused to look in the windows, past the movie theater where nothing of interest was coming, and finally in the bookstore she chose a large paperback novel densely filled with many characters. She chatted with Helen Muskee, grateful that Helen did not know anything about her move, and afterward realized she must have seemed half asleep or feeble-minded because most of the time they were talking she kept frantically thinking, Will I have to tell her, how will I tell her? until Helen said, "We'll have to all get together very soon," and Nancy said, "Oh, we're so busy," and she saw the puzzled look on Helen's face as she turned to go. Then the apartment, more tea, a light thumping and distant whine of vacuum cleaner upstairs, and her book. The first page she read six times as if striking a match again and again. But it caught, held, and even as she began to see and feel those other lives, she hovered peacefully, grateful for being possessed by them.

"Anybody home?"

She looked up. Anna's face was peering in the opened door. It was dark beyond her. Nancy closed the book on her finger. All the windows were dark too. Evening? Night? She looked at her watch. It was seven.

"Come in." She stood up but her foot had gone to sleep and she leaned on the arm of the chair, her leg raised like a heron. Anna came all the way in, closing the door behind her, a pleated skirt swinging above the black, ankle-length shoes, and she was wound in a wide-meshed shawl.

"You warm enough down here? Always hot enough upstairs. Heat rises."

Nancy was rested, at ease, as if she had been sleeping all that time. "Yes."

"I tell Sol again and again, 'You ought to put up storm windows on this house in winter. Saves you money, big old place like this.' Especially when a north wind comes down. These big windows," and she swept a bony hand out of the tangle of her shawl, "they leak."

"But I like the light."

"Where's your boy?" She came into the middle of the room, and when Nancy pointed to a chair, starting to speak, she raised a hand quickly with a nod and perched on the edge of it, the cracked leather of her pointed toes just showing. "You know what I think? I think you got a genius on your hands. That boy plays better than anyone his age should, better than older people do. What're you going to do with him?"

She stared at Nancy, her head turned slightly to the side as she always did, as if favoring one ear slightly, those black eyes not flinching.

"I don't seem to have to do much. He loves it."

"He's a good boy, too, isn't he? Stays out of trouble. You can see that right away. My Luigi is that way. Right from the beginning you could tell. Serious. Tells the truth. *Un uomo d'onestà*, you know what I mean?" and she made a swift motion down through the air with her fingers pursed as if she were tracing a clear, straight line from head to heart. "But Antonio." She shook her head. "Trouble. He eats it, drinks it, loves it. Too much energy, that's all. Can't sit still. Women. Jobs. Never enough of them. My husband used to say, 'Trouble with Antonio, he wants to be everybody, so he's never himself.'"

She stopped abruptly, pursed her lips.

"What're you reading?"

Nancy told her and explained something about the plot, how it was about some families and one woman in paticular who runs away from her husband. Anna listened intently.

"Sounds depressing. How come you don't read something happy?"

Nancy was trying to think of how to explain when the woman fluffed out her shawl slightly to put her hands under it and said, "You run away from your husband?"

"Not really."

"None of my business."

For a second Nancy was irritated, wanted to say yes, that's true, but there was something about the woman that made anger impossible, and by now they knew each other well enough for the question to be justified.

"We're separated. For a while."

"I never seen that work much. I mean, once you're apart, what's to get you together again? But it's always harder on the woman. That's what I think. Men, they got things to do, places to go. Work. Antonio, he left his first wife. Nice girl, Janice, although she wasn't Italian and I told Tony, 'That's trouble.' Nice girl, but a little skinny. I felt sorry for her. I told Tony, 'I don't want to see you for a while, I'm gonna help Janice,' and he stayed away. I had her to supper all the time and she cried a lot the first week, didn't know what to do. But it wasn't long before she stopped coming. Took up with another man. That's the only thing for a woman to do."

Again she stared hard, but this time Nancy could not help laughing, and a flicker of a smile crossed Anna's face.

"Not for a while, thanks. I'm enjoying being alone."

"Good. I like to see you laugh. You ought to laugh more often, quit reading depressing novels. But maybe you like that. Who needs advice? My boys used to come over sometimes in the evening to sit, listen to the radio with me, after their father died. I finally said to Luigi, 'You lonely or something, you need your mamma, you having troubles with Lucia?' He looked at me, surprised. 'No, Mamma, we decided, me and Tony and Carlo that you gotta be lonely all by yourself, without Poppa.' Well, I told him off then. I said, 'Listen, you think I haven't been waiting for you *fannulloni* to grow up and get into your own homes, waiting for when I wouldn't have to listen every night to that junk on the radio your father liked or have to listen to him complain about his bowels all day? You come over when you need me, but otherwise, leave me alone.'" The hands had risen from the shawl and were waving about frantically in the space between Nancy and herself as if Nancy were the puzzled Luigi. "Now sometimes they call up. 'Momma, we want some lasagne. Real lasagne,' or, 'We can't stand it anymore, we want you should take Benny and Joe off our hands for the weekend.' That's all right. You know you're still alive when someone needs you. But I don't need babysitters. Anyway, you ate yet?"

"No."

"I thought. That's the bad thing about being alone. You forget sometimes. Not much fun eating alone. Come up. I got some cannelloni left over. Good stuff."

Nancy hesitated. Partly she wanted to sit with her book. But it was early.

"Your boy coming home? Carey? We'll leave him a note."

"No. He's with his father tonight."

She made three little steps, gently took the book from Nancy's hand and put it on the table, at the same time perching a wiry-fingered hand on her arm. "Come on. We'll stick together."

They climbed the stairs, Anna still holding Nancy's arm, and that was when she showed her age, the legs stiff, her hand grasping tightly, wincing on each step up. "Too bad," she muttered, "that all my boys are married. Except Tony, and I wouldn't wish him on nobody."

Something fragrant was warming in the oven, and later, after Nancy had eaten and had a few glasses of wine and they had talked, it seemed, about almost everything, she went down and sat again with the book in her lap, but not reading, just holding it open. She looked at the lamps and chairs and small objects dimly picked out by the single light. For the first time the room was at least partially possessed by their lives, and she thought, in a voice that sounded as much like Anna's as her own, I'm going to make it, I'm going to make it.

Carey was sitting on the floor with his atlas, trying to find a town in South America, perhaps near the Amazon, called Mburucayao. But he could not find it again. His assignment was to find remote places and imagine what they would be like. He had written down the name in his notebook, but now the town had disappeared in all the other names of cities and rivers and mountain ranges. He looked up at Frank slouched in the easy chair by the fireplace, reading the evening paper and well into his second bourbon. He had muttered something but evidently was not starting a conversation.

The Amazon jungle was purple, the river a pale blue winding into it, veins spreading out into a dark brown strip that was mountains. Large spaces contained no towns at all, or at least none were marked. But he could not find Mburucayao. Had it ever been there? He looked at the piece of paper, the name scrawled in his own writing. He tried some of the others maps of the same area—ones showing minerals or crops—but they were even less detailed. Finally he closed the atlas, took his geography book and began reading the assigned chapter. He was getting hungry, it was past time for dinner, and Frank would have to be reminded, but when he looked up later, his father seemed to be dozing, eyes closed and head back. The chapter was dull, all about making fresh water out of oceans and how years from now the deserts would be green.

Carey stood up quietly and walked around the house for a while, too empty now. A folding cot perched in his own room, and a single bed that Frank had moved down from the attic barely filled a corner of his parents' room. He sat on his cot, its steel mesh sagging deeply. It was cold upstairs because the fire below kept the furnace from going on. If it had not been dark, he would have gone out, maybe tried some sledding on the hill down to the hockey field, something he had not done for years. He switched on the radio that Frank let him keep in his room. Nothing much on, but he listened anyway. Finally he heard some fumbling, pans hitting together in the kitchen. He waited a few minutes and went down.

"Hamburgers, okay?" Frank was standing by the sink flattening some raw meat into patties, but Carey could tell by the motions of his hands, the way he glared at the meat, that his father was drunk, would be for the rest of the evening. "Not so good at this. Give me a hand."

They stood side by side and Carey made two patties quickly, putting them into the pan which Frank set on the stove. He handed the spatula to Carey. "You keep an eye on them. Make sure they don't get away. I'll set the table."

By the time they sat down to eat, Frank had poured himself another drink. Carey was hungry, there was more than enough food, but it made him uneasy to be alone with Frank when he drank this much. The conversation would change soon, and there would be nothing he could tell his father.

One week ago, Frank had ended up chanting, "Why, why, why?" one fist pounding at the side of his head, his flushed face dull, until Carey had been about to yell back, throw something at the wall. But Frank had stopped just in time, looked at Carey as if remembering he was there, and in a subdued voice said, "Sorry. No need to overact."

Now Frank took small bites of his hamburger, pushing it each time to the back of his plate.

"Taste all right?"

Carey nodded.

"Well, your mom's the real cook. But we won't get into that. How's it going, the piano?"

Between mouthfuls Carey talked about his lessons, the concerts, what Newfane was saying about arranging a recital for him soon, but he could see his father was not really listening, that the other topic still lay between them. Carey pushed a wall of words at it, but in the first full pause, Frank said, "She going out at all? With other men yet?"

"No."

"She will, you know. That's what comes next." He waved a hand vaguely. "My fault. I don't mean it's wrong. Can't spend all your time alone."

Carey swallowed, poured himself more milk.

"I know I shouldn't be talking to you about all this. Does she?"

"Some."

"Keeps it to herself, I'm sure. Always had more restraint than I do. But listen, Carey, it's two-sided. I'm telling you all the time how I feel, you can do the same to me."

Carey looked at his father's eyes, then away. Frank meant it, but Carey could not talk to him. Or his mother. Or any of his friends.

"If it seems nonsense to me, it must to you."

"I don't know."

"Well, forget what I asked. I'm not going to ask that sort of thing again. You're not my spy. Just having you come like this helps a lot. Christ," and he banged his glass down, sloshing the bourbon, "it gets lonely in this big place. Too many rooms."

They finished eating, stood together by the sink to do the dishes, and Frank eased up, they joked about other things and laughed.

Carey went upstairs to listen to the radio and from time to time he could hear Frank moving around in the house, finally standing in the doorway listening to the last part of the program, glass in hand. When Carey went to bed he thought everything would be all right. His father said simply, "Goodnight, pal, see you in the morning."

But he was almost asleep, or had he already dozed off? when he heard a shatter, a voice yelling something briefly, and he sat up in the blank silence.

"Dad?" He said it tentatively, knowing it would not carry. Half awake but with precise logic, he told himself that in dreams the voice was not like real talking—it always stuck in the throat—so he said "Dad" again, now wide awake. He walked down the stairs. The kitchen light was on.

His father was sitting on the floor, his back against the counter, and near him was a broken glass, the ice melting in a brownish stain. He did not see Carey at first, eyelids drooping heavily, hands flat on the floor and palms up.

"Dropped the glass, 'm'fraid. Dropped myself, too." He grinned sheepishly.

Carey wanted to turn and close the door. It was an accident—sudden, violent—but he knew his father was not hurt. No, the accident was happening to him, like that time he had been carving in wood and the knife slipped and he was looking at the bone in his finger.

He walked in, found a bag in the back of a drawer, began picking up the glass. Frank heaved up one leg as if to stand.

"Here, now. Do it myself." But he did not go any further. "'Fraid your dad's had a bit to drink."

Carey picked at the slivers carefully, keeping his bare feet away from the liquid.

"Don't cut y'rself."

Frank breathed heavily for a while, his expressionless face staring at all of Carey's motions, the wiping of the rag, the walk to the trash can. "C'mere."

Frank waved, patted the floor beside him. Carey slid down, back to the cabinet.

"Sorry about all this. No good."

His father's hand rose, pushed at the air, then rested on Carey's knee.

"I was thinking, after you went to bed, of my own father, your grandfather, although you never met him. Died when I was a kid. Seven. But you know all that."

"Yes."

"Thinking how I wished he hadn't died, but then, Christ,

who knows. I mean look at us, Carey. Might've been better if I had."

"No," Carey said sharply. "Stop it. Please."

The hand kneaded his leg gently.

"Keeled right over. I was on the porch. I waited on the porch about every afternoon. He'd come home same time. Worked for Wilson and Wright, big contractors."

Frank looked around vaguely. "Where'd I put that drink? Oh. Yes. Busted." He gave a short laugh. "I saw him die. It was Friday afternoon, he came home late, stepped out of the car, waved, had his sleeves rolled up, hot and sweaty, afterward we learned the car'd run out of gas and he'd pushed it a quarter-mile or so—they were lighter then, but still that was work. Then he dropped. I thought it was a trick. A game, see. As if he were pretending, but it seemed wrong to lie like that, face right down, white shirt, on the driveway. I ran up. He didn't answer. I started yelling. Didn't know what to do. Horrible. Mother wasn't home. Should've gone to the neighbors, or rung up the firehouse, something."

He stopped. The hand was a claw on Carey's leg, then he noticed it and relaxed.

"Heart attack. They said he might've come through if help'd gotten there fast, or someone done something. My mother, one of the first things she said was, 'Why didn't you go to the O'Briens? What's wrong with you?'"

"Nana said that?"

Frank gave that harsh, heavy laugh again. "Among other things. I thought for years that I'd killed him. You see, I panicked. Ran into the house, stood in the living room, and my mind went blank. I stood in the middle of the room, and it was hot, so heavy you could hardly breathe, and I stared out the window and could see the front of the car, and him lying there, face down, and I couldn't move."

Carey gazed at his father's face, profile staring ahead, one lip thrust out slightly as if he were stubbornly refusing something, and Carey could not get rid of the clench in his ribs that made it almost impossible to breathe, so he leaned suddenly against him, put his hand on his shoulder, thought for a moment that he would cry, but nothing came except the hot return of his own breath from the sweater. The arm lifted, came around his shoulder and held him, the hand patting in slow rhythm on Carey's side.

"Old history. Long time ago."

The voice came out of the flesh under the clothes. Carey's

eyes were closed. He did not know how long they sat like that, but when the body heaved, he opened his eyes, blinked at the light. Frank was trying to get up.

"C'mon, the kitchen floor's no place to spend the night. Give me a hand, Carey, and we'll call it quits."

Carey stood. His father held up a hand, pushed the floor with the other. Carey pulled, they almost toppled, then Frank was up and leaning heavily on him.

"Phew. Dizzy."

They left the light on behind them, and all the way up the stairs Carey dragged a heavy weight, Frank's arm like a rope over his shoulder.

"That's good enough," Frank said at the door to his room. He turned, eyes wide. "Thanks, son. I'll lock the bottle up next time you come."

Carey lay on his back until he heard the springs in his father's bed give. Only then his muscles began to relax. Mburucayao. He could get up in the morning and look harder. It had to be there. He wanted to write about it. The name began to play its syllables over and over in his mind and his fingers were doing it, like scales. "Ma-bu-ru-ca-yao," and he planted each syllable in a dark earth that spread out endlessly. A brown, swollen river was nearby with silent twists and eddies, and trees began to grow all around him, higher and higher until the sky was only a scattering of blue slivers. When the boat snagged against his bank, he leaned to reach for it, hand spreading its fingers, blue veins growing smaller and smaller, reaching out into the mountains.

# 6

She stood on the lawn under the maple tree, the brown grass
spreading toward the steps and vacant windows. She hoped
no one was watching her from the other houses. The warm
sun, easing through spring, cut clear midafternoon shadows
and pressed an odor of last fall's leaves and dead grass out
of the ground. She clutched her arms tightly to herself even
though she was not cold. All week she had felt shut into a
tight space, and twice she had remembered vividly that incident in her childhood when two children on her block had
been locked in a refrigerator while playing. The pictures in
the paper showed them side by side, knees huddled close to
their chests, and they stared out as if surprised at the sudden
opening of their door. How could she take all those old boxes
down from the attic that they had stored away from their
last move so long ago, fill them carefully with the last of her
belongings, sort through so many mingled possessions? She
did not care about any of it. If only their lawyers could swoop
down and haggle about who should keep this or that.

She walked up the steps, staring at her feet as if snow
were driven against her eyes, turned the key, stumbled in
and, slamming the door behind her, leaned there, head back
against the wood, breathing deeply and slowly. No sounds.
Frank had kept his word, was not there. She was sweating,
thought she might need to sit down. But she made herself
walk slowly from room to room, ground floor first, then up
the stairs, and as she went, her presence was slowly chasing
something in front of her that retreated as she advanced until
there was only one room left, his study, and she turned the
knob, flinched at his chair swiveled toward her, arms reaching for the door, and stepped in, walking all the way to the

window. Whatever she had pursued glided with a swoop where her eyes followed the drop of field, the distant rise and towers, the sky with its feathered clouds. For a moment she lost the defined lines of hedge, path, and etched trees in a simple blur of light.

She packed all morning, room by room. There was less than she had expected—books, clothes, some things she did not even care about. She found a can of soup in the kitchen, there were tea bags, and although she almost felt like a thief, she settled down for some lunch, started to eat in the kitchen but changed her mind and went to sit in a corner of the back porch where the sun, hazy with high clouds, shone in an opaque pool.

Angus McFarlane's head floated past the railings, the collar of his raincoat up even on this day when rain did not seem possible, on his way home to lunch. For five years, whenever college was in session, he had passed one way or the other with such precision that she could keep time by him—to class during the week, to the library on the weekend. A scholar. Famous in his field. Something to do with the decorative tiles of Ancient Greek temples. She had gone to a lecture once, ignored his voice droning on with theory and dates, but loved the slides of lushly colored sites or those tongue-lolling Medusas. She was glad he could not see her. She wanted to meet none of them, to break all connections with this place.

In the last week, the urge to cut clear of everything had been so strong that she knew she would have to do something about it and already she had begun to make inquiries at Bill Stout's office. Now that he was a senator, he would know if there were any jobs open, like the one he had arranged for her friend Molly Caswell, a secretary with some embassy. Only just to see, she told herself. She did not have to take it. But she wanted to leave this town, these people, even her mother and Pop, and memories that seemed to have some edge to them now. To be alone, unencumbered. She put her head back, eyes closed, letting the sun fall flatly on her forehead. Too often in the past weeks she had run into Frank unexpectedly. In the grocery store their carts had locked awkwardly as she tried to pass, and she had not recognized him until he turned with a can of stew in his hand. In the drugstore they had both waited for prescriptions to be filled and had lapsed into the most inane conversation, stiffly correct, but both of them red in the face. Mental space was not enough, distance was what she needed, the sheer physical gap.

She had even thought of going abroad and leaving Carey behind, not with Frank, she would not permit that and her lawyer warned her not to jeopardize custody rights, but Carey could go to a boarding school. She could be off by herself in a new world with new people, maybe in South America; after all she knew a little Spanish from school. But Carey had shaken her out of her fantasies by walking in the door, back from school, confronting her again with his moods—one moment leaning heavily on her, the next angry, remote, still blaming her for everything, or worse, blaming himself. She could not leave him. Anyway, maybe what he needed was to go somewhere too.

A wren fluttered down on the far side of the porch, its lifted tail jerking, head peering from side to side at the patch of sunlight as if it could see something there she could not. She had never traveled very much. There had been no time, certainly no money. Not like Sally and Daniel coming back almost every other summer from some tour—of France, Italy, England—with slides and anecdotes: Daniel holding a squid in Capri, Sally leaning against the tower of Pisa, their guide through the ruins of Pompeii looking disheveled and cutthroat. And what if she and Carey never came back? It happened sometimes. She stood, the bird darted off with a startled chirp, and she went back inside to finish packing.

She opened the last drawer of the dresser they shared, light, nearly empty. They had never bought the big bureau for her own use that they had promised, and instead of each having their own drawers in the single dresser, they had simply divided each drawer in half—an imaginary line that loose sweaters, balled-up socks would not respect. A photograph had slid across from some old shirts and folders he had piled there, so like him not to think of the bureau as a place only for clothes. It was face up, a picture of a long white object, a person. Herself. She held it to the light.

How strange she looked, her hair coiffed tightly, the sleek white dress hanging long and angular over her hips, the sleeves so stiff. A floppy hat almost hid her brow. Her face was barely recognizable, so young, her shoulders slightly hunched as if she were about to laugh, lips lifting, and in her fingers she lightly held a champagne glass. Grass, some kind of flowering tree behind her, a man's back and half his head on one edge, a corner of a table with a fringe of its cloth billowing out in a breeze. She stared but could not recall where it could have been, turned it over, but nothing was written on the back.

She sat on the edge of the bed. It was becoming very important to remember. Was it before she had met Frank? But then why would he have it? She could not recall having seen the photograph. She half closed her eyes, trying to place that tree, the chunk of landscape. There were gardens, trees like that nearby. Her chest tightened with frustration. It was like trying to remember a word when it stayed just around some corner in the mind. She noticed her hand was trembling and she put the photograph in her lap, looking out the opened door into the hallway.

How horrible to think that memory might be like this, fragments boiling up some day in the mind but unlocatable, never quite what they should be. That was herself, but if she could not remember where the photograph belonged in time and space, what difference did it make? That figure might as well not be her. Frank must know, she was sure of that: the hour, the occasion, what other times she had worn that dress, a piece of cloth she could not even remember owning. Had she lost all that time together, all the things he remembered about her or Carey? He would take them with him. A huge piece of her own life had been sheared off.

She put the photograph back, packed her sweaters, and closed the box, taped it, piled it in the hallway with the others. She stood at the head of the stairs looking down. The sun below clung to the newel post and dragged one long stain across the carpet. All those years were wasted and what if she never had the energy to start again? No use for what she had learned of him.

As she stood for one last time with her hand on the banister, that wood familiar and touched so often that it had become an object never consciously perceived, the house itself was slipping away from her like a boat loaded with all those years, their small boxes of days and nights. She touched the nick in the newel post, there since the first day their bed had been moved awkwardly upstairs. She walked along the slim trailing of light to the door, opened it, released the catch on the lock, and pulled it closed. Letting go of the knob was releasing a rope she had held on to for a long, long time. Even the muscles in her hand were strained and cramped.

She passed the maple and looked back at the house crouched with five others along the bank. In the yard two doors down a child was sitting in a bright red wheelbarrow, pounding methodically at something on its side. That would be Gus Morrow. Beside their house were the bulbs she had planted for years—narcissi, irises, day lilies, yet to bloom—and they would bloom, maybe neglected until they choked each other, maybe tended by the next family who lived there, for surely the college would not let Frank stay in such a large house. The Mances and Mitchells had joked once, calling it not "faculty" but "factory" housing—trying, she understood now, to tell themselves something. No wonder she and Frank had so often felt unmoored, their own harried clinging made even more anxious by the lack of anything firm to stand on. And now she was living in an apartment, thinking of traveling to strange places. What in the world was there to hold onto—not memory, not place, not people. She turned back toward town.

She would not miss the college. That was not what made her feel so bleak now as the station came in sight and she walked down through the tunnel. In the middle of it she stood still, looking up at the trembling ceiling as an express rattled through above. When Carey was little he had loved being pushed to the station to watch the steam engines come by, their tall wheels pumped by the rods, the breathing rhythms of smoke making him stare wide-eyed, and above all he wanted to be here, in mid-tunnel when a train went by, so that he could stand in the stroller, small hands pounding at air, yelling at the top of his voice, somewhere between panic and sheer delight. He had looked so funny that she would laugh, and when the train had passed he laughed too, tumbling back in his seat, his cap falling crazily over one eye.

She had taken this whole day off from work, and now she was a little sorry. The afternoon would be long. She walked slowly past Parvins, the banks, Mrs. Hamill's Hardware, where the white plaster horse, flaking badly after a hard winter, stood stiffly, past Nick's Barber Shop, where the china cats perched crazily on the roof as if they were chasing each other in play. She did not turn toward home, but walked into Rosemont, where the stores ended, and then she decided she would go to the church for only a moment.

She had not attended that church often, mostly because for all those years she had rarely gone to any, except with her mother or Pop, since she knew her lapse caused them anxiety. Nothing was old about it, stones too clean and neat, pews not marred by long use. The windows were stained glass but mawkish—large blocks of color so undetailed that there seemed no point to the heavy black strips of lead, the anonymous features of figures who did exactly what was expected.

A service was in progress at one of the side chapels; she found herself a place to sit among the five or six scattered celebrants. There were incense, the bell ringing, familiar phrases. Over the altar a crucifix lifted a brightly bronzed Christ, hung as if clinging energetically to the bars. Her eyes could not penetrate all this veneer, but something stirred and rose. The words again. *Kyrie Eleison.* She closed her eyes and pressed her knuckles hard against her brow. Even that phrase began to drift and float in her mind, needing something to fix it to. Desperately she said the words, as if they were dispersing, a memory looked into so often it was losing its power to evoke. She heard the priest's words, took them in and said them too: *Christe Eleison, Christe Eleison.* For a moment everything in her held in balance, still and peaceful.

As if the photograph were one of those bright dots of Japanese paper she had so often been given as a child that, dropped in water, unfolded and unfolded, pleat on pleat, into water lilies of fire-tongued dragons or impossible fish, she remembered. The lawn stretched green and tightly rolled toward the awning, the guests were scattered in little groups, the women clutching at their hats as the light spring breeze tugged here and there, never defining clearly where it came from. She was at Priscilla Biddle's wedding and had been standing in front of the cherry trees looking for someone, anyone she might know since these were not really her people at all and Priscilla had been someone she met while working in the law office. The photographer had been Tom Caputo, a classmate from high school who appeared behind his camera, hired for the occasion, and the look on her face had been the gathering smile of recognition, even relief. That was all she recalled, not even Priscilla's married name, except to remember that this was before she knew Frank. He had not even been touching her life then.

What was he doing with that photograph? She had some vague recollection of throwing out a whole box of things she had stored, but going through them with Frank and laughing over the old clothes, the silly things she had written in some journals. He had kept this, as if he wanted that part of her too, the life he had never shared with her. She had met him some time that year, not long after, and must have looked like that when he first knew her. Did it make him recall how things used to be?

She could not help it now. All those moments of the years just after that picture had been taken flew at her like a startled flock of birds—Frank with sleeves rolled up, leaning from his Plymouth that always spun them into a countryside for privacy, that night at Valley Forge, June it was, when he brought a blanket and they spread it together in the field below the tier of cannons, and she did not even hesitate when he asked her if she thought they ought to wait till they were married, saying "No," unbuttoning her blouse, not pausing to see if he was joining her, and he never believed she had been a virgin that night, assuming she would have asked him to wait if she had been. And the memory of his body entering hers that first time, the bewildering sense that all their boundaries had been erased and she could no longer distinguish herself from him, rose in her, and also the mere physical sense of her flesh folding tightly to his stiffness, time and time again in all those years. Sometimes now her hunger for the touch and thrust of a man's body was so strong that she imagined some simple, quick arrangement, perhaps with one of the men in her office. But she knew it was never simple.

She shook her head, pressed her knuckles hard into her eyes. She had seen pictures of Frank when he was younger, and knew that will to possess those years: Who was with him then? Why was he smiling, that tennis racket raised like a mock sword drawn, his leg in long white pants thrust forward? Now that photograph of her lay face down in his drawer, waiting to be moved with him, or discarded. But she would keep what her own mind decided to hold onto and give back to her in its own time, not these trivia of chance, someone else's clicking of shutters.

Let go, let go, she murmured, and she was certain she would do everything she could to leave this place for a while, taking Carey with her.

She stayed on her knees for a moment after the service ended. Maybe some day she would even want communion, would be willing to confess. But not now. It was enough to have found those two phrases, holding their place in the mind, the unchanging laws and the love that textured them with mercy: *Kyrie Eleison, Christe Eleison.*

\* \* \*

— 78 —

Carey woke late, relieved to find his mother had already left the apartment. It was Saturday and he was supposed to meet Frank at his office. He went into the living room to practice, beginning tentatively, as if he were picking up some slack, abandoned strings, an old cat's cradle done so often that he might forget. He was working on a fugue now from the "Well-Tempered Clavier," and he had learned how to follow the twisting, raveled maze of subjects, always remembering how Nancy, when he first began playing it, had said, "Isn't it wonderful how just when you think they're going to get hopelessly tangled up, the notes work out?"

She had been angry at him last night. The principal of his school, Mr. Hart, had called before he reached home to tell her how Carey had been caught in the woods with Lisa. None of the students was allowed to go there during recess, but Carey had been certain no one had seen them. They went separately, and when he was screened from the field by the vines and limbs, he walked down without waiting to see if Lisa followed. He tried to think through what he would do or what she expected of him. Sometimes when he touched her now she would brush him away and pout. "That's all you think about," she would say. But if he did not try, she would be nervous, irritable, making him feel clumsy, talking about Pete or Joe as if she wished she were with them. He ducked under the arch of a fallen maple to the circle of bushes and trees and the pool of brackish water that they called the spring. In summer it would be choked with small green plants, but now it was still bare. He heard her footsteps, turned to watch her unbend. She was out of breath.

"I don't think anyone saw. I went back in, then out the other side of the building." She stared at him, and he could not think of anything to say. She stepped closer. His face turned very red and he tried to move toward her as if he did not care whether she was there. But she was looking at him seriously, not as if she would make fun of him.

He put his mouth on hers, they were holding tightly to each other, and not letting go of the back of his head with one hand, she used the other to unbutton her jacket, take his hand and put it up under her blouse, pushing it at her breast. Her skin was so warm on his cold palm that it burned. She was breathing unevenly in his ear, and he rose hard against her pushing body, her legs slightly spread, and knowing he was about to come, he tried to pull away but she fell against him, and when he did, his hand clenched tightly over her flesh, the risen nipple. She was starting to say something when they both drew back at the sound of heavy footsteps, a man's voice. "Carey? Lisa? I know you're down here. Now come on."

She drew her jacket around her quickly, not tucking in her blouse, glancing at the small stain of wet beginning to appear near his pocket, and he had only enough time to drag the corner of his jacket over it when Alfie Hart stooped in, face pounding with blood.

"All right, now up you go, march. What do you think you're doing here? You know it's not allowed."

"We just..." Carey started to say, but Alfie lifted a hand. "No excuses. We'll have to have a talk about this. But you're late for class. Move along now."

So they did, walking single file up the path, Lisa first and Hart panting along in the rear. All the way Carey kept watching her hips move against the pleats of her skirt and he was excited not so much by the fact that she had helped him touch her, as that she had accepted something about his body he had not expected her to.

He waited in the empty classroom at the end of the day, sitting squarely in his desk and facing forward. Hart would come soon and talk to him, Miss Snyder would probably be doing that with Lisa somewhere in the same building. He was not scared. There was nothing they could do, more than make them study during recess or always be in sight of the supervisor. But he dreaded the talk, Hart's heavy earnestness. Just as he expected, the first thing the man said, when he had squeezed himself uncomfortably into the desk beside Carey was, "I think it's time we had a talk about a few things."

Carey kept his hands folded on the desk in front of him, his legs tucked back under the chair. From time to time he nodded or said, "Yes," trying not to taste the man's very stale breath so close to him, or glanced at the frowning face that wanted to look friendly, encouraging; but he did not have to say much for a long time because Hart had worked up a little speech. It was all about how Carey and Lisa were at the age where things were happening to their bodies that they probably did not fully understand, and this especially was a time for vigilance, for understanding that not everything their bodies wanted was to be had—it wasn't, Alfie said slowly, his stumpy fingers meshing and unmeshing like the tines of two forks, quite the same thing as eating or drinking or sleeping which were things one could supply easily and without much thought, but sex, and here he cleared his throat carefully, was something very complicated and society had to regulate it with great care. Because, you see, it had to do with children and marriage and family and basic institutions, and Carey and Lisa were still children really, did not fully comprehend the meaning of their desires.

Carey listened to the voice laboring on through the labyrinth of precautions, his own face beginning to feel flushed with the other man's effort, and yet what he said had absolutely no connection to anything that had happened a few hours ago. The experience of that moment was touching the bare, soft flesh, her hips thrust close to his own and her breath catching as she rubbed, then the sudden, blind rush of his own blood. Hovering over this, parallel and watchful, was a mind uttering these abstract words that he could understand but never feel. He started to interrupt, wanted to ask why this had to be so, but he only opened his mouth and shut it. There was no answer. The trick was struggling to hide oneself from everything Alfred Hart was saying, and clearly the best way to do that was not to ask why, not to let those parallel words and the experience meet and tangle.

Nancy had been no better, although she seemed to be more embarrassed by Hart's call than by what Carey had done. And finally she had said, "Oh, hell, I can't do this right, your father ought to," and that threw them into an awkward silence, as if once more he was being told that he was putting his parents in an impossible situation. At the movies that evening with a group of his friends, he had missed the chance to sit next to Lisa, so that when he had gone to bed, all he could think of was the way her hips had pushed against him, the sense of his own stiff flesh groping through the parting clothes.

He left the house early and it was only a short walk. Even though spring had arrived and the cherry trees were in full bloom, the heat was still on in the auditorium, the air dried and stuffy. Carey walked past his father's office because he could hear voices inside. He knew Frank might go on talking for some time, so he pushed through the side door into the theater. The curtain was open on an elaborate set. He hunched on a dark red, velvet seat. He had always wondered what Frank was seeing in the empty hall. Often Carey would find him there, leaning forward to stare at the stage as if something were happening. Carey tried now, but he could not see—any more than the time his father had started repeating some words from a play by Shakespeare about imagining walls and horses and fields of France. Frank made it sound as if he really saw them.

He walked down the aisle to the front of the stage, the high fringe of curtain straight up and hovering in the dark. He closed his eyes. If he turned, his father would be slumped down in a seat, a distant white flutter of his hand—"Go on, Carey, say them"—and he would repeat his lines like that time he had been in the school play and Frank had helped him rehearse by bringing him there and treating him as he would one of his own students, the hall dim and twisting into dark as if Carey were standing on the lip of a giant conch shell, Frank's voice as distant as the sea.

Voices. Two or three women, his father. Carey did not want to see him unexpectedly, that look that came over Frank's face when he met Carey by chance in town, a flinching before he could smile or put out his hand. He crossed to the side door, circled around to Frank's office, empty now. He could hardly bear to be with his father anymore. It was not the drinking, which seemed to be more moderate, at least in his presence. But even though Frank said very little about Nancy or their situation, Carey always felt there was something he needed that only his son could give him, and often Carey would look across the table to his father's face and see those eyes wide and fixed as if they could never blink, absorbing him, pulling him quietly in and down. What could he do? As if frantically clawing his way up a glassy surface, he would say anything that came to mind, hoping his father would tell him what to do. Had he been responsible and was neither of his parents telling him? Or was it simply that he was supposed to bring them together again but was not smart enough to know how?

The office was very familiar to Carey, as if he had lived there for years—the faintly acrid odor of old wood floors, untouched objects that had accumulated over the years, the chalk dust of the small blackboard that he had doodled on as a child when he came with Frank if his mother was busy. On the wall behind the desk, hung at a slight tilt, was a photograph of his father when he was younger. He was seated in the same chair that now leaned back empty, his hands folded in his lap, and he was staring, eyes wide, mouth slightly opened, either about to speak or just finished. The stare was blank, eyes taking in everything, and Carey could not avoid the sense that Frank, inarticulately trapped and frozen on the paper, had somehow been sucked up from the real desk, was mutely pleading for release. Sometimes as a child Carey had imagined that only he knew the charm, and as he played on the floor for those long hours while Frank rehearsed in the theater nearby, he would write magic nonsense on the board, chanting "Come down, come down," and of course it always worked eventually. Once he had fallen asleep on the floor, waking to see Frank sitting in his chair in the same pose as the figure on the wall behind him, but when he looked at the blackboard, Frank had already cleaned it.

He sat in the chair that creaked stiffly, leaned back until it nudged the wall. Frank's voice in the hallway paused while some woman answered, and then he said, "Wednesday, then," as the door opened wide. He stepped in, saw Carey, and closed the door behind him. "Hello, kiddo."

Carey waved from the chair. Frank looked well, his shirt sleeves rolled loosely, tie pulled down and collar open.

"Thought I saw you by the stage. Hold on a minute."

He started looking through a stack of books on top of a filing cabinet and found a few words which he muttered.

"Right. Want some lunch?" He lifted his jacket off the hook on the back of the door.

"Sure." Carey began to stand but Frank had motioned him down again.

"No. Hold it. Before we go out, I want to talk about something a minute."

Carey sat again but did not lean back. Frank pulled up the chair on the other side of the desk, folding his jacket over his lap as he sat.

"I want to know more about this crazy business your mother is talking about. Going to Rome."

Carey looked at the door and wished he had waited in the hallway instead. "She says she wants to take a job there at this embassy, that..."

"No. I don't mean the particulars. I know them. I want to know if she means it."

"I guess so."

Frank was silent, looked at the shelf opposite him as if trying to find a particular book.

"And you? Do you want to go?"

Carey looked at the ripped side of his sneaker, pressed his foot hard against the leg of the desk. "Mom says there's a good school there, for kids who speak English."

"Do you want to go?"

He knew Frank was staring at him but he did not look up.

"I don't know."

"I won't be able to see you, you know. It's too far away, too expensive for me just to get on a boat and come sometime."

"I know."

"How long would you go for, does she say?"

"No."

Frank stood suddenly, forgetting the jacket that tumbled off his lap. He let it lie where it fell, punched a fist into his hand then walked to the high window beside Carey, leaning there on his elbow, a hand to his forehead.

"What does she know about Rome? Why Rome?"

But Carey's own fist bunched in his lap, his neck tightened. "I don't know." His voice seemed swallowed into his chest. "Don't ask me."

"Look, Carey," and Frank turned abruptly, began pacing slowly along the bookshelf, past the blackboard. "It isn't fair, that's all. It's one thing for her to go off on a crazy trip halfway around the world, but she's taking you away. From me."

"Why do you care?" he blurted, and found himself standing, the chair flung back against the wall. Frank was staring at him.

"What do you mean? Because I'm your father."

"So? She's my mother. Big deal."

Even though he was almost shouting he knew he was not getting anything said that mattered. Where was Rome anyway? What did an embassy have to do with anything he cared about? And why was it the only thing his mother could talk about and now Frank too? First they had torn his house in half, now they were flinging him into a geography he could not even imagine. He saw Frank stiffening, expected him to say something like, "Don't speak to me that way," and then they would spend the next few hours together being surly, but instead he said simply, "Yes, she's your mother. I suspect you almost wish we'd both go away."

"I do."

Frank stooped, picked up the jacket, then turned to the blackboard where he wrote, "Belinda—be back at 3."

"C'mon. Let's eat," and he held out his arm in a cantle so

— 84 —

that when Carey came around the desk his father's hand settled on his shoulder and squeezed him. "Look, son. It's only that I'll miss you."

But Carey would not answer. It was enough to accept the touch of hand without shirking it, to turn briefly in the doorway and see the dimly seated figure of his father hovering over the empty chair.

# 7

"You want to come up? My sons and their wives and kids, we're having a party." Anna stood in their doorway.

"No, thanks," Nancy said. "We're tired."

Carey could hear her visitors, the floors creaking everywhere, light feet running rapidly, probably her grandchildren. The old woman looked at him, and for a moment Carey thought he would say yes. It sounded like they were having fun.

"You sure? We got wine, some good food. Alessandro has just been to Rome. He could tell you some things."

Carey saw by the fixed smile on Nancy's face that Anna was getting nowhere.

"Thanks. But we really musn't."

"Some other time, then," she said, and winked at Carey.

They did not say much to each other during supper. Carey knew that Frank had called earlier. He could tell by the unmodulated tone of Nancy's voice and the way she would stand stiff-backed at the sink, facing out the window, that she was not thinking of the present conversation. But what was he supposed to do now? Frank once again expected him to pull or drag their lives in some direction. Again, he said the only thing he could think of.

"Do we really have to go to Rome?"

She was silent as if waiting for more, but he had nothing else to say, and he knew how truculent even that sounded. Rome was still as unimaginable as a moon, even though she had shown him pictures of walls and fountains and smiling people.

"Carey, it's all done. I don't think we should keep talking about it. The lease is given up, I've told your school, they've started looking for a new secretary at the office." Her voice had begun sternly, as if she were still on the phone, but she breathed deeply and they listened for a moment to the thumps and waves of voices from above. 'I know you'll like it once we get there. You'll have all summer to get used to the idea of going."

"Dad doesn't want us to. You know he says it's not fair, that you're taking me away from him."

"Your father says lots of things that he shouldn't," she said sharply.

Her lips tight, eyes focused on the wall, she might have been looking at Frank's face hovering beyond his shoulder. Whenever he was with Frank, his father was talking to her. Why couldn't they just see him instead of these ghostly confrontations?

"Stop it." His hand swung out, striking his glass of milk and it shattered, spilling a wide delta of white on the tablecloth. As if that were enough to scatter everything that shored him up, he yelled again, "Stop it!"

She had risen with a start, one hand to her throat, her eyes angered as if she would slap him, but she only reached one hand out and drew it back.

"I'll get a rag." She went to the sink.

He hoped he was not going to cry. His eyes blurred, but he fought back, began gathering the large sections of his glass while she was sopping up the milk. When it was clean they sat again, having said nothing while they worked.

"Now then. What was that about?"

"Nothing."

"Stop what, Carey?"

Their dinner was only half eaten, his fork still lying in the congealing gravy.

"What am I supposed to do?" His voice trembled slightly. "What do you both want me to do?" His eyes shifted around the room to find something to hold onto, and when he looked at her, he could see she was too puzzled to speak. "What does he need? Dad. He needs something. I don't know what to do." Now his voice was rising. He swallowed hard.

She put a hand quickly on his arm, stood and came to stoop, her face almost in his.

"You mustn't think that way, Carey. What's done between Frank and me is done. There was nothing any of us could have done differently. At the time. Nothing now, other than what we are doing. I know this better than you."

But he shook his head, his voice lower again. "When I'm over there with Dad, he's always looking at me like I'm supposed to say something or do something, but I never know what. Sometimes I dream about it all night."

"Carey, look at me."

He let his eyes settle on her again.

"I cannot explain this to you all at once. I should have started long ago. Your father always wants something. From all of us. But it is nothing any of us have to give. I don't know what it is. He doesn't either, I think. I tried and tried, and I didn't have it. No one does. I think it's something he had to have to give himself, nothing from us."

For a moment he thought he understood. The words sounded so sure, reasonable. Then they parted, jumbled in his mind. How could someone want something and yet end up having it to give to himself? She was talking nonsense.

"But what about me," he blurted. "What about what I want, who cares about that?"

She was standing now, her hand still on his shoulder and he felt it tighten. "I do, Carey, and I know Frank does."

But that was both easy and angering because it made him feel so awful for even saying it, so he stood, brushing her hand away, and walked to the door. "Then why doesn't anybody do something," and before she could answer, he slammed his door behind him, even slipping the latch in place.

He knew she would come soon. The doorknob turned a few times.

"Carey?"

"Yes."

"Can we talk?"

"I'm busy."

Silence.

"All right. But tomorrow? I have some things to say."

"Okay."

Partly he was disappointed to hear her muffled footsteps go away—what if she had demanded that he open the door? But he was tired. Jittery bursts of restlessness kept rising and he finally left his magazine unfinished, having pecked at five different stories.

In bed he turned on his side to look out the window at the dark of the backyard. Recently he had forgotten how to sleep. Sleeping had always been something that came easily; he slipped into bed, curled tightly into the covers, let his mind skitter where it willed in the images of the day, let those images waver and slide on the watery surface and then it would be there, a blank state broken by a turn and a heave up to heat hissing in the pipes or a door slamming, finally daylight and vague memory of a dream. Not anymore. For the past nights he had lain stiff, eyes burning, mind struggling as if he were trying to stand perfectly still on a dark line in the pavement; and when he did sleep, he woke exhausted, remembering how the face of his father had been waiting in his dreams, staring, concealing something, even though his worst fear had been that it might speak.

He concentrated on the sounds from upstairs. They had begun to sing. What was it all about? His mother had said it was some saint's day. Even the children were up late. He was sorry Nancy had said no. He would not mind watching them sing, and he could tell by their shuffling treads, the billowing tones of an accordion that they were dancing too. Sudden silence. Then a high, thin voice. Laughter. Applause. Someone beating time on the floor. He forced his eyes shut, tried to think of Lisa, but she had started avoiding him recently, as if being caught with him in the woods had been his fault. Anyway, he could not picture her face clearly. They were dancing again. He heard his mother's bed move slightly against the wall behind him. Probably she was also lying and not sleeping. He swung out of bed, tied his bathrobe around him, went out into the living room, and in the dark he thumped against the little table which started to topple but he caught it in time.

"Carey?"

"Yes."

She was in her doorway.

"Can't sleep?"

"No."

"Do you want to try some of my pills?"

"I don't care. If I sleep, it's just as bad."

She took a step forward, but he moved slightly so the table was between them.

"I'm going upstairs."

"What?"

"Well, Anna asked, didn't she?"

"But they must be almost done by now."

They both listened. He did not need to argue. The noise was undiminished.

"Not dressed like that."

"Anna won't mind," and he was already out the front door

and at the bottom of the stairs before her voice stopped him again.

"Carey. What in the world has gotten into you?"

She was in the doorway to their apartment.

"I'll just go up for a minute."

He would have gone anyway, but her slight hesitation was enough, and he turned, stopped a moment to put his slippers back on, and then was on the landing, at the door and knocking.

Anna put a hand to her chest. "We're making too much noise. You want to complain."

The music stopped. All the faces turned to the door. Carey blushed.

"No, no."

She smiled, put a hand on his arm. "Come in. You join us. This is Paolo here..." and she took him around the room where everyone greeted him and no one seemed surprised to see him, even in his bathrobe. Their faced were flushed. Luigi, who had very little hair, smiled hugely, a mouth full of gold chips, and a very stout child was sleeping against his chest. "Welcome, welcome," he said, and the child burrowed closer like a cat. A woman standing beside Carey whose name was Rosa, short and thin-faced but very broad in the hips, said, "We're keeping you up, I bet," but Carey said, "No. I can't sleep anyway," and she nodded. "Come here."

She gripped his elbow and walked him away to a table in the kitchen where there were bottles, glasses, and plates with all sorts of cakes and cheeses and breads. The others began to talk again, and the accordion player, who was blind in one eye, an old man who smiled all the time, began to ripple out more chords, not yet focused into any particular song.

"That's Giggio. You know him?"

"No."

"He's been around for years. Used to be an organ-grinder once. With his father. Been playing for weddings and *festas* all his life. He's Abruzzese too."

They paused at the table.

"Here. You hungry? Thirsty?"

He was not but did not want to let her down.

"You like wine?"

"I guess so."

She blinked often, a nervous tic.

"When you're happy, wine is best. When you're unhappy

— 90 —

too. I know. When my father died, I couldn't sleep for two weeks."

She had poured a glass full and before she handed it to him she gave him a wedge of cheese. "Eat this first. Wine tastes better."

"When did he die?"

"Six years ago. It was a place in Italy. Anzio. Sometimes he was fighting his own people, but mostly the Germans. I finally drank a whole bottle of wine. Cousin Luigi, he came over and held my head all the next day when I was sick."

Carey took a mouthful of the wine, swallowed, and the heat went down him, a little bitter.

"I don't want to be sick."

"We'll keep an eye on you. Your mother coming up?"

"I don't think so."

"Too bad."

They were singing again, and she blinked, smiled widely, poured his glass full, and towed him back into the bright room.

"Here, sit, sit," and she put him on the couch between Luigi with the sleeping child and another woman, older than she, very much stouter, who was singing loudly in a high, wheezy voice.

The child's feet touched against his thigh when Luigi leaned toward him and said in his ear, "We're celebrating tonight because it's my father's name day, you know, like his birthday in our church."

"But I thought he was..."

"Dead? Sure. But so what? Without him," and his hand swung out toward the others and back, "less of this, right? And after all, why not use any excuse for a party."

Luigi plucked his glass off the stand to his right, brought it around and touched it to Carey's, then lifting his hand said, "Drink," and Carey did. He liked the rolling little eyes in the puffy cheeks, and now that he was close he could see the nets of veins that gave them such a reddish tint.

"This is my youngest, Angelo. He likes to sleep," and as if the child had been listening all along his eyes opened slightly, he looked at Carey and then burrowed again into his father's spreading waist. The man shrugged, laughed, patted the boy's back heavily, and joined in the singing in a voice slightly nasal but pleasant and on key. Carey could tell by the way others turned and smiled that they thought his voice the best.

Across the room Anna was sitting perched on the edge of the large mahogany chair, hands on the head of her cane and chin resting on them, and her head nodded slightly from side to side in time with the music. Her eyes moved so quickly from person to person, and her face was so near to bursting into a laugh, that Carey thought she would leap from her chair and begin to dance, and other people in the room began to do just that, finding little circles of space in which to hold onto each other and take small steps in time to the music. Rosa returned, bringing a new bottle of wine around the room, and she filled his glass again.

"For you," she said, "but Luigi drinks too much," and when she pretended to walk away from Luigi's outstretched glass, his legs swung up like a gate to hold her back and she poured his glass full.

Giggio blew out a great heave of air from his bellows, sucked it back in and with a grin, his good eye rolling around next to its milky, stationary companion, he began to slap out a lumbering series of chords and a tune. Everyone was singing again. Carey was bewildered. The wine was beginning to make him warm and floating, but he could not clearly follow everything. Why, for instance, was someone saying in his ear, "Ah, Luigi, what a voice, what a presence. He could have been another Caruso, my Luigi."

A woman came out of the other room and said something to Anna, who signaled him with her finger, so he stood and went over.

"Your mother on the phone. I think she wants you to come down." Her hand was on his where it rested on her chair. "You want to go?"

Carey shook his head.

"I tell you what. Why don't you see if your mother will come up?"

Carey looked at the face closely, bent to it so that he could hear. She made him feel they were plotting together, but he certainly did not want to go down and lie there again.

The phone was in Anna's bedroom, where the coats were stacked on the bed and two or three children lay sleeping in their own nests.

"Carey? What are you doing? You have a lesson early tomorrow."

"I know."

"Well, come down. This minute."

"I don't want to. Anna says you should come up." He spoke

slowly, finding that his tongue was not quite certain where it should go to make the right sounds.

"You thank Anna, but I don't feel like it. Now, seriously, come down."

"No. I like it here. S'fun." He moved too quickly, heard his own slur.

"Are you drinking?"

"Just a little. Some wine."

"Oh, Lord." Now she was mad.

Silence.

"All right. I'm coming up. But I'm coming up to bring you down. If I were you, I'd come on your own. This might be embarrassing."

That only made him angry. "You can't make me."

She groaned and hung up. He put the phone back on its hook, looked at the heaped bodies and clothes. That was when he noticed the long legs protruding from the chair, and a hand moved out of the dark lump, waving vaguely.

"Trouble?" a sleepy voice said.

"Maybe."

"Who was it?"

"My mother."

The hand groped downward, reappeared with a bottle, and the man sighed heavily after he took a swig.

"I'm Tony. I'm also drunk. Sounded like she was giving you a rough time."

"She's a little angry."

"Listen. Mothers are always angry. What's a mother for? They never let up. That's why I'm out here. I'd rather be in the dark with the sleeping kids and my own bottle than out there having my mother give me that 'you're a good-for-nothing' look all night. Families. Jesus, what a mess. You know my mother? Anna?"

"Yes." Carey wanted to leave, to be somewhere less isolated when his mother arrived.

"Never mind. You the boy that lives downstairs?"

"Yes."

"You play a mean piano. Well, have a good time out there. And don't let your mom get to you. Here, shake."

The hand came up and the man leaned out of the dark enough for Carey to see a thin face, sharp nose. His hand was quickly given and withdrawn. "Hang in," he said and slouched back.

"She's coming," he said to Anna, when he came blinking into the light.

*"Benissimo."*

"But she's angry."

The old woman nodded, her smile now pure mischief. "I thought she would be."

His mother would have to dress before she came, so he went into the kitchen and filled his glass again and had a piece of cake too, and went back to the couch. Angelo was gone now, probably to join the bodies in the other room, but Luigi and the woman who said her name was Lucia welcomed him and he was glad to have them on either side. The more he thought of it, the more he dreaded her coming.

She stood just inside the doorway, dressed now in a skirt and sweater. She had not even bothered to put her hair up and it was slung long and trailing around her neck and down the front. She had walked in without knocking, was looking around for him, and the people near the door moved back smiling, waiting for her to say something. He also felt sorry for her; there was only one thing she could do, so she walked over to Anna, took her hand, and stooped to say something. Intense words passed back and forth, then Rosa was there, shyly holding out a glass, Nancy was smiling, shaking her head, Rosa was as smilingly holding the glass in air, and finally Nancy took it. Lucia said with a sigh, *"Bene,"* and when Carey turned to look at her, she put a hand demurely over her mouth and giggled. He laughed too, not quite certain why the conspiracy felt so good or what it really was, other than the obvious fact that he wanted more wine, was wonderfully comfortable, had never liked anyone as much as Lucia or the heaving Luigi, who settled in again next to him with a grunt.

Nancy was in front of him leaning down to speak, her hand tightly on his knee, and she was trying to ignore the two beside him. Carey heard her saying something about, "I mean it, two more minutes and you must go down to bed," but before she could finish, Luigi had nudged him, was saying, "Come, come, up, young man, give your mother a place to sit," and Carey lurched up, Luigi patted the vacated cushion saying, "Please, please," and his mother sat.

When he stood, the room spun, he heard sounds dimly, but everything returned to place and he found himself walking a little unsteadily toward Giggio, whose good eye was peering at him, his face grinning. Rosa was smiling too, and when he turned he could see his mother trying not to laugh. Well, what was so funny? He took refuge behind his glass which he drained, found himself directly in front of Giggio and saying, "Beautiful, beautiful," alarmed that it sounded so emotional, and Giggio cocked his head to one side, bowing it slightly and saying, *"Grazie, grazie, signorino."* Then he reared back in his chair as if the instrument had leapt on his chest and he might fall backward from its weight, and in a voice that seemed to come out of the accordion rather than his wide mouth, he began to boom some song, staring at Carey all the time.

The music beat out a waltz. Carey knew those steps, his feet were starting to shuffle on his own under him, someone at his side said, *"Bravo, bravo,"* and he found himself moving in slow circles in a small space where the others were dancing, his glass in one hand, eyes half closed so that everything spun by in a mist—their grins, their upraised hands. Someone had taken the glass, Rosa, and she stepped into the empty space, her hand on his waist, and they began to dance, her head slightly back and grinning. But when the music shifted, his feet did not know what to do, so she stood closer, her voice in his ear said "Watch, watch," and he made his face stop staring at her ear nesting in its whorl of hair to look at her feet moving in a quick pattern by his. He did the same. "Yes, yes," she said, and before that tune was over, he was making his own feet do it without watching them, even though the rest of his body forgot sometimes how to perch over all that motion and he would stagger slightly.

The music changed, and someone else had taken Rosa's place, the thin woman with the long, sad face, only now she was smiling shyly, and she too had something to teach him. He did not care who was watching anymore, and to Lucia, when she stood before him, her small arms barely reaching him beyond the protrusion of belly and bosom, he grinned and said quietly, "I think I'm drunk," and she laughed, put one hand over his mouth and said, "Dance, dance."

And he did. He lost all sense of time. Giggio's music breathed in and out, lapping up and back like waves, at times he glimpsed the man's face and the shifting faces of his partners, until he heard a clatter of applause around him and he noticed no one was with him, the space of his cantled arms empty, and he had been circling with eyes shut—but for how long, how long? He was standing still and could see Anna in her chair ahead of him, the music welling around him, and she was nodding, nodding in time to it, winking, and he thought the room was pulling away from him but he was only beginning to fall backward. Hands helped him, coming from nowhere to hold him a moment under his arms. When he looked again, his mother was in front of him, but her face was not angry.

"Shall we go down now, Carey? It's late."

Her face was so tired and worn, but flushed with the heat, perhaps the wine; he remembered in a lurch what that day had brought them to and he still felt a jagged corner of anger, but that was so long, long ago, so he reached out, one hand on her hip, the other taking her hand, and she said, annoyed but blushing, "Oh, Carey, really now." He moved his feet, the waltz began again, and she moved with him. *"Bella, bella,"* someone said, and they danced in slow, wide circles, his eyes seeing nothing but her face, and that was all he saw or the last thing he could remember seeing, as if they had waltzed each other off to sleep.

# PART TWO

# Courtyards and Villas

# 1

Standing on the dock, looking back at the boat and surrounded by stevedores, porters, passengers, officials and welcoming families, Carey could hardly breathe, as if all of them
and their possessions had been plucked up and hurled against
a painted backdrop of houses, volcano, blue fire. Even when
he and Nancy and Mr. Mancuso, the head of some department, who had traveled first class, were safely into the waiting station wagon from the embassy and Giacomo began to
drive away, they only moved fitfully through streets where
people walked blindly at the car, ignoring the ceaseless yapping of the horn. From everywhere the new language shattered over him in clusters, signs hung and pointed and
winked with combinations of letters he could not pronounce,
and he could not tell whether the people were happy or mad—
all their tones were torn and violent. Giacomo would turn
slightly, toss some words back, releasing them with a hand
only vaguely connected to his wrist, and Mr. Mancuso would
agree or disagree and usually laugh. The people on foot or
pedaling battered tricycles with sagging loads in front were
moving faster in every direction than the car.

Then came a humming silence, no city, fields on either
side, green or swampy, a shimmering speed that Carey would
never have thought such an old car could attain. Giacomo
hunched over the wheel puffing a cigarette, the shaped trees
lining the narrow road winked by, oxen pulled toward them
around a bend—no room, yes, a yard or two—and without
flinching or slowing Giacomo would slip by, his horn melting

the car through every obstruction. The sun began to set, Nancy talked quietly, and he dozed, later to wake in the dark and stumble into a small restaurant.

They were sitting together at a wooden table in the simple, whitewashed room. A bare light bulb nearby, a candle on the table, gave all the light. As his mind cleared, Carey felt fresh, as if waking after the passage of a thunderstorm. Opposite him Giacomo's lean, very lined face with its dense mustache was absorbed in his work. With knife and fork he was peeling a pear. The yellowish, mottled skin was hazy with water from the bowl he had dipped it in. The fork punctured the swelling end, the knife with deft strokes pared back the skin, baring the white, moist pulp. His long, scarred fingers with gnarled joints moved above the fruit as if molding it until the skin lay neatly to one side. The fruit showed no marks of the knife, he lifted the first forkful to his mouth, and his dazed face was judging. Carey could smell the sweet juice as if his fingertips had touched its slick and beading flesh.

He looked up at the room, the other diners, Nancy beside him. Giacomo was staring at him with kind eyes, almost as if he understood.

*"Prego?"* he said, and moved his plate toward Carey.

With his own knife, Carey cut off a small chunk, forked it into his mouth, and it was so quick and sweet that the corners of his jaw winced.

*"Ti piace?"*

"He says, 'Do you like it?'"Mancuso translated.

Carey nodded. Speaking for the first time in that new tongue, he said, *"Si, molto,"* and flushed red up his neck, but he did not care because Giacomo smiled gravely, put a hand on his arm, and said something which made Mancuso laugh, and he told Carey the man had said he was "truly Italian at heart." Carey only wanted more, not of that particular pear or of the one Giacomo proceeded to peel for him, but of his body new and open and learning its way.

"He'll like it here, I'm sure," Mr. Anderson said. "An adventure. For all of us."

"I guess I was thinking more of an education than an adventure," Nancy said slowly.

"Ah, well. I meant an educational adventure."

They sat in front of Mr. Anderson's "desk," a door lying across two sawhorses, and as he stared, mouth slightly open in a grin, the eyes went blank as if he had forgotten they were there. Plasterers in paper caps were advancing the ceiling steadily toward them. Carey could hear the scrape and slap over his shoulders. The door was disheveled with papers. Anderson's tongue rolled in his mouth and he winked.

"I guess I had expected something different."

"Oh, I see. Well, we're fully accredited, you know. I mean by American standards."

Mr. Anderson, the headmaster of Carey's proposed school, did not look much older than his mother, but he had painfully arthritic hands, knobby joints thrusting the fingers almost at right angles, and he kept brushing the side of his head, a motion between a scratching and an attempt to run those fingers through his wispy hair.

"That's not the problem. I had heard there was already a school."

"Yes," and he pounced on that gleefully, "but there *was.* It's just that this is the first year we've decided to have the upper grades. We have a reputation here. Years of service to the English-speaking community. Thought it our responsibility. Needs of the community. Expand. Prepare them for college..." He grew more incoherent the longer he went on, as if he were standing on the rear platform of a train pulling out. He stopped, the tongue rolled again, and with a deftness that showed he had lived a long time with his crippled fingers, he plucked a cigarette from the mangled pack in front of him. A scratch, a puff, deep intake, and the match, burning down in his hand, was dropped hastily on the marble floor. "Necessitated a move, as you can see. We used to be closer to town, now new address. Via Cassia. But there will be buses. To all parts of the city. No need to worry."

Carey glanced at his mother. She had become more worried the farther from the city the bus had taken them, and had almost turned back when they walked in the driveway filled with the various battered trucks and Vespas of workers. They had stood a moment in shocked disbelief on the rutted lawn of a most inelegant villa rising in square layers to a rectangular cupola, naked in some fields of untended olive trees and vines. The bells and bleating of grazing sheep nearby had blown around them with the dust of a warm wind.

Someone coughed two or three times behind them.

"We have a staff we are proud of." Again the hand rose, this time pulling distractedly at a tuft of hair as if trying to make it longer. "From all over Europe—England, France, our own Italy—our math teacher is American, husband with FAO."

Cough again from above. Then a deep, gruff voice, *"Scusi, per favore, signora e signori, ma..."* and Carey looked over his shoulder to the white-daubed face of a plasterer looming, hand poised to slap the ceiling.

Mr. Anderson popped up, his thigh knocking the door so hard that everything shifted further together. "Perhaps we'd better look about. Come along."

He took them from room to room. None of the furniture had been moved in, and broken windows had not been replaced.

"Neglected for years, but a good structure. Just right for us. Grade school below. Room for upper classes above."

He took them to the top of the building, up two regular flights and then twisting metal stairs that led to the cupola, a room larger than it had seemed below. Some pigeons were still nesting there, and they rose with a clacking that startled them all. Their shoes cracked on the broken glass.

"They promise it will be ready for opening classes. Two weeks. Spectacular spot for a classroom, eh?"

The villa was on the crest of the first major heave of land beyond the city, and a ravine tumbled off to the right. The wind whistled benignly. Carey could see the sheep past the line of cypress trees, a scruffy black dog in attendance, and the falling land swept his eyes off toward the city, the dome of St. Peter's, the towers of a gold and ocher city. He decided he wanted to go to school here, no matter how strange it was. But Nancy, who did not like heights, held on tightly to the top of the metal railing.

"Yes," she said quickly, but Carey could hear the doubt.

Suddenly Mr. Anderson, his eyes wild, tongue rolling crazily in his grinning mouth, drew back one hand in air as if pulling the string, and sighted along an arrow past the other hand that held a tensed bow, out to the fields. It was done so realistically, the arms pulling back with effort, that Carey could not help thinking how painful that would be for his twisted hands. In a high tenor, almost falsetto, he uttered the strangest combination of syllables Carey had ever heard, and loosed the shaft. Nancy and Carey gaped tensely when he turned.

"Homer. Marvelous moment, eh? The words, whole line, sound like the twanging of a bow. Remarkable piece of writing. Onomatopoeia. Know what that is, Carey?" and as he

— 101 —

preceded them down the stairs he chanted back over his shoulder, "'Grate on their scrannel pipes of wretched straw.' Sounds like what it's talking about."

Carey had begun to like him, but saw that Nancy was biting the corner of one lip as they toured the second floor.

"Carey," she said finally, "why don't you look around a little on your own while I chat with Mr. Anderson?"

He went down to the next floor because their voices carried so clearly in the empty rooms. He paused at the windows, taking in each different view of the dilapidated grounds. A gusty rain squall had come up, and the wet glass warped the already twisted olives. He had trouble imagining it as a school, but suspected that was why he liked it so much. He was still confused, although the boat trip had seemed endless and very routine, and summer had stretched monotonously, marked by practicing, his weekly lessons, some evenings of "Conversational Italian" he and his mother had taken at the Berlitz School in Philadelphia. He had tried to learn nothing from that, stubbornly refusing to talk with Nancy when she coaxed him with phrases at the dinner table. Frank had taken a job in Connecticut directing a summer theater, coming home infrequently, but still to argue with Nancy, even more intensely as passports, tickets, all the outward signs of leaving accumulated. Lisa had gone to work in a hotel in Maine, most of his friends had vanished with their families to the mountains or the shore, so that finally, out of boredom, Carey had taken a job as a bag stuffer at the local grocery store. Then they were on a boat surrounded by unchanging bright days, by long heaves of an ocean that seemed to lift them up or down, neither holding them back nor pushing them forward. At the first view of Naples, some of the passengers around him had wept. Carey had felt nothing. But as if the ocean still rose and fell in him, he had been slightly dizzy ever since landing.

He stopped on the threshold of one large room, its blackboard newly installed and the sweet smell of plaster in the air. A man was standing in front of the window, his back partly turned, and his pose was so private and thoughtful that Carey did not want to interrupt. His hands were held loosely behind him, back straight and head slightly bowed, a face looking almost unblinking into the rain. Carey's foot scraped and the man turned.

"Hello?" he said.

Carey stepped all the way into the room. He was slight,

not as tall as Carey, a sharp nose and chin, lips pursed precisely, and spectacles thickly lensed.

"I'm just looking around."

"Going to be a student here, I expect?"

"Hope so."

"Good start. I'm Ian Snyder. A teacher here. This," and he waved, "will be my room."

They shook hands, and Carey waited for him to speak again. He had never talked to a real Englishman before.

"Met Mr. Anderson?"

"Yes. He's talking with my mother."

Ian turned back to the window. "Look. It's rather remarkable, don't you think?"

Carey stood beside him and looked out, but could see nothing more than he had already.

"No, no, there," and a hand gently cupped the back of Carey's head, pointed it down while the other hand gestured toward the tall grass under a particularly writhen olive tree. "See?"

Carey did not find it. Mr. Anderson's voice burst in. "Ah, I see you've found our Ian," and they both turned as if discovered. Ian was introduced to Nancy, Mr. Anderson called Carey a "new student" and he was relieved, in spite of the still hesitant look on his mother's face, to be enrolled. They stood and talked for a while, were on the point of leaving when Ian understood they were still looking for an apartment and he walked down the stairs with them, explaining that he knew someone about to leave, decent apartment on the Gianicolo, Piazza San Pancrazio, one of those new buildings near a convenient bus. After he had written down all the information in a very small, clear script, Nancy thanked him, they both quickly shook Mr. Anderson's bent hand, and found their way out through the lunching workers who stared in silence with the rapt curiosity of cats.

"Well," Nancy said as they rattled back in the bus over the Ponte Milvio, "I hope you learn something there. It seems hopelessly confused to me."

The apartment was small, with a balcony barely extended enough to step onto and look down to the street. There was a wire-cage elevator that was usually out of order, or was even more hazardous if not, because it tended to break down between floors and leave them suspended. From the kitchen window that looked back to the central well and into all the other kitchens, they found a very busy life of cooking, of children tottering about, women calling back and forth, up and down in a tangled network of raucous conversations. They rented a piano for Carey, studied Italian grammar together, tried it out at the local market, and slowly began to gather some sense that they might survive.

Nancy invited Ian Snyder for dinner, their first guest. "After all," she said to Carey, "he helped us find the place." But Carey could tell she wanted some reassuring about the school.

He came precisely on time, knocking so gently that Carey thought the wind as usual was surging up the elevator shaft and shaking the door.

"I'm sorry to be so punctual. For all the years I've been here I can't rid myself of that Anglo-Saxon sense of time."

He was wearing a brown tweed suit, neatly pressed, and he smelled of bay leaf. He already knew the apartment, having visited his friends a few times.

"Did you have a chance to talk to them at all?"

He held the glass of chilled vermouth Nancy had given him, and Carey was still fascinated by how neatly pointed everything about him was—nose, tips of ears, fingers, chin, even the mouth in focusing so precisely on each word—and yet how softened that all was by the eyes.

"No. We only met once. They seemed nice." Nancy had opened the balcony doors and she stood there as an evening breeze billowed the gauze curtains.

"Smells quite good, doesn't it? Ah," and he stepped to the railing, "you see, it must be coming across from Villa Doria Pamphili. Lovely spot. You must try to get in sometime."

They stood together, very tentatively, as if the breeze might flutter them too, and Carey, just behind, peered at the few things he could see as Ian pointed them out.

"They were interesting, your predecessors," and as they moved back into the sparsely furnished living room and Nancy sat so that Ian would also, he talked about his friends. But they had left the place so clean and bare that Carey could not imagine them. Even now the marble floors, lack of furniture, made the apartment seem half-possessed, and he often floated in the rooms as if in a dream.

"And how are you getting on?"

Carey looked at Nancy and they both smiled, as if sharing secrets. But Ian was the first person they had talked with, so they tumbled their confusions out, almost as if confessing:

bewilderments, gaffes of language, chafings that had left them angry.

Ian tried to explain. Carey liked his voice, a clear tenor, cleanly enunciating, but speaking with a cleverness of tone that made the smallest things seem bright and worth thinking about. Nancy began to relax, laugh, started talking about all the customs she had noticed, and for the first time since arriving, Carey was enjoying himself.

Ian asked about the piano in the bedroom and insisted Carey play something. He did—a Chopin étude, and then because he could hear nothing from the other room, a fugue by Bach, and after Ian called distantly "Bravo, more," he even played a Brahms intermezzo. When Ian came to the door, Carey stood awkwardly against the bench and caught it just before it fell. Ian put his arm through Carey's as they went back to the living room.

"I had no idea," he said to Nancy. He became very firm about lessons and a woman he knew. "Mrs. Dorati. Ikbal Dorati, I know her well. You'll have to audition, but I'm sure she'll take you on."

Carey could not help laughing at the name.

"Egyptian. Her maiden name is even more impossible. Can't say it. One of those words you have to swallow halfway through. Married young, but her husband died in the war. At the Ardeatine. She's excellent."

He admitted to being interested in music himself. Voice. That was his principal reason for being in Rome, not his teaching at the school. Trying to make a way in opera. He had hopes, but above all could not think of going back to England, not for some time. "Too tight there for me," and he would not expand on that, his eyes making hard lines, mouth primly drawn.

Nancy went to the kitchen, and for a while Carey and Ian talked, but Carey could tell something was wrong by the way his mother banged around, muttering. Finally she appeared in the doorway, hair wisping out, wiping her hands down the sides of her apron.

"It's the sauce. I've been at it all afternoon, but I can't make it work. Maybe we'd better go to the trattoria instead."

"May I?" Ian stood.

They all surrounded the bubbling pot. Ian dipped the spoon in and took a lick.

"You don't mind?" And even as Nancy reassured him, he

was reaching for the spices, sprinkling and dabbling. He stirred and tasted again.

"Try."

Carey tasted, looked at Nancy. "How'd he do that?"

She seemed a little annoyed, then grinned and shook her head.

"I'm afraid I love to cook," Ian said.

They both looked at her. She had put her hand to her forehead. "The spaghetti. I forgot to buy it."

"Mother." Carey was embarrassed now. After all, this man was going to be his teacher. Ian only found it amusing.

"Carey, you and I will get some. Down at the corner."

"No, you mustn't."

But Ian had his arm around Carey's shoulder, was steering him to the door. When they reached the street and started walking toward the piazza, a fresh September night and the sounds of a very wakeful city around them, Carey tried to apologize, but Ian put his arm through Carey's and insisted that he did not mind, even that he was having enormous fun, the first for weeks since a good friend of his had gone back to Paris for a while and left him quite alone. There was some way in which he said the word "friend" that told Carey she meant a great deal to Ian.

In the bright little store, past the swinging chains of beads, Ian moved at ease, chatting with the proprietor who normally treated Carey and Nancy with aloofness but now hailed him as *"Il signorino grande,"* and Carey watched the items piling up—spaghetti, little rolls, some sconelike cookies that Ian said they must try. He bought a greenish-white flask of wine, "As a welcoming gift," he murmured, and they stuffed their goodies into the net bag they had brought, and paid the signora, who unbent far enough to wish them both a pleasant evening.

As they approached, Carey could see Nancy looking down at them from the balcony. They paused, she waved, they waved back, a bus rattled by, its strut crackling along the wires, and for a moment the space between their fluttering hands spread out and she was not only his mother but an unknown woman, light behind her, beckoning vaguely. She turned back into the lighted room, the net bag swung to rest between them, and Ian's hand touched Carey's shoulder. The scene began to blur and he was weeping, but only with his eyes.

"Well," Ian said, "shall we?" and then, quietly, "What is it?"

Carey shook his head, shrugged, was very angry at himself. What could he say? He could not even explain the strange aching to himself. But Ian did not insist, merely squeezed with his hand. A couple passed.

"All right now?"

By the time they had wedged into the elevator, become stuck on the second floor and scrambled out, they were laughing, and long after dinner was over and he had gone to bed, Carey's face ached as if he had not stopped laughing all evening. He lay with the window open, curtains sagging in above his head. He was not sure what explosion of mood might come to him next. His emotions lately had begun to be like his outer life, unattached, unpredictable. Where were they coming from, these longings, pits of need, rushes of wanting to give with nothing tangible to offer, nowhere to go? He pushed back the covers, lay naked in the light from the street, looked down the long stretch of his body to the standing flesh and held it, closing his eyes, using the image of a woman he had watched on the bus that afternoon to relieve him of only one of a thousand hungers that pulled at him now, even in dreams.

He was less sleepy than he had thought. Was it the city itself that disturbed him? He had never imagined it would be like this—fountains, like that one of Triton blowing a conch, his dwarf torso merging so imperceptibly into fish, or all those watery, unfocused creatures rising from pools and wellholes into another world, holding their jets, commanding or chasing. He could never tell when one thing would turn magically into something else, women into fish, men into horses, hair into horns, feet to hooves, and even a stone boat in one square quavered half under water, worn and yellowed by centuries of foundering. They entered his mind until even when he was awake he expected his eyes to follow the bare back of a street worker down to coils of serpents, expected faces to grin and spout wide, clear bands of water. Nothing was what it seemed to be.

One day that week Nancy had let him wander alone while she was at work, giving him a map and telling him to start at the doorway of a church near the embassy. It was early still, tables stacked at the café across the street. She waved, and for a while he watched her walking away.

He was not prepared for all the bones, or for their guardian who sat in front of a small table scattered with postcards and momentos, an old man in a drab, brown robe, tonsured head nodding as he mumbled to himself, his hand playing with the rope of belt in his lap. He hardly looked up as Carey walked past him into the corridor and maze of remains: stacked skulls, hipbones, shoulder blades, the butterflies of vertebrae, and clad in the same robes as their guardian were the skeletons of monks, grinning, bowing, trying to look at ease in their deadly oratory. The lights farther along snapped on, he heard the slap of the monk's sandals as he shuffled back to his chair, and Carey took a deep breath, walked all the way to the end slowly. Soon those twisting baroque arrangements began to be merely decorative, even to have a kind of exuberance—a bursting flower of vertebrae and leg bones, petals of shoulder blades, and in its center a skull. For a moment his own bones seemed delicately etched as the skeleton of a fish against the red velvet of flesh; he was thrust out of his body to see it as an indifferent arrangement of parts that could at any moment be reshuffled. But when he turned, the living monk at the end of the corridor was standing, hands folded, his hood fallen low on his forehead, so like his dead brothers that Carey was eager to get out. He did not leave any money and thought the monk muttered at him.

He stood in the sun for a moment. Across the street the waiter unstacking his tables, the strollers on their casual way past the newsstand, were only bones barely disguised by flesh and clothes, and he could not remember where he had seen such a frozen sense of reduction before, and then did—those films they had shown at school of the pits, corpses stacked naked and stiff in their grinning contortions, the piled wheelbarrows, the lampshades. He had walked for a long time trying to forget.

He was losing any sense of when he saw things, how images of the place became fixed in his mind. And lying in bed, letting them rise, he could almost think the city was a landscape of his own mind. Most places were not like the chapel of bones, images stared at directly, but were seen vaguely in the corner of the eye, then rose in a dream, insistently waiting to release or bear unexpressed feelings. He might think he was leaning like all the other people on an iron rail and looking at a ridiculously overstated collection of statues and false rocks, of pooled water, of laughing foolish people throwing coins over their shoulders, might think he was listening only to a confused tangle of languages. But a few hours later, with eyes closed for a moment, he would see a huge stone figure pointing menacingly at the slithering water, hear words indistinguishable from the sound of its falling, and a gushing power would be exposed, bubbling up and out from darkness into a seemingly blue and innocent fall day. Beyond the long stairs and spoked wheels of a square with its pointing figure of a man on a horse, he had found the fragments of a huge statue in a courtyard: the colossal bend of an elbow, a knee sitting by itself, a hand on a pedestal with its finger pointing up, up at nothing, and the head cut off at the collarbone, eyes half-lidded as if the giant were slowly waking from stone, face streaked with the darkness of his dreams. Was that really the Emperor Constantine if he appeared so often to Carey as he woke in the morning, feeling his own body spaced into separate pedestals, half dreaming? Was that statue less real than the old beggar with no legs who rolled in his rags on a wheeled board past an obelisk, or the pit with stumped columns, its temples without altars or roofs, filled with cats staring, preening, rising slowly from stone and ivy-like creatures magically called up from clay?

During the morning that he had visited the chapel of bones, lost in spite of his map, Carey had wandered through the arch of a building and entered a courtyard where a fountain, barely flowing, its water dripping and oozing through cool, green plants, was spilling down a wall and over the edge of its basin into the sun. It defined a space so quiet that every drip echoed; Carey sat on a stone bench. The windows were discreetly shuttered and the whole building seemed to sleep. He looked carefully over the map, traced street by street the way he had wandered. When he looked more carefully at the fountain he saw it was an old sarcophagus and the busts of a prim-looking couple stared out through the moss. Some birds fluttered and hopped in the pebbles, very distantly a woman's voice began singing, and he relaxed, hunched his elbows down on his knees, holding so still that the birds pecked close to his feet. And even when he thought of it now, the water was not the confusion of shifts, but the quiet music of deep sleep.

# 2

At first everything was too close to her. Turning off any of the main streets was to enter twisting and narrow lanes where buildings corniced, arched, and pillared, pushed and leaned in, and once she tried to walk straight through from the embassy to the Tiber and found herself winding in a labyrinth that mocked attempts to find a way out. Or the Tiber bent back on itself, as if to keep the bridge to the Trastevere forever just out of reach. The people around her were happiest when pushed together in groups, would gather tightly on street corners even when there was space available, as if they needed the touch of bodies to reassure them. On the buses hands rode over her like water, down her hips, along her thighs, and once an old man who sat in the seat she was crowded against had put his palm flatly on her calf. He stroked it gently, absentmindedly, his toothless lips sucking in and puffing out. In buses she learned to find corners, handbag clutched in front of her both to protect herself and its contents. Even when she sat down some man would stand so that his hardening genitals rubbed against her shoulder as the bus rattled and twisted up the Gianicolo. If she shoved back, resisted, glanced angrily, the men always looked shocked, bewildered, as if their bodies did that out of pure habit, and she came to see that it was a half-waking activity for both men and women, their minds hovering off in other thoughts or fantasies, no sense of personal invasion there at all. They had simply been rubbing up against another body all their lives.

But her own body could not accept this. It sent her warnings all day, shocks and flashes of nervous intensity. She felt every glancing touch because everything around put her sensuously on edge: those fishy men in fountains, bodies glistening, holding their jets of water pulsing in some breeze, the fruit on stalls, ripe and pulpy, persimmons and figs splitting and viscous, a sun that would press down like the palm of a hand on her upturned face when she walked out on to the Via Veneto to start home, a licking heat that made her want to lie without clothes in some private place, taking it in. The nights were almost sleepless for her now. She would rise to stand by the window in the dark, naked at last, Carey safely sleeping two rooms away, and the breeze from the villa would be full of the scent of rotting flowers, would billow the gauze curtain that she would catch and hold against her breasts, avoiding the dreams that would come later, waking her finally to a body fully roused, her hands groping, and dawn beginning to rise palely from every rumpled object in the room. She would lie half dozing, wondering what this place was doing to her, if the fierce isolation she and Carey shared was working on her mind, and she would at last sleep deeply, to wake moments later to the alarm.

They treated her with kindness and her job was not as demanding as working with lawyers at home. There were many little breaks to take coffee, push aside the stacks of meaningless paperwork, but most of the employees on her level were Italian, and although they spoke English well, they tended to talk among themselves in their own language. The men and women above her had their separate social world, and because she was only a secretary, even if a high level one, she rarely saw them after work. Only one of her fellow workers, an Italian named Alberto who was hired as a cultural consultant, seemed interested in her, and he had even taken her out to eat a few times during their long midday break. But everyone was kind. "How are things going?" Mr. Andrews would ask, or the ambassador, an old gentleman with a flushed, veinous face, would say, "Now you must let my wife know if there are any problems. She would love to help out." But they were all married, and she knew there was little way for them to include her in their lives. So she always said, "Everything is going wonderfully." She rarely thought of home, almost never of Frank. He had written only once, a letter to both of them, and then there was silence. She had not written back, although she encouraged Carey for a while to send postcards. Sometimes when she and Carey ate at the trattoria near their apartment where they went increasingly because of her inability to deal with cooking

— 111 —

after work, she would look at him, invariably devouring his pizza, the glass of wine she allowed him from her *quartino,* and she would panic to think that they would spend years like this, locked into each other's lives, recluses in a landscape overflowing with people.

When they went to St. Peter's one Sunday, so many people had already arrived that they had to work their way slowly in the door and up the huge nave until they were packed close to a barricade. She could feel the crowd surging in behind her, an impenetrable mass that they would never be able to retreat through, and she looked back only once at the thousands of faces turned forward, gaping and talking. She clasped Carey's hand to be certain they would not be separated. But she was more excited than afraid. They had come before when there was no Papal Mass, and the place had looked too big, too tortuously decorative to be real. Now the writhing columns of the baldachino, the twisting clothes of statues and bright rays of gold rose out of all the anticipation and murmur.

But they were still far away from the altar, and she could barely see the small figures when the Mass began, or hear bursts of the choir over the constant hubbub of the crowd. She could hear just enough from time to time to let her know what part was being celebrated, and the devout around her ignored the casual conversations nearby or small children on their fathers' shoulders. She watched them, the old women in black with lace handkerchiefs on their heads, rosaries in hands, and she too murmured responses. She glanced at Carey, thinking how odd it was that her own child was so foreign to all this, had never more than touched on these rituals in which her childhood had been steeped. He peered around, taller than most of them, or dropped back his head slowly to stare straight up. She decided she would have to tell him more about it all, take him to services. The music welled up and over them and the faint whiff of incense drifted by. The crowd was pushing, pushing, as if somewhere far behind a wall were compacting them.

The Mass was over. Some physical wave was riding back and forth through all the bodies around her and she held Carey's hand more tightly. Way up toward the altar there was a blare of trumpets, the cockaded hats of guards appeared in the aisle beyond the barricade, and distantly a domed and richly brocaded hat was bobbing like a thumb of light. The hat rose higher as it neared, and under it was the sharp thin face of a man with steely glasses, his two fingers raised. The crowd pressed relentlessly. They were yelling something that rolled toward her until even the people beside her were saying it. *"Papa, Papa, viva il Papa."* He was riding on a chair held on poles, carried on the shoulders of stern-faced men.

The crowd pressed the breath from her, and she could not move, could not defend herself against a body pressed flatly to her back, hands clutching her hips, the ridge of the man's penis thrust against the crease of her buttocks. She tried to jab back with her elbow, but it was locked in place by the screaming woman at her side. The man was pushing at her, his hands rolling her slightly back and forth, and his breath was in her ear, he was saying the words too, but in a whisper, *"Papa, Papa, viva il Papa."* She tried to scream, but the chair was high over them now, the glint of his round glasses blanked his face, the fingers were directly over their heads, looking more like a warning than a blessing, and everyone yelled with their faces twisted up like hungry birds. Lips were wet on her neck, the voice moaned, a last convulsive shove forced the thin cloth of her skirt into her cleft. The chair was past and already the crowd loosened as if some of them were pulled along by a magnet. She was sweating, faint, her own throat beating as if she had wakened from one of her dreams, but she felt sick. She twisted as soon as she could, pulled at her stuck skirt, but already the people around her were shifting away, and directly behind were only a frail young girl in white communion dress and cap and her mother, busily straightening her daughter's crushed ruffles. The rear of a brown suit, a humped back turned off into the crowd and Nancy shuddered, touching the back of her skirt as if she expected to find a slime he had left on her.

"What's the matter?" Carcy was saying, and she leaned for a moment on his shoulder.

"I think I need some air."

They pushed slowly out to the square where people were spilling over the cascades of stone to the fountains and pure gold air was washing down from the autumn sun. She breathed, her body as exhausted as if she had lain tightly clasped for hours by one of those half-fish men of the city's fountains.

"So many cruel and self-indulgent faces," she said.

Ian nodded. "But when you go out again, or tomorrow, I suspect you will see them everywhere. No togas, but these old Romans are still with us."

The busts of Roman emperors, their wives and families, stared at them from every direction in the dimly lit room.

"He is the worst, though, don't you think?" Ian paused to put a fingertip on the portrait of a young man with wispy sideburns on a very modish, unintelligent face. "Elagabalus."

The marble eyes stared back at her so knowingly, as if including her in their depraved world.

"But I didn't bring you here to depress you. Come."

He led her to the window where they could look down on the lighted square, the statue of Marcus Aurelius holding his hand out over the white-gloved policeman who was chatting with some friends. Perched on the cornice of the opposite building was a huge moon.

"It's not quite real," she said.

He laughed, that high, precise burst that she had come to like.

"Nothing is in Rome, Nancy. On our level, anyway." He paused. "On theirs," and he jerked his hand back toward the portraits, "which is the level for everyone who really lives here, it is—too real."

A guard sauntered through reminding them that it was time for the museum to close, so they walked slowly down the corridor and the wide stairs, past Marforio reclining sadly in his watery bower, and out into the white spokes of the square.

"Come. With a moon like this, it's obligatory that we look at the Forum."

She did not object. She had seen Ian often enough the past few weeks to feel at ease with him, was pleasantly relaxed from the dinner at a small restaurant nearby. But she was not prepared for the view over the most familiar of landscapes now made thoroughly new by the moonlight on pale columns, collecting in pools in the hollows, splashing the jagged, menacing cliffs of the old palaces.

"It doesn't matter how often I've seen it," he said. "It never fails."

A cat skittered by their feet and she jumped, grasping his arm tightly. He laughed but she sensed again how it made him uncomfortable to have her touch him. He always stood well back from her when they returned to her apartment, said goodnight very formally. She took it for an ingrained English reticence.

"Ian, it was such a good dinner. And I'm grateful to you for helping."

— 114 —

"Helping?"

"You are able to tell me so much, and I *have* begun to feel cut off, just Carey and myself. That's not very good."

"When school begins, that will change, won't it? For him certainly."

"For you too?"

"For me too."

He leaned forward on the railing, and she put her hands on it too.

"Your friend will return?" she asked.

He did not move, but his body had stiffened as if he were merely bending, not leaning in a relaxed way. He had never mentioned his friend but Carey had told her, and as if the past few evenings of intimacy made her want to clarify all that, she had been waiting to mention it.

"I'm not sure that will happen."

"I'm sorry. Carey said you were used to being together often."

"We lived together."

"I see." But she was not certain she did. So she said quietly, "You can tell me about her. It's all right. Maybe even better that you do?" She was embarrassed. Had the wine made her too relaxed? After all, he had only been friendly to her.

"Him."

"What?"

"Him, not her. I live with Pierre Leiberg."

She put a hand on his stooped shoulder. "I'm sorry. That was a foolish bit of prying."

But he had not relaxed. "Not foolish. I'm grateful you brought it up. I was hoping you would. We can't continue without some clarification."

He stood as if to turn to her and make a speech. But he only stared, one hand still on the railing, glasses showing two moons where his eyes should be.

"I'm very fond of you, Nancy."

She could not help smiling and knew it was light enough for him to see. "I'm sorry. I'm not mocking you. But you'll have to admit that sounded very English."

Again he did not answer and his lips pursed more stiffly.

"What I'm trying to tell you is that Pierre and I are lovers."

She saw his face set and waiting.

"I am sorry, Ian. I don't think I made that any easier for you to say."

Still he hung there as if she had not found the right words to release him, but she needed to catch her breath first.

"It's all right, Ian."

"You're not," and he paused, his face at last more expressive, "upset?"

"Not at you."

"Thank you. One never knows."

They both turned and began walking back and he talked about it to her in a rush that found them eventually sitting in a small bar on the Gianicolo, and she was surprised she did not find it hard to listen since for a moment in the taxi she thought she would never feel the same about him. But much of his reticence dropped now, and he ranged from bitterness when he talked about his native country to anguish whenever he mentioned Pierre. Finally she began to talk about Frank, as if she owed Ian something. It was very late when they stood outside the apartment building, and for the first time he hugged her to him and she held on tightly.

"If you'd rather not, we could just go back to the apartment."

She and Carey stood in front of the entrance. They had finished a brief visit to the Villa Giulia where Carey's growing impatience with museums had whisked them along, his sullen shrug the only reply to attempts on her part to interest him in various objects. He had finally wandered on ahead and been looking down on her from the small balcony when she came to the recumbent statues of an Etruscan couple, tightly side by side on the lid of their common coffin. Above them, hovering as if he were about to take flight, Carey was staring down, as lean and brooding as some of the boys his own age that lurked in the streets outside. She had held perfectly still as if her own movements might frighten something away. The smiling couple, hands extended, cast around them a sense of awkward composure, of interrupted privacy. In this city of gesture so extended that it curled back on itself, of displayed exuberance that seemed acted only to conceal some lassitude, these two were too real in their homely affection. And what was Carey looking at so angrily? When he saw her staring at him over the couple, he said, "Aren't you coming?" She could see it was no use, so she skipped the rooms of vases and walked up to the second floor, looking at the map quickly to see if there might be someplace else nearby that might interest him more. His school, delayed by the final stages of repairs, would at last begin in three days, and she was eager to end these restless weeks in which he played the piano or moped around the house. Now they paused at the gate to the zoo.

"No, it's all right," he said.

"I only thought it might be more interesting, and it's too early to eat."

He was looking sullenly past the turnstile to the grounds. Somewhere distantly an elephant began to bellow and the lions, closer by, began their deep coughing that gathered into a roar. As they wandered up the recently cemented path, she tried to put out of her mind the man who sold them tickets. He was perched high on a table pushed to the grate, his legs ending in stumps, and he had only one arm. Such sights were nagging, insistent, but after the first few days of shock, she had begun to avoid looking closely at them, even to the point of getting off her bus one stop beyond Piazza Venezia and walking back to the other bus in order to avoid a particular cripple—his face half blown away so that eye, cheek, and caved-in jaw were melted into one drawn, sinewed piece of raw flesh, his legless body on an old dolly. His arms would wave like polyps as the wordless voice moaned for coins. *"I mutilati di guerra,"* Ian said they were called.

The sign at the crossroads was in Italian. She made Carey read the small arrows pointing to various animals and he guessed most of them. Perhaps it was the sun, the trees around them, and lack of people that relaxed them at last. She translated the large sign which explained in very flowery terms that the recent "disruption" had interrupted the smooth functioning of the Zoological Society, that numbers of species had died and not been replaced, that the pressing needs of the human population must be served first, but that surely one day the Roman Zoo would once again flourish as before, known throughout the world.

"What disruption?" Carey said as they headed toward the lion cages.

"The war, they mean."

Few of the signs had been changed. The lion was claimed to be from Italian Ethiopia. His mane was tangled, fur torn out in places, and he lay panting, ribs moving sharply under the taut skin. He did not even bother to look at them. The leopard paced with his head down, avoiding a large, fly-specked pile of spaghetti in the corner.

"Jesus," Carey said, "the animals too?"

She did not answer, afraid to have to say that they probably were given only that, and some of the food in the other cages looked no better, as if the animals were being fed on the garbage from city restaurants. The elephant was dusting himself, swaying slowly from side to side as small birds pecked at his mounded droppings. "Not much of a zoo," Carey said, and then Nancy tried to explain how the city had so many other things to take care of, but he interrupted her with "I know," as if he did not want to know. In some of the empty cages cats had made their homes, coming and going at will through the open gates. They sat for a moment on a bench in the sun by the seal pool. There were no seals, no water in the cracked cavity except the last brackish pools of some recent storm.

She said, "I guess zoos are a kind of luxury."

But he was thinking, hands clasped between his legs. Finally he blurted, "You'd be doing the animals a favor if you shot them."

She knew he was nettling her on purpose. "I don't suppose being shot is ever a favor."

"You know what I mean."

But she was thinking how odd it was that in this one place more than any of the others they had been, a place where human beings never lived, they were staring directly at the war, as if that bare pool, its rusted and tilted sign, were the recently bombed remains of some tenement. "*I mutilati di guerra, i mutilati di guerra,*" kept chanting through her mind.

"Did you see the man in the ticket booth?" Carey asked without looking at her.

"Yes."

"I can't stand them. It makes me feel crawly all over. They're everywhere. I wish they wouldn't ask for money. Do you give them money?"

"Sometimes."

"I don't. I just want to get by. Then I feel awful I didn't."

She did not answer. He was staring at the pool now.

"People do terrible things to each other. Do they have to?"

She wanted, more than anything, an answer, and whirled through all the old evasions—because we suffer, because we don't know what we are doing or why God made us so blind and violent, because pain is the price exacted for what tenderness and love we secure, *Kyrie Eleison, Christe Eleison;* but her voice would not speak, as if her own face were torn and shapelessly healed, her tongue as useless to her as to the

— 118 —

cripple she avoided. She reached out an arm and put her hand on his neck. He did not draw back. "I don't know."

They were interrupted by a couple who had approached so slowly and quietly that they had not seen them coming. They stood shyly in front of the bench as if they were sorry to bother them, but the man rattled off some phrases about a camera he held toward Nancy. She was puzzled, shook her head.

"*Ah, scusi,*" and the man grinned broadly. "*Americani?*"

"*Si, si.*" Nancy nodded effusively.

"*Allora,*" and the man, speaking slowly, using his hands and the camera, let her know he wanted a picture taken of himself and his wife, his very recent wife, he said proudly, and the woman stared at her toes and grinned. They were both young but very stout, with flushed red cheeks and hard-worked hands. Nancy took the camera and Carey stood so the couple could sit on the bench. The man put his arm stiffly behind his bride and she sat as if fearing to fall backward. Nancy pushed down on the plunger, but at the same time the man's face started, his other hand fluttered up.

"*Ah, Signora,*" he explained—her thumb, it had been over the lens.

They were all laughing at her as she looked ruefully at the little box and blushed.

"My son is better," she explained. So she gave it to Carey, and he clicked it. The man and his wife stood and shook their hands with a small bow, gravely polite. He said as if deeply embarrassed, "We are grateful," and Nancy thanked him.

She walked with Carey slowly back to the gate, turning once to look down the dim path, hazy now with the midday sun, its dried bay leaves perfuming the air, but the couple had vanished, and she could not help thinking of their lives, of some long, curving motion they were beginning together, and she wished she had told them, "Good luck."

"Don't look up yet," he said, his hand loosely holding her waist.

She was dizzy from the wine they had consumed in a long meal in the piazza outside the church. The man, Alberto Benedetti, had been very attentive, very witty, and she had not minded how long it took. Only now, in the dim church so musty with old incense, so cavernously empty, did she feel quite drunk. But he was as steady as he had been when he had met her at the bus stop that evening, not even unbalanced when he genuflected and crossed himself quickly as they entered the nave.

"Stand on this small spot."

The pavement focused into a brownish circle of marble. He spoke English perfectly, learned it, he had admitted, while interned in England during the war. It had made his hiring by the embassy as a consultant on cultural affairs easier.

"Why here?"

"Because. When they made the illusion, this place is where it is to focus. You must be standing in the right place."

He had not removed his arm, although she could tell he was being careful to touch her very decorously, nothing insistent. He was northern Italian, born in Turin, with something French in the sharp-featured face, the light hair—but the eyes, the gestures were unmistakably Italian, and especially that genteel but teasing manner he had come to treat her with when at the office. In those long lunches, she had come to think of him as someone she knew quite well.

"Lean back, and look up."

She did, letting the arm hold her as she swayed her head back, eyes wide. At first everything was very dim, but there were a few lights tilted to shine up onto the distant ceiling. What she thought she saw was the cupola and a dome rising away as it did in St. Peter's, and as she leaned even farther back, a blue sky with clouds and figures rising into it, their feet and robes in an upward rush, and angels and saints sitting on cornices were looking into a heaven that made her feel as if she could fall up and up. She could not help laughing, and knew that without his arm she would certainly fall.

"Who is it?" Her neck began to ache but she did not want to turn away.

"San Ignazio. Saint Ignatius, I believe you say. Entering Paradise."

"I believe it." She looked down, straightened up. "It's very ugly, but very wonderful."

He laughed. "Vulgar, maybe. Not ugly, surely. The Jesuits would not want it to be ugly. Appearances are important to them, you know."

They sauntered farther up the nave.

"You saw that was not a dome?"

She stopped. Unsupported this time, she looked again. It was true. The dome was painted on a vaulted ceiling but wherever she stood it rose away into depth.

"Tricky, tricky."

They walked down a side aisle and out again into the night. The little restaurant was at the side of the piazza beyond the church steps, and a square was formed by three perfectly adjusted, curved buildings and the looming façade of the church—too perfectly formed, Nancy had decided as they had eaten and she kept looking at it over the potted hedges that separated them from the night traffic. It was a small stage set and the program should have announced, "Rome, 1827—Enter the Count from the left, Countess from the right."

"I've forgotten my lines," she said.

"Pardon?"

"Just thinking to myself. This square makes me feel as if I should have a part to play, some tragic or at least passionate speech."

He smiled. "It is most artificial. But attractive?"

"I guess. It makes me uneasy too. Like in there. Everything is trying so hard to make you believe something. Anything."

He was standing close, and she had forgotten that his hand had not left her arm as he helped her out the door. Now it moved easily around her waist again.

"Nancy. I want to tell you something."

"That's better," she said, and was laughing a little as she turned, the arm actually pressing her against him, but she saw he was not mocking at all, and only had a brief second to stop laughing before his mouth was on hers, his other hand on her back. Dizzy, she put her head down slightly, her forehead resting on his chin, and let him talk.

"These times we have been together, they mean a great deal to me. I am certain you know. I want you to understand that. And also I hope to be more than just your friend."

He was doing it quite awkwardly, she thought. She had expected this kind of move soon, but she had imagined something more suave, more seductive in a place where seduction would make more sense, not in the middle of some baroque square where waiters at the nearby restaurant were moving away tables and chairs as they closed for the night. For a moment she thought she would be angry, as if cheated. But no, although she wanted something not too deep, at least it should be genuine. The hands were gently moving over her back. How good that felt, even the touch of his breath on her hair, and she let her own hands flatten out on his shoulders.

"I think I already am," she said slowly.

He moved his face away, let one hand come under her chin to gently raise her head. She let him press the small of her back so that her hips rode hard into his, shut her eyes, the old rush of blood she had not known for so long, so long, and when he turned, she walked down the steps almost leaning into him, the lights spinning slightly and she said, "Alberto, Alberto, so much wine," but his only reply was to turn her to him when they stood in the street and hold her again, more insistently.

So when the taxi wound out through the narrow streets to the Corso and up the hill in the opposite direction from home, she only put her head down on his shoulder; when the cab stopped and he paid, leaning in the window while she clutched her arms to herself in the cooling fall air, she did not mind, and she said as he fumbled for a key, "Where are we, what part of the city?" and he said, "The Parioli." Shyly, turning on the lights, he murmured, "My apartment, you like it?" and she nodded, blinking in the light at a much too fastidiously arranged living room, too clean, too shining to be much lived in. For a second she thought dazedly of Carey. Should she call? But she let go of that too. He was safe. She was tired of always thinking of him.

She saw herself briefly in a mirror as they passed through the hallway to the bedroom, her hair untucked in places, and the eyes looked hard at her as if to say, "Think, think," but she turned away. She asked him to leave the light off, and he opened the windows, then she let him undress her, which he did very gently, did everything slowly as if they had all the time in the world, and for a brief second when he entered her, his body a strange naked presence, she came fully awake, sober, even startled as if she had forgotten what it was to part and close on that column of flesh, and then she clasped her arms and legs around him, tightly, opened her mouth wide to his, and moved toward all his thrusts.

They were praying eternally, a devotion to the sacrament that was never interrupted, two nuns in pale blue and white relieved at regular intervals by two more nuns, like soldiers at a nation's flame. Nancy sat in the dark little church and no one but she and the nuns were there. Between herself and them rose an elaborate screen that did not conceal their quiet figures but only shielded them as if they were the next layer of sacrament and she should be praying devotedly to them.

But she was not. She found it peaceful here and had learned, on those days when her work was particularly without meaning, or her patience with a restless Carey waiting for her at home was thin, to stop for a few moments, walking quickly past the cascading Fountain of Trevi and the parked stands of mute horses, their faces smothered in blinders and feedbags.

It was Monday, Carey would be starting school at last tomorrow, and she was certain that one deep breath, one hard look at where they were, would suffice before some new and easier way would begin. She suspected that was merely wishful, but something had to be different; even the fact that he would have an audition soon with Ikbal Dorati would help. She and Carey were simply out of phase and that made him like a large weight tugging against the new motions of her own life.

But she could not tell Carey about Alberto. Not yet. She wanted it to be a telling, not a confession, and she still was too unclear about what it all meant. That first night she had dozed, then woke sprawled to his second gropings, alarmed to see the room rising dimly out of a grayish light, his own face clear now, blurred only by its closeness to her own. He was less gentle, more insistent, as if his need had grown, not diminished, or as if there were no need now for any *cortesia*. But since that matched her own eagerness, she did not care. She was much more aware of small details: the hardness of the flesh along his waist that she had expected to be more loose since he was not a thin figure, the hint of some spice in his hair that she could not place—cinnamon, nutmeg? He rode home in the taxi with her, face less guarded, eyes as puzzled as her own must have been, and all that morning she would pause from time to time trying to see his face, but she had lost it temporarily, could not even think how he looked at work. "Some party," Carey had said suspiciously over breakfast. She had not bothered to go to bed, but was sitting by the open balcony doors when he woke. Like a girl younger than her dour-faced, sleepy son across the table cracking his boiled eggs, she wanted to take him by the hand and stand in the sun at the balcony breathing deeply. But she laughed instead. "At least it's Saturday." For the rest of the morning as she dozed and woke to his practicing, Bach and more Bach falling around her in fugues she never stayed awake long enough to hear resolved, she thought of interrupting him, of letting him know that she had a lover. He was old enough, wasn't he? Better they should always be open since there were just the two of them in this world of strangers. But guiltily she realized that was not true. There was a third person now, shadowy, still blurred in her mind, even though her body kept dreaming it all again vividly, the weight of his body released totally onto her as they both cried out in that tangled bed.

She loved the shade of blue the nuns wore, pale but bright, and against the stark white of collar and wimple, in the pure light of fluttering candles, it seemed to be the translucent stained glass for something shining within them. Or was she supposed to think of the sacrament beyond them as casting its own light like a sun that they were making visible for her by kneeling between herself and that chalice, that bread? How could she feel so peaceful looking at those colors when she could no longer believe in what they were doing? She tried to think she believed, wanted to slide forward onto her knees, something the whole slant of the bench urged her to do.

They moved at last. Two other nuns had come to stand directly behind, and they stepped up to the empty places and kneeled, settling quietly as birds on some nest. Nancy dimly saw one of their faces, surprised at how old the woman was, and remembering how cramped and arthritic kneeling could become even when she was a child, she knew that what they were doing was not a comfortable thing.

As punishment for what? How saintly she had felt extending those moments on her knees, especially on days when she had cramps, as if making that even more painful erased the "impurity" of her body. The old angers rose, against those mumbling men who had listened bored, surely hearing far more vicious sins than she could offer up as a child and teenager, yet *her* sins, suffered with every fear of damnation, made even more fiercely painful by that childish fear than for someone older who had sinned and confessed and sinned again; anger against the men who had burdened her body with a lead shield of detestation for its blood, let loose without her will, and its need against which she clenched her knees to her growing breasts, trying to clasp deep away from her hand that new soft wedge of hair, those lips that petaled out to her dreams.

Yet she saw in those nuns the old "wish," the same goal she and every other girl child in that church had hoped to fulfill, waiting in the darkened bedroom for days, some even for months, after careful prayers, after keeping the mind pure for weeks, for the spirit to descend, some angel of mercy announcing an end to all the waiting for the word. She had known soon enough Saint Teresa was someone else's pattern, and as she and her apostate friends grew into their bodies, they became conspiratorial, thinking of the sisters as women to be feared, identifying their devout peers as spies, at last thinking of confession as a place to drop placebo sins, mere vanities and minor indulgences.

She stared at their backs. So all these things she thought she had long grown away from, even believing to have become a pale Protestant or maybe a pseudopagan, were not going to let her alone anymore. She had been naïve to think something so much a part of her childhood could vanish forever, and this city, so thick with that way of living, had to demand something of her, would not let all that sleep. Even now, more sternly straightened in her back than she needed to be, pushing against the thrust of the bench, she longed to slide forward, let her words touch that gawky, garish figure of a Christ some recent donor had nailed to the false marble wall. The bitterness of her old rejections was strongly tasted, but she sensed they were simple, too easy, the motions of an adolescence that had to make up its mind or sink in confusion. One way or the other, rejecting or accepting, the vision could never again be simple. No ritual ever was, she thought as she stood, whether it was the curved devotion of those nuns or the ancient spreading of her body to the gestures of Alberto's thrust and moan.

She paused at the door to look back. Uneasy as she was from all these new things only half pondered, that lurking sense of peace had not left her, here, or in her memory of what she had seen when sitting by the open balcony when the pines were pure bursts of greenish gold in a rising sun—as though no matter which way she went, beyond everything there must be a God who meant them to live this way, tangled in wonder.

# 3

"And this," Mr. Anderson said, winking at them all, his hair no less awry than when Carey first met him, "is Signor Cortese, I should say Il Conte Cortese, who will be teaching some of you Latin," and in a burst he began intoning, "'*Arma virumque cano...*'" and continued until the count's smile and his cocked, interested expression could not be held, and many of the students began to fidget.

One by one he introduced the teachers sitting in a row at the front of the room. The noise of some game being played by the lower grades drifted up the marble corridors, the students' names were called and they stood awkwardly, postures not helped by the desks borrowed from the lower grades. Carey could barely squeeze his legs under when he sat. Anderson named their various nationalities, obviously proud that there were so many. Most were Americans, some English, and the boy next to Carey, pale-skinned and stocky, blushing profusely as he stood, was introduced as Yugoslavian. The Australian's name was Fiero Caffaro, and he corrected Anderson boldly when he put the accent on the first syllable instead of the second. Carey decided the girls were not very good-looking.

For the first few days, Carey felt shy, in spite of Ian, and he could not seem to avoid the Yugoslavian, Mladen. The boy's surliness annoyed him, and he suspected it was supposed to—a tough-guy pose that was too showy. But he was strong, a compact, short body and fists that did not show bones when he clenched them. Because he had spent five years in New York City while his father was with the legation there, he spoke English easily. He would set himself on the balls of his feet when he said something as if he expected to have to punch someone, but at the same time he would be blushing. As if he could tell Carey was uneasy near him, Mladen stuck with him, talking at recess, whispering in class, demanding Carey either insult or accept him. That only made Carey more stubbornly ignore him.

The Latin class was held in the tower. Only four students were well enough prepared to study Virgil with the count—Mladen and Carey and Fiero and a girl named Amy, whose curled and bobbing hair and broad face gave her the nickname Goldilocks. She hated that, but Carey would say it anyway, teasing her as if they were back in grade school. She was bright and too aware of it.

He had come up early from recess. He liked that room, and sometimes he would climb alone to look out over the fields to the city, through air, as fall advanced, that lost its haze and more sharply defined the distant buildings, and he would try to identify them, thinking of the streets nearby where he might have wandered.

Mladen's head and shoulders rose from the hole in the floor where the spiral ended. He grinned. *"Dov' é il conte?"*

Carey shrugged and turned partly to the windows. "Don't know."

Mladen uttered a steady stream of Italian and came the rest of the way up, swinging over the railing. Carey was certain Mladen knew how much the other students envied that ease with languages.

"Want to unpin the table?"

Mladen had discovered that trick and they had pulled it earlier in a history class downstairs with Mr. Johnson, a lantern-jawed Englishman still blinking and unnerved by the war; "Shell-shocked," Anderson had told them angrily after the table had collapsed under Johnson's books when he set them down, and pale, clutching his head, he had left the room with a thin, high wail like a punctured tire. Nobody had laughed much except Mladen, but Carey had thought the laugh was forced, as though not to laugh would have been some kind of defeat.

"I'd rather not," Carey said to the window.

"I'd rather not," Mladen mimicked primly.

"I've got nothing against him." Carey liked the count—tall, constantly smiling with some private amusement, but very quiet and serious when he read Virgil or listened to their struggling translations.

"C'mon," and Mladen was already stooping under the table, pulling at one of the pins holding the leg in place, "don't be such a goody-goody."

"Oh, leave it alone. It's simple-minded." Carey turned to the window again.

Footsteps flicked on the iron treads, and the thin face of Fiero appeared, but Mladen spun Carey around, hand tight on his shoulder.

"What did you say?"

"It's a stupid thing to do."

The back of Mladen's hand slapped across Carey's face so fast that he was still not moving when he began to taste the blood on his teeth.

"I'm not stupid." Mladen's face was swollen red.

"Hey," Fiero's voice said from somewhere near their ankles.

Carey put out his hand and grabbed a bunch of Mladen's shirt. They stood here, breathing heavily, and Carey was not certain what should come next. Mladen tried to get loose. Carey held on. They began a clumsy circling, knocking over chairs, still staring, panting, not speaking. When Mladen's hand swung again Carey was ready, blocked it with his free arm, and then they were grappling, wound tight, down on the floor, rolling against table and chairs. Two heads were staring at their level, Amy's wide blue eyes joining Fiero, then the count's voice, his tall figure was over them, and his hand twisted at Carey's collar. Before they were separated, he flailed out one good swing that raised a mouse on Mladen's forehead. He had been strong, hands that bruised when they closed on Carey's arms.

"Stop," the count kept saying.

Mladen was wild-eyed, arms shaking.

"Get your hands off me," he said to Cortese, and he swung, a fling of his arm that missed his head, and suddenly Mladen had been struck hard by a slap from the count's open palm.

He held still. "You hit me."

"*Silenzio*. Sit down."

Carey's knees weakened. He found a toppled chair, righted it, and sagged down. Mladen was cursing, some of it recognizably English, like "wop" and "bastard," some of it Italian, and what he could not understand Carey assumed must be Yugoslavian. The count raised an eyebrow but did not move. Carey had never seen such a rage before, but it began to run down, and as it did Mladen backed away until he stood against one window as if afraid everyone would jump him.

"You're cowards," he said to the count. "All of your people were yellow. You fought for the Germans and then you ran, ran, ran."

But the count was walking around picking up the spilled books and chairs. He turned to the two pale faces still barely risen into the room.

"Come up now," he said quietly, and with a whirl that placed him directly in front of Mladen he said firmly, "Sit down."

Still breathing heavily, Mladen moved to the chair next to Carey and slumped into it. The others came up and sat too. None of them were looking at each other. The wind rattled at the panes and subsided. On the stairwell Ian's voice said, "I say, what's up? What's the racket?"

*"Tutto a posto,* Ian," the count said precisely, and there was no reply.

Again silence. The breathing choked a few times next to Carey and when he turned slightly he saw Mladen was crying, almost without sound. More than anything that had happened, that shocked Carey.

"What is this about?" the count said.

Carey shook his head. He could have said something about the table, but that did not seem connected to it anymore. Amy stood, her moony face like a mask.

"I want to go."

"Sit," the count said impatiently, and as if her strings had been cut, she dropped back into her chair. "Mladen?"

"Why do you hate me?"

Carey had to turn away from his eyes. "I don't."

"You do, you do. I try to talk to you or anything and you won't. You insult me, you hate me."

Carey did not know what to say. The count cleared his throat. Fiero had his face propped on his folded arms and was staring sideways out the window. When Carey reached to put his hand on Mladen's arm, he shrugged slightly but turned his face to look at it, cheeks blazing up red again. The count was opening his book, riffling the pages.

"Book Two. *Conticuere omnes intentique ora tenebant."*

"I'm sorry, Signor Cortese," Mladen said very plainly. "I've never forgotten what they did to my cousin. But it wasn't you. Or the Italians."

The count stared at him, lips smiling archaically under eyes that seemed to look back and back inside.

*"Va bene, giovanotto mio. Sunt lacrimae rerum."* He looked

down to his book and continued reading for a while before he asked Fiero to begin translating.

At the end of the day Mladen and Carey rode the school bus to Piazza Venezia together, talking quietly about things that did not matter. When they were about to go to their own separate buses, Mladen took Carey by the arm.

"Wait. I want to tell you."

They walked into the little graveled park near Trajan's column, where prisoners and soldiers and chariots were winding their way endlessly up toward the incongruous figure of St. Peter. Mladen picked up some of the pebbles and tossed one between his feet from time to time as he talked.

"They drove into our village early in the morning, just before the sun came up. The partisans had left that night, knew the Germans were coming because it was the only road through and no one could stop them, not enough men to hold off those cars and tanks, so the men went up into the hills, leaving us behind. There was my mother and brother and cousin Ljubo, he was staying with us for the summer, and my grandmother. I was six and I sat on our doorstep in the dark and even before the sun came over the field you could hear the motors, and a few fast cycles came through, then the tanks and trucks, and they went right to the square and rang the bell and made all the people come stand there. They asked questions. They asked my mother where Father was and she said she didn't know, maybe dead because she hadn't seen him for years. Lying, of course. He'd been with us that week, but we'd all been taught the same lies so we knew what to say, and I remember they made my grandmother come, made her stand even though she hadn't been out of bed for half a year. Then they said we were lying, and they built a huge fire in the middle of the square and they took old Bunic, our mayor, and made him hold a piece of iron that they'd heated, and he yelled and begged but wouldn't tell them anything, so they put a gun in his mouth and shot him. Most of the back of his head went off and some of the people nearby were wiping at themselves and getting sick. Then they walked around and stopped by us, and they grabbed my cousin Ljubo. One of them brought out an ironing board and they tied him to it, and the head of them said we could stop all this if we just told them where our men had gone, but no one spoke, so they put the ironing board slowly into the fire and Ljubo was yelling all the time until they stuffed some-

— 130 —

thing in his mouth. When I looked at my mother she wasn't crying but she had bitten all the way through her lip."

His voice stopped. Carey did not speak. He felt sick but was almost angry, wanted to believe it was all made up. Mladen stood abruptly as if he were afraid Carey would say something. He dug in his pocket and pulled out lire.

"I'm hungry."

They pooled their cash and bought some pastries and then went home. On the bus, winding slowly up the hill, Carey looked at the people who touched against him, polite, thinking their own thoughts, and he could not help wondering what memories, cruel, implacable, were eating away in spaces that could never be refilled.

"Now," Mrs. Dorati said, and leaned close over Carey from behind so that he could see her face from the corners of his eyes, and her hair, musky with some perfume, brushed his ear. She spoke with only a slight accent that he could not identify. "Don't be nervous. Just play," and her fingers drummed a quick arpeggio on Carey's shoulder like a bird running along the sand.

He had come to the audition expecting to be very nervous. Nancy and he had followed the twisting way past the Palazzo Cenci to Via Catalana, up the musty stairwell to the imposing door with its brass nameplate, into the marbled hallway and beyond to the large room darkly draped, its piano hulking at the far end. But in spite of all that seeming heaviness and solemnity, after only a moment of conversation with her, he could not be nervous. Nancy was; he could tell by the way she hung back slightly, answering Ikbal's questions too quickly. But most of the time lately she had seemed either jittery or preoccupied.

Ikbal Dorati was not imposing: a sparrow in a black dress, long black hair swung around to one side of her head and hanging down over the pale white skin of neck and collarbone. Ian had told them she was only twenty-nine, but Carey had not realized how young she would seem, and then he could not believe this was to be his teacher or that she was the famous pianist they had heard so much about. As they sat stiffly in their chairs before she asked him to go to the piano, he kept wondering how anyone so petite, with those frail hands, delicate cheekbones and black, sunken eyes, could control that concert grand beyond them.

Her hand left his shoulder and she walked away to sit in

a large brocaded chair that nearly swallowed her, quickly crossing her legs, holding her long fingers in a tent in front of her mouth. Beyond her, on the sofa, Nancy sat trying not to catch his eyes, as if she could fade away into the upholstery. They were both waiting, those two women in line, Ikbal intently becoming a listener, his mother trying to hide her concern—their faces blurring in the dark room into two pale marble busts.

He began with a prelude and fugue. When he finished he glanced at Ikbal, but she merely nodded. Nancy was staring at the back of Ikbal's head. Then a Beethoven sonata, and he had a little trouble in the second movement but found his way out. She had moved now, was leaning forward slightly in the chair, arms clasped to her waist, and she was staring at his hands. As he was finishing a Chopin nocturne she stood and came silently across the carpet until she was behind him. He was distracted but kept on, smelling that spiced perfume, certain she was breathing close to him, and then the piece took over and he forgot her. When it was done he drew back his hands and they started trembling.

"Please stand for a moment."

He did, his body feeling very lumpish. She sat. He wanted her to say something, not to be swept off the stool, and he even thought of shaking that slim figure he looked down on, the straight back, harped curve of hips. Her eyes were closed for a moment, hands in her lap.

"Like this," and her hands rose, held still for a moment over the keys. The wrists bent supplely, hands fell, and she began playing the same nocturne. At first he could not hear it, was annoyed. Why not just say she didn't like how he had played if she didn't? But he began to hear what she was doing, and he knew that was what he had wanted but had not accomplished, and the more he listened, the more he wondered bleakly if he ever could.

When she had finished, she paused for a moment to let the last note fade, released the damper pedal and swiveled to him on the stool. Her hand leapt from the keyboard to take his firmly by the wrist.

"Do you see? Toward the end. You do wonderfully until then. But it must gather like that, not pause or fall into phrases. Like a wave. Up onto the beach, all the way up, *then* subsides, so, gently. Dies." She let go of him and stood quietly. "Now, sit."

She leaned over him, her arms came down from his own shoulders on each side of him, hands positioned on the keyboard.

"From here," and she played a few measures, then stood back.

Carey began. She spoke behind him. "More bass there, now the inner voice, bravo," and awkward as he felt, he began to hear it growing. Toward the end his hands seemed to belong to her. When it was over, she touched him on the shoulder again, her voice over his head speaking to Nancy, and he watched his mother's face.

"A very fine talent. We will work together well."

"How wonderful," Nancy murmured, and they left the piano, to stand for a while in the middle of the room, talking randomly, but Carey was numb.

At the door she turned to him and for the first time laughed.

"You look very tired."

He nodded, but was puzzled. Something had come over her after she laughed. She had seemed so intense, carried along by a deeply controlled energy that had pulled a similar response out of himself. That was why he was so tired. Now she had retracted far into herself, face becoming expressionless, a posed portrait.

"Did you like her?" Nancy asked, when they sat for pastries at the café nearby.

"She's much better than Stafford. And prettier."

He blushed, but she was smiling in such a way that he could tell she did not really know what he was thinking, that ever since the door had closed behind them, he had begun to wait for the week to pass, and even now he could feel the light touch of her hand on his.

Ian gave him a yellowed volume, Schubert's *Winterreise*, with threads wisping out along its spine, and said, "Let's try these sometime."

They went into the empty room to use the school's mangled piano. Carey stumbled along through the music, but he was listening too much to the firm tenor voice, not big, but very precise and expressive. Finally he took his hands off the keys in midsong.

"I'm butchering it."

Ian pulled up a chair, leafed the book back to the first song.

"They're hard. Remember I've known them for years."

The door opened for a moment behind them, then shut again. They went back to the first song. They did it again after Ian translated the German. Carey could tell he was playing better by the way the voice began moving more freely, and he followed its hesitations, glides, diminuendos.

"There." Ian sat again. "Would you like to work these up? I'm thinking of a little concert next spring. Just for some friends. And their friends."

"Yes."

"I know Ikbal won't mind, but I'll ask her, if you like."

He had forgotten how well Ian knew her. "Mother was surprised how young she is."

He nodded. "Prodigy. Born in Egypt, Egyptian father, Armenian mother. Taken to Europe early to study and gave her first recital when she was six. Imagine," and he went on listing her accomplishments. But Carey was not very interested in them. They were mere facts. Finally Ian closed the music and handed it to him. "Recess is almost over."

"The Ardeatine," Carey blurted, and Ian looked puzzled. "You said her husband was there. What was it?"

He spoke more precisely, as he tended to when he felt something strongly. "Not very nice, I'm afraid. Late in the war, March 1944. The resistance trapped and killed thirty-two Germans on the Via Rasella, downtown Rome. You know it? Opposite the Palazzo Barberini."

Carey waited.

"They decided a fitting response would be about ten to one—ten Italians for one German. Rounded up three hundred and thirty-six people into trucks, very much a random job, took them out the Via Ardeatina and gunned them all down, then caved in sand on them."

He turned toward the window that looked out onto the old olive trees, and his voice became much quieter. Carey was almost sorry he had asked, had that sick lurching in him that came now when these unexpected tales of violence were revealed, but this was about Ikbal, and he thought there would never be any way *she* could tell him.

"She'd married quite young. Nineteen. He was older, Piero Dorati. Almost twice her age. A violinist. Good, not great, but excellent chamber musician. They were very happy. He just chanced to be walking home that day from a rehearsal. Quartets. There wasn't much in the way of music going on then. It was hard enough to find some food, some heat—to survive. But he and his friends practiced, as Ikbal did too, and they would all get together every few weeks and give free concerts in one apartment or another—just to keep in shape and also to help the people around them, reminding them of other things."

He put one hand on the windowpane, scratching a small chip of paint, then clasped both hands behind his back, still looking down on to the trees as if he could see something there.

"She even remembers it was Beethoven he had been playing that week. The A minor, Opus 132. He was first violin, and having trouble with the last movement. He was herded into the trucks along with the others, none of them knowing what was going on. One of the soldiers took his violin and threw it on the sidewalk. The case sprung open. They found it there later. She says that must have been the part that truly disturbed him. Someone was looking down from one of the houses on the street and remembered a man who kept begging the soldiers not to leave his violin there. It was raining."

The buzzer broke over them with a prolonged rasp. Recess was over.

"For days she didn't know what had happened. No one did. But it was all pieced together soon."

"I'm sorry," but Carey said something only to fill the space. He wanted to say that to her.

They walked to the door.

"She was twenty-two then. And she's very tough, active. You mustn't think of it in the wrong way. There was so much suffering for everyone here. It helps to have other people around you who are also recovering." With the door opened, he lifted a finger and said, "Practice."

He liked Mladen best when only the two of them were together—swimming at the Foro Italico, that already decaying, white-stoned sports center built by Mussolini where his obelisk rose like a stark finger, its base splashed day after day with the bloody paint of graffiti, or wandering around the city, or sometimes taking a bus out to the beach at Ostia. He would be less brash, and under his noisy acts Carey found him very shy. But he also deeply mistrusted the people around thim, and was better at seeing through the con games that Carey mistook for kindness or interest. He tried to explain the Trieste problem; all Carey could understand was that it made Italians and Yugoslavians hopelessly angry with each other. But when they had someone else with them, Mladen would start posturing again, blustering into scrapes they were lucky to escape from.

"Why do you act that way?" Carey asked him one Saturday morning as they waited for a bus at Ponte Milvio. The evening before, when they were supposed to be at a party and instead had spent the time wandering on the Via Veneto, Mladen had seen two men on the lower end of Via Bissolati, daubing some slogan about Trieste on a wall, had made a dash, kicked over the can of paint, been pursued, but dodged through the traffic. The men had backed off gesturing and yelling. Fiero had been impressed, Mladen paraded for the next hour like a cock, talking about how Italians never fought it out and were full of threats and gestures only, but Carey knew that if there had not been so many people around, they would have been in trouble.

"I don't know. I don't do it to prove anything to you, Carey. I don't seem to have to do that. But I can't stand it when we're all in a bunch and nobody's any different."

"Different than what?"

But he stared at his shoes. "Than anyone else. When I'm with Fiero, or in classes, or just riding in a bus, sometimes I feel so lonely."

At night all the energy of the city held under during the day broke out, as if the contrasts of light and dark—black sky seeping down to exaggerate each baroque volute and scroll, the light that splashed up from fountains and walls—gave the people who lived there the setting for their need to act and strut. At first Carey was surprised that Nancy let him go out so freely at night, as long as he was back by ten or so. But all those lights and people made it safe, and she was often out herself, later than he was; he became used to half waking when the key rasped in the tumblers, the door squeaked open, and he would turn back to search for an interrupted dream.

He loved those nights with Mladen and sometimes Fiero. Always there was a sense of potentiality, as if whatever they wanted might be theirs at any moment. They began wandering into the dark, still alleys that dropped into silence, uneven cobblestones, stale cooking smells. One narrow street they took for a shortcut twisted on and on, voices from open windows high above fading off, sounds of traffic far behind them smothered. The street became much too narrow for cars, cats skittered off into a darkness they began to grope through, and the blank wall of a building ahead cut them off. They were whispering now. Fiero thought they should go back.

A door was flung open behind them. In a square of white light, bare bulb, a wedge of woman was hulking, her arms bowed out around her breasts and hips. Even if her legs were fat they seemed much too small to hold her bulk, and her hair stood out like a black halo. She was wheezing.

Her voice was more howl than words. An arm rose, cut out toward them like a scythe, sending a shadow to their feet.

*"Vuole?"* the voice said, then grunted a short chain of fierce snorts.

They backed off toward the blank end.

"Owww," she moaned again, and stepping up onto the threshold, hurled her shadow on them.

Carey was backing off faster, almost against the last building, when she heaved herself into the street and stooped, they turned to run, and the alley crooked suddenly to the left toward bright lights of some street. She howled again, a stone smashed and rolled near them, they sprinted all the way to the end like spooked horses in a dark field.

Carey called her the Troll Woman and they made plans to go back and bait her, but they never did. He saw the street by day a few weeks later and it seemed smaller, nothing like the alley in his dreams that followed, ones he would wake from, heart thudding, certain his room was full of her.

As if hopelessly fascinated, they began to watch and even bait the prostitutes. Some of them they did not dare approach—the muffed, coiffed, high-strutting birds of the Via Veneto who perched and preened on the curbs like tropical rarities. They would approach close enough to hear the haggling with a customer, enviously watch them hitch their skirts high over their tawny thighs as they straddled a Vespa. Some of them they began to recognize and make names for. But they would talk with the ones who fringed the Villa Borghese, who stood around their fires of old packing cases and cartons in the chilly night, warming up between stints in the bushes or nearby hotels.

One night Fiero, urged by Mladen and made plucky by hogging the flask of wine they had snatched from a party earlier, made an offer. She had come out of the bushes near the edge of the Galoppatoio, a tall, mountainous woman made more fierce by the eyebrows plucked and replaced with crudely drawn, upswept slashes, by the way her face exploded like an ostrich head out of the collar of a pink, feathery muff.

*"Quant'è?"* Fiero shrilled, and she turned to him grandly as if surprised such a small creature could make audible noises.

"How much you got?"

"A hundred lire," Fiero blurted, stepping closer.

She put her hand on her hip and her head tilted back in a laugh that looked more like she was preparing to gobble him down.

"For a hundred lire I'll watch you piss in your pants, monkey."

"A thousand."

She was not laughing anymore, half turned, hand still on hip.

"First time?"

Fiero did not answer. She came close.

"A thousand, then," and her arm had him around the waist.

Fiero, barely at the height of her shoulder, looked once back to them fearfully, and then, as if being carried off by a wave of breasts, rolling buttocks and thighs, was borne down toward the bushes.

Carey saw the branches take them in, heard her mutter some command, a squeal as if someone had stepped on a dog's paw, and Fiero was running up toward them over the moonlit grass, holding his pants up as he stumbled on, and she lurched out behind him, laughing so hugely that she could barely stand, and they had to sprint to catch up with Fiero when he passed them at a dead run.

They tried to soothe him and let him know how brave they thought he had been to go that far. But he kept saying incredulously, "She was trying to put me in her mouth."

When he left them early to go home, Mladen and Carey continued on down the Via Veneto.

"Jesus, look at that one," Mladen said.

Across the street a woman in a bright red dress, as large as a gladiator, was stalking past the kiosk, and cars were honking as they passed.Carey watched her for a moment and then walked on, passing one of the café's where chairs and tables were still out under the awnings and within the shelter of potted hedges in spite of the lateness of the season. Mladen caught up with him, and as he turned to say something, Carey saw a face at one of the tables that seemed familiar, then, shocked, knew it was his mother. He stopped, began to go toward her. But he was not supposed to be there. She had not seen him, and he glimpsed her through the branches of the hedge. She was with a man and they were not watching the sidewalk or street but each other, leaning forward and talking intently. The man's hand with its lit cigarette waved from time to time emphasizing something. Nancy's posture, leaning into the table, made this all seem habitual, accepted. He began to feel left out, and when the man snuffed his cigarette to hold her hand in both of his, Carey nudged Mladen into crossing the street.

"What's wrong?" Mladen asked, as they drifted toward the Trevi Fountain.

The air was dank from a rain that had borne down some of the last leaves and they clung to the sidewalk in soggy, sharp-smelling clumps.

"Nothing." Mladen had never met his mother and Carey decided he would not tell him.

"What's eating you?" he asked again later.

They sat for a while on the edge of the square watching the few tourists fling coins. Suddenly Carey wanted to tell Mladen something, anything to express this loneliness he had begun to feel. So for the first time he talked about Frank and his parents' divorce, and he found himself trying to explain why he thought something should have been done by him, but Mladen was only puzzled.

"Do what? I don't understand. It was their business."

When he reached home, Carey found a note on the table saying there were éclairs in the refrigerator. He was glad he had arrived first so that he could turn out the light and undress and lie in bed thinking for a while. He could send another postcard to Frank tomorrow, but decided not to. The last four had gone unanswered. He was too tired to figure out why he felt so sad. He dozed and woke to hear her return, and when she walked into his room far enough to be certain he was safely in bed, he did not let her know he was awake.

# 4

Alberto had never met a woman he felt more like telling the truth to, but when he was alone with Nancy and he would open his mouth to speak, something in him would say, "Not now, soon. First we must get to know each other well. Then she will understand." He would see her face in the dim light on the pillow beside him grow puzzled, her hand would touch his cheek, she would say, "What is it, Alberto?" and he would smile, say, "Nothing. I love you," feeling her eyes tug at the words he had almost said. Those words he did say had been spoken often enough before, but now even they came slowly, as if he were saying them for the first time.

He tried to understand what in her demanded this openness from him. Was it that she was so honest with him? She seemed to hide nothing at all, and at first this had shocked him. After making love, when they would lie quietly together in some rented room, because they had never gone back to the apartment in the Parioli, a place, he had explained, that was not his at all but his brother's, she would turn her face to him, and he would feel her eyes searching his face quietly and she would start speaking. She would say the things on her mind, reactions to him, their situation, all the intense and ambiguous flow of her thoughts, all the part of her mind that Alberto had always believed were the secrets of a life never, never shown. They were the things that one learned to monitor almost with objectivity in oneself, but never to show to others, because they were knowledge out of which one acted and others must never know the reasons for actions. That was survival. Sometimes her quiet murmuring to him, her pauses that he was supposed to fill, delighted him like the prattling of his own children when he would hear them in another room.

But at other times he would think, this is only a show of truth, this is an American woman, and they are all this way—their "openness" is only the ultimate disguise since it enables them to believe they have seen and dealt with the truth when that frankness is only a tone, an attitude. But no, that was not true of Nancy. He had spent time with other American women. She was being honest, and at times he could see this was even a struggle for her, but that she was determined not to evade.

Sometimes she would pay for the room, sometimes he did. She did not question him further about his "brother's" place, and he sealed that over in his mind, only trying to bear with him the fact that he had invented this brother in Rome and he must not forget. The nearest brother lived in Milan, but he would be able to handle that soon by saying he had moved. He vowed to avoid the usual nets of deception, this would be the only small lapse, and it was not truly harmful—simply much easier to leave the whole thing that way than to explain that the apartment belonged to his friend Costantino for whom Alberto did small favors from time to time in the embassy. Costantino was kind in his repayments, had been out of town for the weekend.

Alberto knew most of the *alberghi diurni* nearby, and she did not mind the other clientele, the fast-moving traffic of women and tired men, the bored, unshaven clerks. But that too, he could not understand. She was so much tougher than he expected. Some new shock would take her—"You mean those are all prostitutes? Working all day too?"—and he would think, Now she will be disgusted, this will be too much, but after a silence, her face thoughtful as she slowly removed her stockings, eyes taking in the bright veneer of a glass-topped bedside table, the tilted drapes and pocked marble of floors, she would somehow fit it in, angry, perhaps, or merely sad. "Alberto, tell me, does it all begin when you are boys, in this the kind of place you know you will be coming to, with one of them?"

"There is a story, you know, an old one about the Irish father and the Italian father," he said. "When your son comes of age in Ireland you take him to the pub and get him drunk. In Italy, you take him to the whorehouse." He lay on his back listening to the heavy thump of passing footsteps, desultory voices. It was midafternoon and they had both left work early.

— 141 —

She had claimed, with a natural guile that now puzzled him because he had discovered how finely she could lie, that she was not feeling well.

"Did your father?"

He felt her voice as much as heard it since her head lay on his chest.

"No. Actually it is only a story. It tells the truth about the way we think, not what we actually do."

She laughed. "But aren't they really the same?"

"Not often, or maybe it doesn't matter. Maybe it is saying that when we go to the prostitute we feel as if our fathers have taken us there because we know they went, and the prostitutes know that, and we feel as if even this prostitute was our father's, and it is all in the family. And our wives know too."

She placed her face on his shoulder now, breathing on his neck. "How strange. Is that truly expected when you marry?"

He thought for a moment. Now? Is this a good time to tell? But he concentrated on the question, shook his head. "Not for oneself. Again there is a difference. You say, 'Yes, that is the way it is in everyone else's marriage. But mine, of course, will be different.' And at the church, as you stand there and she is all in white and the priest is blessing you, all your family of aunts and uncles and cousins behind you are saying, 'You are different, holy, pure, at last.' In a few years it happens, and you are bitter, but you and she have this to fall back on now, you see? 'I am simply like everyone.' The consolation is there. After all, humility is a virtue."

"For her too? You really think there's a consolation for the wife too?"

He sensed her anger and his own wish to hunch his shoulders, lift his hands in bafflement, say, "Eh, *bene,* but that's the way it is," but instead said, "That is when she truly becomes the mother, you see? Not just when she has the children. But when the husband also becomes the child, someone she must bear with and above all forgive."

She laughed sharply. "Ah, how nice. The Madonna."

He lifted his hand from the bed and let it stroke quietly along her side, the curve of her bare hip. He would tell her something out of his own life.

"This is what happened to me when I was a young man. I had hopes to marry. But I did not yet have a job or the money to have a home and her family was not wealthy anymore either."

"Were you married?" her head shifted, turning up her face, attentive now.

"That's not the story. This girl and I were very pure. We thought we were, and yet we wanted each other very much. We would go for long walks on her uncle's land in the country near Turin, he was a farmer, and we would stop in the grove of trees by the river and would touch each other all over, and finally we knew we could not wait for those two years until I would have saved enough money. We had to make love. But I was upset, I confessed it to my priest."

She leaned on her elbows, staring down at his face closely. It made him uncomfortable that she could see his face while he talked but he went on. "He said this: 'My son, you must not do this thing. You must help her come chaste to your marriage. You must remember that she will one day be the mother of your children, and you will want to have her come to your marriage bed pure and whole.' I felt tortured. I knew we would not be able to control ourselves. I cried out, 'What can I do? I cannot stop myself.' He said, 'You must help save her. You must go to the other women. This is simply a physical urge. You must get rid of it with the women of the town. Bear this impurity for her and confess it and the Lord will forgive you if you do penance.'"

"No."

He looked at her now. His voice had become bitter at the end, surprising even himself.

"It is the truth."

"But that's crazy. You are saying the church supports prostitution."

He grunted. "These are both very old and established institutions. You must remember they have gotten along with each other for a long time."

"I don't believe you." Her face was still frowning, angry. He smiled slightly, enjoying the irony that the first clear anecdote he had told from his own life was not to be believed.

"Did you do it?"

"No."

"Did you marry her?"

But that was enough truth telling for one day so he said, "No," looking toward the ceiling where the fins of a long-broken fan hung motionless. "Her father arranged a marriage with a wealthy family from Milano. We were not allowed to see each other."

"How sad."

— 143 —

"It solved the problem."

Her hand moved over his chest. She put her head down on it again.

"I would not want to be a woman here."

He laughed. "But you are a woman, and you are here."

"I am a woman," she said quietly. "But not really here."

They were silent for a moment and he wanted very much to say, "Yes, I know, and I am a man, and I am not really here too," but somehow that made him feel a pain as if he wanted them only to be a man and a woman and here, always here, and her hand was moving over his chest, his belly, and he rose to meet the soft folding of her mouth.

He tried to imagine what her son would look like. He had come as far as the door to the apartment house, had waited in the street below in a cab for her, but had not yet been allowed to go upstairs. "Have the cab honk," she would say, or they would kiss once more in the early morning while the driver stared ahead motionlessly, his meter clicking. Alberto rarely took the cab back into town. He would ask the driver to drop him at the bus stop halfway down the hill, and of course he did so, used to that kind of economy from male fares.

His own son, Giorgio, was only five, and Alberto did not see him often. Sometimes he came close to telling Nancy about his family in Rome, but if he could not yet tell her he was married, how could he reveal that Assunta, the mother of his children, was not even his wife? As for Susanna, who had run away so long ago, he did not know where she was. He had thought of divorcing her, or at least having the marriage annulled, but he reminded himself of how difficult that would be in this country. With Assunta it had often been convenient that he was married, and he liked the fixed memory of Susanna, painful as it was, a relationship still established by law standing far behind his children, Assunta, all the other women in between. He imagined meeting Susanna on a street in some city, her face and body youthful and unchanged, and he would follow her through twisted streets to wherever she lived, would watch her come and go.

When he and Assunta had decided to live apart, he had left her with the apartment, the children, which was only right, but it meant that his life in the past year had been nomadic as he moved from one *pensione* to another, never quite committing himself to leasing a space, never certain that he was really leaving her, and some weeks he would return. She would meet him at the door, look wearily at his suitcase, make up the bed in the extra room, and Teresa, who was three, and Giorgio would hang on him wherever he went in the apartment, holding tightly as if afraid that even in that small space he might disappear. She had taken no lover in that time, but held back from him now, not strong enough to forbid him to enter, not weak enough to accept his presence, and, after the first few times, past hoping he would stay permanently. Sullen, her face set against him, she would talk, cook, help the children pretend that Alberto was only coming and going like this for a while, and when they were alone together she would sit in the living room on the edge of the wicker chair, her arms tightly folded, listening to him try to explain his confusions, listening him into silence.

But he was still thoroughly attracted to her, and the more her mouth pouted or set itself firmly, the more he wanted to put both hands on her cheeks, to run his hands back through that dark tangle of hair and combs, pressing his lips against her clenched mouth until it opened to his tongue. And sometimes silenced at last, he would rise from the sofa where he always hoped she would sit, and go over to her and she would say, "No, Alberto." As his hands groped over her neck, her shoulders, she would lean her forehead against his belly, saying, "Please, please," and although he was pained at his own bullish insistence, he would pull her, even carry her to the bed, and she would let her body go slack, not keeping him from stripping her as if she were a doll or an old, helpless being, her eyes staring beyond him to the ceiling. "Oh, Lord, oh, Lord," she would mutter, but she was always ready for him, finally would move against him, once in a fury pushed with her hips and feet and rolled him over, rode him, moaning, her fists beating indiscriminately on his shoulders, the pillows, as if she raged only from the waist up. Then she lay heavily on him, not letting him out of her, waiting as if in a deep sleep for him to rise again, and when he did she moved in long slow heaves, her face buried against his neck. He knew this could not go on, was an agony for both of them, a circling pattern of estrangement and forgiveness, their bodies doing penance for the sin of his absence.

Usually she would lie at last apart from him, breathing quickly like a trapped animal, saying, "Go now, please, sleep in the other bed or I won't be able to stop. I can't bear to touch you in my sleep, it wakes me," and he would because

— 145 —

it was true for him too—they could not fall peacefully to sleep anymore in the same space, would only want each other again and again until he could not bear the ache of rising to her hand, her mouth, the dry heave of his coming. "Why do you sleep in the guest bed?" Giorgio would ask at breakfast, and Assunta would say, "Because he must work late at night, Giorgio, and Mommy must sleep." After a few days, as if they both remembered why they had tried to separate before, she would ask him to go, or he would pack his suitcase and leave when the children and Assunta had gone to the park.

But he would not be able to return to the *pensione* he had last inhabited because it would be full of the memory of his loneliness that had driven him out and which he feared would do so again. This time, he would think, I'll find an apartment, and he would look carefully at the ads in the *Messaggiero* or on the bulletin board at the embassy. But there were too many reasons not to rent—he had to keep supporting Assunta and the children, and apartments now took very large down payments—and when he would finally go as far as looking at one, some fierce sense of the irrevocable nature of being there would come over him and he would begin sweating, his face flushed, would try to say suavely that he would speak to his wife and certainly call back that evening. He would go back up the dark stairwell of some class C *pensione*, past the dreary breakfast room, to sit hunched in a humped and sagging chair, waiting for the sunset and some excuse to go out and walk.

He was certain all this was known to no one but himself. The same instinct that protected all his inner self had kept him from letting even the embassy know he was married when he took the job there. Americans had no way of understanding this need for privacy. Luigi, who had worked for them in Naples, warned him, "Don't let them know you have a family. They will invite you to their homes, you will have to have them to yours, they will give gifts to your children, make them come to Christmas parties. They have no sense of decency, these Americans. They must know everything, love everything. They are greedy to love."

But now he found himself as curious as they were reputed to be. He wanted to see this boy, Carey. He wanted to talk to him, not about anything personal, but to sit with him somewhere—partly because Nancy talked of him so much, but mostly he sensed Carey must have something to say, to show inadvertently, that would help him understand this woman. Because he wanted to, and that had never been the case before. Sometimes he thought he simply understood all there was to know about Assunta, but he doubted that too, and he had never wanted to anyway, did not even now when he had enough distance to feel curious at times about what Assunta would do with herself. Or the other women, like that Englishwoman, Gwyn, he had lived with in Zurich all during the war, who had taught him such perfect English, and whom he did not mind making into the false image of "internship in England." After all, she was a form of entrapment. He had not wanted to go back to his native country because he was not in the least bit attracted to the blustering of Mussolini and his dreams of empire as dilapidated as some Roman bath, or the partisans' stealthy knife work. All his life he had struggled to escape those needless bludgeonings of this group or that, the toughs in the streets of Torino or Firenze, or the police in Calabria where he had once journeyed with his uncle. And she was demanding as any prison guard, but rich, biding her own bitchy time until "they stop dropping those bloody bombs on London." She had been tortuously neurotic, of which the perfect image for him was her preference to stoop in bed on all fours, her butt thrust up, while he rode over her back like a dog, indiscriminately thrusting. Even that strangely innocent, girlish part of her that often exorcised her demons, nestling her close to him in such a way that he knew why he stayed with her, did not make him curious. To ask her why she could be so purely gentle and sensuous and then so driven would only have led to explanations, and it had been enough to taste her bitter ravings without having to know why.

Now there was a woman he wanted to know—not even for the sake of understanding or being better able to keep her. It was a simple, clear wish to fall down through layer after layer of clarity, peeling back his own furtive wrappings. But because he had never wanted this before, he had no way of knowing how to begin, could only clumsily follow her graceful motions, trying to unfold with her. He would say, "I love you" to her, and be puzzled to discover that he meant it, even more confused when she would put a hand over his mouth and shake her head slightly, as if gently reproving him for speaking out of turn.

Finally he decided to see this boy even if Nancy did not know. He waited for a Saturday morning when she would have to go to her office and work overtime. It was raining, one of those windless drizzles falling straight down out of a seamless gray sky. He stood under his umbrella by the kiosk across from their apartment. He had an explanation ready in case she saw him, but with his umbrella, his hat pulled tightly down, he suspected she would not know him and he was right. She appeared in the doorway, looked straight up at the sky, bowed her head, pulled up her collar and began walking quickly toward the bus stop at the other side of the square. He stayed until he saw a bus come between them. When it left, the sidewalk where she had stood was empty. He went in to the café where he could stand by the window and sip espresso. It was warmer there and for a while he conversed mindlessly with the woman at the register, her pinched but friendly face rising white and pasty out of a black smock. When a boy came out of the doorway Alberto picked up his umbrella, but it was only a child, and dressed like an Italian. Yes, it was terrible that this kind of rain, too much like December, had come so soon, and hadn't the leaves died early this year? All very hazardous for the health, and he too had noticed a certain susceptibility of the lungs under these conditions—coughing, all that dampness.

At a certain point he sensed that staying any longer would seem unusual, so he dropped some extra lire in the woman's dish; she murmured, *"Grazie,"* and *"Buon giorno,"* and he went back to stand near the kiosk. The rain had not altered. This might be futile, the boy might never come out, and he had decided that at a certain hour he would go. Already he felt quite absurd, and yet what kept him there was curiosity—increasingly not the original motive of wanting to see Carey, but a curiosity to understand why this had become so important to himself.

He always had a sense of power in watching someone who did not suspect his presence. He had found that out many years ago when he followed his wife's first lover before Susanna had run away, not with that man, but another whom he did not know about. Even now he could feel the shocked desolation of returning to their rooms in Firenze, the note carefully sealed in an envelope and rising out of its perch on the telephone, pointed side of its rectangle up like a piece of shattered glass. He had stood looking across the room at the telephone, and even though she had taken almost nothing with her, the rooms were empty. That envelope had to be murderous in intent, but he had walked over the marble, lifted and opened it carefully with the knife to avoid cutting himself on the thin, stiff paper. That man's name was Raimondo, and Alberto had never heard of him, did not know how his wife could have met him, except perhaps at her brother's house in Pisa, where she sometimes went when Alberto was traveling.

Curiously, he could not now recall the name of the lover he did know about. He had worked at the local office of the Ministry for Public Information which even apolitical persons like Alberto knew was an organization used by Mussolini to keep watch on cities and towns. He had followed them to a *pensione* near the railway station, where, paralyzed between rage and fear of blundering about from room to room without finding them, he had waited outside, in a rain much like this one, but in his suit only, soaked, shivering, until the man (Ugo? Francesco?) came out, stood for a second alone under the canopy, groped out a toothpick which he placed in his mouth and rolled around, then walked away. Alberto had hesitated. So. They had decided to leave separately. He would wait for her. But quickly he crossed the street and began following the man. If she were to come out the door now, he might simply, brutally, take her throat in his hands and wring it then and there. Susanna, pert as a small bird, eyes always moving flirtatiously, even when he was the only one in the room with her—his only bride.

The man walked slowly, carelessly. Alberto came close enough to him to hear that he was humming quietly to himself, and when he turned his face at a street corner, Alberto could see the way he worked the toothpick around with his tongue as if he had enjoyed a full dinner, wine, excellent service. He passed him once quickly and turned back to see if the man would recognize him, even bumped into him slightly to make certain he was seen, but the face only showed annoyance, said, "Watch it," sullenly.

The man began to walk more aimlessly, pausing from time to time to look in store windows, and Alberto, to his bewilderment, noticed that he was looking at the women closely when they passed, realized they were in a section of town where many of the whores solicited, and finally the man put out his hand and stopped one of them. They talked briefly, and she shook her head a few times, then nodded. Alberto felt sick, as if the man had approached Susanna in this way, as if perhaps she were nothing but a common prostitute—and what gross appetite could the man have? Or was it some perverse pleasure in going rapidly from a tryst with a lover to purchased lovemaking?

They had turned and started to walk back toward him, were almost past when Alberto reached out and put a hand on her arm.

"Hey," she said. "Can't you see I'm busy?"

"How much?" he said.

The man was frowning. "C'mon, let's go."

"How much is he paying you?"

She shrugged, mentioned a price.

"I'll double that," Alberto said.

She looked at him, then the man. She smiled, gap-toothed, a coarse grin. "What is this? A joke? Are you friends?" Her face settled into a hard, businesslike manner. "Listen. Both of you for that price, if you like. Together or separately. But no tricks. I don't like this."

"I don't know him," the man said.

"Triple the price," Alberto said harshly, feeling his words as if they were fists he was smashing at the man's face.

He gestured with one hand, raised his eyebrows. "So? Help yourself."

Seeing one of them slipping away, she put her hand on Alberto's arm. "A deal."

For a moment they stood there, then the man said, *"Buon appetito,"* and walked away. Something rose sharply in Alberto's chest, all the muscles in his shoulders tightened, and then he was merely staring at her, that broad, gross body, the battered nose, and he was calm.

*"Andiamo,"* he said to her, and they went to her little room nearby, she stooped to clean herself at the bidet while he took off his trousers, not bothering with more, and he made her stand and lean with her elbows on the little bedside table where her cheap reproduction of Bernini's Saint Teresa perched, while he groped into her from behind, finally whirling her around in the last moments and taking her face in his hands, coming in her mouth while he called out, "Susanna, Susanna," shrilly at the untouched bed.

A tall, gawky figure was in the doorway, bareheaded, dressed in a windbreaker, old basketball shoes. Alberto could not see the face clearly at that distance, but he was certain it had to be Carey. The boy was carrying a small canvas bag and he turned, walked slowly off toward the bus, began to break into a lope when the crackle of its strut on the wires approached. Alberto had to spring to get there in time, leaping up on to the steps, folding down his umbrella as the doors hissed shut. The bus was nearly empty, and he sat behind Carey.

He tried to look at ease, cleared a small space on the fogged window to peer out at the street, but when he saw that Carey was not paying attention to anything around him, he stared straight ahead at the back of the boy's head. His heart was racing. What was it? The hair was tousled, a brown that glinted here and there with some dark shade of red, a neck slender and straight, and when Carey turned his head toward the seats across the aisle, gazing absentmindedly at the old woman and child who were gaily chattering, Alberto absorbed the features hungrily—a long, slightly flared nose, mouth he recognized as being like Nancy's in its tendency to curve down slightly in repose, and above all the steady unflinching eyes staring out of those sunken but delicately boned sockets, eyes he wanted to look into directly. What he did not recognize in Carey he thought must belong to the father, but he could not help seeing Nancy lurking, half formed in the face; or, gradually, as the boy's features assumed their own independent shape, he dizzily saw Nancy as a pale imitation of the boy, and he wanted simply to take those shoulders in his hands and hug the other man to him, because he saw him suddenly as a man, not a boy. Perhaps it was the hand that raised to flutter through the wet hair, a hand that looked much older than the rest of him—long, slender fingers, not the flesh of children's hands that kept their baby fat for too long. And what he felt for him was not what he had expected, not a bewildered sensuality from knowing the body of Carey's mother, but the same yearning, giving tug that came when he lifted Giorgio, when those small, tight arms choked at his neck. He wanted simply to bend forward, say in that whorled ear, "Son, my son."

When Carey stood to get off at the Piazza Venezia, Alberto did not rise. He watched the straight back move forward, the lurch of the bus heaving him off balance and Carey quickly recovering, watched him stand poised by the doors that hissed open, his leap out into space, a wall the only thing left to view, doors slapping shut. Alberto turned his face to the window so no one could see him weeping.

"Please, Alberto, not quite yet. I want just a little more time."

He was angry at her, but bit it back. He drove fast, staring ahead as if concentrating hard on the road.

"Why, Nancy? What is it that makes this so difficult?"

He suspected he should gracefully let the whole subject drop, bide his time. They were doing all right and he did not need to insist as he had, a pressure represented by this journey in a borrowed car out into the landscape to Tivoli. He had arranged it, with her hesitant agreement, as a means of meeting Carey—a day's outing to see the fountains, the gardens. But she had been waiting at the doorway when he drove up, her sweater over her arm. Now he glanced at her, saw she was thinking, but her jaw tensed in a way that showed she was also stubbornly firm. He veered quickly around a Vespa, both of them honking noisily at each other. He thought how strange it was that already in the small amount of time they had spent together, there was an intimacy that couples of long-standing shared, a knowledge of each other's moods, slight irritations.

"Because this is more serious than anything has been so far, since I left Frank." She swiveled slightly on the seat, tucked one leg under her so she faced him, knee jutting forward against her skirt. "Other men at home were easy to introduce. They were casual. But I couldn't do it that way this time. And Carey knows something is going on."

Alberto laughed. "I should hope so."

"How do you mean?"

"You are out often very late, or you are away on a Saturday or Sunday. He must know a great deal. Or he is not observant."

"But he hasn't said anything yet. I never know with Carey. Sometimes I think he is just very self-involved, that he is thinking of himself or his music, and that everything out here has faded away. He concentrates so. His father is that way too. But suddenly he will say something and I realize he has been watching all the time, thinking about other things but watching also."

Alberto sighed, shrugged resignedly. There was no point in pushing. "Some other time."

Her hand touched his arm briefly; he took his hand off the wheel and groped it over hers.

"It will have to be soon, Alberto. I know that. He is very busy now with school and new friends and his music, and for the first time since we started living alone, I think he seems fine. But I don't want too many strange things to come on him at once."

Alberto nodded. He decided not to add to the conversation.

This part of her he was less interested in knowing. He wanted to meet Carey, but he did not want to hear about him from her, and when she would go on about Carey, using his interest as a way to muse about her son, Alberto would grow silent, wanting the topic to shift. He simply did not understand or want to know more about her "motherhood." She was so different from any mother he had known, so analytical, so able to confuse herself with conflicting ideas of "what should be done." He wondered if sons in America treated their mothers with the same baffled watchfulness.

The car belonged to the embassy, and from time to time he was permitted to use it if he could claim he was doing some "fieldwork." He was careful not to abuse that privilege, and in return had discovered that his boss did not inquire too closely. He liked to drive and thought himself skillful, would cut at high speeds past the small trucks or wagons, gear down smoothly at intersections, and always found the quick response of wheel and foot and hand a pleasure. So he could not stay angry with her. And besides, the dreary weather had evaporated as it always did, leaving a warm fall air, spritzy with the evaporating moisture, heavily laden with the pungent drying of fallen leaves. It was that time of year he loved most to go out to the small hill towns of the Castelli Romani and walk through the twisted streets, pausing to watch the grapes being pressed beyond the opened doors of basements, the workers grinning, juice spilling underfoot and already turning to vinegar on the stones.

They wound up slowly through the town, still shattered in places by the bombings that had broken out sudden views of busily decorated wallpaper, a sink clinging to its pipes like a drooping flower, a shocking intimacy that always disturbed Alberto, and when he had seen some similar ravages in his childhood, the aftermath of World War I, he had always wondered with fear and disgust what it would be like to wake in the morning, the walls gone, other people gaping in at the private sanctuary, like a dream of finding oneself naked at a public gathering. They parked in the little square, bought their tickets, and wandered slowly down through the gardens, level by level.

She kept breathing in deeply. "What is it? That smell?" "Bay leaves," he would say, or, "Mint, growing there by the small fountain," and she held onto his arm, sometimes with both hands when she was particularly enchanted with some cascade or jet, and he told her what he knew of the villa's history, quietly marveling himself at the old views of water tumbled and thrown and forced in every imaginable way—thundering high jets that constantly shook the ground when the water reached its pool again, delicate trickles through carefully tended beards of vegetation, even water brightly streaming from the engorged breasts of smiling sphinxes—as if water were the only reality and those trees, the patches of earth and greenery were drifting endlessly downhill. "Oh, Alberto," she said, her face leaning on his shoulder as they sat on the bottom terrace, the water behind them, the olive trees falling away toward the fields and the old ruins of Roman emperors, the palely orchered walls of Rome itself wavering through the mists, "it's like a dream, but I don't know if it is good or frightening." She held his hand in her lap, its palm against the wedge of thighs and belly, and he wished they were in one of those fields below, naked in the sun.

They went to his favorite restaurant for lunch, drank too much, stumbled back out into the sun, found the Rocca Pia and chased each other high up into its towers to look dizzily over the town while she said, "Look, I can fly, I can fly," and he caught her arm as she lurched against the parapet, laughing, sending small pieces of mortar out into the air to the patchy field below. Back in town where they came to an open door and men twisting the long handles of the screw, she would not be stopped, walked in, and the men grinned but were decorously polite, insisted on having her taste the sweet pure juice of the grape, showed her how they pressed, saying *"Guarda, signora, prego, guarda,"* over their shoulders as they walked slowly around the huge, slatted drum. When they were back in the car again, she sat still beside him, her legs tucked up and head resting on the back of the seat, but her eyes were open, and when he would turn quickly away from the road to see if she was sleeping, she would smile in a slow, dazed motion of her lips, eyes wide as they sometimes were when he made love to her.

They had just entered the Porta Maggiore. Alberto leaned forward slightly, pointed to the baker's tomb, started to explain, when out of the corner of his eye he saw a woman's face, a man who was hurling himself head first into their windshield, and even as he groped for the brake, something struck their side dully, the man crumpled his shoulder into the windshield and bounced absurdly across the hood, and the woman disappeared entirely. The car stopped, even the

— 154 —

motor dead, and in the brief silence that followed, before the man began to roll toward them on the hood, groaning, his crooked jaw spewing blood, Alberto noticed that Nancy had heaped against the dashboard, the top of her head against the windshield that was webbed in the sun like a radiant halo, her body lax as a rag doll.

# 5

In the middle of his lesson the phone rang. Ikbal hung it up after a brief conversation and did not come back to her chair but stood in the doorway. Carey saw the expression on her face and stopped playing.

"I'm afraid I have some bad news." She walked the rest of the way in and stood with her hand on the music stand. "That was Mr. Benedetti who called."

"Who?"

"A Signor Benedetti. Do you know him?"

Carey shook his head.

"It's about your mother."

Carey stood. He did not like her tone of voice.

"There's been an accident." She put a hand on his shoulder quickly. "No, no. Everything is all right. Sit. He was driving her home and they ran into a Vespa and they've had to go to the hospital. He's fine and they don't think anything is wrong with your mother, but they are checking. She asked him to call and say you were not to go home until they call back."

He could not speak. Someone was knocking. She stood him up again, put a hand on his cheek.

"He said very clearly it was nothing serious. Not to worry."

He nodded, ashamed to think he could cry.

"*Si, si, vengo subito,*" she shrilled at the door, and then put his arm around her waist and walked him past the door and down the narrow hallway. "Now come. You sit back here in my bedroom where the other phone is. Answer when it rings, and then let me know what they say."

In the bedroom she let go of him and with another quick touch of her hand said, "Don't worry now," and left. He sat down, heard the door open and the voice he recognized as the very dapper Italian boy, about his age, who often followed him.

The phone sat inertly. He tried not to look at it and also to avoid those swift backwashes of panic. Why had he never worried about her? He was angry, as if his worrying might have kept her safe. She so surrounded him with warnings about himself that he always thought he was the one in constant danger. He imagined a Roman street, the smashed Vespa. He tightened his hands on the arms of the chair as if the room were traveling at high speed with nothing to brake it. He closed his eyes and pushed back as best he could. Hold on, hold on, he said to himself as he did when he was sick to his stomach and did not want to vomit again, and he tried to listen to each note in the badly mangled rendition of a "Gymnopédie."

The phone rang distantly in the hallway. He groped the receiver off the hook, said *"Pronto,"* heard a strange woman's voice say, *"Chi parla?"* gave his name. She said, *"Momento, prego."* The phone clicked at him in a regular pulse and then Nancy said, "Carey?" and for a moment he could not answer through the lump in his throat.

"I'm all right. Can you hear me? I hope Alberto didn't worry you too much."

Alberto? But he could not hold on to that.

"How are you? What's wrong?"

"I don't want you to worry. You must do what I say." Her voice sounded different, tense but slow. Drugged? He waited.

"Carcy? Are you there?"

"Yes, yes."

"We had an accident. I'll explain all that later, and I was shaken up a little, and nothing's broken, just bruises. Do you understand?"

"Yes."

"They're keeping me here overnight. But nothing is wrong. It's just to be sure. Now listen. I don't want you home alone. I've called Mladen's parents. You're to go there for the night."

"I'd rather be at home. I'll be all right there."

A voice interrupted in Italian from somewhere and then was cut off.

"Carey?"

"I'm here."

"They're not going to be home until nine. You're to stay

at Ikbal's until then and they'll stop by and pick you up. Go on to school with Mladen in the morning."

"Why? I don't want to be with them."

A moment of silence. Then her voice was sharp, high, not angry but borne along by the same panic inside him and he could not breathe listening to it. "Please, Carey. Do what I say. It's like a nightmare. I want to know where you are. That you're safe. With other people. Please."

"Yes," he said to silence that voice.

"Let me speak to Ikbal."

He put the phone down, went and stood in the door to the parlor. She was waiting in the middle of the room.

"She'd like to speak to you."

Ikbal went to the phone in the hall. Carey stood there, not looking anywhere in particular.

She was saying, "Yes, yes, certainly," and then, "Your mother wants to speak to you again."

He took the phone.

"Do as I say, promise?"

"Yes."

"I'll call at Mladen's before you go to school."

He blurted, not caring if Ikbal could hear, "But can't I come? To see you? Now?"

"No. It's too complicated. I'd worry about your coming and going. Alberto is here."

"Who is Alberto? I don't care about Alberto. I want to be there."

"I'll explain. I promise." There was a dim voice and then she continued, "I have to go now. Don't worry," and the phone clicked dead. He put it down, did not turn to see if Ikbal was still there but went back quickly toward the bedroom, the hall already blurring. He hung up the other phone and sat on the edge of the bed, hoping he could cry, but he was too tense and instead listened for a while to the unrestrained boredom of Satie.

He could hear their voices very distantly, then Ikbal playing some of the same passages—it had to be her because the piece was so much better played. Gradually the room around him began to intrude, and he sensed how private it was, compared with the only other room he had seen, the parlor with its furnishings, rugs, drapes that showed something of her taste but nothing so personal as the small articles scattered around this room: the man's face posed and highlighted in its gilt frame by the bedside, the brush with silver handle elegantly embossed that lay across the dressing table scattered with boxes and small bottles. Their perfumes and powders vaguely filled the air. He began to walk around the room—to the window that looked out on to the cornice of a nearby palazzo and down to the cobbles of an alley that crooked out of sight, to the huge armoir with half-opened door, the dresses, coats, filigrees of satin pushing out like milkweed about to burst its pod. He went back to the picture by the bed, picked it up and was holding it when he heard her. She was standing inside the doorway. He put the picture back carefully.

"My husband. Wasn't he handsome?"

That was hard to tell. The photographer had worked to make it true and the pose was too stiff. But Carey said, "Yes."

"Your mother seemed fine."

"She says so."

"You're worried?"

He nodded.

"I'm sure she sounded fine. Let's cook some dinner."

She stood with her arms folded, waiting for him.

"I'm not very hungry."

She waved a hand. "Come, come."

His arms, legs, dangling hands were suddenly awkward. He wanted to handle it all smoothly, say yes, carry on, but his eyes were beginning to water. She took his hand.

"Sometimes I wish my father were here."

But he could not continue, so he just shook his head and she reached up to smooth a hand through his hair, gently covering his ear for a moment.

"I am sure she is all right. Or they wouldn't have let her call." She put her arm around his shoulder, her face very close to his. "Some dinner would be good for both of us. A drink, maybe?" She kept tugging him out into the hall. "You can watch while I eat, if I can't make you hungry."

She moved easily around the small kitchen, plucking food from the crouched refrigerator, breaking eggs deftly with one hand while stirring with the other. She sat Carey at a table among the neat bundles of ingredients.

"He's terrible, that Riccardo, isn't he?"

Carey grinned.

"You see, he's a prince, and one doesn't say to a prince, 'You can't play very well,' because his father is a prince too, and his father also is a patron and on the board of this and that. Like your own count's family used to be."

"My count?"

"Conte Cortese. The teacher."

"You know him?"

"Of course. Rome, you know, in some ways is a very small town. Do you like the count?"

"Yes. But I don't know if he's a very good teacher."

She had reached some pause in the cooking, sat on one hip on the edge of the table, arms folded.

"He has never taught before. Never had to. He truly is a count. There was even a pope on his mother's side, and too many cardinals. He's simply not used to working."

"Then why does he?" Perched like that her face was above his and he noticed for the first time how sharp her widow's peak was, how clearly it defined the midpoint of her face, the way one eyebrow drew upward when she smiled.

"They haven't done well, his father's side of the family. They made some wrong choices. Your count was harmless, carefully watched by all sides during the war, but choosing to do nothing at all, that we know of. The rest of the family wasn't harmless at all. They supported Mussolini enthusiastically—until they saw how vulgar he was. Then it was too late." She hopped nimbly off her perch to rescue a small pan from its burner. "It's hard for someone of his background to get a job. They hold it against him."

"How?"

"That's not quite right. Actually, being a count is too much in one's favor. They don't like to see one working at just anything. They expect him to hold his position, his dignity. They don't want him to be like the rest of them, in spite of the fact this city has been full of fallen nobility since time began."

What was happening in the various pans began to make Carey very hungry.

"Do you like vermouth?"

He wanted to be sophisticated and say yes, but decided in this case it would do no good. "No."

"Wine?"

"Yes."

"Good. Then I can have some vermouth."

He drank the first glass quickly, she put the flask on the table beside him, and for a while some crucial event happened in a small pan of mushrooms so that they could not talk. Carey was relaxing, as if his bones were spreading slightly as he sat, and he watched her figure, softened by the wool

pleats of her skirt, move quickly from table to stove. She had
put on a pair of slippers and they flopped from her bare feet,
slapping as she walked. When she leaned over the table he
could not help looking down the billowing front of her blouse,
quickly, fearing she would see his eyes.

"And how is Ian?"

"Fine."

"And the Schubert?"

"Not so fine."

"You mustn't let him down, you know. He'll make his
concert seem trifling, but it means a great deal to him. Some
of those 'friends' he is inviting are important. Maybe for both
of you."

That was the first time he had thought of it as a true
performance and as something that perhaps they were doing
for him as much as for Ian. He blushed, then blushed harder
because his face was signaling how much he was thinking
about himself, so he said, "You know each other well, don't
you?"

"For years now. Actually, I even met him once before the
war, when I was playing in London. I was sixteen."

"How old is he?"

"Why do you ask?"

"I don't know. It's hard to tell."

"Thirty-seven, I think. He's very fond of you." She cleared
the table. "Do you mind if we eat here? Or if I do. You won't
mind watching me eat?" She was smiling, teasing, setting a
fork and knife in front of him. Suddenly she leaned across
the table, her hand fluttered through his hair, came to rest
behind his ear again. "It's all right, Carey." Her face was
serious now, eyes looking at him intently. "Really. I know
it is. You mustn't worry."

He swallowed. The wine was making him feel flushed all
the time. He liked the touch of her hand on his head.

"It's so hard to understand," and he kept looking at her
eyes. "One minute nothing is wrong, the next, everything.
So quickly, and you can't do anything about it."

She nodded, leaned all the way to his face and kissed him
on the forehead, then she was away, and turning to the stove.
She said nothing for a few minutes, seemed to be busy filling
their plates, and when she had set one in front of him and
filled his glass she said quietly, "I know."

She sat opposite him, leaning on her elbows. "Anything
missing?"

Carey could not answer because he already had a mouthful of the most delicious omelet he had ever tasted.

She kept filling their glasses whenever they were almost empty. For dessert she took a *crostata* from the cupboard. Carey became very talkative. She wanted to know all about his schools, about his home. When she asked, "And girl friends? Lots of girl friends waiting for you at home?" he shook his head, said, "Nope," a little guiltily, remembering he had not written to Lisa at all.

"Oh, come now. You're being modest."

"No," and he heard his own voice being much too stoic. "I am too busy. Music and all."

She clucked and shook her head. "Too busy for women. Poor Carey," and when he saw her face he could not help laughing with her.

"Will your mother remarry?" she said after a while.

"I don't know." Into the silence that followed, slightly giddy and watching her stare absently at the table, he blurted, "Will you?"

Her hand stopped turning the stem of her glass.

"I don't think so. It has nothing to do with Piero, my husband. Being married was hard enough even then, you see, although we loved each other very much. It is very hard," and her voice grew softer, almost too low to hear, "to have both a thing to do as demanding as performing, and a marriage. I joked with you about your girl friends, but I suspect it is not all modesty. There must be some truth in it. You would not be as good as you are unless you had already given up something." Her hand waved slightly, returning to the glass. "At this point, for me, it seems easier to be unattached. I move about more freely. My time to myself. Do you understand?"

"I think so."

Although he could tell at certain points that it called for an effort on her part, she told him a little about Piero and herself, and finally the way he died, but the story became very factual, even more spare than what Ian had told him. They were silent for a while. Carey had drunk enough so that he was not bothered by sitting there with her, just breathing.

She stood so suddenly that he thought maybe the doorbell had rung. "Come on, before they arrive, let's do some Mozart."

She held out her hand and they went down the hall and into the parlor, so dark that he had to stand dizzily in the middle and wait for her to grope to the lights for fear he

— 162 —

would bowl over something. She opened the music, sat beside him on the bench she had moved up so they could both sit down. She clasped her hands over his and said with that unflinching stare, "Carey, I will tell you something. I don't know what it is about you. There is a quality you bring. A gift."

He let his hand rest in hers, holding still, wanting to tell her he felt as he had once in a booth in Atlantic City when a fortune-teller, a real gypsy, had held his hand and spoken in such a way that he could hardly breathe, even though he could not clearly recall the words afterward. He tried to say something, but closed his mouth because there was nothing to say, and she smiled, butted his shoulder with her forehead and said, "You are catching flies."

They began adagio, but could not slow down for long. His pulse was racing prestissimo. He could not hold her at a distance, any more than he could care about the unwritten notes flung in by his racing, careless fingers. "Poor Wolfgang," she muttered gaily.

When Mladen and his father came to the door, knocking like evil messengers, when they sat in the car and barely talked except for the report from Mr. Makarovic that he had called the hospital and his mother was fine, even later when Mladen and Carey were alone in his room and Mrs. Makarovic was kind enough to make Carey feel at home by coming in to kiss him on the forehead as he lay on the cot, he let them think his preoccupation came from worrying about his mother. But all the time that he was closing his eyes on the slightly whirling shapes of the dark room he was imagining that small figure leaning all the way across the table, both her arms around his neck, this time her lips on his.

But that night he also dreamed again of the Emperor Constantine, giant face with half-awakened eyes, finger lifted to warn him about something. His blackened lips were sealed. Carey stood out in the square of the Campidoglio under the rider whose gesture of command was so gentled by his sad face, and a voice told him to gather the body of Constantine. It was not Aurelius speaking but his horse. He tried to make that other emperor's body come together. If only the missing pieces would scrape heavily from deep under some field or palazzo, foot and elbow and thigh dragging over and uprooting the cobblestones on the way, to arrive at the inner courtyard. With a groan the giant would stand, the lips would open, and shaking the air, the terrible secret of his dream would come down. Carey both wanted that and feared it. He worked, for what seemed the whole of his sleeping, to tug and drag and lift the pieces from wherever he could find them, his own heavy breathing and groaning, the grate of stone on stone, being the only sounds in a vacant city.

All that Nancy saw in the moment the accident took place was the woman's face. She heard Alberto begin to explain something about a tomb, his hand rose, and as if he were conjuring it up, the face, wide-eyed, beautiful and young, floated into the side window. She started to say, "Look," but her own body floated free also, and pain exploded on her head.

She could not have been unconscious for long. When her eyes cleared, she was staring hard at the chrome line of a windshield wiper, but all she could think was that someone must have thrust something equally hard through her forehead. She shifted slightly and found herself face to face with a mask of pain worse than hers—a man's face, wide-eyed, mouth crazily askew, blood gushing along his outstretched tongue onto the glass of the windshild. She was dreaming, she was certain, but when she said, "Oh, no, oh, no," her voice was her own, loud and clear, not the smothered distant murmur of dreams. There were hands on her shoulder, Alberto's voice saying, "Don't touch her, don't touch her," but she lurched back to get away from the other face, her body jammed into the seat, and she was looking out through a pulsing brow at Alberto leaning in to her from her side of the car. She held her hands up toward the shattered windshield as if she could push it all away. "What happened, what happened?" she was saying, and she leaned to one side and vomited swiftly, a straight gush onto the driver's seat. Hands leaned her back, and through half-closed eyes she saw some white figures moving around, the man from the hood was walking unsteadily between them, and Alberto kept saying, "Sit still, it's all right now."

She let herself go limp, started trembling as if she expected to be thrown forward again at any moment. When she closed her eyes she felt the whole world was moving, might stop suddenly, walls, people, vehicles falling in on her head. She opened her eyes wide, fixed on an unmoving point. But when they helped her into the ambulance she had to close her eyes to avoid the sight of things gliding by, and she held onto

Alberto so rigidly that hours afterward she could see the small half-moons of her fingernails on the back of his hand.

By the time she was being X-rayed, trundled around in a wheelchair, she had lost her dizziness, nausea, even some of the fright, and she wanted them to let her walk but they insisted and Alberto said, "Please, Nancy. Do what they say." He came with her, talking quickly to attendants, secretaries, making out papers. She reached out and touched his arm from time to time, grateful he could handle all that. For a brief space she had lost all comprehension of the language. In fact, as she sat on the table in the X-ray room, her head a simple throb, too numb for sharp pain anymore, she could not quite remember what city this was, where they had just been, why Alberto spoke Italian so fluently, why she had not been driving, why her head hurt so. When all that ignorance caved in on her and she realized she should be afraid since maybe she did not even know who she was, and she pushed back by saying in a half whisper, "Nancy, Nancy Mitchell," she remembered everything, closed her eyes, again felt her body relax. The hands of a doctor were on each cheek, moving her head slowly from one side to the other. She said, "How are the others? The man. The woman. Ask them, Alberto."

He knew already. "They will be all right. The woman was not hurt. She hit the side of the car with her shoulder. The man broke his jaw. They must not have been going fast when they hit us."

"They hit us?"

"From the side. I couldn't see them in time."

He described it to her, and she had to be quiet while the doctor felt around her neck, her head. They took more X-rays. Alberto kept talking, either to them in Italian or to her. She could tell he was pushing out his nervousness by talking. They took her up to a room with a bed, a crucifix over it bearing a very hieratic Christ, a droopy-eyed Madonna over the sink. She saw her face in the mirror, a great red splotch of bruise and lump over one eye. She turned away quickly. "How ugly," she said. Alberto waited outside while the nurse helped her out of her clothes and into a white smock that tied in back. She had not worn one of those since Carey was born.

"Carey," she said, as soon as Alberto walked back in. She was sitting on the edge of the bed refusing the nurse's obvious attempts to get her to lie down. "I have to go home, Alberto. I can't stay here."

He said something to the nurse, too quickly for Nancy to

catch although she was understanding most of it again, and the woman argued back, shrugging.

"Please," and Alberto put a hand on her knee, "she says she was told you must lie down now. At least until they know more," and he helped her, lifting her legs as if she were a little old lady. She lay back into the pillows.

"I won't stay, Alberto. I can't."

She did not understand what this new panic was, as though what was happening to her was only an emblem, a hint of what might be happening to Carey at any moment. When she closed her eyes something large and black, formless but fluttering, swooped down past her, striking her head, thrust her aside to get at Carey who was somewhere just out of the corners of her eyes. It was the swiftness of its motion that terrified her. Even now he might be clawed, mangled, hurled headlong from some height.

"Please," she said, opened her eyes, puzzled to find the lights on, Alberto there with two doctors and they were all talking very politely, Alberto repeating, *"Si, Dottore, ma certo, Dottore, dunque . . ."* and when they saw she was looking at them they all smiled.

"Good news," Alberto said, "the X-rays show no fractures. Only bad bruises."

"Then I am going," and she started to sit up, but they were all frowning, and she almost laughed, they were so easy to affect.

"No, no. They want to be certain. You are to stay here tonight. You must."

She sat there, stubborn, crossed her legs, tucking her smock close around her knees, feeling it spread coolly in back, and they negotiated with her. She won the telephone calls. Alberto helped her into her shoes and stood beside her at the phone. On the way he offered to pick up Carey and take him home, but she said, "No," so quickly and firmly that he did not argue, and she was sorry, afraid he had known what she was thinking—her fear that there would be another accident. She had a crazy idea that automobiles were hunting them down.

When she came back to the room, feeling like crying because of the desperation she had sensed in Carey's voice that she had not been able to dispel, she was surprised to see she had not noticed it was a double room and that there was a curtain with another bed beyond it where someone now was humming softly.

"Really, Alberto," she said crossly. "This is absurd. I can go home now."

She saw his face as if for the first time since the accident, and he looked very drawn, pale. She sat on the bed, making him sit in the chair nearby, and she put a hand on his cheek.

"You're all right?"

He took her hand in both of his, kissed it. "It was terrible. For a moment, the way you were lying there, the window broken, I thought you were dead."

She shook her head slowly but could think of nothing to say. What if she had died, if Carey had been left here in this strange world without her? She shuddered. "I hate this. I want to wake up."

She thought she was going to weep, and that doing so would be a great relief, but it did not happen. Instead she veered sharply in the other direction and laughed jaggedly.

"I've much too hard a head, Alberto. I'm afraid I hurt the car badly."

He smiled. "Does it hurt?"

"Some."

"It should be all right. They gave you a shot of something."

She did not like the fact that she could recall nothing about a shot. She was very, very tired, and he pulled the covers over her when she lay back and she was already drowsing when his voice said, "I will come back early in the morning to take you home, don't worry, sleep well."

At first it was not clear to her why Pop or her mother were digging in the yard. She was looking down on them from behind the curtains of her bedroom in Philadelphia. Pop hunched forward in his wheelchair, his back to her, and he kept lifting a posthole digger with both arms and plunging it straight down into the earth beyond his feet. From time to time he would pause to hold his head back, gasping like a fish. She wanted to tell him to stop, was certain the violent exertion would kill him. But her mother was there and seemed unconcerned. She too had her back turned, was kneeling on the rim of the widening hole, scrabbling with her bare hands, pawing the earth up in handfuls with a ferocity that had made her sweat a dark patch along her back. Her hair straggled limply down her neck. She would turn to Pop, sharply commanding. From time to time the face of a woman, young and beautiful, would float up along the window just beyond the glass, blocking Nancy's view of her parents, and she would motion it aside impatiently. The woman was trying to say something, her eyes wide, but Nancy was afraid her parents would hear so she kept putting a finger to her lips. The face would slide down the glass, slowly rise again, so the next time it rose she let it go all the way up the window where it caught against the upper corner and hung bobbing and helpless.

They had found something. Pop threw the digger to one side. Her mother leaned so far down that she almost fell in. Pop was reaching stiffly down with both arms, waggling them like a child that cannot reach what he wants. Her mother slowly, straining, lifted something. Nancy pressed her face to the glass. It was a box in the shape of a confessional. She held it tightly to her with both arms and then laid it on Pop's lap. His hands scrabbled wildly over the little doors, looking for a clasp, until she brushed them aside, flicked the hook that held it closed. They both turned, looked up at the window. Her mother's face was haggard, waxen with effort, her hands dangling at her sides like muddied roots of some plant ripped out of earth. Pop's hand groped in the box and he lifted something. The earth around it began to fall away. They were both looking at her, grinning, either meanly or proudly, Nancy could not tell.

It was Frank's head. The eyes were closed, the features barely discernible through the soil. A large bruise was on his forehead, but she could feel it and knew that he could not. Pop held the head up high in both hands, he shook it, his lips were saying something, but Nancy could only hear the shrill crying of a gull. The face in the corner above her slid down, was blurred by being so close on the other side of the glass, but with a snap, it disappeared, and she felt it wrap tightly, wet and warm, around her own. She put her hands to her face, began to grope desperately for some seam or crack where she could insert a finger to pull, reeled back into the room, her own voice held in by the tight-fitting mask. "Uh, uh, uh," she was saying when she rolled over, eyes wide to the bluish glow of a night light on the table beside her, the bright aluminum of a pitcher. She held perfectly still, her face sweating, trying to catch her breath and slow her pounding heart.

She turned on her back, threw the sheets off, letting the air cool her sweat-soaked body. For a few minutes her head pained her so badly that she thought she would be sick, but that either subsided or she grew used to it. She knew from other times in hospitals that this was partly the effect of whatever drug they had given her, that when it wore off the body had built up none of its own defenses against the pain and had to do it all at once. She did not want another shot. She did not want to sleep again if such dreams were going to come to her. Even now she could still vividly remember the raised head, the smothering numbness of the mask. The images began to subside, the pain settled into a throb. She put the shifted pillows back on top of each other so that she could lie with her head and shoulders slightly raised.

The woman in the bed beyond the curtain stirred and moaned once, surprisingly less like pain than sexual satisfaction. Nancy wondered what was wrong with her. She had no idea what time it was. Later, when the woman began talking, Nancy thought she must be awake, trying to say something to her through the curtain, but she realized by the fragmentary sentences that she must be having a conversation in her sleep. She listened more closely, believed for a while that the woman was talking to her father because she kept saying, "Pappa," and then by the increasingly fervent or contrite tones knew that it was the pope, finally a pope named Silvestro. The woman's voice swung wildly from shame to bitter mocking and back again, a tidal wash of words that Nancy could not follow, although it sounded to her like the tones the women in the outdoor markets would take in haggling with the butcher. Finally the woman said, *"Basta, basta così,"* and stopped. For the rest of the night she rested peacefully.

Nancy only dozed from time to time. It was not just avoiding dreams that made her struggle against sleep, but something was trying to come clear to her about the accident and her fear. She poured herself a glass of water, pulled the sheets back over her legs. For the first time in weeks she thought of Frank with longing. It was not sexual or the clear sense of loss, but a wish he could be there to comfort her now. He had always been good at that, as though he knew best what to do, what to provide for her at the moments when she was physically helpless with a bad cold, or that time she had broken her ankle. That was why living alone was so wrong; she would always want that sense of someone else to touch when waking from a nightmare, to give herself over to when sick or helpless. She had always thought that was weak, childish, and fought against it even when it was happening. She was certain now that it was necessary and natural.

But how was she going to tell Carey about Frank's latest letter, that he had decided to move to California, to direct

— 169 —

some repertory theater there? Perhaps she would just show the letter, but it was obviously meant for her, so self-justifying. She could not help wondering if there was a woman involved, one of his students. California. She could not recall his ever mentioning that possibility. Was it simply another one of those things they had never talked about? Perhaps he had always wanted to go there. Or had he grabbed at any job as far away from Philadelphia as possible? She had put an ocean between herself and home. She could hardly blame him for leaping a continent. But the idea of California did not appeal to her at all.

For a moment she imagined them arguing about going there, as if they were still at home and he were telling her they had to move. Then she was describing the accident, and that conversation too slipped into an argument. True, she had not willed that accident this afternoon. She and Alberto and the other couple had met like Frank's car and that dog long ago. Tired and confused as she might be at times, she did not want to die. She certainly had not wanted this night; and she could have died.

Dead. She sat up, her head pounding. For a while she was terrified as if she had waked from some dream and could remember nothing of it except absolute fear. What she was feeling had nothing to do with any argument with Frank. She was touching death itself—but as if it were something the mind could not contain but only glimpse, someplace where all emotions, all knowing, were drawn in, condensed into one.

She lay back, breathing deeply. She did not even try to find that moment again. She let go of it and all the things she had been thinking, and gradually her body relaxed, her face cooled, as if she had come out of a fever. A calmness made her mind very clear, but for a while there was nothing going on there but an awareness of calm. Gradually her mind stirred into thoughts again. She would never know what had happened to Frank and herself, how much they had created, how much had been waiting for them. She saw him standing on the porch, one hand leaning on the pillar, and he was about to turn and speak, but it would not matter what he said. Somehow she had gone beyond their old arguments. They would not be talking to each other anymore.

She was waiting for Carey when he came home, sitting on the sofa with a blanket over her legs. She watched his expression when he looked at her head, saw him try not to

— 170 —

keep staring at it, and so she said, "It's awful looking, isn't it? But it's really all right."

He looked so awkward that she moved her legs and made him sit on the sofa. They talked about anything she could think of asking, about the Makarovics, school, until he was more at ease. He began asking questions about the accident, the hospital, why they had kept her there. She found she needed to describe it all to him, and on the way to the restaurant he listened eagerly while she chattered on, words tumbling.

She knew perfectly well that they were both skirting the figure of Alberto and all she could finally say was, "I want you to meet him soon," but he did not seem to want to discuss Alberto yet, and anyway, their usual waiter was much too solicitous, had to sympathize with the details of the accident, report on his nephew's collision with a taxi.

Walking home she could not help putting her arm through Carey's and he took it, folding it tightly against him as if that were all he wanted now.

# 6

Carey stood outside the door to Ian's apartment. It was partway open, and what kept him from knocking was the tone of the voices—heated, overlapping, moving excitedly through English, French, Italian, so that he could not catch distinct words. He and Ian had always rehearsed alone. Finally the voices stopped after Ian said something in French, lashing and spiteful.

He walked quietly downstairs to the courtyard, thought of leaving, but he had looked forward to the rehearsal, so after a few minutes he walked back up, whistling loudly in the echoing stairwell. But the door was closed. He knocked and it opened before he finished.

Ian poked out his sharp face. At the far end of the room, flipping through a magazine that was lying on the lid of the piano was a tall, very thickset man with rounded shoulders, and when he turned he showed a face to match—heavily molded nose and lips. But his smile was shy.

"Carey, I'd like you to meet my friend, Pierre Leiberg. He's just come back from Paris."

They shook hands and the man said, "I have heard much of you."

While Ian was serving them tea, they talked about music, about Pierre's Paris, somewhat stiff gulps of conversation in which Pierre often had to refer to Ian in French for the correct English expression. He liked Pierre at once. That heaviness of body that at first seemed menacing was undercut by the man's own sense of its awkwardness, so when he smiled, his hair disheveled in a way that showed it always was, he was more like an oversized, stuffed bear. But both Ian and Pierre were restrained, and when Carey began to spread his music on the piano stand, Pierre said quietly from the doorway that he would return later, Ian asked sharply when? and Pierre only shrugged, turning his open hand in the air. Carey concentrated on the music, but Ian was making mistakes, his attention wavering.

"Sorry, a bit weary today." Carey decided he looked it. "You've not forgotten this Saturday?"

Carey tried to remember.

"Our little trip to Hadrian's Villa. Do rémind your mother."

Carey was certain Nancy had forgotten, but said nothing. That would be her problem.

"I'll pick you up. Now that Pierre's back we can take the car. He'll probably be coming too."

That evening Carey listened to Nancy present some excuses to Ian as nimbly as if she had not forgotten. Something unexpected had come up. "A reception at the embassy, some senator visiting," she said with all the offhand boredom he knew she would have felt if it had been true. Even though he could do that himself now, he was uneasy to hear her perform so well and wondered if Ian could catch it or not. Maybe it was something people simply did even though everyone involved knew it was unreal. But why bother? And he was going to argue with her when he decided he was just tired of it all. Let them. If they needed to do that it was none of his business. He heard them decide that Ian and Pierre and he would go anyway, and if she could get free she would come too. Before she hung up, he began practicing.

He and Ian went alone in the small gray Peugeot that Ian and Pierre owned jointly. A wicker basket with lunch was on the back seat, "Enough," Ian said with a small twist of his mouth, "for four." But Carey decided he was more comfortable with Ian alone anyway.

The day was fiercely clear, cold in the shadows but warm in the sun, with a slight breeze that hinted of distant snow, "Probably from the peaks in the Abruzzi," Ian said. For a while as they wound out through the city traffic, they were silent, then Ian began questioning Carey about the villa, did he know this or that? and finally, seeing how little he did know, he told him as much as he could about it and Hadrian and the youth Antinous, and three or four times repeated the words of *"Animula, vagula, blandula,"* trying to get Carey to translate it, making him dope out the words he did not know.

— 173 —

Carey wondered if Ian was disappointed that Nancy had not come. He knew they had not seen much of each other recently and that this person Alberto was taking more and more of his mother's time. "I'm sorry Mother couldn't come."

Ian was wearing a bulky white sweater with a turtleneck that almost rose over his chin, and his head swiveled in it to glance at Carey, eyebrows lifted.

"Nothing's wrong, I hope."

"No. You aren't angry? I mean we did plan this sometime ago."

"Heavens, no. We'll go again sometime. This spring, maybe when the flowers are out."

His tone was truly casual. The hills ahead rose crisply out of the slight haze, the distant line of Mount Soracte was edged in snow. Ian drove with both hands on the wheel.

"Actually, I'm sorry Pierre couldn't come along."

"Is he going back to Paris?"

"Not immediately. He might, though. He is working for the Jewish orphanage here. He was an orphan himself."

When they had parked, Ian lifted out the basket, and for a while they wandered in the ruins, almost deserted except for some bored guards who stood here and there with hands behind their backs, or a couple feeling their way along with their guidebooks. The air was sharp, with sudden cups of sunny warmth in the twists of old walls where iridescent lizards clung and waited. Ian knew all about the place, explaining with emotion as they entered this gaping square or that, raising the roofs, domes, and marbled walls back into place for Carey, who could tell he was listening to something the man cared about, and he did not interrupt.

By lunchtime they had wandered well up on to a hill, and they found a hollow there, facing the sun and out of the breeze. They put the basket in front of them and looked out to the slope falling away toward the tumble of ruins in gray-green foliage of early winter and the dark, almost too perfectly coned cypresses. They could not say much at first. Carey was too hungry. Ian drew the cork and they had some glasses of Frascati, still chilled. Every so often the breeze would rustle through the grass nearby, but it never reached them.

"Pierre and I met just after the war," he began, although Carey could not quite see any connection to an immediate comment. "In Rome. He had been in the French underground. He was actually born in Belgium, he thinks. He fought most of the time in France after the occupation. He had some horrible things to tell about, wasn't very well for a while. He had always believed up until the war that his parents were still alive, that they had merely abandoned him, or lost him rather than dying. But they were Jewish. He says the death of that hope was the worst thing that happened to him, even though he knew it had probably been unreal all along. He found working with the orphanage helped. He's good with children, you should see him," and Ian laughed. "He takes them to a park on Sunday afternoon sometimes. He's so like a big child himself. They love him."

"Why does he go to Paris?"

Ian poured more wine. "He has friends there. Perhaps a job soon with the UN. He's thinking about it."

Carey felt drowsy. When he looked at Ian he was surprised to see his face reddened.

"Look, my dear Carey. I will have to tell you this if your mother hasn't already, and I suspect she would not. There is no point in having lies between us."

Carey was edgy now. He suspected that Ian was going to say something about Nancy and himself and that he would not know how to handle it. What if the man asked him about Alberto, or wanted him to be some sort of go-between?

"We're lovers, Pierre and I. We have lived together for some time. Does that shock you?"

Carey could not answer.

"Can you understand that?"

He shook his head slowly.

"I imagine not. Are you disappointed in me? Don't answer that. Not for a while. Let me talk to you."

As he did, Carey watched Ian's hand flutter nervously around the rim of his glass as if trying to find a place to light. Ian now seemed someone unknown to him, as if the word "homosexual" that kept slipping into his mind when he turned to look at Ian altered the person. But in talking, Ian had become very gentle, all the sharp, pressured feeling he had shown all day gone from his face and voice. He talked on about himself, about how ashamed his own country had made him feel, how furtive his life had become, of meeting Pierre and how happy they had been for years, of someone else who had known Pierre in the war years, a Spaniard, and how Pierre had traveled to Greece for a while, leaving Ian behind. Things had not been the same since. Carey followed the words with embarrassment, as if he were overhearing something he should not, but he looked for Ian in it all, trying to understand those jealousies and fears and the one anxiety above all others, now that the other man had disappeared— that Pierre would move to Paris. Ian hated Paris, could not bear the idea of living there.

"I simply detest Parisians."

A small bird perched in a dead bush near the rim of their hollow, turning his head to one side as if listening. When Ian put a hand on his, Carey wanted to pull away.

"Just for a moment."

Ian's hand moved slowly up and down his arm. He raised it to Carey's chin. He had put his glasses aside and his eyes were unfocused, wide. The hand moved over his cheek. When Ian's face approached, Carey was too surprised to avoid the kiss, a pressing of lips and slight rasp of whiskers on his cheek as Ian brushed against him afterward, and then Ian sat back.

Carey had never been kissed on the lips by a man. He could not accept it, and in that lurch he drew his knees up to his face, clutching his legs. He wanted to be far away. What was he supposed to do? If Ian touched him again, Carey would hit him. He did not look up, but thought for a minute until he had a way to say it. "Why does everyone seem to want something, but I don't know what? And so do I, but I don't know what either."

"I did not mean that as a demand. I thought," and his voice was brittle, "it was more in the nature of a gift."

"But I don't want it," Carey said, and then he did look up and was sorry because Ian was so pinched, his lips pursed, eyes squinting out over the fields.

"Sorry. It really wasn't very fair. Look. We'll forget that happened?"

Carey nodded.

"Still friends?"

"Yes." Then he blurted, "Does Mother know?"

"Yes."

"I wish she'd told me."

"I think it's a measure of her trust in me that she didn't."

"I think she doesn't tell me lots of things." He recalled Frank's letter she had shown him that morning. If there were things he could not understand, it was partly because they were kept from him.

"But, now that we are on the subject, I hope you will keep

this to yourself. Your mother is very understanding. Most people aren't."

Carey was tired, so tired that he wondered if he could make it back to the car. But he did, and by the time they had reached Rome, they were talking, planning their next rehearsal.

That night as he lay in bed, Carey wondered about what Ian could mean by "understanding." That had to exclude him, because although he might accept the fact that Ian was homosexual, he could not "understand" it, any more than he could "understand" his father saying he was moving to California. It was a place Carey had never been and could not even imagine going to, and when he asked his mother if he would visit Frank there, she did not seem to know. "I'm sure he will be writing you soon," she had said. Once again he was looking into water, looking at the lives of people he thought he understood but watching them twist off into places he had not known. He thought, as he always did now in moments when his mind moved freely, of Ikbal; but would her face too some day shift and change as she opened her mouth to tell him something he could not have guessed? Ian came to him that night in a dream, his wide eyes half sleeping, body slowly falling away into the melded coils of a water serpent. As Carey reached to close Ian's eyes, his own fingers grew webbed and undulant.

# PART THREE

# *Figures in a Dance*

# 1

"Do you really love my mother?"

Carey's words echoed in the damp and brightly lit chamber of the tomb, and the guard impatiently rattled his keys at the doorway. Nancy was in the field above, trying to find some warmth in the sun even though Alberto had said these were the best of the wall paintings.

He looked at Carey sharply, and the hands he held behind him flinched. "Why do you ask?"

"Because I need to know."

"I won't harm her," Alberto said softly. "Are you worried?"

The guide blew his nose, muttered at the air, *"Fa freddo oggi."*

"Do you love her?"

"But of course," he said with one hand flung out, palm up, his shoulder shrugging down, and Carey knew he had been defeated for the moment. Hands in his pockets, beginning to feel the cold penetrate so that he shivered, Carey said, "I hope so," intending a menacing tone.

Alberto glanced sideways with a puzzled smile. How often Carey had seen that look in the past weeks, in restaurants, museums, wherever they went together now that Nancy had decided to let Alberto Benedetti and Carey "get to know each other." Carey wanted to, even sensed Alberto was willing, but they were both baffled. Alberto would sometimes tell him what he found amusing in the manners and quirks of an American teenager. Carey did not quite dare to express how uneasy he was made by the man's punctiliousness, charm bordering on duplicity, even his elegance.

"But come," he said, and he put a hand on Carey's elbow, "we will talk about all this later, you and I. In better surroundings."

The guard was not interested in their problems. He cleared his throat again, rattled the keys. Alberto whirled.

*"Ma che c'é? Abbiamo pagato, no?"* and suddenly they were erupting at each other, the guard denouncing the waste of electricity, Alberto saying he had a right to look without constant interruption, the guard spreading his hands and arguing tentatively because he did not have his tip yet. Alberto spoke rapidly about how the working man in central and southern Italy had no concern any longer for the job in itself but only for his own comfort and that they all had the mentality either of thieves or "big-do-nothings." The argument stopped as quickly as it had begun when Alberto turned his back and the guard shrugged, sputtering a few syllables under his breath. Nancy appeared in the wedge of sky at the end of the stairs, stooping.

"Is everything all right?"

"Yes, yes, Nancy. But do come. These are some of the finest."

She descended, her coat pulled tightly around her, and Alberto, in a gesture Carey only accepted for his mother's sake, put an arm around each of them and began explaining the things he wanted them to notice. He was talking about the garlands of flowers and fruits, but Carey saw only the figures on the wall nearby.

He had not been prepared for these curved, domed burrows, the loops of vines and gay animals, bright ochers and yellows beginning to fade but still more like the decoration of a nursery than a grave. On the wall over the hard rock couches for the dead feasters, men and women were dancing, and one couple took him along with their flung-out prance—the man still holding a wine jug in one hand, his red skin bare, other hand held up, one knee raised while his body, on a thigh as stout as an unformed lump of clay, drove forward toward his companion. Her own hand and knee were raised even higher in balance to his steps, her white flesh veiled in diaphanous folds. They stared without expression, as if seeing each other far inside themselves. Carey could imagine the shallow drums and a voice somewhere, as bare and nasal as the singing by those women in black who passed under their windows in early morning with laundry on their heads, wailing the sun awake.

"You like them?" Alberto was saying in his ear.

Carey nodded, sneezed, and they retreated, past the guard who made a great show of locking and sighing as he trudged up the stairs afterward. They only looked at one more tomb, but by the time they exited, Alberto and the guard were frantically agreeing over the disregard that the present government had for the working man, and what was the awful war for anyway if it left the people in a new form of slavery? Carey was always annoyed that these people could move so quickly from anger to affection, or any of their emotions could dissipate by mere expression. He could not be certain what was real to them.

"What's wrong?" Nancy said as she and Carey approached the car while Alberto settled accounts.

"Nothing. I'm hungry."

But even after the trattoria and its good spaghetti, he was surly. So he was quiet all the way to Orvieto. Nancy and Alberto sat in the front of the car, borrowed again from the embassy, its windshield repaired, and from his seat behind them Carey stared past their heads that kept turning to each other as they talked. He was irritated that he allowed himself to feel neglected, but at times they seemed to forget him. Then his frowning silence would gradually intrude on them. In the beginning she had told Carey she wanted his advice about Alberto, but he could see she was past the point of needing that.

They drove away from the coastal plain, began the gentle lifting and turns past hills with their bare, gnarled vines pruned back for winter. He resented most of all being taken away from Rome for the weekend, away from the possibility of seeing Ikbal, of running into her "by chance" at the little open-air market near her home, of being called to come down to her apartment and play some four-hands because she was bored. He came with Alberto and his mother as reluctantly as a scuff-toed child.

*"Guardate, amici."*

He had been dozing and the command sat him up. Ahead a small mesa thrust up from the fields, and it was walled, topped, and towered with a town.

*"Orvieto. É magnifico, no?"*

He pointed out the line of the funicular cutting up from the railway station, and then they came so close that the cliffs were rising over them and they began a winding ascent to the town. In the *pensione* down the narrow street from the Duomo, they settled into their rooms. Carey had one to himself. He had certainly expected Nancy and Alberto would stay together, but her slight hesitation, nervous glance at his face as she and Alberto were shown to the room, made him self-conscious. He was glad to close the door, to sit in slatted sunshine. When Alberto dropped by in his bathrobe on the way to shower, asking Carey how he liked his room, he shrugged, said it was fine, was relieved when Alberto flopped off, shutting the door behind him. But he was angry at himself for being such a brat.

It was cold, only a week away from his Christmas vacation, and on that rock where the houses were crowded together and the squares were far more niggardly than in Rome, they walked in shadow even though above them as they strolled listening to Alberto, the sky was an unmarred, polished blue. The sun sparked and dazzled on the face of the Duomo, but inside the heaped stones was a blunt dampness that numbed his fingers, and he told Alberto that he thought the figures of the dead rising from their graves in Signorelli's frescoes looked like muscled worms, not people. He managed to have something critical to say about everything: the well was full of rubbish, the statue of Maurizio was useless because it was out of order and would not stroke the hours, the restaurant with its blazing fireplace was too hot now that he had put on two undershirts.

So the next morning when they proposed a walk down to the Etruscan necropolis and Carey said he had seen enough old graves, they seemed relieved, although Nancy took him aside and told him to try to cheer up a little. He could tell by the way she looked at him that she had made up her mind what was troubling him and was not going to mention it unless he did. But just because he had in his pocket that letter Frank had written him, did not mean what she thought. He only wanted to read it again, carefully. He was not thinking of Frank as much as Ikbal, and he certainly was not going to mention her to Nancy. If only he could keep his imagination from presenting him with the wildest possibilities, as concrete in detail as the sound of her voice, the touch of her shoulder on his as they sat together at the piano. Better to let Nancy think he was preoccupied with Frank's letter. But that night he had hardly slept, and when he did, he dreamed that Ikbal was calling, the phone was ringing in their empty apartment; she would change her mind, there would never be another chance.

He sat for a while on the steps of the Duomo, watching the few tourists trudge in and out. They were mostly French and had arrived on a chartered bus together. A high thin haze had dulled the blue, but the air was warmer, settling toward rain. He was very restless, thinking too much of the evening to come when they would be safely back by the frozen Maurizio. He began to wander, going anywhere the road went, not caring if he was lost. But he kept crisscrossing the same alleys, suddenly coming up against the same small opening, a retaining wall before the sheer drop. Finally he was on a road that began to descend sharply between the houses, twisted, then slipped out through a gate.

For a while he watched some men trying to train a very spirited horse, its mouth lathering from the cruel, deep bit, hooves weighted to make its gait mincing. In the fields the sun was heavy and warm, and the smell of the dead, dry weeds and manured fields made him drowsy. He walked on past the riding circle, left the wider road for a narrow lane that wound uphill into the fields. In only a short time he could look back on Orvieto. It seemed miles away, an impossible construction. Some cattle came lumbering down, the herdsman twitching lazily at them with a stick, and he nodded at Carey. He kept on, past some farmhouses, up into the fields until the lane became dirt, then tracks in the ground, finally ending in a wooden fence. He sat on the gate for a while, staring at the city.

It hung glazed as in those hard, enameled paintings they had seen in the museum. Somewhere below it Nancy and Alberto would be looking at tombs. In his drowsiness, Carey began to lose all sense of who he was or why he was there. A flock of small brown birds fluttered up nearby to peck and cheep. The sun and smell of that earth could have been anywhere. He tried to think of them all—his mother, Alberto, Ian, Pierre, Ikbal, even Frank, and he only saw them remotely, as if he did not care. He tried to think of the house in Pennsylvania, no longer theirs, but even though he could see rooms and windows, he felt nothing. All the people and places he knew were objects, and he could simply get up and walk away. He too was a separate thing sitting on a fence in the middle of a field looking at an unbelievable town on a rock that he could never have imagined a year ago. It was as if he had stepped into the future, but before it had acted

— 184 —

itself out in any way, and he was as far away from himself now as his old house was—everything was part of another life.

The letter was already rumpled and torn, the ink even smudged by being carried so long in his back pocket. He read through the first few paragraphs quickly, all about Frank's trip west in the car, how it broke down, the Indian reservation, facts that seemed as neutral to Carey as a geography lesson. Then the tone changed, and that was no longer a text, but his father's voice.

"...and California was the best thing I could think of, Carey, the other side of the country, with people I have never known, a city, San Francisco, I have only seen in photographs. The theater is supposed to be adequate, we will be starting from scratch, a chance to make something and do it well. I will tell you something, son. Those days were awful for me after you and your mother moved, and then again, after you left for Rome. But looking back, most of my life seems that way. I think sometime last year, I knew I had a choice. I could kill myself, or I could find a way to go on. In any case, it had to be a new life. I've chosen California..." and the voice went on for a while, stating that he expected Carey to visit when he could, if he wanted, until it seemed to submerge again into the details of arrival, descriptions of a city with hills and tramcars and a new ocean. Carey folded and slipped it carefully into the back pocket that had a button. Frank could have killed himself. Why didn't he explain that more fully? How was it that Carey had never even suspected his father felt that way? Ever since he had read the letter, Carey had imagined himself in bed at the house, a crash waking him, but this time not the dropping of a glass. On the kitchen floor, stretched onto a dark stain, was his father, face down, a white shirt soaking in blood, or was that his father's father drowning in sweat? and he could never get beyond the threshold of the room, as if plateglass held him back.

He climbed off the gate and settled into the grass, looking down the valley that turned sharply to the right. He could go there, could go anywhere he wanted. He was sure he had foreseen sitting like this years ago, and that he would do so again and again. His life was like a picture of a picture within a picture, receding infinitely. He could not move. The birds rose and veered out of sight as if strung together on unseen wires. He closed his eyes, dizzy. In one wheeling moment he dwindled to absolutely nothing, then dispersed so that he was equally certain he was everything—the vanished birds, the grass, even the distant tower of rock.

He dozed and woke to find his arm numb from lying on it, the sun well down toward the hills. He would write his father soon. Maybe he would ask him if he really meant that. It did not seem possible that anyone could choose to die, especially anyone he knew. He began walking back, kept taking any lane or path that edged toward Orvieto. But after a while of turning here and there, never finding a path that went directly toward the town, he was not any closer than when he had started. He walked faster, beginning to sweat. A dog burst down the road from a farmhouse, a black scurry of howling, and he jumped across a fence into a field to protect himself. The dog followed for a while, coming close and setting its front legs, teeth bared, growling.

At last the road straightened, scarcely more than a cobblestoned path between two high walls. It dipped, then rose up the small slope before the scarp where it seemed to have nowhere to go, but he kept walking, more calmly now. The wall crumbled, disappeared as the road began to climb. Tucked to the side was a small stone hut, hardly higher than the outcropping in the field around it, but an old man sat in front at a table, a gray dog stretched out in the dirt by his feet as if dead. For some time Carey had heard his voice singing in an undulating whine, then had seen him waving at the air. He had a large flask of wine beside him, and the sun, almost touching the distant line of hilltops, was burning directly into his red face. He began to wave and beckon, his voice saying something that ended in a long howling "uuuu" as if calling to the sun itself and not Carey. He became more insistent, leaned out over the table, both arms raking. Carey turned in the little path to the shelter and the old man sat down again, quiet, his toothless mouth in a grin.

Carey could not understand a word. The lack of teeth, a heavy tongue that hardly moved at all in spite of his constantly changing face, jumbled the sounds, but he must also have been speaking in some dialect because words began as if they might be understandable and were cut off, elided with sudden weighted syllables more like grunts. But his meaning was clear. As if he had been waiting for someone to happen by, he had an extra glass, a littly hazy from being long unwashed. His dog raised its scruffy head, then went back to sleep, blinking when the flies came too close to its eyes.

Carey took the glass, pulled up the wicker chair. He was not afraid of the old man; the creased, brightly veined face was friendly. His age was impossible to guess. The ground nearby was grazed down by a sheep or goat, and there was a metal rod in the earth, a tether, and droppings. Carey was thirsty and drank, and the wine burned at first, almost peppery. He understood one question after the man repeated it, and so he said, "Carcy, Carey," slowly, and like a child amused by a new sound, the man repeated his name, "Carey, Ca-rey," and Carey felt as if he were hearing it for the first time.

After grinning and nodding for a while, and since there was no hope for further conversation, the man drained his glass, stretched out a hand toward the sun that had just touched the land, and began singing in a phlegmy voice. His guttural words had a strange dignity, as if he were singing a hymn to that light, huge and orange and tamed now that they could stare at it directly through the wintry haze. Carey watched him for a while drawing deep gasps into his short, thick body, then drank, listening to the song, watching the hill cut more deeply into the falling sun.

Before it disappeared, Carey stood. The song stopped and the man poured himself another glass. He offered more, but Carey shook his head. The man's hand came out to him and grasped Carey's wrist.

"Buon viaggio," he said with a sudden clarity, and Carcy thanked him, pointed up the path saying, "Orvieto, per Orvieto?" and the man nodded, smiling, and said, "Si, si, sempre avanti." Carey was dizzied by the fumy wine. The path, which had appeared to end hopelessly in rocks, twisted up steep ramps cut out and carefully fortified centuries before. He turned at the last gate in the wall before the park ahead, and he could still hear the voice singing another song, probably to the darkness that was already in the distant valleys and narrow streets of the town.

They were waiting for him impatiently, a little worried. He told them about the old man, but nothing else. The proprietor of the pensione said, oh, yes, that was the crazy Greek who had wandered in to squat there years ago, everyone knew him, and even the Italians could not understand him very well.

He settled into the back of the car again. It was easier to

talk to them, even though he was annoyed at the long, overly lyrical account by Alberto of the tragic death of Etruscan culture at the hands of the dour and dutiful Romans. But he could ignore that; they were returning to Rome.

# 2

"I guess I don't believe you," Nancy said, and stared at the ceiling to avoid his eyes, knowing that when confronted with any statement that plain they would flinch to the side, and their one moment of turning away would make her mistrust his next words even more. Sometimes she thought that talking with Alberto was like scrambling up a glass wall. Here he was suddenly admitting he had no brother in Rome, that apartment they had visited belonged to a friend. Then, as if he wanted to tell all, he was admitting he had a family—two children, a wife. But even as he told her, she found his words so unhalting that she wondered if this confession was only concealing something else.

He stirred but did not answer. It was early afternoon and they lay together in the Pensione Bellavista Milton, so named, Nancy had discovered by asking the desk clerk, because it had a fine view of the Borghese Gardens and because the English poet John Milton had stayed there—neither of which facts seemed true to her. Usually the view from their window was of the inner air shaft, rank with the fumes of kitchen, sewer gas, decomposing paper, and the building was surely not old enough to have been standing when Milton visited Rome. But it was conveniently close to the embassy and they came there often during the siesta when the embassy offices closed.

"What does it matter, though? I do not lie when I say I love you. What I am doing now is no lie. I am with you."

They both lay on their backs, side by side like a heraldic king and queen ensconced memorially in a chapel. Only their hands touched, and now he clasped hers more tightly. She knew that old evasion, the plea for the absolute present. "I am feeling what I feel now, I am true to the moment, I am in a state of truth." But that neatly excised the awareness of past and future, the pressure of both on a moment more fragile than such a statement admitted.

"It's not that simple. I can't even hope to know you if all I know is now. This." Her free hand swept in an arc over them, gathering in the cracked ceiling, the dulled brass of a chandelier hanging by naked wires.

"This 'knowing' you keep talking about. Sometimes I have trouble understanding it." The way his hand clenched slightly did not seem an outwardly directed gesture.

"It's not just your past, Alberto. Although that is a problem. You are so vague when I ask anything about that. But even the present. What you call the present is only the slight surface of time when you and I are together, touching. I really know nothing even about where you are when we aren't together, why you are so vague about all that."

"Why do you want to know?"

His voice was growing hostile, but she was angry now too.

"It's not fair." She released her hand, rolled onto her stomach to lean on her elbows, face staring down at his. "You are curious about me. You wanted to meet Carey, to come to our apartment, to ask about Frank. I want to know the same things about you. To have an equal knowledge."

"That sounds possessive." He was not looking at her, his hands behind his head. "You are saying if you know these things you will 'have' me."

She thought she would hit him. What he had said seemed insulting. But looking at his clenched jaw, the surly frown, she was more shocked than angry. Maybe she had been wrong, maybe he had nothing specific to hide, only a fear of losing parts of himself, of being owned. She could understand that. She still kept back some large part of herself, not wanting to give it up, rooms in her house that were only for her to sit in during quiet moments. But how could revealing of mere facts jeopardize that?

"No," she said quietly. "I don't want to own you. Any more than I want to be owned by you."

He turned to her quickly, and she was in for another shock because now his face was slightly pained, as if he had assumed all along that was not true.

"I suppose not." His hand untucked itself from behind his head and he ran it over her cheek. "I imagine it will be best if I tell you more. So I will."

He turned his face away but left his hand gently stroking her neck, and began to talk again about his wife Assunta and the children.

"But you've not been divorced?"

He laughed sharply. "That's not really possible for us, you know."

"And you see her sometimes?"

"Yes. But to see the children, I must."

"Do you love her still?"

"That's all over."

She could not discover what difference all this made. Not yet. He was waiting for her to say something.

She was not at all concerned about the other woman, even if he was lying about how he felt. She wanted to know more about the children, about what kind of father he was. She had always expected there were other women, and if it was a wife, that was almost laughably more respectable than what she had imagined.

"Tell me about them. Teresa and Giorgio, I mean."

His hand stopped moving. She had done it again, surprised him. She was probably supposed to ask about Assunta; and she suspected he was prepared for that. His lips tightened. Her own anger lifted again. He was always prepared. Nothing made him more uneasy than not being ready. She was about to say something to him about that when his face turned abruptly, his mouth slightly open and eyes unveiled, a look she had always wanted to see.

"I love them."

She felt perverse enough to want to call that sentimental. She already knew how hopelessly maudlin these people were about children, how they spoiled them and regarded them indulgently from the confessed sense of their own sins, and as he went on to describe them, haltingly, as if the language he knew so well was deserting him, she saw the expression become truly sentimental, the words lapsing into Italian, becoming more and more trite. But that first look had not been, and with a twinge she admitted she might indeed be a little possessive, wishing he had been able to say those words to her as honestly, just once.

There was a knock on the door, a voice telling them what time it was and Alberto answered, thanking him. He swept the sheet off and started to rise. But she did not want to leave. Not yet. She saw the naked body stretched leaning on a crooked arm, his taut flesh, lax horn of his penis. She grasped his face in both her hands, pressed it down and back into the pillows, kissing his eyes closed. His hands grasped her shoulders, moved up and down her back. She lay fully on him, pressed her tongue deep into his mouth, holding fast to his head now, and suddenly she wanted to be him, lying on his back, rising to the chafe and pressure of a woman's body, his two hands pulling her thighs open, lifting her hips enough to let him thrust into her, then the hands gripping, spreading her buttocks, pressing her deepr and deeper onto him, and in only a few moments she cried out in wave after wave. She rose, looking down on his arched body, and his eyes were closed, head thrust back. She tried to plunge behind that mask, to be rooted in the shaft of flesh her own body folded around. She rode him slowly and held his hands to her breasts, saying his name with her own eyes closed.

The portiere, standing by the gate with his hands clasped behind his back, bowed slightly to them as they entered, and when Alberto said, *"Buona sera, Giuseppe,"* the man's face lost its mask of mere politeness and smiled widely.

*"Ah, Signor Benedetti."*

They exchanged one of those brief, broken-handed touches, a few words about their health, and Alberto and Nancy walked into the first courtyard, circling a small round of box hedge, pebbles popping under their feet, and ascended the wide marble stairs leading up under the façade.

It was an opening of the annual art show at the American Academy, traditionally hosted by the ambassador. She had not dressed up so much since coming to Rome, had even indulged herself in a new dress, silk and pleated, flowing back slightly now in the gust of wind that eddied in the doorway. In the still, inner courtyard were the last stairs to the rectangular garden where the arched portico covered the various works of art and the sound of the fountain in the center splashed under the murmur of voices. They had been, until this evening, very careful about their public appearances, acting friendly but maintaining the guise of mere co-workers. But they had decided to come together, and as if that made appearances unnecessary to her, Nancy now clung tightly to his arm as they walked around the various displays, a glass of wine in hand. They recognized some of the people, fellow workers at the embassy, or couples Nancy had met through the school, but Alberto also knew many of the Italians there, those obviously wealthy men and women; or so it seemed to Nancy by their exquisite clothing, the perfectly adjusted coiffures, but above all that almost immobile, haughty expression, always poised and weary—faces, as Ian had warned her, that had been cast from the marble busts of the Roman Empire's lords and ladies. In fact, she could hardly concentrate on the art, and would stare at a statue or painting only to conceal the real focus of her gaze on some creature of high fashion shrugging as she listened in as bored a manner as possible to a thin-faced gentleman who did not even bother to look at her as he talked. Very few people were actually studying the art. They strolled by each piece slowly as if it had been placed there merely to give an excuse for a promenade, a greeting, a knot of conversation. She could pick out the artists themselves, dressed too carefully for their disheveled beards, their faces uneasily caught in discussion, eyes tugging right and left, obviously trying hard not to look in that corner where their own work was hung or pedestaled.

They were slowly returning to the long, white-clothed table to refill their glasses when she thought she recognized the slim, straight back of the man ahead of them and as he turned, jostling his elbow on her so that his wine spilled slightly over the back of his hand, she said, "Why, Ian. Hello."

He was in the process of excusing himself, recognized her, smiled genuinely and said, "Nancy." But his face became expressionless as he saw Alberto, and Nancy, holding her glass out to the waiter, said, "Alberto, this is my friend Ian Snyder, one of Carey's teachers. Alberto Benedetti."

At first she thought they must be trying to insult each other because Ian lifted his other hand merely to hold his wine in both and they inclined their heads at each other stiffly, saying, *"Buona sera."* With eyebrows raised slightly, mouth pinched, Ian said, "How nice to see you again."

"You know each other?"

They moved away from the table to make room for others until they were standing near a group of figures in bronze, perhaps dancing, their arms and legs tied in knots, more like a Laocoön without serpent, but flesh as plastic as snakes.

"Yes, yes," Alberto said, "we've known each other for some time. And how is the opera world?"

Nancy watched them carefully. She knew them both well enough to sense the tension in their manners: Ian's enunciation overly clipped and sharp, Alberto's mouth slightly turned down as if he had tasted something bitter. They carried on a very wordy conversation, each one completing a paragraph before the other would begin his, as if they had worked it all out beforehand, or it sounded that way because all the phrases were so worn and trite that they were saying nothing. This, she supposed, was the height of hostile politeness, but she had taken enough wine on an empty stomach, had tasted enough of the evening's artificiality not to want the people she knew well to fit so comfortably into the mold around her. There was every reason for these two men to be more cordial to each other, so in a pause where they both stiffly sipped from the rims of their glasses, looking fixedly over each other's shoulders, she put her hand on Ian's arm, laughed, and said, "Oh, come on, you two. You look as if you're about to have a duel."

Ian's face blushed. He looked at her, blinked, and said, "Sorry." Nancy was stunned, feeling she had hurt him deeply in some way. She reached her hand out again, but only the fingertips brushed his sleeve as he drew back, although he may have been turning slightly to make way for a portly gentleman. Alberto laughed once, said something rapidly in Italian that sounded as if he were accusing her of being a voyeur, then she realized it probably translated "clairvoyant," and Ian said quite clearly, "Yes, she has remarkable powers."

At this point she was almost beyond controlling her anger. Not only were they in some concealed way brutalizing each other, but they had begun to talk about her as if she were not there. She looked rapidly from one to the other, and she must have taken on a furious expression because Ian suddenly put his hand on her arm, and said, "I am sorry, Nancy. Let me excuse myself to wander around. Signor Benedetti and I are well acquainted, and I'm sure he can explain it to you amply," but the last words hardened again, were certainly as much directed to Alberto as herself, and as he said, "Good evening," to them both and turned away, Alberto muttered something.

She glanced at him, turned to pick up another full glass, put her arm firmly in his and tried to direct them toward the fountain. Many more people had arrived and they had to move slowly. He pulled back, finally not moving.

"I want you to come somewhere where we can talk. I want to know what this is about."

He looked at her, that sullen, languid droop of eyelids. "Nancy. Come. There is really nothing to explain. We have met before and do not care for each other. It is very simple."

She had been irritable all day, was tired, had even scolded Carey for not waking himself on time that morning. She should let it go. But she felt as stubborn as an insulted child.

"You're lying."

She did not say it loudly but she could tell by the glances of other people nearby that their poses, expressions, were becoming unusual.

He sipped his wine, said quietly, "I think you're becoming a little hysterical. This doesn't seem like you."

"But it certainly seems like you."

His eyebrows lifted slightly, he shrugged. "Would you like to go now?"

"No. Thank you. I'm having a good time." But she turned, began edging away, felt his hand on her arm.

"Where are you going?"

She was no less angry, but cinched it in coldly so that her voice was perfectly even, and she managed a smile let down like a visor. "I am going to look at the art which is after all what we supposedly came to do. But no one seems to be doing it. And I'm tired of your secrets. Please go along when you feel like it. I am very close to home."

She whirled, awkwardly nudged the back of a tall, bearded man who turned a smiling face quickly to her as if she might be a friend, but she slipped on past him without even excusing herself. She half expected Alberto to follow her, and after she had found her way to the portico where fewer people were, she glanced back. Of course he would not be there, would be too conscious of how absurd that would look. But she was relieved, truly did want to be left to herself for a while. She ignored the people. They only seemed to keep her anger up. Gradually she felt quieter. Beyond the arches of the portico the fountain, lit brightly by a single spotlight, was splashing irregularly, and the balmy air lapsed down from a velvet square of sky. She breathed deeply, sipped the wine—white, probably a Frascati— began to concentrate on the art. She did not like the first group of paintings, either too rigidly abstract or vaguely familiar—definitely student work. The sculpture along the wall seemed better, and at the last turn she could not stop looking at one piece, a figurine of a woman. It changed aspects completely as she circled it. From the front the woman seemed at rest, solidly looking earthward. She was pregnant, naked, her body ripely sloped toward the modeled earth she stood on. Her arms, held out slightly in a curve, seemed to be reaching downward as if to gather something growing up toward her. But from the rear, her arched back, taut legs, the slightly angled neck with its high-gathered hair, were full of motion, a dancer about to leap, not weighted by her body at all but capable of springing free from all bounds, and the earth at this angle slanted away, urging her upward. Nancy kept circling the figure slowly, then stopped, amused to think that she was gradually performing her own slow dance, the ritual motions of an observer.

"You like her?"

Ian was by her shoulder. She started to speak but he said quickly, eyes down, "I'm terribly sorry about that silliness. We don't behave well when taken by surprise."

"But what in the world was that all about?"

Ian cocked his head to one side. "He didn't tell you?"

"He may," she said half-heartedly.

"Some other time. I believe I saw him leaving."

She was a little disappointed. She had hoped to feel composed enough soon to find Alberto, perhaps change the subject by showing him this statuette. But she was not worried. It was their first major argument, but she was sure he was leaving mostly in order to avoid a more embarrassing scene. He thought her at least that unpredictable.

"Then you must tell me," she said firmly, but he held up a hand.

"Hardly my show."

"I mean it. If he decided not to, that's his business. I'm depending on you."

She saw he was uncertain.

"Will you walk me home? Now? I'm tired of this. You can talk to me on the way, join Carey and me. We're going out for dinner."

He looked into his wineglass. "Very well."

The ambassador was at the top of the stairs with a little group, hoping to begin the speechmaking soon, and the guests were beginning to gather, so they slipped down and out the front gate just in time.

"An odd place, this Academy," Ian said.

But she let that go and waited in silence as they walked slowly up toward the Porta.

"This may take a little while. I didn't realize you knew Alberto or had..." he paused.

"Become his lover? Or he mine? Yes."

"The problem is an old one between us, and I want you

to understand that I do not know the man in any other way than this, so what you know of him is equally valid."

Again she did not know how to help him.

"Alberto lived with my sister, during the war. In my terms, I'm afraid, lived *off* my sister."

"In England. While he was interned?"

Ian stood, glanced at her, and then walked on.

"I'm afraid neither of them was in England. They were both in Zurich. My sister had married wealth, her husband had died in the early days of the war, and she could not bear England after that, went with her money to Switzerland. She never was very stable, I'm afraid, but..." and he shrugged.

They were passing slowly under the street lamps toward the high terrace, and already the lights of the city below were spreading out beyond them.

"I don't know why I should now, or should have blamed him for anything then. I suppose he had his own reasons, may not have been simply a parasite."

Nancy flinched at the word. She was trying to gather the details together and make them adhere to her conception of Alberto, but they would not stay put.

"And remember Italians were our enemies too, although we had nothing like the sheer hate for them that we had for the Germans. But we knew about my sister's life from others, and she flaunted it also in letters home. I m afraid neither of us was good to our parents in that respect. Her promiscuity in the months after her husband's death was well known, and my homosexuality was never hidden from them either. I imagine they must have deserved some of it or we wouldn't have been that way. Especially my mother. However."

They had reached the balustrade and the breeze was chillier now, so that Nancy had to pull her shawl close around herself and fold her arms.

"I think they did terrible things to each other. And I even think she loved him, although he was far from constant either. I was very close to my sister."

"What was her name?"

"Gwyn. She died. On the day of the German surrender, she killed herself."

"Oh, Ian."

"She left no notes, letters, explanations. But the people who knew her said it was perhaps just as well. She had tried before and failed, in fact rather purposely setting up situations where she would be interrupted. This time she was determined. I think I understand, especially the day. She must have felt that the world of war, living in a little pocket of Zurich surrounded by chaos, was the only possible image for her life. She wouldn't have been able to stand peace. Although I sometimes think that if she had known how violent our 'peace' would be, she would have stayed."

"I'm sorry." Nancy had almost forgotten about Alberto now. It was Ian's life she felt pressing her in that clipped, understated tone.

"I went looking for Alberto. I knew it was crazy of me. Gwyn had her own problems, and he couldn't have hindered or helped them. But I had been told he had left her when the end of the war was in sight, and I simply wanted to tell him what a cad I thought he was. Yes, cad. Pure Edwardian dramatics." He paused, and when she shivered, put his arm around her and held her close to his side. She leaned on him. "I caught up with him in Venice, of all places for a full-fledged melodrama. He was sitting in St. Mark's Square, alone fortunately, although I knew he certainly wasn't wealthy enough to be enjoying that particular café—so he had either made a catch or was setting himself up for one."

"Ian. Is that fair?"

"No. You're right. I seem to be judging him harshly. But bear in mind I mean it less harshly than you might think, in spite of my sister. Because we all had to make our way after the war. My dear Nancy, if it is time for confessions, let me admit I had my eye out too, and at least once depended on my good luck or looks." He squeezed his hand on her arm, then held still. "I didn't know quite what to do. I challenged him. To a duel."

She pulled back her head, trying to see his face. "A duel? How quaint. Then this evening?"

He laughed genuinely. "It's awfully funny, isn't it? Both then, and this evening. Imagine how ashamed I was for a moment, how I thought he had told you already and you were mocking me. But immediately I knew that wasn't like you."

"Go on."

"That's really about all. Of course he did not accept. He laughed. I tried to get at him, but the table was between us, I was quickly restrained by others. It was a very odd scene, because when the police came, he argued them into letting me go, said it was a matter of the heart, which anyone forgives in Italy. Then we were left alone, standing in the center of the square. I knew I didn't want to kill him or any of that nonsense. He just disgusted me. But we began talking. We must have wanted something from each other, but did not know what. A clue? Did we feel that if we understood Gwyn we would understand ourselves? We took the same train that evening from Venice, he to Rome, I to Florence, and all through that night we talked. There is something easy about dealing with someone when you share a mutual distaste for the other's being, and have admitted it openly. But I don't remember anything significant in that conversation. At least for me. We avoid each other, have met occasionally in Rome, as this evening, and we can be quite civilized. I knew he had a family somewhere in the city." He paused.

"He has told me."

"Good. Then he is honest with you."

"Perhaps."

"But neither of us wants to see each other. And in public, unexpectedly, it always feels to me as though someone has ripped off a carefully healed piece of flesh. I have to assume it does to him too. I'm sorry you had to see all that."

She only nodded. She wanted to know more about Ian's sister, but he turned slightly, she straightened up, and they began walking toward home.

"I wonder," she said, "why I don't feel changed about Alberto. Why I still wish to see him, now, tomorrow."

He tucked her hand onto his arm.

"You must love him."

"I don't know. He is very complicated."

She began to walk faster. "Come on, Carey will be impatient," and as if welcoming the change in topic, they talked about Carey all the way home.

When Alberto called late that night, she decided to say nothing about her conversation with Ian, at least not on the phone. He was sorry. She was sorry. They both admitted their behavior had been exaggerated. Yes, she had noticed he was gone and had left soon afterward. Sitting in her nightgown in the dark room, Carey long since asleep, she was aware of a strange unreality—her half-wakened mind, Alberto's voice interrupted by brief cracks on the line, a draft of cold air from some open window reminding her that the weather had retreated from its unnatural warmth of that evening. It was one of those moments when she rose up out of the tangled coils of her life to look around, her own clear voice saying in surprise, "What am I doing here, in Rome, in a dark room, talking to a man I hardly know, but love?"

The next day it seemed easier to let her new knowledge of his past go undiscussed and their reconciliation that afternoon left little time for conversation anyway. From time to time she found him staring at her, but whether he was suspecting she knew something or simply fixing a new intensity of focus on her, she could not tell.

# 3

Carey knew something was wrong at school, but no one was explaining it to the students. The teachers were inattentive, and meetings were held almost every night with parents and staff. Some of that leaked down, but only vaguely. A "reorganization" was being planned and a group of parents was angry about something. His mother never went to meetings, and Mladen was no help either. Even Ian shook his head when Carey asked him one day on the bus, and then turned to look out the window.

"I guess you'll know soon enough," he murmured.

Mr. Anderson looked more and more distracted, was seen mumbling in the hallways between classes, tweaking at his wispy hair. Once he poked his head up into the tower in the middle of Latin class, and because they were silently writing a quiz and his back was turned in the final screw of the staircase, he did not see them. His head and shoulders held still, he sighed heavily, his voice said something like "Can't get a hold on..." or "Damn it, I told 'em..." and then he scraped down again. Already the shell-shocked Mr. Johnson had vanished in November, his whereabouts unknown until two weeks later when a postcard of the Statue of Liberty was sent to the school from New York with his name scribbled on it and nothing else.

Slowly, in the last three weeks, one of the teachers had made her presence felt in almost every classroom, even though she only taught geometry and American history. Roberta Wise was the wife of an American official at FAO, and her two children in the lower school, a boy and a girl, had become the terror of Carey's bus—not because they were tough or mean, but because their brattish babbling was protected by that firm, implacable presence of "Mom" Roberta who always seemed to be there to back them up.

But Carey learned his geometry. He and the others had to. Grudgingly, they admitted that other than Ian's classroom, hers was the only place they learned a subject. She was broad-faced, perfectly groomed, always thinly smiling. Carey was tired of hearing parents call her "very capable." But she was steady, neither cruel nor affectionate, a patient but unceasing pressure that Carey found far worse than the count's petulant scolding when they could not conjugate, or Anderson's bleak sigh when they did not respond to the beauty of some poem he recited by heart. She managed to visit every classroom in three weeks, sitting in the back of the room, her attempt to be unobtrusive making her even more present. Carey watched Ian under the fixed, archaic smile on her listening cocked head become more brittle, witty, English than the worst parody of him Fiero sometimes performed. The look Ian gave to the back of her head as she walked out when the bell rang could have blackened marble. When he saw Carey staring at him he tried to smile, but it was only a wince.

The day before Christmas vacation an assmebly of the whole school was called "to clarify the situation." They gathered in the large dining hall, where the piano had been pushed to one side, the tables stacked, and chairs set in neat rows to face a table where Mr. Anderson, Hollister Brewster, who was chairman of the board, and Mrs. Wise were seated. Anderson looked as if he would be overwhelmed by his nervous twitches, or his neighbors might be in danger of a jab or kick from one of his misplaced limbs as he crossed and uncrossed his legs, thrust a hand up and behind his head to rub it, threw out an arm to the left to get his cuff away from his watch. He lit a cigarette with a sweeping strike at the box in spite of one half-smoked and still fuming in his ashtray. The other teachers were standing along the back wall. Everyone was more quiet than usual.

In his best Oklahoma drawl, Mr. Brewster delivered Christmas greetings from the trustees, then a little speech about how fortunate they were, the Americans, and he made it seem that everything around them in an impoverished, blighted country was put there to remind them of the superiority of the "American Way of Life," and they must be grateful for that, especially since it was having such good effect in helping poor Europe accomplish an "Economic Miracle" of recovery, until Mladen had to sit on his hands, his face scarlet.

"It is, however," he said finally, "with some sadness that I must announce the resignation of Mr. Anderson as principal of the school."

No reasons were given. The words coming to them were praising Mr. Anderson, but Carey could tell something was wrong. The man was fidgeting even more violently. Mrs. Wise would be the new principal, effective immediately. She too was praised, and she became statuelike, her smile etched in stone. Mr. Brewster was finished. Mrs. Wise would address them. She shifted to stand.

But Anderson was up, his face ashen.

"Sit down," he said to her firmly.

She did, without looking at him.

"I have not resigned, they have kicked me out," and he leaned down on both his bent hands, his body suddenly calm. "That's all right, I just don't want you to have lies. Schools are not for lies. They say there is not enough order, discipline, incentive here. They are going to give that to you. I wish them good luck, truly I do." He looked around the room vaguely as if trying to take in all their faces in his unfocused gaze. Carey wondered if he might draw his bow and shoot some Homer at them, but whatever had seized him to speak, left, and he looked very tired. "Goodbye," and he sat as abruptly as he had stood.

Mrs. Wise rose. She was calm and addressed them as if she had followed Mr. Brewster's speech without interruption. She was grateful for the honor, the trust, the responsibility, was sure they would move on together into a new semester, would build an "ongoing tradition of excellence." Whatever tension had been drawn by Mr. Anderson was unstrung by her smooth and endless speech. They went to lunch subdued, almost indifferent. "Well," Mladen said, and shrugged, "it's vacation anyway."

"What will happen?" Carey asked Ian as they rode the bus.

"We shall see. You Americans are very strange at times."

"How?"

"You have a mission."

"What's that?"

He looked ahead five rows to the back of Mrs. Wise's head. "To have things your way."

"Gone. To the school. Another meeting," Pierre told him. "He said to say sorry. A note."

They stood in Ian's living room. Carey had come to know Pierre well enough in his visits to Ian to feel at ease with him, had even joined them once for dinner. Pierre stood wiping his hands on a dishtowel, grinning. "All the time now, meetings, meetings."

The note was jotted in haste, excusing, setting up another day, saying he had called but Carey had already left, which he knew was true since it was vacation and he had left early to wander around. Ikbal was in the north for a series of concerts, and sitting in the apartment made Carey nervous.

"Look, you boy," and Pierre threw the balled-up towel onto the distant counter. He had a way of calling Carey, "You boy," his own form of familiar address. "Come with me. I am going to Piazza Navona to buy gifts, for Hanukkah—then to my children."

He put on an old khaki U.S. Army jacket and they walked out into the damp day, cloudy and on the verge of rain.

All the booths were up and open, closing in the long oval of the square, trapping the writhing figures in the fountain. Balloon men with their families were working portions of the square, and some of them also held up pennants of the various soccer teams. But Pierre was only interested in the booths that sold wooden, hand-carved *presepio* figures.

"I get something for each one. Thirty. You help keep the numbers."

The vendors were calling to them. Pierre would hold up a figure to judge its carving, laughing when he found something he thought well done, and he bantered easily with the old man on his stool who pressed them to buy.

"Look at the face on this one," and he showed Carey a shepherd, hands held to his heart dramatically, eyes and mouth wide, obviously lost in amazement at the sudden brightness of a messenger angel. Carey thought it strange to look across the counter at a swatch of kneeling figures, then a patch of angels, of Marys, of Josephs, of sheep—multitudes of little figures, each meticulously and uniformly carved by hand—and there were also the cork-roofed sheds, the little cribs, even a cow being milked by a very happy and buxom peasant girl. Soon he was picking up the ones he liked too, showing Pierre and even tugging at his sleeve with impatience to show him a find, and Pierre had to remind him that his children would only want the animals or perhaps some shepherds, that Joseph and Mary and the child were of no importance to them. Halfway around the square they bought a cone of hot chestnuts and sat on a bench to peel them, scorching their fingers, eating and chatting, Pierre beginning to lapse into various languages. But Carey was used to following conversations with small holes in them. Pierre bought a balloon and tied it to the button of Carey's jacket. Its string plucked at his ear and tugged lightly, a little impatient to be off but somehow also an expression of Carey's mood—lifting, bobbing—and it reminded him briefly, not even sadly, of the times that he and Frank would go to the county fair.

They did not buy things at the booths where the faces of the proprietors were bored or sleepy. They paused long with the ones who talked or laughed or were flippant: the old woman who nipped from the wine flask on the bench behind her and sang some filthy mountain song at them as they looked over her sheep, something about what the peasants were doing in their fields that night, or the skinny, toothless man who insisted loudly that Pope Pius himself had bought one of his angels last year to make into a cardinal. But above all Carey liked the way Pierre laughed, his huge shoulders shaking, shaking his head as if he must stop, he must stop laughing, but oh, he couldn't help it. And suddenly, as he stood with a naked Christ child no larger than a peanut curled in his palm, Carey remembered why Ian loved the man.

When they had finished buying, having long ago lost count and continuing merely for the fun of it, they sat on the bench again and counted their booty. Carey had chipped in with his own money although Pierre had refused at first. They had almost two gifts for every child, so they went back to their favorite stall and bought five more. The old woman Pierre called Mother Befana laughed and leaned forward with a large bear painted black, and dropping it into the sack with great seriousness said, "For the children, in the spirit of Jesus," and they thanked her.

The children were waiting beyond the gate in the courtyard of a building pink-tinged with white lines of concrete, an absolute monotony of rectangular shape beginning to crack and peel badly, a style that Ian had told Carey was "fascist architecture."

"Pietro, Pietro," they called, and a rush began for the gate.

They were dressed uniformly in smocks and pinafores, even though all boys, their bare, knobby legs ending in heavy institutional shoes not seeming to fit anyone well, like hand-me-downs in an enormous family. Some of their heads were shorn and spotted with medicine. The women watched and one of them came over quickly, smiling, to open the gate.

"We told them at breakfast, as you see," she said in Italian, and the gate swung open.

Pierre handed Carey the sack, stepped in and was immediately tugged about and weighted down, and he stooped to lift two of the smallest, their eyes wide as they curved away from him to stare at his face, and some of the older ones kept up a chant of "Where are the presents, where are the presents?" while Pierre laughed, his face red, muttering, "No, no—no pulling," but not as though he meant it.

When they quieted down he said that this was his friend Carey who had helped him, and their grave, silent faces took him in. They began their chant again and Pierre took two of them by the hands and said, "Avanti," and they all swarmed through the doors into a hallway smelling of ammonia, down its echoing reach to a large room of battered wooden chairs where a branching candlestick was standing on a table.

He took the sack and put it on the table and then sat in front of it, and they gathered in a tight semicircle. The woman who had let them in stood in the back of the room, her hands folded.

"You see," he said, and held out his hands flatly, "no gifts."

One of the older boys, standing in the last row, pointed and frowned. "No, you don't. We see the sack."

"Those are my boots in case it snows."

They laughed, high, excited, as if trying to see who could laugh the loudest. Suddenly Pierre twisted his hand, made a fist, opened it, showing a 100-lire piece in his palm. He flipped it high in the air toward them, a shining blur that rose almost to the ceiling and then came down to their raised hands.

"I have it," and one boy lifted it high.

"What will you do with it?"

Carey could see this was something Pierre did often and that each child had already thought out what he would do if he caught the coin.

"Buy more candles," he said solemnly, and the others liked

that idea. The boy took the coin back to the woman and then sat down again.

At first Carey felt out of place, but Pierre insisted he sit beside him and they began to hand out the presents they had paired and wrapped in pieces of tissue paper. Pierre knew each child by name, and gravely, without hesitation, he called them up to him one by one and handed each his present. The child would go back to his place, holding it tightly, not removing the wrapping until everyone was served. Then they unraveled them fast, squealing, milling around, making sounds for their animals, and while they were lost in playing with those small wooden objects, Pierre wandered back through them to the woman and they talked together.

"Do you see my bear?"

A boy with a very round but monkeylike face, stood at Carey's shoulder and he held out the bear the old woman had given them. Carey took, admired it, and put it back in the waiting hand.

"I have a horse from last week. I kept it and didn't trade like the others." He peered at Carey very directly. "Where do you come from?"

"America."

He pursed his lips. "I don't believe you."

"It's true."

"Then speak some American."

"What do you want me to say?" Carey asked in English.

He nodded. "All right. Then you are. Are you one of us?"

Carey was puzzled.

"An orphan."

"No."

"Do they have orphans in America?"

"Yes. They do."

"Pierre is an orphan," and he looked at Carey as if wondering how he could not be one if Pierre was. "But I used to have parents. I just don't remember them." He paused as if thinking. "They took them away from me when I was too little to remember. The Germans took them some place to kill them with a lot of other people. I went to live with Nonna Bagnoli. They gave me to her to hide. When she died, I came here because there was no one else." But his own story was boring him and he lifted the bear between them. "What shall we name him?"

"You do it."

But he insisted. Carey thought for a moment, almost gave

up, then said the first thing that came to mind. *"Orsa maggiore."*

He grinned. "Like the stars? The big bear in the stars?" He laughed and ran off with the bear raised. *"Ecco. Guarda qui. É l'orsa maggiore. Guarda l'orsa nel cielo."*

They left soon. Pierre looked tired. He stood with Carey for a moment at his bus stop. Carey wanted to let him know he was glad to have been taken along, but everything he started to form into words sounded sloppy.

After a silence Pierre said, "They are all right there. It's better than the place I was. Sometimes I think I like living in Rome because I feel almost as if I am still in the underground. Being Jewish in this city can be like that."

"Does the church help that place?"

Pierre looked at him sharply. He snorted. "Help? It helps by not preventing us, I guess. But this pope has washed his hands often." They both saw the bus coming so he patted Carey quickly on the shoulder and said, "So, you boy, I will tell Ian you see him Monday."

The bus drew up, the doors unfolded with a hiss, and lifting on Carey's elbow he urged him up. From the back window Carey could see the man slouch across the street to his own bus stop, hands thrust over his belly in the pockets of his jacket. All the way up the hill, looking down the curving and diminishing street, Carey thought of how his father might have killed himself, and then Nancy might have died in that accident, and he would be an orphan now, riding a bus in a city he hardly knew.

Remembering the bustle and stir of Christmas, for the first time in months Carey was homesick. Nancy and he did what they could, but they were looking at someone else's rituals. The rows of mosaics and gold leaf on the coffered ceiling sparkled and shimmered on Christmas Eve at Santa Maria Maggiore when the lights burst on, and they heard the sound of hundreds of people around them sucking in their breath all at once. But that was new to him, only a curiosity. The single greeting he received from friends at home was a charred Christmas card from Lisa, the first word from her since October, and it had survived the wreck of a mail plane. He suspected she had stopped writing for the same reasons he had—boredom at finding new words to describe how much he missed her when he did not really think of her much anymore. Except in dreams and fantasies. But that was an extension of her body and what he had learned from it. He looked at every woman now with the dim knowledge of Lisa, wondering if they would feel the same to hold, if their breasts would be shaped differently. His whole body would ache when he sat opposite some woman on a bus or was pressed close to her indifferent flesh by the crowd.

Late one evening, on his way home from Mladen's, he had walked away from his bus stop to the corner where three whores were resting against the side of a palazzo. He had never dealt with them alone, always Mladen or Fiero had been there to play games. Now his heart pumped wildly. One of them saw him coming and stood straight, preening, pulling at her skirt, striking a manikin's pose with one leg thrust out. He walked up to her, stood only inches away. She stared at him through half-closed eyes, waiting for him to speak. He swallowed. Her breasts were loose and nippled against her parted dress, her belly a ripe mound. He wanted to touch her. But just as quickly as he had crossed the street, he turned and walked back, and the other two laughed, said something jeering to the woman he had stood by, and she in turn yelled some insult at him. He was glad the bus came before he had to turn around, and all the way home he imagined himself telling the other women off, rescuing her from their taunts, and they would go somewhere to make love all night long. On the bus, rattling and half empty, he had to sit down to hide the lift in his pants.

But the worst of his dreams were when Lisa would suddenly come to his bed. He would turn restlessly, then feel something nudging the side of his mattress. He would open his eyes and her naked thighs would be in front of his face, the dark wedge of hair musky, and he would look up the standing column of her body to see her distant face staring down at him, her lips gathered in a playful kiss. He would place his hands on her buttocks, kiss her belly while she put her hands on his shoulders and moved her hips slowly, and she would shift toward him on the bed, the covers falling away from him, would flow down over him like water, moaning until her face was next to his. Suddenly the face would not be Lisa's but Ikbal's. Her hands would take his head and lift it slightly, her dark hair falling all around them like a tent, and as he thrust at her she would say, "Yes, yes, yes," until he woke, his own voice whimpering the words, his sheets and belly wet. Those dreams would not leave him all the next day, and he was almost glad she was still not back from her concert tour because he was afraid he would not be able to hide his thoughts.

But he was lonely for her. At the newsstand near the embassy he bought papers from Milan, from Verona, from Padua, looking for reviews, announcements, and when he found one he labored secretly over it with his dictionary, furious at the flowery meaningless phrases. Under all those words he could never find her. They could have been talking about anyone.

The day after Christmas as he was practicing, Nancy brought him a letter and put it on top of the piano. He finished memorizing the last few measures. It was from Ikabl. The postmark was Venice, where he knew she had been three days earlier.

"Dearest Carey, have you missed me? Are you practicing?" And she described some of her concerts, a badly tuned Steinway, a limousine that took her to the wrong hall in Torino, a drunken gondolier. She wrote in English, but he found it strange how much more awkward it seemed than her speech. "I will be glad to be home soon and to see you again," the letter ended. He wanted to write back, but he had no address.

Over the next few days he reread the letter carefully. "Some day when I am returned and this time is still fresh in my mind, we must talk, long and much about this life of performing. You must not let me forget how I feel, because this may be your life some day, and I should let you have no illusions." He wanted to talk with her about all that, and much more. He imagined so many scenes of her return that he began to think it would never happen.

Fiero had taken a trip to England with his family, and Mladen was bored. He and Carey would meet often in the afternoons at the Foro, or wander around, maybe going to a movie. He was convinced that Carey knew something about the school. His parents had almost taken him out because his mother had gone to a meeting where Mr. Brewster had made some general comments about "our responsibility to educate our students from some of the Communist-dominated countries in more than the three R's." Mladen gave Carey a very aggressive history lesson in the difference between Tito-ism and Communism. Carey was careful to agree, although he knew nothing about it all and did not much care.

They were walking toward the Campidoglio to go to the

museum, something their parents had insisted on for a change instead of the movies. Carey had decided to let Mladen read Ikbal's letter, maybe to let him know how he felt about her, certainly to see if Mladen saw anything unusual in it. He wanted someone outside to tell him he was right. Mladen stopped abruptly at the bottom of the Cordonata.

"How often do you and Ian rehearse?"

"Once a week. Maybe ten days."

"Then you're close."

"Yes."

"Buddies."

Carey did not like being set up with this heavy-handed logic. He knew the next statement would be, "Then he must tell you things about the school," but instead Mladen looked at him hard.

"Are you queer?"

Carey was too surprised to answer.

"I mean it. Are you both queer?"

He shook his head.

"*You're* not, you're saying. But you can't say to me *he's* not. They say Ian is a homo."

Carey paused, nodded again, and for a second he thought that was a mistake, but Mladen was serious, even afraid of him in some way.

He seemed a little relieved and they began to walk slowly up the ramp.

"Jesus, and you still hang around with him? Doesn't it give you the creeps? I mean, I've seen him myself. Once my folks and I saw them, him and his boyfriend, at a restaurant. They didn't see us. I knew he was queer then."

Even by listening to Mladen, Carey felt as if he were doing something wrong to Ian. But he needed to get through all this, to show Mladen the letter.

"He doesn't bother me, if that's what you mean. He's never touched me."

"But don't you worry? Don't you sometimes think he might?"

"It isn't that way."

Mladen was quiet for a moment. They stood at the top step between the giant figures of Castor and Pollux.

"You know, if they knew, they'd fire him."

"Who?"

"Wise. Those people."

Carey put a hand on his arm. "You won't tell anyone what I've told you?"

He shook his head.

"Even your parents?"

"No. Although I bet they know."

They walked on toward the palazzo's door, and Carey said, "I shouldn't have said anything."

Mladen shrugged, then stopped again. "One thing more. How did you know? What makes you sure?"

"He told me."

"Why?"

"Because we're friends. He didn't want any confusion, I guess."

They passed Constantine, who still held up a hand in warning; maybe, Carey thought, only gesturing to the blank stones across from him.

"You're strange, Carey, but I'm fucking glad you're not queer. That would have finished it for us, you know."

"You Serbo-Croatian jerk."

He looked at Carey with his red-faced smile and jumped him on the stairs laughing and hooting until one of the guards yelled down to them that he would call in the police from the square unless they behaved.

But Carey still did not feel right and as they wandered around, making jokes about the nudes or herms or even the inverted tents of the wolf's breasts, he decided he did not want to show Ikbal's letter, that he would never talk to anyone about her. He let Mladen wander ahead of him and for a long time he stood in front of the figure of a dancing maenad, her down-thrust face expressionlessly rapt, knife flung wildly over her shoulder, in her falling arm the severed hindquarters of a fawn, and her garments swung and rippled like waves of her own violence breaking out. He could hear the scraping of Mladen's shoes in the next room, and suddenly he was frightened as if in a dream—such absolute silence surrounded her frozen agitation, such muted intensity was held by everything he knew, his friends, school, even Alberto and his mother, and finally himself. Pieces, shards, the torn edges of stone were in every room. He pulled Mladen along by the arm, saying he was hungry. Mladen did not mind. He had not found any pretty girls to follow around in the museum.

Bored by the Veneto, the Borghese, the well-lit promenades, Carey and Mladen began to wander more and more in the darker areas of town. There were few lights on the fringes of the Circus Maximus and the bushes were tall and thick. They would walk beyond the obelisk of Porta Capena to the Baths of Caracalla and massive chunks of shadow. The whores knotted around the fires that splashed on the ancient brickwork, their limbs and grimacing faces. As they passed a dark niche someone would mutter, a hand thrust out, or the pale faces of two intense talkers would go dead at their approach, watching them pass stiffly on. For Carey the danger was close to some lurking fantasy. At any moment it might happen, as if by some dark fish lunging out of shadows he might be carried off into something terrible he did not imagine, a place with everything he dreaded yet wanted.

But afterward he would remember how no one much cared. The women might try them from a distance, hiking a skirt up in those tongues of light until he and Mladen were close enough to reveal their gawky arms and legs, their blank and staring faces, or some man might straighten up from a tree he leaned against with his bicycle, holding out something in his hand, but he would withdraw quickly. Mladen always spoke in low tones, as if they were conspirators or half asleep.

They had just passed the obelisk. Mladen was more jumpy than usual and kept looking back, often did not listen when Carey said something. Finally he stopped walking.

"Don't look back now, but in a moment. We'll walk on. Tell me if you see a little man with his hands in his jacket. He's very fat."

The figure was standing on the curb staring off to one side.

"You see him? He's been walking with us since Piazza Venezia."

"Oh, c'mon." Mladen liked to play games, sometimes to trick him, often just inventing a melodrama he half believed himself.

"I mean it. Look," and he grabbed Carey's arm, making him sit on the bench beside him. "Keep looking at me as if we're talking, but watch now and tell me what he does."

The man looked like any other stroller, except he was out of place there. He seemed to think of something and paused, stroked his cheek with a hand, and then he lit a cigarette, the match flaring out a round face with thick-lensed glasses. Carey described all this to Mladen sotto voce, and how the man now leaned against the bus stop sign.

"C'mon. Watch."

Mladen stood and they walked on, the ruins beginning to loom nearby, the first fire to their right. When Carey looked back the man was still coming behind them at the same interval but always managing to look on the point of going somewhere else.

"I think I saw him this morning too," Mladen said. "Near my house."

They began to walk faster. Carey was trying to get hold of himself, as if he had waked in the middle of the night to sense a stranger moving about in his room.

"Why? What is it?"

"My father told me we should be careful. The Trieste thing."

A car drove past slowly. At the open intersection ahead it made a circle, then drove back on the other side of the street, its occupants staring at them. Mladen grabbed his arm. The car had pulled over to the side of the road. The little man, hardly taller than the roof of the car, was standing close to the driver's window, talking. Mladen turned quickly.

"Don't run yet, it's too soon. Start when I do."

Carey already was out of breath. Something moved in the shadows of the nearest wall and he shied.

*"Buo' seraah,"* a cracked voice wailed, a pale hand and leg thrust into the light.

They were almost at the intersection. Carey was certain he could hear the quiet purring of the car behind them.

"Cross the street, run up there. *Now!"*

Mladen burst to the left, Carey followed, heard a shriek of spinning wheels, an engine accelerating. They were across, the car spun into the open square, already one of its doors opening, a man jumping out, the car trying to cut across in front, but Carey was on the sidewalk. He could hear someone else running, and then he shut down every sense and pursued Mladen's driving legs, and there was not enough air for him to breathe. The car was behind them again, Mladen swerved, the sidewalk widened, and they ducked through the beaded doorway of a small bar.

They stood panting, staring at the startled faces turned to them from the bar, then they faced the doorway but no one came in. Mladen looked out.

"The car's across the street."

Carey heard some words behind them, laughter. He wanted to turn and blurt something to them, make them help.

— 214 —

"Tell them to call the police," he said to Mladen.

But Mladen made Carey promise to keep quiet and stand in a corner near the door. He bought a slug and went to the phone.

By the time his father arrived, Mladen was enjoying the adventure, swaggering a little, but Carey was still jittery. Every face in the room seemed hostile to him, and he expected them all to turn at some signal from the doorway and put down their drinks. Instead someone treated him to coffee. A man with a broad toothless smile said he was glad to see an American, and in broken English learned, he said, in a prison camp near Pisa, praised the brave General Eisenhower.

His father was angry and Mladen became truculent.

"Absurd, absurd," he said, trying after his first outburst in Yugoslavian to use English so that Carey could have a share of his anger. "I have told Mladen he must not put himself in such jeopardy now. We are getting threats each day at the embassy. And so. Now you see I was not joking, Mladen. This is serious."

But in the safety of the car as they wound up the Gianicolo to take him home, Carey wondered if they had made it all up. There had been no car, no fat man when they left the café. Couldn't that car, the chase, the stalking figure, have been something they invented? At the worst, maybe the men in the car wanted their money.

Mr. Makarovic insisted on taking Carey upstairs and on speaking with Nancy, who stood in the hallway in her slippers and bathrobe, face becoming more vexed as he politely explained.

"I think we'll have to keep an eye on these boys for a while," he said before leaving. "I don't know what they could have been doing way out there."

Nancy thanked him. They went in, the door shut behind him, Carey tried to go into his room, but her voice stopped him.

"I think we need to talk."

They went to sit in the living room. As they passed her room, Carey saw she had been reading in bed, the covers disheveled, book spread-eagled where she had set it down to come to the door. For a while her words were what he expected, chiding him for wandering out there, asking if they did it often, what were they thinking of, didn't they know a city could be dangerous? He did not say much. He thought she was a little suspicious of what he and Mladen might be thinking up, as she probably had been ever since a few nights ago when she and Carey were walking home together from a concert, and a whore, very drunk, clutching the torn neck of her dress tightly against the cold, had accosted them, saying that she was "more attractive than that one, and younger besides," and whatever it was, she'd charge him less. They had laughed about it after the first shocked moments when they had passed on, but Carey knew that his mother saw how available all that was, especially when she said thoughtfully as they jiggled along in the bus, "Does that happen to you often?" and he had said the worst thing possible: "I don't know."

But now he was tired, and very confused. He mistrusted everything that had happened that night. Had he and Mladen really been afraid, or had they merely wanted to be? Had those men been after them or had Mr. Makarovic scared Mladen so much that he could invent a whole drama out of the chance harassment of some thugs? He wanted it to be a real adventure, but the stronger that desire became, the more he suspected he could be inventing it.

"Are you listening to me, Carey?"

"Can I go to bed now?"

She was sitting very straight beside him. He could see she wanted something from him, a reassurance, a pledge. But he felt stubborn.

"First I want some answers."

"I don't have any."

"You owe me some."

He did not answer, and he could tell he was not hiding his anger very well.

"Carey, dear, what is the matter lately? You seem so quiet. We don't talk anymore."

"You're not around much."

"I guess that's fair enough."

"Besides, I want to be left alone."

"I don't think you should be alone so much. I'm sorry, but I'm worried. That's all."

"What for?"

"Something's on your mind. I want to know what it is. To help you, if I can."

This was an old argument, her fear of his solitude, but that only made it worse. She had always needed to know his time was full, tucked down at the edges, not free to "just drift." But he was even more afraid she suspected there was a person filling those seemingly blank spaces in his mind and days and he did not want her to touch that in any way.

"It's none of your business."

"Don't talk to me that way. I've had more than my fill from you tonight."

"Then let me go to bed, dammit."

She slapped him. It stung, but he tried not to flinch. She had never hit him before. Her voice said huskily, "Don't speak to me that way," but her face was wide-eyed, shocked.

He said nothing. She gripped her hand tightly and it fluttered. She let go and it rose quickly to touch him where she had struck. She blinked. "I'm sorry. Tired. We both are. But sometimes lately you are so exasperating."

"How?" He was surprised how choked his voice was.

"Oh, look at that trip to Orvieto. You were so mean. Alberto was trying so hard. It's not easy for him either, you know."

Carey shrugged. It was not the blow that left him still angry.

"Maybe I don't like him."

"Why?"

"He's a phony."

"That's not fair. You hardly know him. I'll tell you what I think, Carey. You made up your mind not to like him from the start. I think you're jealous because for the first time you can tell this is someone I really like."

"I hope you do."

"Why?"

"If you didn't I suppose what you're doing would be wrong."

"Go on."

"That's all."

"No. I mean, what are we doing that would be wrong?"

"Sleeping together."

The hand came loose, he tensed to be slapped again, but she did not. Immediately he wished she had. He felt awful about saying that because it was nothing he really meant, more a way of slapping back.

"I guess we'd better talk about this some other time." She stood. "You have to do something now, Carey. You have to remember that I am like you or any other person, not just your mother. I don't know what I'm doing any better than anyone else, and all this is terribly confusing. Be as angry as you have to be, but don't expect me to be perfect."

He could have given in then. He did not really want to

leave her with that. But at the same time he did not want to tell her anything about what was really on his mind.

"Can I go to bed?"

She nodded, he stood and walked toward the door to his room, each step away from her making him feel more hollow.

"Carey?"

"Yes."

"Promise me we'll talk about these things again, soon?"

He nodded, closed the door between them, and as soon as he could, he turned out the light and sat naked on the edge of his bed. The dull light from the window caught the spreading ivory of the hulking piano, the book of opened music. He heard her turn the lights out and return to her own room. He lay on his back for a while held in a fierce stiffness like some knight in armor. He would not give in, would not give in.

# 4

Too early in the morning the front doorbell rang. A bright, cold sun cut shadows on the marble floor and Nancy held still, dazed by standing suddenly, her eyes blinking at the contrasts. The buzz was insistent.

The portiere's wife stood smiling, apologetic, her hand thrust out with a white enevelope.

*"Mi dispiace, signora, ma c'é un telegramma."*

Nancy took the message, told the woman to wait, and brought back some lire for her to take to the messenger below. She closed the door, turned to find Carey standing in his bedroom doorway, eyes blinking. She was afraid to open it. Like phone calls in the middle of the night, telegrams were not to be trusted. The words were the usual poor phonetic rendering of her own language, but she read it out loud: "'Arriving Rome night of January second. Staying at Imperial. Hope to see you, Stafford and Alice.'" It was postmarked Naples.

"But that was yesterday," she said.

Carey was frowning, took the telegram. "What are they doing here?"

Over breakfast, the sunlight reflecting off china and chrome, making dazzling pools where it struck the marble, they tried to imagine Stafford and Alice in Rome. Nancy was glad they had something else to talk about because the previous evening still hung over them both, but she could tell he would not want to discuss it. The resistance in his face held his smile to a mere flicker.

"Strange, isn't it," she said. "But I'm not sure I really want to see them."

"We have to."

"I don't mean we won't. In fact, I'd better call immediately. But that all seems so remote now."

"What will we do with them?"

So she coaxed out a few ideas of places to go, decided to call and see how they felt. She dialed the Imperial. Yes, please wait a moment, they were certain to be in their rooms still. She found herself talking to Stafford, his voice a little crisp but relieved to make contact. It was odd about the telegram, sent three days before. Not odd at all, Nancy said, laughing. They were lucky to get it before the Newfanes left. Which would be how long? Well, they weren't sure, and then followed brief explanations: he and Alice feeling pent-up at home, needed to get away for a while, Europe seemed good, take in Italy, never seen it before, lovely time on the boat. And here was Alice. Solid. Her sentences in square chunks followed by silences that Nancy was supposed to fill, but found she could not. She was certain she sensed something strained in both their voices. Perhaps weariness? Silence. Yes. They were both tired. A touch of seasickness for Alice on the boat. Naples, well, Naples was difficult at times. Then Stafford's voice with a suddenness that could only have been from seizing the phone very eagerly. Could they all gather for dinner? Nancy hesitated. Then plunged. Yes, why not all get together at a little place they knew. Pierluigi's. Very authentic. And she and Carey would be joined by a friend of hers. But in the meantime perhaps they would like to see Carey, an excellent guide to the city. As she said it she saw him throw his eyes upward, his old "Oh, Mom" look that she had not been given for months, but he nodded. Fine, fine, and Stafford promised a good lunch for his services. Wouldn't she? But Nancy was sorry. Errands. Her day off. There seemed to be nothing more to say and she promised Carey would be there in an hour.

She could tell that Carey minded less than his balky movements indicated. He dressed slowly, went downstairs first to check the mail, brought her nothing but the latest electricity bill. He was at the door again, jacket slung over his shoulder.

"It's too bad Ikbal Dorati is out of town. We could ask her to come."

"Why?" He looked ferociously at her, and she wondered if he would go on to say something angry. Evidently she was not to make suggestions.

"Stafford might enjoy meeting your new teacher."

He was biting the corner of one lip, staring past her at the balcony. "They wouldn't like each other."

She smiled, imagining how true that was. Stafford would be very defensive with anyone so accomplished in his own art.

"Carey, please be careful." That was her only overt reference to the previous evening and she watched him choose to ignore it.

"I need some money."

She found her purse. "Don't let them pay for everything."

He held out his hand, she put the money in it, and for a halting moment she saw him standing completely apart from her, as if the square of sunlight he stood in and the dark cut of the doorway's shadow falling across their hands put them in two different worlds. He did not seem to notice, turned, glanced back once over his shoulder as he closed the door, waving slightly with his free hand. She stared at the bright stone where he had stood. Slowly she moved her hand out across the line of shadow into the light. It cast a long-fingered image on the floor.

She turned quickly and walked to the balcony doors, opened them and stood carefully looking down. He appeared below, standing on the curb before crossing the street and beginning to walk very slowly, hands in pockets, down the sidewalk. The man in the kiosk must have said good morning because Carey's voice, wordless, only its tones, carried back to her. She watched him all the way down to the piazza's edge, then he sauntered out of sight, but she was seeing something she did not know how to explain at first, a kind of physical presence and motion that she had not seen so clearly before. The lanky stride, the slight twist to his shoulders as he strolled along, above all the lithe, tight motion of his hips were no longer boyish. That was still to be seen in the lean and bony frame, the much too youthful neck; but his motions were set now, and would be this way forever. If it was like her gait, she could not tell, and it certainly did not seem like Frank's, he had always come down hard on his heels, his hands never in his pockets when he was going somewhere. She put her hands to her face, over her eyes, still trying to catch some afterimage of that walk. It was simply attractive, a motion of body that in any other male she would have seen as sensuous, did see now, until she resolved that sexual tone into a small, intense pain of separation, some last membrane cut between them.

She put away the dishes and went out to sit on the couch. The air coming in from the balcony was fresh and warmed by the winter sun. She would call Alberto soon about tonight. He would come or not as he chose. But first she wanted some silence. She wanted to fill it with clarity. She closed her eyes, breathed deeply. If only she could rise, perhaps to hover on some balcony overlooking the plan of their lives, like that huge plaster model of Rome at the height of the empire. She would look down on their small figures wandering in the maze of streets and monuments, would smile to see them bump and grope, then reaching with a long pole she would prod them in the right way toward...what? Her own image collapsed. She opened her eyes.

All she could imagine was a city with no destination, streets and walls and alleys ending in fountains or the brick grimed by centuries. It was not that she was trying to find a way out, or in, or around. Maybe at most she feared reaching out and no longer being able to take Carey's hand. Then she would need that balcony to stand on and look around for him. At times like this she thought the city was too perfect an image of her mind, all their minds, as if Rome were the human brain itself, a convoluted surface of skittering figures and fruit and all the traffic of conscious motion, but with layers beneath of time older than memory, dark stones with forgotten languages, springs of water never rising to the sun but heard in the deepest basement of some ruin, and then a final immovable silence.

How would she extricate herself enough to see clearly what they should do? Her body pressed closely to the ripeness of fruit stands, the human crush of odors in a bus, as if lovers wrapped arms and thighs around and penetrated her everywhere. She wanted to see Alberto, herself, Carey in clear diagrams with arrows: "You can go this way or that—Plan A, Plan B."

She untucked her leg, let her numbed foot gather feeling, and walked to the kitchen to make some tea. Lately she had begun to believe that the only way she would be able to deal clearly with their lives would be to leave. Even being alone as she was now did not seem to help. What if the problem was simple, merely that as long as they were in Rome, there was no solution? When they had first arrived, the idea of leaving had been something to combat since it was fear of the unknown place and of their isolation. Such a retreat she could label cowardice. Now it was harder. The divorce decree was final, Frank had moved, and Philadelphia would be a very different place. As for Rome, she had made contact with the place and its people, and now it was a matter of how much she wanted that to get under her skin. Would there come a point when it would be impossible to go, or too difficult to extricate herself? And Carey. After scenes like last night, after watching him make another leap into a life less and less attached to hers, wouldn't it be better to at least watch him become more unknown in surroundings more known? It was all so blurred, unfixed, shimmering.

She lifted the strainer, smelling the grassy steam of tea, then let it down again to steep further, and as it often happened now, as if the only clarity available in such a place as Rome were memory, she saw the yard stretching to the broad-limbed maple, the slope of hill beyond, and she was standing on the porch, a bright sun so dazzling her eyes that she had to shade them to see Carey hanging upside down from a limb, swinging slightly with his arms extended toward the ground. She could not tell his age, or when this was, or why she was asking him to come down to the ground. Perhaps fear of his falling, perhaps to tell him something. She leaned on the stove for a moment, trying to understand why such a simple impression that she suspected had not done anything to her at the time should rise now with such clarity, but caked also with so many layers of unfocused intensity. She wanted to reach forward with her arms and hold his figure tightly to her, still small and weightless as he seemed at such a distance.

She went to the balcony with her cup of tea, sipped it, then tilted her face up, eyes closed, letting the sun fall flatly on her skin. She breathed in deeply. No matter how baffled, sometimes she could not imagine anything better than this, being alone, lost in herself.

"S'accomodi, s'accomodi." Franco bowed them to their places, slapped the table perfunctorily with his white cloth, and was quickly at her shoulder to help Nancy take off her coat.

The room was already crowded. They had met by the Palazzo Farnese, Carey coming with the Newfanes whom he had not deserted all day, and Alberto arriving at the last moment just as Nancy was deciding he would not come. They had strolled slowly down the Via Monserrato, trying to be politely conversational in the push and jostle of traffic and passersby. Yes, they were much taken with Rome, but above all by the expertise of their young guide who even spoke this terrible language so well.

Now, in the lighted room as they resolved the problem of where to sit, Nancy was certain her intuition had been right—there was something overly stiff, even taut, about Stafford's motions, and Alice was very subdued, not looking at anyone for more than a moment. They both carried their portion of any conversation, but never turned to each other. Alice moved brusquely to the other side of the table opposite Stafford. Nancy looked at Carey, he caught her glance, the gesture she made of putting her head slightly to one side as if asking him a question, and he shrugged quickly as if to say it had been odd all day.

The wine appeared immediately at Alberto's order, and he began to coax Stafford into conversation about their boat trip. Alice wanted to know the names of some shops, the best area for shoes, and Nancy, beside her, did her best. But then it was time to translate the menu as Franco hovered, a little annoyed that they would even consult it, but Alberto explained that their friends from America wanted to know all there was.

"It wasn't so much the rough weather I objected to," Stafford continued, "as the awful service. The ship was a mess, simply a mess."

Alberto commiserated, Carey played with his fork. Nancy leaned to him, speaking quietly.

"You had a good day?"

They were near enough to a loud table to make their own conversation private if they wanted. He looked quickly at Stafford and Alice and said, "Okay."

"You went places?"

"Vatican, Forum, taxis all over. Wherever they wanted."

"Is everything all right?"

He leaned closer to her, staring down at the fork he twisted around in his fingers.

"Weird. Talking only to me all the time. Never each other. They always wanted to go different places. I had to choose."

The antipasto arrived and she did not want to risk more so she smiled and touched his hand briefly with hers. She could imagine him touring around all day like an interpreter. He looked tired. Alberto and Stafford were discussing the disorderly conduct of southern Italians and she could tell that Stafford was restraining himself from condemning Italians in general. At home he had always appeared very cosmopolitan, but here his dark blazer, the ascot, that rigid back, were the waxwork pose of what an English gentleman should have been twenty years ago. Old movies. What startled her most of all was to see how quickly Alice drained her glass of wine and poured more, already twice since it had arrived; Alice who always seemed so calm and set.

"So you decided on a vacation?"

The woman looked up quickly, an olive impaled on her fork. "Yes, why?"

"Such a surprise to see you."

Alice laughed sharply, ate the olive, spit the pit into her palm.

"Surprise for us too. But it seemed necessary."

Nancy wanted to return to shoes, anything to avoid the whiff of some anger she thought private and did not want to share.

"Why Italy, I don't know," Alice continued. "I favored Mexico. Always wanted to go there. But we must take a boat instead. Tour the Continent. His idea."

Even though Stafford was listening to Alberto, Nancy could tell by the strain in his eyes as they flicked slightly toward them and away, that he was taking in both conversations, and Alice spoke louder than she needed to.

"To tell the truth, Nancy, you see it's more than a vacation. I had a little breakdown. Travel. Good idea, travel. Diversion. Like what they used to do for silly young ladies when they chose the wrong man."

Stafford had stopped even trying to pretend to be listening to Alberto. He stared at her.

"It was good advice. Dr. Tilson," he said firmly.

"Your advice. The two of you." Alice drained her glass, reached for the decanter. His hand held it by the neck.

"Not too much, eh?"

She tugged and he let go, his face flushing slightly.

"Both of us, really," he said to Nancy. "Needing a rest. A change. You know."

Nancy felt helpless. She wanted to agree with both of them and find some impersonal ground for conversation. Such poisonous bitterness she did not want to taste further.

"Very restful," Alice was saying as Franco substituted some fettuccini for her half-empty plate. "Tell them how restful Naples was, Stafford."

A man behind them let out a great burst of laughter, and

Alice grinned maliciously as if he had understood her thoughts. Stafford turned very palely to Carey.

"I'm sorry we won't have a chance to meet your new teacher. I remember hearing of her."

Alberto leaned forward as if trying to push back a great weight. "Yes, yes. Mrs. Dorati, superb," and he proceeded to enumerate her accomplishments while Stafford, his head held as stiffly as if it were on a pole, shifted his eyes around the room uneasily. Alice seemed content to wind her fettuccini around her fork. She leaned to Nancy, speaking so low she could barely hear.

"I'm sorry. Really, I am. I will try to keep myself under control. You see, control is everything. I'm trying very hard. There were these terrible dreams for a while and I'm afraid once or twice I simply found myself interrupting Stafford's lessons and saying awful things." Her upper lip was sweating heavily and Nancy tried to find a moment to say something sympathetic, but there was no room. "Stafford lost all patience with me, and I don't know what I'd do without him, really..." and Nancy was alarmed to see how scared and frail the woman looked, her face almost cringing. But quickly she gave a sharp laugh, took another drink, and said, "Except go to Mexico."

They were all eating, and Alberto caught Nancy's eyes, turned his mouth down slightly with eyebrows raised, then leaned forward to tell them one of his anecdotes and even Stafford laughed. Well into the next course, Nancy could hardly believe what had gone on before. They were simply a group of friends in a restaurant. Carey told them about his school.

A singer and guitarist wandered in, recognized Nancy and Alberto.

"Some nights," he said as they played, the singer rolling his head from side to side as he stood behind Alberto, "when it is not crowded, we dance a little when they sing. Especially when it is warm enough for us to be eating outside. But it is too crowded tonight."

"Just as well," Alice said. "Stafford hates to dance."

"Yes," he said quickly. "Always have. Ever since dancing school. Hated it."

"Actually he just hates to stand up and move his body around with other people. Too inhibited. 'Fraid of making a fool of himself. I'm not. Love to dance."

"Well," and Alberto pressed some lire into the hand of the

singer who was still in some endless verse about the sorrows of unfaithfulness, "I wish we could."

"Can anyway." She was standing with her hands out, large and circular hips swaying cumbersomely. The guitarist grinned, his partner blew her a kiss, Franco clapped from the doorway and someone at a nearby table said, *"Brava, bellissima."*

Stafford's face was crimson. "Sit down," he hissed.

She stared at him, her hips stopped moving, her arms descended. Nancy watched her uneasily, but the woman sat as quickly as she had stood. The musicians shrugged, thanked Alberto, moved on. For a moment no one said anything. Stafford's hand had started trembling slightly on the stem of his glass.

"That was good fish," Carey said loudly.

Alice poured herself another glass. "Do you have a girl friend, Carey?" She leaned forward so she could see around Nancy.

Carey opened his mouth to speak, but he never did more than gape. The hand that held Alice's wineglass had darted and the contents of the glass were in Stafford's face. He blinked, blindly groping for his napkin.

"Now you tell them," she said in a toneless, low voice, leaning her head toward him. "Tell them about your girl friend in Naples."

Stafford could see again. Franco hovered nearby, a nervous look on his face, but Alberto gestured quickly to him.

"I think maybe we'd better go," Stafford said.

"Or shall I?"

"Alice, please."

She laughed again. "A chambermaid. Can you imagine anything so trite?"

Nancy knew she must look like Alberto and Carey, perfectly still in their places and wide-eyed. Stafford spoke to his plate.

"She has these delusions, I'm afraid . . ."

"Delusions? Is it a delusion to find your husband firmly planted between two thighs and his pants around his ankles in midafternoon in a hotel in Naples?"

Alberto looked as if he might laugh, but instead he made another motion with his hand and when Franco approached, he said simply, *"Il conto, Franco,"* but the waiter must have had that already in mind and slipped Alberto a piece of paper.

"Alice, I don't think these people care about our squabbles."

Suddenly the woman's hand was on Nancy's arm like a claw. "Not true." Her face was puffing, eyes beginning to tear. "They do. Old friends. Even in Italy. It's true, Nancy, this cheap, fat floozy of a chambermaid rutting in a bed with him when I was supposed to be at the museum and he said he had the shits, and why did we ever come to this awful place anyway?" She put her face in her hands for a moment, then dropped them both to her lap, her face drained. "There, that's over."

Nancy had put her hand under the table, found Carey's and gripped it. She actually felt a little sick. Alberto stood, leaving money on the table.

"Perhaps a little fresh air?"

They went out to the street and Nancy breathed deeply. They walked in a slow group along the high bank of the Tiber. Alberto pointed back up the river to the lump of light and brown stone that was Castel Sant' Angelo, the final spread wings of Saint Michael. "Delivered the city from the plague," he was explaining and they all pretended to listen. No one suggested stopping for a drink or going somewhere else. "We'll need some rest," Stafford said as if to their unspoken thoughts. "It's off to Florence tomorrow."

"I can't wait for Paris," Alice said almost as if she meant it.

At the bus stop they shook hands. Alice kissed Nancy on the cheek shyly and muttered "Sorry" in her ear, but Nancy could only smile in return. She watched Stafford shaking Carey's hand. They separated and Stafford was saying something about practicing hard when his voice choked, and suddenly he had stepped forward, placed both hands on Carey's shoulders, hugged him very quickly. "I miss you," he said, and Nancy, for the first time that evening was sad, even more so when Alice's voice by her shoulder said tonelessly as if talking to herself, "He's always wanted a son."

They watched the Newfanes step up into the bus, already uneasily looking about to decide what the next move should be, and then they were gone.

"Come," Alberto said, "I will treat," and they walked to the nearest bar where Carey told them everything strange that had happened that day.

"Do you think," he finally asked, "it's true what she said about Naples?"

Nancy shook her head. "We'll never know." She was drinking sambuca, pushing aside the coffee bean they called "the fly" with the tip of her tongue. She wanted to say that she did not care to know. But when she looked at Carey, his face was staring past Alberto to the counter where a woman was leaning, her tight-bound hips plush and creased.

"I hope so," he said. "For his sake."

Alberto was shaking, and as if they were children who had been held back too long, they began to laugh uncontrollably.

# 5

"Come in. Come in."

Ikbal took Carey's face in her hands and kissed him. He could not hold back, and both arms slipped around her. His music tumbled, he hugged her, and afraid he had gone too far, he backed off so suddenly that she staggered, breathless but laughing.

"You big bear," and she put her arm through his, leading him to the couch. "Look at you. Don't you ever stop growing? It's only been four weeks and you've grown at least a foot."

He could not answer, laughed, shook his head, only wanting to reach for her again. She had come back unexpectedly and called. "Come, bring your music. Play for me. Let's talk."

In spite of her laughter, the ease with which she touched him, brushing the hair away from his eyes absentmindedly as she asked one question on top of the other before he could fully answer, dark circles were under her eyes, a drawn and weary look to her mouth when she paused.

"And your *Winterreise?* How does it go with you and Ian?"

"Ian says he has never sung it better."

"And Pierre. You've met him?"

"Yes." And he told her about the orphanage.

"You know about Pierre and Ian too, then?"

"As much as Ian told me."

She held his music on her lap, pulling together the various sheets that had come loose in falling.

"How is it you can deal so well with all these things? You are much too old for your age."

He wanted to say it all then, to tell her how much older he could be if she would let him.

"Never mind. Play something. Mozart."

She stood. He did not want a lesson in music. He rose slowly to take the books, was walking to the piano when her voice stopped him.

"I can't bear it, can't stand hearing another piano."

She strode by him quickly, slammed down the cover so hard that the sounding board picked up a muddied echo of all the strings. Her back was to him, but the hand that rested its fingertips on the music stand was trembling. She was looking out the window.

"It's a fine day, isn't it?"

"Yes."

"Do you have to be home soon?"

"No."

She whirled, smiling again. "Then come on. We'll have a picnic. We'll go out the Appia and sit in a field in the sun and have a long talk. *Va bene?*"

He nodded. She bustled around in her kitchen plucking up this or that, making him write down a list of what they should buy while she filled a small net bag with wine and some wrapped utensils and half-loaf of bread. All the time he tried to watch her hands or be looking at her face when she turned, but he could not keep his eyes off the contours of her slim body as she spun and stooped and reached like a dancer.

"There. You carry everything since you are the man." She held out the bag.

He barely managed to say "Yes" before she was off again, pulling on her coat, scarf, urging him downstairs and to the market for cheese and fruit, and soon they were on a bus, rattling off through the Porta San Sebastiano. He recounted his adventure with Mladen, emphasizing the dangers, and she frowned, told him they were silly to take such risks. Didn't he know how indifferently cruel such people were, especially the political ones? But he did not mind being scolded by her, enjoyed her concern.

They went as far as the last bus stop and began walking. Smothered in her long, tight coat, its large collar up, even though the sun was so warm to him that he wanted to take off his sweater, she seemed very small, and they walked along side by side, each holding a handle of the bag so it swung between them.

"Have you been out here?" She peered at him over the top of her collar, her voice muffled into it.

"No."

"Lovely, don't you think? It was even better ten years ago. Less was paved, fewer cars."

But only two had passed and some Vespas scooting out or back carrying a hunter or goggled farmer with his spraddled woman clinging behind.

They walked for a mile or two and turned off into a field on a cart track that wound up among some ruins onto a mound of soil, the base of a ragged medieval tower. They sat and leaned against it. His trousers were covered with burdocks, and he picked at them on the fringes of her coat that she had spread to sit on. It was very warm facing the sun, the road so distant he could barely hear the traffic.

"I came home early because I couldn't do the last concert."

He waited for her to continue, but she started wrestling with the cork.

"Here, you do it."

The cork released with a jerk that made his arm fling back and he beat his funny bone against a rock. He hopped and giggled in pain while she tried not to laugh. She insisted on a good sip of wine to help the pain.

"For a moment in Milano, I wanted to be performing, and I was playing well again. But the rest of the time I was fighting. I was pulling out notes like nails, one at a time, no sweep, no wholeness. I didn't want to be doing it."

"Why?"

She had leaned back, her hands folded in her lap. He could understand what she was saying, but could not quite feel it—the idea of the music dying like that. He could not remember a time when it was not there, waiting for him. She turned slightly to look at him.

"I hope it never happens to you. Because I think it's for you like it is for me, or it will be. Everything else can be fine in our lives—health, enough money to live on, friends, peace in all things, but if the music isn't there and going well, nothing is right. We are a little sick without it. Do you know?"

"I think so." What had come into his mind was how he had felt the past weeks without her, and that sounded like much the same thing.

She looked out across the field. "I don't know why it goes. I can't even tell when it will. That's the crazy thing about concerts. You sign up to do them months, years ahead. Oh, I never doubt I'll play, and play well. I did this time. We get professional about that and know all the tricks. I can do it for them. But if it's not there for me, if I am not the instrument the music is passing through, then it is no good, only fingers."

A large crow flew raggedly into sight pursued by two smaller birds rising and diving. They watched silently for a while and concentrated on lunch, passing the bottle back and forth. He sensed she had more on her mind but did not know how to help her. After they had finished eating, they leaned back with the bottle between them.

"They were angry at me when I cancelled. I said I was ill, would be sure to give them a very reasonable contract next time." She pulled at a stalk. "Right now, I am not interested in a next time."

The hand was shaking slightly again.

"Perhaps I need a rest. I'll start by thinking of it that way. It isn't the music, Carey. I still love the music. I will tell you something you'll think odd. Yesterday when I reached home, I sat down, last night it was, and played through the program, all of it, as if I were there. And it was all right again. The connections. I think I'm merely tired of playing for others. I want to be alone for a while."

She drank from the nearly empty bottle, then handed it to him, smiling.

"But that's the catch. When it is good, I want to share it with others—and there we are again." She shook her head violently as if flinging off her thoughts. "Now. Have I said enough to make you wonder about this life you want?"

He took the last warm gulps of sharp Chianti and stood the bottle up, glistening and empty. She rose, held out a hand.

"Come on," and she pulled him up.

Her sleeves rolled, hair tucked under the collar of her shirt, she hiked up her skirt, pranced down from their mound and began running over the hummocked earth. She stopped suddenly, held out her arms and turned and turned, a pirouette flinging her skirt out like a disk from her waist and when he caught up to her she stopped, the cloth gathered in wild pleats, and she pushed him with both hands, said, "Catch me if you can," running across the field toward distant trees where a flock of small birds were rising and falling like motes of dust in the branches. He ran, tripped on the uneven ground, rose, ran on. She was fast, her arms swinging, her hair loose now, white legs flashing from the buckling flutter of skirt. He caught up to her finally, grabbed her arm, they lurched, were into the grove of trees, leaned panting against a trunk, and he did not care—with the wine, the sun, her heaving body backed against a tree, his own hands flat on its bark as if he had caught the tree, not her—he kissed her. They looked at each other, gathering breath. She did not seem surprised.

She reached up and held his face between her hands. He strained forward, wanting to kiss her again.

"Wait," she said. "Come. Sit down."

They sat in the crisscrossed shadow of the bare tree and the birds fluttered like loosed leaves dropping from branch to branch. He sat forward on his knees, feet under him, still holding her hand, not knowing what to do.

"Carey, have you ever made love before?"

He shook his head, afraid to speak.

"Don't you think this is all a little too much? I mean given your age, mine?"

He could not look at her anymore but had to stare out over the blurred fields, back to their tower. If he only knew what to do or say. Her hand touched his chin and turned his face to her.

"Don't look so sad. You must talk to me now."

"I love you" was all he could say.

"È serio, allora," she murmured, and when she leaned forward to kiss him again he held his breath. She stood. Her hand urged him up, he rose, and she let him hold her tightly for a few minutes.

She turned, and still holding one hand started to tow him out. He moved his feet reluctantly.

"Come."

"Where?"

"Back to Rome."

She kept walking. He stopped and she did too rather than break the link.

"Why can't we stay?"

She put her arm through his and stood closely at his side.

"I don't want to make love in the middle of a field in broad daylight."

He followed her, fearful that at any moment something would happen to the world to keep time from moving. They walked back and collected their belongings at the tower, strolled to the bus stop, and he tried to think of something to say but could not. Finally as they were waiting, the bus gathering shape distantly down the road, she said, "Do you feel a little silly?" and he nodded, and they burst out laughing

— 234 —

so hard that the two or three people there looked at them as if they were crazy.

In the bus she looked past his face, across the aisle. "Do you know, when I'm in this kind of mood, when I feel so empty, I do almost anything to cover it up. Even though I know that's what I'm doing."

He was afraid she would change her mind before they reached the city, and he should never have said he had not made love before because she might not want him, so he said, "I lied to you. I made love before. Once. It was..." But her hand was gently on his lips.

"I shouldn't have asked. That's your secret."

She looked out the window and held his hand on her lap. Every object in the world around them and flinging past was unbearably swollen, lifted into intensity by his fear that she would change her mind. The city dragged against them, a dream of running through water. And what would he do now that he had lied and would face her naked, not knowing what to do?

In a daze he walked beside her through the square, up the stairs that were totally changed. He stood in her bedroom bright with sunlight, shyly taking off his clothes, waiting to be certain that she was too, and even before they touched, when he saw her move naked toward him, his flesh rose beyond his control and he could not hold back. He was embarrassed, but the way she laughed let him know it did not matter. They lay close for a while and she let his hands wander over her, her breath and lips against his neck, and then he was ready again and when he entered her she said his name, they looked at each other and he closed his eyes, her body moving to his rhythms.

For a few moments before he left he sat with her in the kitchen. She made some tea. He wondered how she could move about so easily, as if her life were the same. Even his voice seemed changed. She smiled when they reached the door, put a hand on the back of his neck and kissed him again.

"Am I all right?" he said quickly and his face burned.

She laughed. "You have some things to learn, perhaps."

"Teach me."

"Practice," she answered, handing him the music he had nearly forgotten.

But he was also afraid, and the joking was not right. He had come so close to her that he could not tell who she was anymore, or who he was—all boundaries, all points of reference wiped out. She no longer was limited to a name, a finite body. She was everywhere because she was in him. Now they were standing in front of a door, and he was Carey Mitchell again and she was Ikbal Dorati, but both of them wholly changed without his knowing in any way what was different. He was almost eager to go, to sit somewhere alone, catch his breath, try to find something to hold onto.

"Come tomorrow. We have our music to do."

One thing more rose in his mind. "Are you sorry?"

She stared at him, put her hand on his neck again, her forehead against his lips.

"No, Carey," her voice said.

But walking slowly up the hill toward home, he wondered what else she *could* say.

That first morning, waking with the early light seeping in his window, Carey wanted to touch her, to have some certainty that he had not imagined it, or worse, that she had not regretted. But he could do nothing but wait for his lesson that morning, wait for the slowest of suns to creep up against the backward pull of the eastern horizon.

Finally the bell jangled far inside her apartment, her footsteps clicked to the door, the bolt slipped back. She was not looking at his eyes but to the side of his face.

"Come in." The voice was clipped, the smile too fixed. He stepped in, the door closed, he turned and his hand rose, but she gripped him by the wrist.

"Wait. Not now. I need some time, Carey. I think we've made a mistake."

He could not speak and something was falling away inside him. She dropped his arm, turned, that lithe figure walked ahead of him to the parlor and he went to the piano, opened the music, began playing—but his mind was still at the doorway, looking for some way to change it all back.

She sat nearby. As usual, she prompted, urged, cajoled, had him stand while she played, listened to him imitate her phrasing. She had chosen him to go to Naples in March where a concert for pupils of various teachers would be held, and now she referred to it often. "This isn't far enough along," she would say.

But by the end of the lesson he was dashing the notes wildly into the space between them, certain that nothing could change this, and then the doorbell announcing the next pupil cut whatever strings had kept his hands moving. She was looking at him as he stood to shuffle the music together.

"I'm sorry, Carey. It's no good."

Them? The music? He could not look at her and held his hands still.

"I mean the lesson, I should have called."

He stepped toward her.

"Please." She put a hand flatly against his chest. "I told you yesterday things might change, quickly."

The doorbell rang again. He thought he would break, but did not want to betray her. They walked side by side to the door.

"I'll call."

"When?"

"Soon." Her hand touched his face. "I promise."

She opened the door to a bright-faced, ringleted girl whose polished voice sang, *"Buon giorno, Signora Dorati,"* and she bobbed in a half-hearted curtsy.

He walked home. A note from Nancy said she would be out to dinner with Alberto. He lay on his bed and tried to close down his mind. But he could not lie still and so he paced from room to room. He wanted at least to walk outside, but what if she called? In the early afternoon he opened the balcony door and looked out over the street, then down to the pavement below.

He would call, do something. He had the phone in hand when he imagined her voice. There was nothing he could say. He sat down at his desk and tried to write a letter. But after a page, he ripped it up. He stared at the wall seeing every seam in the plaster, and he was frightened of his own mind, the way it would go on thinking, imagining, insisting, when all he wanted was for it to turn off or think of something else. He had never so completely felt how powerless he was to make it do anything. With a dizzying glide it began to hover, play over, rearrange the memories of that morning. He should have done this, said that. Surely this gesture, these exact words would have changed her mind. What if, what if.

He was not hungry. He found an opened bottle of wine, and gulped down two tumblers of it. It had started to turn sour but he did not care. He flung the balcony doors wide open, could tell by the slant of light that it was late afternoon. The Vespas and Topolinos were buzzing back into the city, his mother would be leaving work soon but not coming home.

He poured another tumbler of wine, drank it in sips. His mind was beginning to slow down, leave him alone.

But then he saw her, felt her—hair and skin, and her eyes half closed, her bare legs around him and all the long touch of her naked body. She became someone totally outside of him again, another being as far beyond him as that distant tree in the park, and he knew for certain that he could lose her. He said her name.

Later when the phone rang he came to it as if from a deep sleep.

"Carey?"

"Yes."

"How are you?" Her voice was so disembodied.

"Awful."

A silence.

"Can you come?"

He left a note. Meeting Mladen. He named a movie. If the bus had not come soon he would have run all the way, did run after he jumped off the bus, through the winding streets, up the stairs, and she must have heard him coming—the door opened as he spun onto the landing, he lurched in, arms stiffly held out. The door snapped shut and she let him hold onto her for a long time as if he were drowning, would never find enough air.

She was nervous at first, and as they lay together on her bed she turned a dull blue pack of *Nazionali* around and around in her fingers. Sometimes her face could look so sharp.

"We have to come to some understanding, Carey, some rules. About calling. About coming."

He nodded. He would take any restrictions rather than return to the hell of that morning. She snuffed out the cigarette and looked at him.

"I will need some distance at times. Privacy."

He closed his eyes for a moment. Her bare body so close to him made it impossible for him to listen.

"Do you understand?" Her hand touched his neck.

When he opened his eyes she was lying close, face to his face. Her hand began riding slowly up and down his bare back.

She taught him more than how to touch and turn and touch again. He began to know how to hold into himself that white hot center of need he felt for her, to face it down each day, even to enjoy it for its own sake and bear it with him over the long days that often passed between their meetings. He learned when to call and how to, even when to reach out to her and when not to, though he might be in the same room with her. On those days when he saw that mood in her, the dropping away when her body was left far behind by some inner retreat, he would let the music between them suffice, would play for her as best he could and leave, accepting her simple announcement of their next meeting. But he hated those days, would go rambling home, always walking rather than taking the bus even if it rained, seeing everything as drab and unpossessed, mere façades for an endlessly gray, winter descent of rain. But as the weeks went by, he learned to endure those moods because they passed. If he could not be with her, he preferred to be alone. When he was with others, he was afraid that something in the way he acted or talked would show how much he had changed, and he did not want anyone else to enter their world. Next to being with Ikbal, there was nothing more perfect in his life than thinking of her.

# 6

Carey could tell they were working harder at school, as if every teacher had been instructed to increase the homework, to harass them with tests and quizzes. A tautness around them made the bells for class changes harsh, made their recesses full of frantic play. They kicked a soccer ball in the courtyard in violent determination, compared scores of tests as if they were the true index of their selves. Only the count stayed unchanged, his quiet, ineffectual rambling through the sixth book of *The Aeneid* so slow-paced in comparison to the other courses that it seemed indolent. He was brought down from the tower room as though Mrs. Wise thought lowering him from that aerie would plug him efficiently into her machine. But he became even more sardonic, remote, in that room on the second floor where, in the long pauses between phrases as Carey groped for words, he could hear her beginning American history class yapping and shrilling out their answers. The tower was locked up indefinitely since Mrs. Wise said it was "unsuitable for concentration."

She talked to each student individually in those weeks, to discuss the quality of work and "to get to know each of you better," as she had said in a general assembly when she sat half smiling and solid as a sphinx. In each of the first classes students were to repeat the Pledge of Allegiance to the American Flag. "Those of you, of course, who are not American citizens will not be required to," she said calmly, "but we would like you to see what an American school is like." "It never was one," Ian said sharply that afternoon to Carey when they were rehearsing. "It was always a school for English-speaking students." Carey could see the place was getting on Ian's nerves. When it came time for his own interview, he too was nervous. "Sit down," Roberta Wise said, and gestured him toward a cane-bottomed chair beside the desk in the principal's office. "Carey Mitchell," and she looked up at him over the papers in the open folder, presenting her broad-boned face. Since she had him in geometry class he thought that an absurd opening.

"Well, let's see if I remember correctly now. Mother works at the embassy? Mr. Andrews' office, I believe."

"Yes."

"I've met her briefly. In fact I know Don Andrews quite well. He has excellent things to say about your mother's work."

Carey was glad, but not certain he liked the tone, as if she and Andrews had decided to hand out a citation.

"And your primary interest, as I recall, is in music. A pianist. I confess to eavesdropping once when you and Mr. Snyder were rehearsing downstairs. It sounded quite good."

"Thank you."

"You study with?"

"Ikbal Dorati."

"You *are* accomplished, then."

She held a pencil by the tip and eraser between her two fingers as if she were a lathe.

"I hope we'll be able to talk you into performing sometime for us at general assembly. We're hoping to have some of our more talented members of the student community share their interests. We find it encourages the other students. I'm sure a little recognition would be pleasing to you?"

The smile she gave him filled the space he might have entered with a reply.

"And I also hear that you and Mr. Snyder are preparing a concert for this spring?"

"Yes."

"Perhaps that might be a good thing for us to hear, a chance for you to run through it in public."

He could imagine the look on Ian's face if he suggested it, so he only nodded.

"I suppose you have to see quite a bit of each other?"

"Who?"

"Mr. Snyder and yourself."

Carey shrugged. "We have to rehearse. When there's time." He thought that was clever since she was probably trying to tell him he spent too much time on music and not enough on his schoolwork, something he had heard from teachers like her for years. Her face had gone a little blank, as if she were looking through him to something he could not see.

"And how are things for you here? Any problems? Questions? Do you feel you are adjusting to your life in Rome?"

Yes, he was adjusting, he told her. They chatted about the oddities, but he did not like doing it with her. With Ian or even Alberto such a conversation had a sense of humor, as if they were admitting that the foibles they saw around them were just distorted versions of their own. But hers was a real distaste.

"And when do you think you and your mother will be returning?"

"Returning?"

"Home. To the States."

"We don't know."

"Well. Why should you? At any rate, when you do, I think you'll find yourself prepared to enter the educational world back there. That's what we're aiming for now that we've got things tracked again. No plans for college, then?"

"Not for a while."

She began tapping with the eraser on the glass top beyond his folder. They chatted more about some of the changes, and she admitted competition had increased. It was not hard for Carey to see that she was uninterested in criticism of the changes, but wanted to justify them, and she had considerable praise for the virtues of competition. There was a pause, then looking a little perplexed for the first time, she said, "Carey, one thing. I'd like to ask you a few questions about Mladen. You are good friends, I believe."

"Yes."

"Well, I hasten to add that I'm not prying, and you don't need to answer any questions if you think I'm treading on confidential territory, but we'd like to be a little more helpful to him."

He did not answer. For the first time since entering he had a sense of some possible violation that he did not want. Lately there had been conferences in her office with the perpetrators of this or that piece of mischief, and a heavy emphasis was placed on "telling the truth," which usually meant "telling the truth on" someone.

"It's just that often he seems very resentful, separate from us all, and takes an attitude, a tone that doesn't seem very helpful."

He tried to look as blank as possible.

"You haven't any idea what's on his mind, do you? I mean, he hasn't expressed any areas of friction?"

"No, ma'am. None I know of. He doesn't like…"

"Yes? Go on."

"Things that are phony."

"Phony?"

"Like when someone says they're tough and they're not. But that doesn't have much to do with school."

"No, it doesn't. Does he talk much about home? His parents or way of life in Yugoslavia?"

Carey shook his head. "No. His father's a diplomat, you know, and…"

"Yes, we know."

She waited, but he had nothing more to say.

"So, Carey," and she stood. "Thank you for coming in. This has been very helpful."

They walked together to the door, her heels snicking on the marble beside him.

"And please, do think of this as a place you can come if you have any problems. At all. I've a boy of my own, you know." And she put a hand on his shoulder. He tried very hard to smile on the way out, but because the interview was over, it was too difficult.

He sat with Ian on the bus going home that day, and Mladen perched over his shoulder in the seat behind. As usual he could see her sitting up front, bending from time to time to chatter with her children. Ian caught him staring at her.

"Had your appointment?" His lips were pursed so that he would not laugh.

"I don't like her," Carey said quietly, and Ian looked as if he might say something, but instead he put a hand on Carey's for a moment and turned to the window.

Mladen tapped him on the shoulder and they yelled to Giorgio to stop so they could get off to go swimming. Carey waved at Ian's face, pointed and smiling beyond the glass, and perhaps it was only the aftertaste of his interview, but he felt some vague loneliness in that view of window, face, unfocused eyes. They raced each other to the Foro. Mladen won.

All the time they were swimming and playing around, Mladen kept watching him as if curious, and knowing how different he must seem, his mind always veering off to think

— 243 —

about Ikbal, Carey swam harder, made Mladen race him. Afterward they bought some pizza and walked slowly along the Tiber, talking about anything that came to mind. Near one of the bridges Mladen made them follow two girls who had smiled at them and now walked ahead, looking back from time to time.

"C'mon," he said, and they were off on one of their old chases.

But it did not interest Carey anymore. The girls walked faster, Mladen kept on, Carey's feet tired and he wanted to sit quietly in some nook of wall to eat. Near the synagogue the girls both turned, laughing, said something, and began running—the last taunt of the game. Mladen took it up, darting across the street. But Carey stood there and let the traffic pass. Mladen was waiting on the sidewalk when he finally crossed.

"Jesus, Carey. Move it."

But Carey shook his head.

Mladen shrugged. "They looked good to me."

They walked in silence to the little park by the temples and sat in the sun, spreading out the pizza, dividing it up evenly with Carey's pocketknife.

"We've seen worse, you know." His hair was standing in two peaks, dry now but tangled. "Listen, Carey, I want you to level with me. Do you like me anymore? I mean, are we still friends or has something gone wrong?"

His face had flushed up scarlet and he was staring down past the food in his hands.

"Yes, we are. I'm just tired."

"Don't keep saying that. Everybody around me has excuses. What the hell's going on at school? Do they tell you? Doesn't Ian? It's not just you, Carey. Everyone. They're treating me weird, and I can't get an answer. Wise, she watches me all the time. She listens when she passes in the halls. I know it. And it's not just me. Something weird is going on there, don't you know?"

"Ian doesn't tell me. And I don't think it's just you. She was spying on me today."

"Then what is it? The other day Wise had me into her office, the second time in a week, and she offered me some tea and didn't really have anything to say. We just sat there, talking about the weather or a class, and she'd ask me a fishy question or two, and all the damn time it was like she expected me to say something, but I didn't know what the hell it was."

Carey thought for a moment, then he told Mladen how she had asked about him, and Malden blushed again and said she had asked him about Carey, and at first they laughed, but then they became dizzy trying to figure it out and lapsed into silence. They finished eating and he leaned back.

"Sometimes," Mladen said, "I think there's trouble and they're not telling what. Sometimes I'm scared."

A cat, then two, began circling in at them warily. Mladen took the crusts from the paper and threw it to them.

"Carey, are you sure you're not keeping something from me?"

Carey felt a surge of words, the need to let them out. He trusted Mladen. But he could not do it and when the words stayed in him, he felt as if he had betrayed Mladen and that made him angry.

"For Chrissakes, why do you keep bugging me?"

"Sorry." And Mladen stared at the cats while Carey felt rotten. Mladen had always fought back. "I guess the damn thing at school is really getting to me."

It was all right after a while. They stopped in at the little church across the street and horsed around sticking their hands in the Bocca della Verità, that round blank face of shock with scarred lips, wide, broken eye, as if lie after lie had been stuffed into his maw until he could only gape. They watched some tourists take pictures of it, and finally a father came with his little daughter on their way to pray and as they were going in he playfully took her hand and thrust it at the mouth, but she screamed and tugged back and began crying so that he had to lift her, saying soothing things while he glanced at Carey guiltily as if asking forgiveness. On the way to the bus they talked about Fiero, who had not come back after Christmas but returned unexpectedly with his family to Australia, and they thought of writing him some wild tale about the whores. As Mladen was about to walk away he punched Carey on the arm lightly and said, "Old buddy, I guess it's just you and me, now."

"Look, there's Ikbal," Nancy said.

Carey and his mother were sitting well back in the concert hall behind the overthrust of the balcony. He had not recognized Ikbal in the dimming light. She had passed up the central aisle nearby and was making her way toward the front, her shoulders bare, hands in long gloves. She had her arm linked with the man beside her. The performers appeared to the rattle of applause. The silhouettes of her and her companion stalked briefly across the background of lit stage and bowing musicians and then they dropped from sight.

Carey did not hear the music. He hoped the lights would never go on. He had no idea what to do with the pain that made it impossible for him to breathe. Before this he had been jealous of her music, jealous of her pupils, jealous of the book she was reading, of anything that had nothing to do with him. But this was the first time he had been jealous of another man, a real one. He decided immediately that she loved that man, and tomorrow when Carey went to her, she would tell him. The stranger would be there, very stern and composed. Carey's mind split and frazzled into quavers of anger and the music played itself out. Everyone was applauding again as the lights flared on.

"Do you want to wander a little?"

Carey shook his head. He wanted to crawl under the chairs ahead and even had his program in hand to drop if they came along the aisle so that he could crouch down and grope for it on the floor. But there was no time. His mother stood.

"Ikbal," she called firmly. "Signora Dorati."

They paused at the end of the row. He stood, Nancy urged him forward, and they bunched together in the aisle while people on their way out moved patiently around them.

"Cesare, I'd like you to meet Nancy Mitchell and this is her son, Carey, the young pianist I have told you so much about. Cesare Orsini."

He had a sharp, almost hooked nose, and when Carey shook his hand, his grip was a half-given clip of the fingers.

"A pleasure. I have heard you are a virtuoso. Perhaps one night we will be coming to hear you."

"But you will, you will," Ikbal said smoothly. "He'll be accompanying Ian this spring."

"Ah, well then."

Carey was trying to listen, to answer him, not to look at Ikbal, who he knew was staring at him. Cesare and Nancy passed a few meaningless phrases back and forth about the performers, and when he finally found the courage to look at Ikbal she had turned to take the hand of a very stout lady who had tapped her arm.

"But," and Cesare glanced at the man pausing behind him, "I fear we are impeding. Ikbal, my dear, we should move. Won't you join us?" He took Ikbal's gloved hand to set her in motion and turned before Carey or Nancy could answer. Carey's eyes met Ikbal's briefly, but she was in mid-reply to the woman and he could see nothing special in her face for him.

Nancy offered to buy him an *aranciata*, but he refused and sat, pretending to read the program notes while she stood, and he was relieved when she saw a friend from the embassy and went to sit for a while with the woman and her husband. He did not let himself look up as the people filed back. He tried to hear every note the musicians played, and he was right to dread the loneliness of his bedroom even more than the concert hall. As for Ikbal and Cesare, he was certain where they were. All night he could hear her voice moaning to Cesare, and finally Carey wept bitterly.

He had to force himself up the stairs and he stood outside her door for a few minutes, unable to lift his hand. Faintly through the wood he could hear the piano, and from some floor above came the sound of sporadic hammering.

The music stopped when he knocked. She was alone, closed the door after him, slipped the bolt. She was smiling. He could not understand. She seemed completely unchanged.

"I have our tickets for Naples, our reservations in the hotel. Do they make you nervous? It won't be long now."

She gave him the envelope to look through, urging him forward in the living room, chatting on about how many other teachers and students were coming. But halfway to the piano she turned him by the shoulders so that he had to look at her.

"Confess. Why are you drooping today?"

He looked anywhere but her eyes.

"Come." Her tone had more edge to it.

"Who was he?"

"Who?"

"That man last night."

"At the concert? You mean Cesare? He's an old friend."

He did look at her then, angrily.

"Are you jealous?"

"Why not. Do you love him?"

She looked as though she could not decide to laugh or frown.

"Of course not. But what if I did?"

"But you made love, didn't you? You went to bed together."

She slapped him once, so quickly that he hardly skipped a breath.

"That's for the ugliness of your thoughts. But also because you mustn't ask me questions like that."

"Why not? Don't I have a right?"

He was not going to cry or accept that stinging cheek in any way. He had done his crying that night.

"No. You haven't. You don't own me."

"What am I, then? What do you want me for?"

Her face was suddenly very gentle. That hurt even more. He wanted her to tell him, not to fuzz off into some hidden place. She took his hand, started pulling him toward the bedroom.

"We need to talk, Carey."

He jerked back. "No. I want to know what I am to you. Don't you love me?"

She put her hand on his neck, bending his face toward her.

"Yes, I love you. But there are some things you will have to accept or we should stop, now."

"Other men you love?" He still did not touch her, her hand firmly on his skin.

She nodded. "Perhaps other men. I have different needs. They take nothing away from you."

He stood there. Her face was listening, waiting, and he had taken her words far down inside as slowly as stones falling through water, and then he was weighing them, poised impossibly, and the thing he called "love" that he thought was single and whole, split. He wanted nothing but to dance with her in some magic circle that no one else could enter.

"Why?" he said quietly.

He wondered if they had been looking at the same thing. Her other hand went up to his neck, they stood there with their cheeks touching, and then he went with her to the bedroom, willingly.

Later they dozed and Carey woke to see her face for the first time in sleep, relaxed, shockingly girlish. He was no longer in any way embarrassed with her, and when she woke to find him lying propped on his elbows, staring at her naked body, she laughed.

Later she said, "If what I ask of you hurts too much, you mustn't allow it to go on."

He believed her, but did not see any solution in her words. Being totally without her was more painful than anything he could imagine. "I don't want to talk about that."

But she was looking past him at the window, her eyes unfocused. "Some day you'll have to go, or I will."

At least he could assume he would go with her, so he said, "Where would you go? I thought Rome was where you lived."

She lit a cigarette, then propped her pillow against the headboard. "Some day I will go back to Egypt. I know that. I belong there, even if I left when I was very young. Many of my father's people are still there, and I know it is my country also. Some day I think I will give up all this performing and teaching and go there. But when I think that, I'm not sure what I will do."

"Have you gone back?"

"A few times. It's not a very good place to be, right now. Very confused. Corrupt. But I have friends who tell me this will change one day, before very long. I only hope it will not be too violent."

He was not prepared for this hidden attachment or the seriousness of tone. She was usually so glib about the things she cared for, as if afraid of any sentimentality, although once when he told her that, she had said, "No. It's a way of not showing God what you care about, because if he knows, he'll take it back."

"We lived in the city, in Cairo. It's a big, dirty, confused place, but I love it, that chaos. Worse than Rome. But my uncle used to live in the country and we would go there often. You know I was remembering the other day a lamb he gave me, or he called it mine because it was born one week when we were visiting, and every time we came back that year I'd be in charge of it, and he let me give it a name. Then one day, in the late spring, I woke up early from a nap and went out into the yard and wandered off toward the fields where I wasn't supposed to go by myself, but it was hot, and I wanted to be under the big tree near the trough. I came down over the hill and saw my father and uncle working over something under the tree, and Uncle had a knife, and then I saw it was my lamb. They were going to kill it."

She stopped to put out the cigarette, looked at his face, and smiled.

"No, it's not what you think. Oh, I was upset for a minute and they saw me and told me to come down. My uncle explained that the animal had reached the time when it should be killed for eating, and he asked if I wanted to stay or go back to the house. I stayed. The blood bothered me at first. But they did it cleanly, they did it with a kind of gentleness of purpose, and it seemed right. Do you know, I even ate some of it. I think I understood things on the farm, immediately, in ways I never did in the city. Things just seem cruel in the city. Unnecessarily."

She put the ashtray on the table, then lay back quietly for a while. He did not ask her what she meant.

All the way home Carey thought over the things she had said about them, especially about other men, and it all blurred brightly as if he were staring at some new light that hurt more than it clarified.

They were all going to Naples for the concert. Ikbal was to go with Carey two nights early since there would be a chance to practice briefly in the recital hall. His mother and Alberto would come down for the evening of the concert, stay that night, and bring him home the next day. Even Ian and Pierre decided to come, although when Carey mentioned Alberto, Ian seemed reluctant but would not explain. "Well, well," he said, "I do have to find out how good my accompanist is." But Carey knew they were all trying to help him.

He had not been to Naples since they had left the boat, and that already seemed like a long time ago. Nancy went with him to the terminal where Ikbal was waiting, and she suddenly was reluctant, insisting on standing around in the compartment until Carey was afraid the train would leave with her, and Ikbal kept saying not to worry until Nancy stopped, smiled, and with watery eyes said, "Now, don't be nervous, Carey, and remember we'll be there and see you Friday." Carey told her he thought she was more nervous than he was, and they all laughed. She stood on the platform until they slid away.

He had spent most of his time imagining the concert, seeing himself again and again on a huge stage exploding with white light, confronting an endlessly receding black instrument, and somewhere beyond a sparkling fringe of bulbs was a viciously silent crowd of pale, staring faces. But now that Ikbal and he would be alone for a few days and nights, the concert seemed less important. She sat opposite him, her back to the forward motion of the train. She had brought a book and held it in her lap under her clasped hands. He leaned forward, touched those hands with his in one of those odd moments when he saw her so clearly—her pointed brown shoes, one knee bare where the pale blue skirt had opened slightly, her face staring sleepily out of the window—almost as if she were a photograph he could look at with painful slowness. Her body was completely at ease in the gentle shifts and rolls of the train gathering speed. When he touched her he wanted to give her something, to pass it unspoken from hand to hand. Her clasp broke, her fingers closed over his and she smiled sleepily at him.

"Your mother is a good person. I like her ways."

He did not answer, but she did not seem to expect him to.

"I don't suppose she knows, does she? For certain."

He shook his head. She closed her eyes for a minute.

"Trains always make me sleepy. Do you know, I was thinking of my first concert. In Europe. I started much younger than you. That was because of my father. He had been a violinist, a good one, but had to give it up and make a living when my brothers and I were born, and then my mother was so ill. I hated it, most of the time, as a small child. Hours, hours, at that thing, and my hands were too small for what I already wanted to do, was ready in my mind to do, but also I couldn't understand why my father was doing this to me—only me, because he didn't try with my brothers, you see. He was too bitter. He said the same thing would happen to them that happened to him, but I was a girl and I would marry someone who would support me, so I didn't have to worry. And he often said that in front of my mother. They seemed to need to hurt each other sometimes."

Her book slipped from her lap and she reached for it, putting it on the empty seat beside her.

"It was in Paris. I was seven. I wasn't frightened. But I was very lonely. My parents could not afford to come, so they sent my brother with me, he was fourteen, and we were to stay with a cousin. I thought I was lonely because I wanted my parents to be there, but then I felt even lonelier when I realized there wasn't anyone who could help me. My brother and I invented a little man named Wolfgang Sebastian Beethoven who would be sitting invisibly on the edge of my piano and pulling out all the notes. Before I walked out on the stage my brother was standing in the wings with me and he said, 'Look, Wolfgang is waiting for you, he brought a rose,' and he described him to me sitting there, a rose in his teeth, legs crossed. I guess I did all right. People will forgive a lot if you're seven."

"How about if you're seventeen?"

She leaned forward and put a hand on his cheek. "Everything, everything is forgiven if you are seventeen."

She sat back, took up her book as if she would read, and then looked out the window for a while.

"The last of the aqueducts," she said vaguely. "My brother's name was Mamoun. He became an Italian citizen. He died before the war."

Some people came into their compartment at the first stop, so they were quiet most of the way, and she slept for a while.

To keep appearances they had separate rooms, but they were adjoining. The hotel was on the bay with the Castel dell'Ovo in sight. The city looked so different to Carey that he could not believe they had docked there. The colors were subdued, the water greenish rather than the blue he remembered, and the crowds, the noise, were not remarkable to him anymore. Only Vesuvius brought everything back to mind clearly, and it hovered there as always, now rimmed with snow, still smoking in barely visible wisps.

She knew the city well, and showed him some things that afternoon. It began to rain hard in the evening, so they ate in their rooms, and he kept going to the balcony windows to look at the lights on the quays and along the shore streaking out into the black water or equally watery pavements. They drank their bottle of wine, and for the first time in his life he spent the whole night with a woman, waking from time to time to listen to her breathe, to touch her lightly, to hear her rise in the dark and return. He turned to her as she whispered, "Shh, sleep, sleep."

He was disappointed in the concert hall and tried to fight it back so she would not see. The room was small, crowded with folding chairs, and the piano was not raised on a stage or dais but merely stationed at the front of a room that was obviously used for something else most of the time. But he liked the instrument, and when he sat at it, seeing all those chairs stretching off, suddenly noticing that the ceiling was coffered in gold and delicate, ornate chandeliers hung in the shadows down the length of the hall, he felt it was enough to handle. When they left, the next performer was waiting impatiently out in the hallway with her teacher. He could tell that even though she pretended indifference as they passed, she had been listening at the door.

The rest of the day was free, and the air was clear, balmy now that the rain had stopped, turning the sky to a blue less intense than he had seen before but rinsed and clean, tinting the water palely. She bought tickets for a tour of various sites, and so he had a glimpse of Cumae, of Solfatara, and down the road to Pompeii. Perhaps it was only his gathering nervousness, but everything, in spite of the day so clearly edging into early spring, had a slightly ominous air; the crazed old woman gathering sticks at the mouth of the Sibyls' cave, the sulfurous, rotten fumes rising from a ground that melted and heaved, the dead town broken out of the encrusting mold of the mountain that smoked above it, and those curled, hardened bodies, sleepers turned to rock, some of them caught in the toss of their worst nightmares. He was glad to sit in the little restaurant they found by the shore that evening, talking about all they had seen and her memories of that city some years before. She would recall something in great detail, her face taking on so many of the emotions she described. For brief moments he would be dazed and silent, aware that no one had ever talked to him with such intensity before. Once that night he woke to hear her talking in a dream, her words unclear but urgent, and he lay awake thinking how much of her life was unknown to him. There were things she could tell him, as she had recently, about her past, but even as she did so, or now as she slept, she possessed a life he could not see. He remembered one night years before when he had been sleeping in the same room with Frank and heard him talking in his sleep too. Suddenly Carey wanted her to know what he was thinking, and that he was lonely, so he woke her gently.

She left him alone the next afternoon. She said it would be good for him to get a little nervous, and she had to visit with some of the other teachers. He read, walked around, sat in the sun on the balcony, spent some time in the lobby. It was not nervousness that was finally reaching him, but boredom. When Ian called they talked a long time, and then he talked to Pierre. They were in a *pensione* near the concert hall. They wished him good luck. Just before he and Ikbal left for the hall, Nancy called, and he could tell by her breathlessness that she was almost crying so he laughed and told her to cheer up.

There were only four performers. All of them sat in the front row alone. Carey could not stop staring at the program. He had never seen his name printed so elegantly before. He was to play third, after the intermission. All the pieces that the first two performed were familiar to him, and he could not understand why they played so slowly, why he could hear each note drag through. He waited and waited. There was intermission, and he looked on with envy while the two who had finished were crowded around, congratulated. They chattered excitedly. He stood for a while with his mother and Alberto, his mouth so dry he could barely speak, not hearing anything they said and dropping irrelevant comments that only Alberto could pick up with any grace because Nancy was preoccupied, pale, her hand constantly tucking at her hair. He left them and went to sit in his chair some time before the intermission ended with blinking lights. In the darkened hall, with its squeaks and shuffles as the audience settled down, there was only one thing left to do.

They applauded, he bowed, he remembered to readjust the stool. How desperately he wanted to try out a few chords casually, to let out some of the tension that turned his fingers to willow branches, and for a moment he could not remember where he was to begin, what he was going to play, who he was, why he was sitting in light in front of a stretch of ivory and ebony, that formal design cut so deeply into his brain. They were waiting. He was waiting. He released his arms which had an idea of where to go and took him along.

From then on no one else was there to bother him, hardly even himself. Only at times, between movements or in tiny gaps where he let his mind almost flirtatiously play with the idea of where he was, they were there and he was playing to them. But he shut them out, a few slipped notes, a scramble to regain his balance warned him to concentrate. They were not to applaud until he had played all of his pieces. Between Beethoven and Chopin he heard them fluttering their programs. He wanted to turn and yell, "Tell me, for God's sake, how am I doing?" He was afraid to look, certain they would be staring dully at their feet or slumped dozing in the chairs. He was coming to the last measures of the nocturne and suddenly he did not want it to end, wished the phrases stretched on into new pages. But there were his hands in his lap. Silence. His legs worked, stood him, let him bow, strode him back to his chair, stood him again, and yet by the way they trembled were letting him know he must pray for an end to the applause. It did stop, the people were murmuring, and then they were beating their hands for the other person, and he did too. He heard little, though. She seemed to play terribly fast and was through the whole of a Beethoven sonata before he had begun to concentrate, and then he was thinking of being where she was and he lost his attention again and it was all over.

They stood together in a tight circle and he wanted to reach out and hold onto Ikbal because he was lonely and tired. They told him how fine it was, but that did not matter at all; it was over, and he was in a blank space, drained, useless. Ikbal was staring at him, although saying something reassuring to his mother, and he knew she was trying to tell him she understood.

"What is it, what is it?" he asked her as they were alone for a moment on the steps outside waiting for the others to join them so they could walk down to the sea and their restaurant. "I only want to cry, or..."

"Or?" Her hand was on his.

"Or do it all again."

Quickly she leaned into him, kissed him on the cheek.

"Then you are hooked," she said, and before he could answer, Pierre had jumped down the stairs, grasped him around the waist and lifted him, his arms squeezing out Carey's breath, and when he put him down he said, "You skinny pianist, you boy."

He felt better soon. They had reserved a table at their restaurant and the place was full, the lights on cords swinging when the sea breeze wafted in the partly opened windows. They ate and drank, and Ian, happier than Carey had ever seen him, told story after story. Soon Nancy was gaily drunk and when she was not laughing or saying unexpectedly clear and funny things, she leaned her head on Alberto's shoulder. At first Carey thought Alberto looked stiff and uncomfortable, but then he too leaned forward, said something quietly to Ian, and they looked at each other silently for a moment. Ian began to laugh, Alberto did too, and although the laughter was excessive, Alberto was more at ease.

The musicians came in off the street, a violinist and guitarist leading a blind accordian player who also sang. Pierre called them over. They sat down to play what he asked for, country songs, ballads in the Neapolitan dialect, and he told Carey what they meant. They all pushed back some chairs with the help of the waiter who was standing nearby and enjoying the music too, and when Pierre asked for some other tunes, the blind man smiled and nodded and rounded his mouth in song, leaning back, back until Carey was afraid he would fall off the chair. Pierre asked Ikbal to dance, and Alberto danced with Nancy, and then Ian with Nancy, and

Ikbal with Alberto and Carey with Nancy and even Pierre with Ian, both of them laughing, and finally Carey was dancing with Ikbal and he was dizzy, dizzy, with the wine and happiness and music and everyone around them smiling and urging them on, and he said to her eyes as they whirled in that blur of light and air, "I love you, I love you," and it seemed as though they danced all the way back to bed.

# PART FOUR

# The Mouth of Truth

# 1

"I think we should go home, Carey. Sometime this summer."

It was April, spring rising everywhere, and they were sitting in their trattoria on a Sunday night.

"Why?"

"Oh, homesick, I guess."

But he knew better. She had only moved the food around on her plate, was drinking more than her share of the wine.

"C'mon."

"I'm not sure we should talk about all of it, are you? I just don't think things are working out very well."

"You mean Alberto."

Paolo, their waiter, was removing the plates. "You have no hunger tonight?"

She shook her head.

"Some fruit?"

She ordered some, keeping Carey company as he ate whatever rum-soaked cake they had that night.

"Partly Alberto."

"You don't like each other anymore?" But then he recalled that she and Alberto were leaving for a three-day weekend in Siena and Florence.

"No. But there's no way it can work out."

"Because he's married?"

She smiled tightly, shaking her head. "It turns out to be a little more complicated than that. He *is* married, that's true, although he hasn't seen his wife now for fifteen years. She ran away with someone years ago."

"But I thought..."

"So did I. No, he's not married to the woman he sometimes lives with. She's just the mother of his children."

"He told you that?"

She shook her head. "Ian did. I made him."

"But how does Ian know? What has he got to do with all this?"

She waved as if that were not important.

"They knew each other long ago. That's another story. The point is, I sometimes don't know what to believe. Especially with Alberto."

He was having trouble swallowing and poured another glass of wine. The expression on his mother's face was no longer wry. She looked dazed.

"The son of a bitch."

She leaned forward. "That's not right. It isn't the deception that troubles me. Oh, when I found out that woman isn't really his wife, I was hurt and wondered if he was pulling all sorts of tricks on me, but what difference do those facts make? Wife, mistress, whoever she is, she's the mother of those children, and he doesn't want to leave them. He decided to tell me he's married because it's the same, in terms of what he is free to do. And besides, he *is* married, and I don't want to marry *him* anyway," and suddenly, in spite of herself, she was laughing and he was too. When they stopped she thought for a moment and said, "No, what seems to trouble me is the way that everything has no clarity. I don't think Alberto is deceiving me as much as he is deceiving himself. That's what makes it all so muddled," and then she repeated vaguely, "so muddled."

While she groped for her money to pay the hovering Paolo, who was all solicitations, adjusting the sweater that lay across her shoulders, warning against the fickle winds of spring, Carey tried to straighten out his feelings about Alberto, but could not. Even though he had begun to enjoy the trips the three of them would take, he always held something back from the man, as he held something back from all that confused and shifting world around him. It was not his world. But leaving was out of the question. He wanted to burst out angrily at her, to say, "So you're tired of Alberto. Well, I won't leave Ikbal, do you hear?" But he would have to find other ways.

"So you want us to leave, soon," he said as they walked slowly back, veering together through the gate into the Gar-

ibaldi Park as if they both knew they would talk better out-
doors in the half dark of the balmy night.

"Yes. I can't stop wanting to see Alberto if I'm here. Leaving would seem to be the best way."

As they passed through the gate, he was already beginning
to invent a plan to stay behind, even if she left.

"But that's not all, Carey. There's more. Much more."

"Go on."

"For one thing, I think being here is like stopping a clock.
We're not really solving anything. This isn't our world. It's
lovely, fascinating to live in for a while, and I don't mean we
aren't learning a lot while we're here, but it's not ours. Everything here, like Alberto and myself, is just paralyzed."

He did not feel like arguing. He wanted to hear all her
reasons before he began trying to talk them down. Above all
he wanted to be able to agree with them as valid for her, and
prove they did not apply to him.

"And I don't think it's all that good for you, Carey."

"How?"

A bicycle hissed by, its light wobbling.

"We have to think of your education."

"I'm working on my music."

"Well, also you don't have many friends your own age."

"I never had much time for that at home either, you know."
There he was arguing anyway. He could not help it. She had
made up her mind, about him as much as herself. "And my
music is certainly going well here."

They stood in the dusky clearing of the overlook, the city
lit up and spreading out into a starry sky, the trees by the
river winding darkly. Something in the small laugh she gave
when he said that, warned him.

"The music is fine. But I don't know what to do about the
rest."

"The rest?"

"About you and Ikbal." She did not say it harshly. It was
a simple, pensive statement.

"What about?" he murmured, hoping she meant something else.

"I've known for some time. How could I help it?"

"Ian told you."

"No one did. But Lord, does he know that too?"

They were silent for a moment. She slipped her arm
through his.

"Maybe I was not certain until the concert. But I had to

know then. I knew you liked her, but I always thought it was just infatuation. But a woman doesn't touch, hold, dance with someone like that unless she's familiar with much more than his mind. I'm sure, Carey, she must have known I would see it that night, and decided she did not care."

He thought that possible. Ikbal had said something once about how she did not intend to go out of her way to be deceptive.

"I'm no one to babble about the morality of it all, am I? Terrible to have given up a parent's one most infallible argument—morality, guilt. But I keep telling myself you had to grow up sometime."

She paused, but he could not speak.

"Maybe I can see something that you can't, or won't, admit. What's going on between you and Ikbal is hopeless. Like Alberto and me. Maybe more so, because we understand that, even when we're together. Surely Ikbal knows. Does she say it to you, I wonder? You see, down past all those confusing problems of morality, I'm just afraid of seeing you hurt. What you have with her has no future. Soon it's going to be holding you back, or you'll get in deeper before she has to drop you, and then it will hurt more."

He shook his head. "But I love her."

She touched against him, then stood free, leaning on the balustrade.

"I know you do. But I'll tell you something," and her voice became firm, "if I have to fight her, I will. I'll risk that. I still want to keep you from being hurt in ways that might last—and as long as I can, I will. I'm more than a match for her."

He clenched against that stiffened voice in her, as if her hand were trying to hold him under water. He pushed back.

"No."

"No, what?" Her voice went blank.

"You stay out. It's none of your business."

He knew the way her jaw would be tensing. She folded her arms.

"I guess I'm making it my business now."

"You can't. You'll ruin everything. It's my life."

"I'm your mother. It's very much my business, and you are not old enough to talk about *your* life in that way."

"What are you doing? We don't need you messing things

up. You can't stop me. It's not like you and Dad. You can't make me do anything."

He stopped. He did not know why he said that, why Frank had even entered his mind. She unfolded her arms and sucked in her breath.

"Explain that, Carey Mitchell."

"You can't tell me what do do. I'm on my own."

"Are you, now? Explain, please, what you mean about your father. About how I treated him."

"Like you treat me sometimes. As if you know me so well you can tell me what to do or not do. As if you are looking at me all the time and I can't get anything out or done because you've already made up your mind about it."

"I did that to your father?"

"That's what he said, wasn't it? He used to say you were trying to control everything."

"Not quite. I used to say a person could try to control some things. He used to say no one could. An old argument."

"I don't care. You can't control me."

"Carey, I don't want to."

By the way his name was spoken, ripped and torn at the edges, he knew that he had spoken too strongly, but he did not want to say he was sorry. She put a hand on his arm and starting off toward home as if they wanted to get away from that view, they stepped off the curb with a jolt like two blind people without canes.

"You meant all that. And I'm going to think about it."

They were almost to the apartment when he finally answered. "I'm sorry. Dad's not part of this."

Her voice was calm, a little distant. "But he is. And I was foolish to think those arguments were over. Well, I have the advantage of practice."

They walked up since the elevator had its usual sign saying it was broken.

"We'll talk some more. And if you have Frank on your mind, I'm not surprised. You probably ought to see him soon. This weekend I'll be telling Alberto that we will leave. I hope you'll tell Ikbal too."

"Why do you keep on with Alberto if it seems hopeless? Why are you going on this trip?"

She paused, her back to him as she opened the balcony doors.

"Because. Nothing would be more hopeless than not seeing him."

But that weekend he did not say anything to Ikbal about leaving. He wanted to think.

When he strolled back to the bench near the edge of the terrace where his mother and Alberto were sitting, he knew they had been talking about him, but he was surprised to hear Alberto say quietly, "Perhaps he should stay. Of course I wish you both would, but if he wants, I think I can help."

Carey looked quickly at his mother, Nancy looked at Alberto as if she could not decide to be puzzled or angry, and she said, "What are you saying?"

"There's something to what he is telling you. He's doing very well. You exaggerate about this little thing of the woman, Signora Dorati. It's his profession we are really talking about."

They were on the Palatine, sitting under the trees of the high parapet overlooking the Forum and the Capitoline, and already three or four cats had gathered nearby, mewing and stretching out in the sun. Nancy waved a hand in exasperation.

"Oh, how like you, 'Little thing.' Do you really think that I could go off, thousands of miles away, and leave him with some unscrupulous, mad pianist, and..."

"And your crazy lover." He smiled slightly.

"He's hardly seventeen."

"Eighteen," Carey said firmly, remembering his birthday would be soon.

"Never mind. Not old enough."

"But," and Alberto looked at neither of them as he spoke, as if addressing the cats, "about to be a fine artist. He needs every opportunity. And besides, you know this woman cares for him."

"No," and she shook her head so furiously that her hair flung around as if in a wind. "I tell you no."

Carey left them again to look down over the dizzying edge. Below, the rubble of scarred walls and shattered columns was being crisscrossed by slow-moving groups, or stragglers with books in hand. From time to time their voices surged up in a breeze that shivered the bay leaves. He could hear Alberto and his mother talking behind him but did not want to join the conversation. He could not control his need for a quick, simple answer. "Please, Alberto, you stay out of this,"

— 263 —

he heard Nancy say at one point, but he was trying to adjust to Alberto's being *in* at all. The man stood so far outside of him and his dream, beyond Ikbal and the circumference of their private world. Suddenly he was elated. What if that trough of columns and old roads, those spreading hills of tinted walls and pines and tufa banks were to be his home. He had never thought of it in that way before. Rome had always been only a city they had come to visit.

Alberto's hand was on his shoulder and he turned. Nancy stood behind him, but Carey could not stop looking at Alberto's face, his fixed, uptilted lips and wide eyes, and when he said, "Splendid view, isn't it?" Carey felt as if the man were offering it to him. They walked down the steps, past the grotto, to the exit. His mother had to go back to work even though it was Saturday, some preparation for a special visitor, and they flagged down a taxi for her. "Now, no conspiracies," she said, as she took her seat in the cab, and then she was driven away and Carey glimpsed her watchful gaze.

"Let me take you to lunch, eh?" Alberto said.

Carey consented and they began walking around the white bulk of the monument. He could never quite tell if the self-consciousness he felt when left alone with Alberto was only his own or whether Alberto imposed it on him. But something in his attitude now annoyed Carey even more, as if by taking his side Alberto had entered into a compact with him. The man put his hand on Carey's arm from time to time, his jacket thrown casually over his shoulders, his dark glasses thrust back over his forehead. But there was something nervous, uneasy, in the way the hand would grasp his elbow, the eyes would move about from street to passer-by to traffic and back to Carey's face to settle unblinking. After the burst of freedom he had sensed up there, Alberto was a weight pressing in around him on all sides.

"Perhaps I have been wrong to even speak to Nancy about all this," he was saying as they worked their way across the streets. "It is between your mother and yourself. But not entirely. This other person, Signora Dorati, and I, too, have something to say."

"Say?"

"Yes. We are involved also."

Carey wanted to tell the man it was none of his business. But he bit his lip. What could he say? It was no longer just himself and Nancy. They turned into the smaller street toward Piazza Campitelli, stood aside for a passing car. The clean white tablecloths and tubs of hedges were ahead of them. Alberto stopped him, a hand now tight on his wrist.

"Look, Carey. I will be honest. I want your mother to stay. I don't want to lose her. She says you will go soon. If you stay I am certain she will too. I am eager to help you." At first the eyes would not settle on Carey's and the mouth smiled wryly. "We can help each other, I believe."

"But why? How can I do that?" he said, and the anger rose. "What do you want her to stay for? You're married. What do you want?"

Alberto was shaking his head slowly. "I had forgotten how harshly the young can judge. Yes, I am married. There are difficulties. But what about yourself, my dear boy. What about you and a woman fifteen years, is it, older than you are?" The expression was not mocking. "As to what I want, can you say what you want? But perhaps that seems an unfair question. After all, I am older. I should be able to articulate some of that. Come," and again the hand brushed Carey's shoulder, urging them on to the restaurant. "We can talk at last about all this."

Carey saw the waiter at the cleft in the hedge eyeing them expectantly. He needed someone who could help him express all these things to Nancy. He and Alberto, working on her, plotting it out. He stood still in the middle of the street.

"I can't. I promised to go somewhere."

They faced each other.

"Come, now. I won't keep you long. Don't you think it would be better for us to talk?"

"I don't want to talk."

"I see." At first Carey thought the man would be genuinely angry. His jaw set as if he were biting down hard. But his face softened, the eyes looked at him absorptively. "Please. Let's not even talk of all this. We will talk of other things."

"I'm sorry. I really can't."

"You don't understand, my boy. I care for you. A great deal. I need to know you better. I can help. I feel like a father to you."

"But you're not."

Carey backed away slightly, shaking his head. Alberto pursed his lips, shrugged.

"*Ho fatto una brutta figura,* eh? Well, let us part in a friendly manner. Some other time. *Ciao.*"

He held out his hand, Carey shook it, the man swung it behind his jacket to clasp his hands together and sauntered across the street where the waiter, who seemed to know him, smiled and bowed him to a table. He did not look back and Carey left the square quickly, feeling insulted but not able to find any specific words or gesture to blame that on.

He sat for a while on the wall by the Tiber, watching its green waters part around the island. Ikbal was waiting for him when he came, late.

"I won't go," he said stubbornly to the face where it lay dimly on the pillow in her darkened room. "She can't make me." He had told her some time ago that Nancy knew about them, and Ikbal had not been upset, had only turned to him a little later to say, "I hope we won't have to go through one of those silly scenes, your mother and I."

Ikbal's eyes were closed. He could not tell for a moment if she was asleep or thinking.

"Do you want me to go?"

She turned on her side to look at him.

"That is up to you."

"Then I'm not."

She nodded. "There are all sorts of reasons why you shouldn't. Above all, your music. It's just beginning to go well. I've heard good things from the Naples concert. There are people I could bring you to and you are almost ready."

But he wanted other reasons than those from her.

"I'm going to tell her that I am staying. To work on my music. I don't need school."

"If you are sure that's what you want, Carey. I will help."

"Help?"

She laughed. "Do you think food will fall on you from heaven? If you stay you will need someone for a while. You will have to come live with me. At least until we can find other help for you."

"How?"

She waved a hand impatiently. "I know certain people."

He had never felt more sure than when he left her that evening, and he tried to work it out now clearly in his head. But there was not much time to think. As if the season itself were pushing everyone along, his life and the lives of others around him were moving too rapidly. More and more often Carey was a truant from school, wandering about in the city, sitting in the sunshine that arrived washed and fragrant out of a mild ocean where it had slept for months, and he sometimes lured Mladen into joining him. But what was it behind the mask of all that sun and blossoming that made him edgy, made both of them uneasy as if they knew more than the season was changing and they were helpless to avoid it? They talked endlessly about all their plans, fumes they puffed out across the years ahead of them, and they were always to be in touch. But at the same time Mladen had begun to bring a camera with him wherever he went, taking pictures of the things he and Carey had come to love, as if he had to catch hold of them in some way before they vanished, and again and again Carey was included in the frame, standing between the admonishing hand and stern face of the fragmented colossus still ungathered in his courtyard, leaning toward the Bocca della Verità as if trying to see beyond that cracked lip, beyond the fear of lying, to all the unmasked truths. The season wheeled on—azaleas on the Spanish Steps, the concert with Ian in only four weeks. He could not be close enough to Ikbal's body as if all those tricks the earth was playing around him were there to drive him to that one place. But something was slipping out of his cupped hands. He dreamed that brother Mladen, his love Ikbal, friend Ian were climbing up a vine toward light, but it grew too fast, its leaves making shadows on their eager faces.

"Who told you these things?" Alberto sat very stiffly, hands folded in his lap.

Nancy, next to him on the bench, tried to gauge the expression on his face, but his profile revealed nothing. Footsteps crackled on the pebbles of the path and one of her fellow secretaries appeared around the hedge, waved, and as if sensing they were in some kind of intense conversation, walked on.

"Ian."

He sighed as if to say, Who else?

"So. And now you know my past—"

"Pasts," she corrected, but he kept on—"and what difference does it all make?"

"None. Except I wish *you* had told me."

"Is there anything else? Surely this has nothing to do with your going?"

"Very little. We're leaving because we don't belong here."

He placed his arm along the back of the bench and his hand touched her shoulder. They made no pretense now about their relationship while they were at work. No one cared, and besides it was spring, Rome, and she had already let Mr. Andrews know she would be leaving.

"I will keep trying, you know. To persuade you not to go. Carey will too."

She shook her head, took his hand from her shoulder, and brushed it against her cheek. "No use." She hoped they would not go through the motions of those arguments again. But the more certain she had become, the more briefly she expressed her reasons, and that exasperated him, so that lately even he had begun to refer to her departure only in feints and jabs.

"I suppose I should be annoyed with Ian. He gossips."

"No. I pried. I knew he knew more."

"Would you like to know more about Ian and me?"

His tone was slightly mocking, and she wanted to say no, but he continued. "Ian and I both loved the same woman, in a way. It gives us some shared past, a brotherhood."

"You mean his sister."

"I see we have no secrets."

She did not answer. At moments like this, when Alberto was meshed in a tangle of obscure facts, she would think with relief of leaving. Both men could recite the other's past with such indifference that she knew what was left to them now were merely shared facts. They could speak of the woman with intensity, but the other man was a point of reference, a history.

"How strange," she said.

"I suppose it is."

"No, I mean how the past becomes a 'thing.' Or parts of it do. The parts we think are most terrible or memorable lose all their feelings. They just sit there and the things we don't even know are important are stored and then years later they open up and hurt or seem funny."

He nodded, continued as if he had not heard her. "For a while he blamed me for her death." He described how that had changed gradually, as if their shared memory of her made them brothers, a little hateful to each other. But now she really was not listening. She was wondering what years from this moment she would recall of it, if anything. Would the woman who had appeared a few moments ago, her hand lifted, a vague smile on her face, walking in her light dress on tiptoe to keep her heels from turning on the pebbles, come back to her with a meaning she had not known, bearing a gathered sense of the whole day, week, months, in her brief gesture? Angels and messengers suddenly seemed to surround her: trees, the angle of a wall, the shadow of a statue were the conveyors. What she looked at steadily would have been burned out in the moment, and what was being gathered in the corners of her eyes would return, bearing gifts. She saw him staring at her, knew she had been silent too long, took his hand from his lap and as if there were nothing but the simple touch of his moving fingers she said, "I love you. Now."

That evening she took the bus only to the Trastevere and decided to walk up the hill. It was hot, the buses full of stale air. She stood looking back at the bridge. For days she had intended to walk over to Ikbal's apartment, to sit down with her and talk. That would have to come soon. No matter what Carey would think about it. But each time she did not quite feel strong enough, and this would take energy, some sharpness of wit. Or was it that she simply did not want to sit with the woman, in her physical presence, thinking of Ikbal and her son as lovers? But she thought of them almost all the time anyway. She twisted her way through the narrow streets to the base of the hill and began the climb up the winding stairs.

She did not see the couple until she was almost next to them, and she walked so slowly, so quietly that they had not heard her coming. A boy and a girl, fully clothed, lay stretched out in the grass beside the path. He lay on her and they were laughing quietly at something, looking at each other's faces, his hands in her hair. She kissed his nose, he said something like, "Careful now," and when they both heard Nancy, their faces turned to her, wide-eyed and smiling. His hips had been moving against her and now held still. But they did not look alarmed or even embarrassed. Nancy kept walking, tried to look away, but the boy said simply, "Buona sera," and she answered.

The girl put a hand across her mouth, and as Nancy turned with the path she heard them both laughing again. But she felt like laughing too, and what puzzled her even more was the flush of heat in her as she came up toward the pounding waters of the Fontana Paola, imagining those two young lovers perfectly naked in the grass and she stepping forward to put her arms around them as if she could hold them together, become both of their bodies, tangling around them like a vine.

# 2

All that afternoon Mladen had looked vacant, a little pale, for no reason Carey could locate. They met near his house and walked around for a while since it was too early for the party they were going to. Mladen was still truculent, said he had gotten into a bad argument with his father by insisting that the Yugoslavians ought to let go of Trieste. He laughed harshly and admitted that three hours before he had wrangled bitterly with the janitor of his building, taking the opposite side. But even as he talked, he seemed to be watching for an opening, as a boxer might through lifted gloves.

They reached the apartment late. The party was already frantic; doors to the balcony three stories up were open, some singer was lamenting at such a level that his words were distorted into noise, and their host Greg was leaning against the rail, his back turned, whinnying at something, flailing with his beer can. Greg's parents always spent evenings out with friends when their son had a party. Carey had seen them come home drunk, bleary-eyed, talking incoherently through the mush of their numb lips, and they would start dancing with their son's friends or sag off to bed.

"Shit," Mladen said.

Carey had started up the steps and turned to see him still standing on the sidewalk, hands deep in his jacket pockets, his face looking up.

"Let's forget it, Carey. I can't take that crap."

They took a bus downtown and started walking around in the old city, and all the way Mladen rambled on angrily about the stupidities American kids liked, and Carey thought of reminding him of the new leather jacket with studs that his cousin in New York had sent, but he did not feel like an argument.

They sat for a while in the Campo dei Fiori. Carey was content to hunch quietly for a while, watching the men clean up the trash from that day's market, brushing the garbage in one pile for the trucks, putting the old crates together near Bruno's statue, where they would burn them. Mladen would get up and move around, but when Carey asked him if he wanted to go on to someplace else, he said no. Finally he came back with a flask of Chianti he had bought at the shop nearby and they opened it and began to get high. He fidgeted less, although he was still gloomy. They had a good back-and-forth with two gypsy brats who wanted some cigarettes, and even after they had no luck the boys kept watching, wherever they were in the square. The fire was lit and the breeze blew it up into a blaze until the heat reached them. The uneven cobbles, high fronts of the buildings, the hooded figure of Bruno staring morosely—all began to move and shiver, and the sparks scattered in bursts.

"I might as well tell you." He glanced quickly at Carey. "Well, don't you want to know?"

Carey nodded.

"I told them."

"Told who? What?"

"Wise. I told her about Ian."

"Told her what?"

"That he's a queer."

"But why?"

"To get them off my back, that's why. She and Brewster or all those parents. Whoever they are."

He sat up stiffly, his fists clenched. At first Carey thought he was going to take a swing, but he opened out his hands, reached for the flask between his legs and had a mouthful. He handed it to Carey.

"It's no good. I could get angry at you or those bastards, but it was wrong of me and I know it. I don't know why I did it, exactly. She made me feel so strange all those times I talked to her. I mean, it was as if there was something wrong with me and she knew it but wouldn't tell me what. I know there's that stuff about my being what they call a Commie and all, but I got some of that in New York before. She kept on about Ian. Never anything direct, and wanted to know how good friends we were and all, and then she'd talk about something else. Sometimes she'd ask about you, and then you and Ian, nothing very clear or direct. It was getting creepy."

Carey had a drink. He was beginning to feel awful.

"This morning I got angry. I said, 'I'm sick of this. What do you want to know?' So she just smiled and said, 'I think there's something you want to tell us, Mladen. About Ian,' and so I said it. 'He's queer. Now are you happy?' and she tried to make me talk but I wouldn't say a word more, and wanted to give her the finger, but," and he looked at Carey sideways, his hands folded together as he leaned forward on his knees, "she had me. The bitch."

"What will they do?"

"I don't know. But I bet they'll be talking to you."

The fire was burning down now, the smell of pine slats mixed with the rot of burned vegetables. Already the upper stories, the torso of the statue had returned to the night.

"But why, Mladen? They're mean. They'll do something awful."

"I was afraid. You see I could tell they already knew, and I guess they must think you're queer, and I was afraid they'd think I was too."

He was looking the other way when he spoke. Carey never felt more like punching him than he did then. Hard, a full smack in the face. But he did not, and suddenly by Mladen's posture he could tell he might weep, and so he tried to tell him it was all right. Mladen quieted down and they finished the bottle. For a while they decided it was all silly, something they had exaggerated, especially after they had a funny conversation with a crazy whore who thought she was Marilyn Monroe and could hardly say the name. But the wine began to work off and they had to go home and they tried to keep up some bravado, but the look Mladen gave him as Carey stooped at the window of the bus was of panic, as if he had to be sure Carey was still there.

Mrs. Wise called him to her office early the next afternoon. He thought she looked more tired than usual. She was not smiling.

"Sit down, Carey."

She kept her back stiff, hands symmetrically holding a blank piece of paper on her desk.

"I'm afraid this won't be particularly pleasant."

He wanted to tell her that already it was not.

"I'm going to ask you a frank question and I expect the truth from you."

She had been staring past his shoulder. Now she focused directly on his eyes, and Carey tried to turn his flesh to concrete.

"Have you ever had homosexual relations with Ian Snyder?"

He only blinked, keeping his eyes on hers. "No."

She stared for a moment longer, then looked at the piece of paper she had laid on the desk and was smoothing with her hand.

"Of course, if you are lying, things will go hard for all of you."

He wanted to ask what she meant by "you" but held on.

"The next question you'll have to answer honestly too. But I want to warn you that on this matter, we are already firmly in possession of the facts. Mr. Brewster has been looking into things for some time, and we know a great deal."

"Then why are you asking *me?*"

A low knock on the door. She rose. "Corroboration, that's all." She opened the door and Hollister Brewster was there. They spoke quietly to each other and she closed the door and introduced Carey to him. He held out a hand and Carey shook it but did not get up. He had begun to sweat heavily. She went back to her desk and Brewster sat in the chair beyond her.

"So. This is the young man." He looked at Carey as if that small fact had much behind it, leaned forward slightly, elbows on the arms of his chair, and with one hand he absentmindedly twisted the cords of his string tie.

"It's all right," Mrs. Wise said. "He's not been approached."

"You're sure? You don't have to be afraid, son, you know. This sort of thing happens, and you're young, and we can get help for you. We just need to find out how far this has gone."

Carey began to be queasy as if closed up in a car on a winding road. Mrs. Wise did not wait for him to answer.

"I'm going to ask you, Carey, whether you have any knowledge concerning Ian Snyder's homosexuality. Now, bear in mind we do know some things already. We even know the name of the man he cohabits with."

Carey wanted to laugh. That much was such common knowledge. Almost all of the students by now had met Pierre at the bus stop or when they went to museums as a group.

— 273 —

He wondered if they could be serious. But they were. He could not laugh.

"I'm not going to answer any of your lousy questions."

Her expression did not change. She stiffened in the shoulders. Brewster looked at her then back at Carey.

"Now look here," he said, but she put up her hand.

"Never mind. We don't really need his answers."

Brewster crossed his beefy legs. "Young man, I think we're going to have a lot to say to you in the next few weeks." He leaned forward, frowning. "Listen, son, I hope you know we're on your side. We have a lot to fight for, and we're really united in needing to help each other out of tight spots. Let us help you."

Mrs. Wise bowed her head slightly, shoulders still tense, but her voice was quiet, and some of the words that came out were mumbled and lost. "Sorry, Carey, it's not a pleasant thing, and I don't know how to make it clear to you, but..." and after a few syllables she stopped, although her lips moved slightly. But in a few seconds she had looked up and said, "I guess that's all for now," and he stood. She let him out and he went back to his classroom.

He tried to whisper to Mladen, but Ian made them be quiet. In their last period, a study hall, Ian was called out of the room and he never came back. When the bell rang and Carey reached the bus, Ian was already sitting there, alone in the middle, the younger children beginning to climb in, and his face, as if underwater because of reflections on the window, was absolutely still in profile, staring forward. He turned, eyes wide, mouth slightly open as if he had run out of air.

Carey sat beside him and Mladen perched across the aisle. The secretary dashed out to say Mrs. Wise would be staying for a while, so the bus started off. Ian put a hand on his arm and gave it a gentle tap.

"Were they hard on you?"

"No." Carey looked at him now, but he still had his face slightly toward the window.

"Good. But they probably will be, in their own way. They tried to give me some nonsense about how you had told them this or that, but I knew differently."

Carey flushed. "They lied."

The hand gripped him firmly. "I know. I told them so, and they admitted you and Mladen had not been 'helpful.' Now don't worry. Do you know what? They had me watched, followed, all sorts of guff. One of those agencies, Ponzi. Brewster kept saying, 'We have the facts, Ian, right here,' and he'd pat his little briefcase."

Carey said something obscene that he thought covered the situation, and Ian turned, then looked like he might laugh.

"Yes, 'fuck them,' indeed," he said.

They were silent for a moment.

"What will they do?"

"Do? They already have. The board met last night. I'm fired."

Carey imagined his hands grappling with Mrs. Wise's throat, Brewster trying to beat them apart.

"Now, look," Ian said. "Let's not be silly. This is nasty, but not the end of the world. I had it in mind to quit this year anyway. I've enough to get along with for a while, and Pierre and I are thinking of moving to Paris. And besides, the rest of the world, fortunately, is a little more grown up than your people."

Carey knew he was making it sound smoother than it was.

"But what do they think they're doing?"

Ian sighed, took off his glasses to clean them with the neat triangle of his handkerchief. "I don't know. I guess they're making Europe safe for Americans." When he had pushed them well back on his nose again, he said firmly but without animosity, "They are sick, very sick."

When he told Nancy she threw the book she was reading across the room, then went to the phone and looked up a number and started dialing, but she hung up before she had finished.

"I guess I'll cool down, first."

Later she called Mrs. Wise and wrote letters and even talked with some of the people at the embassy, but by the end of the week she was very depressed. "The problem is," she said glumly to Carey one evening, "most people seem to agree with them."

But at least she made them leave Carey alone, except for the hard time he had with his schoolwork. He could not do it anymore, and increasingly he would get to the bus stop early and walk away.

Mladen and Carey played hooky all afternoon, sneaking away from a school expedition to the ruins of Ostia, taking the train to the end of the line and the beach. Bright sun, warm air that must have been blowing straight from Africa, wild chases along the beach at nothing but flocks of gulls or their own shadows—shoes off, pants rolled to the knees, even finally flailing off into the waves—nothing could wear them out, and in the evening after they came back to Carey's home together and raided the icebox, Nancy seemed glad to hustle them off with money for a movie. Carey always felt lifted and free when Mladen was like that. Even Nancy could not help reaching across the table at him to ruffle that already wildly disheveled hair.

They went to the movie, some Italian comedy about two sailors transported to Ancient Rome, bumbling around with emperors and gladiators and very bosomy concubines. They wandered for a while afterward, up the Via Veneto, back down past the Palazzo Barbarini, and they turned down the Via Rasella, intending to go and gawk at the Trevi Fountain.

A car idled down the street behind them and stopped. Carey looked at it, and when he turned back, two men had approached at a run from the other end of the street and stood blocking the way, slightly out of breath. The car doors opened and two more men stepped out. Their faces were impassive but watchful of the street around them. A woman walked briskly by on the other side and then they were alone.

"No noise, please." The shortest one, round face with a small mustache, spoke in Italian clearly, precisely, as if talking to children.

Carey was scared. Their motions were firm and unemotional and he felt as if he were being treated like an object.

"Which is the Slav?"

"In the leather jacket," the small man answered.

One of the men twisted Carey's arm up behind and pushed him against the side of the car so that he was held there awkwardly, his own unbalanced weight increasing the tension on his arm.

"Quiet," the voice said in his ear, "and you will not be hurt."

Mladen had said nothing. The other three stood near him, and he looked around as if someone could help.

"You are American?" the voice said to Carey again, casually conversational in tone.

"Yes."

He clucked his tongue, switched for a moment into uneven English. "Too bad. I don't want you should get the bad idea of us. These things are of importance, though. Bigger than us, each one. But the Americans, now—*gli Americani sono generosi, simpatici.*"

Some small creature in Carey, heart pounding, wanted to cajole, beg, thank him for liking Americans, ask him to please not hurt him. Mladen jumped but he no more than took a step into air and they had him, two holding his arms, and the one in front smacked him hard across the face—all so quickly that it was graceful as a practiced dance. But when they turned slightly, Carey could see Mladen's face, mouth open, nose bleeding heavily. His eyes crossed Carey's but did not seem to know him.

"We are sorry," the stout man said, the one who had struck him. "But your people have made this necessary, even in these small ways. Now listen, my sardine, carefully. We're going to let you off easier than some. But afterward you're to tell your father, and he is to tell the ambassador who will surely know who else to tell. Trieste belongs to us. We will stop at nothing."

Mladen was panting heavily now, staring past Carey.

"You understand?"

"Yes," he grunted.

The little man nodded. The other two took Mladen to the car beside Carey. One of them held his twisted arm and made him lean down slightly, and the other took Mladen's free arm to hold it like a bridge between the fender and hood. The little man who had gone to the trunk of the car came back with a crowbar and raised it over his head quickly. Carey yelled, "No," but the bar came down with a thwack and Mladen was screaming in a voice Carey did not know, doubled over on the cobbles. They pushed him away, the car started, Carey was thrown against the wall, and then they were gone.

Carey kneeled by Mladen. He still screamed, holding his arm. The forearm was bent in the middle like a broken stick. For a moment he could not think of what to do. He did not know this person who was suffering so horribly, and he even imagined that the only way to deal with such pain would be to kill him, quickly, his hands over that mouth, holding in the shriek. But instead he was yelling also, then standing in the middle of the street and turning from window to window. Some men came, and an ambulance, and he went with them, but before he climbed in he had to turn and vomit. In the ambulance they gave Mladen a shot to quiet him. Nancy arrived, and Mladen's parents, and they stayed at the hospital until the arm was set.

In the early morning, Nancy and Carey were told to go home. Carey tried to tell Mladen's father, but he said, no, they must not talk about it here, and the police said they would question him again later. Just before he left Carey went in to see Mladen lying on the bed, his arm in a cast, pale face puffed and sleeping under his shock of hair. He could believe none of it, and he wept as if a hook were being pulled up out of his gut.

Mladen was no longer allowed out at night alone. In a cast that went from shoulder to his still fingers, which began as gleaming white and was soon decorated with every kind of name and emblem, he chafed and played at being angry that his parents treated him like a child, although Carey was secretly glad of those restrictions and knew Mladen was too. In front of others Mladen talked about how he'd like to get hold of the chickens that did it, but there was no pretense between the two of them. They were both hurt, shaken and uneasy. Carey was surprised to see that for all his bantam bravado, Mladen had thought the rest of the world's violence was as showy as his own, and that underneath, it too would be gentle and considerate. In that first week they talked until they were beginning to invent details, and as soon as they found talking did no good, still left them with a brutal silence to deal with, they stopped.

Carey did not feel like wandering anymore. That old easiness of random movement, floating around from street to street through pools of light, had vanished, and in its place he moved purposefully, uneasy at the shadows, trusting no one. He knew rationally that there was no danger for him—those men were not any more interested in him now than they had been that night. But it did not matter whether the violence was directed at him or not. He had discovered something savage, larger than anyone, was waiting to break out, and he might by chance be there to take it, or almost as awful, merely to see it. History seemed to be something that used people, and this was a different randomness than the one he had loved.

Sometimes he would wonder whether it would not have happened if they had stayed home that night, or walked a different street, and then he would remember that dog slanting suddenly across the road, its tongue out from running hard in the fields, and the car's shuddering stop. He could not recall what Frank had said, only the initial certainty in his own mind that it did not have to happen—they could have stayed longer for lunch, or slept later that morning, or—and then by going back and back in time, those casual motions of car and dog had become fixed, unalterable.

Mladen came and went in an embassy car, and out of school Carey saw him at his apartment where always at least one beefy, bored guard in his baggy, mid-European suit was sitting or walking armed in the lobby, and if they went to the movies, they were accompanied by one of the guards. Carey came to know them by name, and even if Mladen was the only one who could speak with them fluently, they recognized Carey and managed some small talk in Italian. Mladen's family was making plans—they would go home for the summer, probably Mladen and his mother would have to stay on alone when his father came back to work, but maybe by next fall, they said, things would cool down over Trieste.

Carey was sorry for them. Sometimes they seemed to be living in a prison even though they were the victims, not the criminals. Gradually he and Mladen began to see less of each other. Carey could not help it—being with Mladen only heightened his own uneasiness since the knowledge they shared was one they both wanted to avoid. Mladen started out of boredom to flash into rages at his mother, even when Carey was there. The Makarovics talked about leaving sooner than they had planned.

For Carey now, everything was slipping out, away, quietly slackening and leaving huge spaces. He dreamed that his emperor moved farther and farther apart, his huge head carried out on a black stone boat into the sea while the hand stood in the wet sand, pointing away.


When Carey reached Ian's apartment the door was open. All the shades were up, the curtains drawn back, windows thrown open, and the May sun wrapped in its air of the warmed city was blinding, reflecting off the polished marble floors, the glass of lamps and objects scattered around the room, with a painful glitter. He blinked, putting a hand on his forehead to shield his eyes. Everything was sharply cut out by the light: the piano, a standing lamp, a chair, and three people as equally fixed in place as the furniture. Carey knew two of the silhouettes: Ian with his back turned, head slightly bowed, standing by the tip of the piano's bend as if he might have been shoving the instrument into place; Pierre in the middle of the brightest spot of sun on the floor, his huge arms hanging slack, body toward Carey. But his head was turned to the man Carey did not recognize who sat in the chair, one leg up under the other, an elbow on the armrest and hand holding his chin on its fingertips, a gesture so whittled and spiked that he took on the central focus, as if all the crystalline and shattered light had been brought by him. They did not move and Carey was stunned by the dazzle.

The stranger muttered something in a soft but somewhat nasal voice, a language Carey did not at first recognize. Pierre turned slowly away and went to the window as if intending to shut it, but he leaned there instead, looking down. When Ian turned, Carey could tell he had been weeping, face puffed and distorted. Still no one had spoken to him.

"Come in. We were expecting you." Ian's voice began uncertainly but cleared itself. "Manuel, this is Carey, our *wunderkind*. Manuel Artaria."

The man did not untuck his leg but extended an arm, so that Carey had to make a brief, awkward clasp of his left hand.

"They tell me you are excellent," he said in chiseled Italian.

Now that he could see his face, Carey could tell it was older than Pierre's and Ian's, but with a fleshy kind of handsomeness— large-lidded eyes, a pendulous lower lip and cleft chin—features far more blunt than his pose and silhouette had seemed, a face that almost mocked his small-boned, elegant, very slim body.

"We'd better go now," Pierre said. He stroked a paw roughly back through his hair, "Hello, you boy." The attempt at a smile made him seem more weary.

"What? I'm not to hear the Schubert, then?"

"I'd prefer that." Ian stood very stiffly beside Carey.

Manuel unfolded and rose. The leg he had tucked up was slightly shorter than the other and when he walked he did so with a jerk, his face assuming a tense droop to one side. "Come, Pierre. We can all talk later at dinner. I wish to go to the Museo now anyway."

Pierre followed him, glanced at Ian, who watched them both as if he wanted something more than this, but when he saw Carey staring he pursed his lips. They paused together at the door.

"Well, Ian," and Pierre did not look at him. "Around eight? At Ranieri's?"

"Yes."

The door shut. Carey took the music to the piano, Ian turned to the window and then back as though struggling not to look out. With his back to Carey, who sat and began playing, Ian stared toward the mirror on the opposite wall, and after a while he moved slowly as if looking for something and stood in front of it for a long time, hands clasped behind his back. Carey wanted to go over to him, but Ian looked too completely self-enclosed to be touched. Finally he turned and came to stand by the piano, his face pale but perfectly composed. Carey stopped playing.

"Sorry that you had to come in on all this. I imagine I owe you some explanation."

"What's wrong, Ian?"

When Carey said his name, he looked at him instead of the wall above, and his tone of voice became less clipped.

"He's leaving."

"Pierre?"

He nodded.

"Why?"

He raised an eyebrow, jerked his head as if Manuel were still in the chair.

"Him."

"But why him? He seems so mean."

Ian shrugged. "Who knows why we love what we love?" He said more angrily, "Oh, it's been going on for years. I'm certain I told you. Manuel's the man Pierre was with in Paris for a while. But I had heard he'd gone away. They had an argument. Pierre said it was all over. But it wasn't. They've been seeing each other off and on most of this year. Funny, I didn't even suspect."

He turned to the window, this time to put a hand on the sill and lean there. The sun lit up his hair and for the first time Carey noticed how it was slightly tinged with red.

"They're going back to Paris. Together. Of course, Pierre doesn't want me to come."

"What will you do?"

"Not go," he said quickly. "Not go."

"I'm sorry."

"Perhaps they won't go either."

He put a hand on Carey's shoulder with something like

a smile but in a very pale face, and he said, "Come, let's hear it."

They knew the music almost by heart now and went through without stopping, better than they had ever performed it before.


"I'm going with you."

Carey was about to leave for his lesson and he stopped with his hand on the banister.

"Don't."

"I have to. We need to talk."

"Shouldn't you call her at least?"

But they had started down already and Nancy said crisply, "I believe she'll be there."

Ikbal saw him first, squinted at the figure behind him, then half smiled as if this were long expected.

"Do come in," she said to Nancy, and she had a few parting words in French for the very serious gentleman who was on his way out. She closed the door, kept her hand momentarily on the lock, then said, "Shall we sit in the living room? Or we could go to the kitchen and have some coffee."

"That would be fine," Nancy said, and as they turned to go there, Ikbal put her arm through Carey's.

They sat around the table in the kitchen so polished and clean that Carey often thought she must eat there only when he came. Now she moved quickly about the stove, measuring the coffee, letting the water run for a while from the tap. When the pot was on, she sat with them, arms folded.

"Where do we begin?" she said.

Nancy and Ikbal stared at each other briefly, and for a moment Carey wished he were not there.

"We could talk about how I am ruining your child."

"Please." Nancy lifted a hand as if she were warding off a blow. "I don't want to talk about all that. That's done."

"Finished?"

"Obviously not. But accomplished. I've had to accept that much."

"So."

Carey sat there, tangled in the back and forth of gestures and looks. He could tell they were almost unaware of his presence and that whatever was going on, he was, for a while at least, an onlooker, a mere subject of conversation. Ikbal was momentarily confused, as if she had expected the conversation to go a different way.

"I don't want to discuss why a thirty-year-old woman might want to be the mistress of a young man nearly half her age. You have your reasons."

That almost brought him in, but he let Ikbal's silence restrain him.

"I want to know some other things, clearly and simply."

"Go on."

"My son says he will not leave Rome. That he is going to stay here and you are encouraging him to."

"Yes."

"I've told him I want him to come back with me. He pointed out I can't make him." She looked at neither of them and moved her finger in a slow circle on the tabletop, making a maze with some spilled water. "Maybe he's right. I guess I know that if I or someone else can't persuade him, it's no use. So that means I have some decisions to make. I could leave him, trusting that all this is something in himself he *does* understand, that it goes beyond just you and him. Or I could stay myself, here, with him, for his sake." She was looking at Ikbal now.

The pot began to perk and Ikbal swiveled in her chair to turn down the flame. "Do you think I can answer that?"

"I don't know you very well. I don't know how much imagination you have. So I'm telling you what it is like, how it is to have a seventeen-year-old son you love more than anything on earth, who's your only true family and has helped you through the worst of things, how it is to see him growing up suddenly, perhaps too suddenly, at any rate so quickly that you don't know whether to hold on or let go."

Carey had expected anger, bitterness, a chill back and forth, not this calm revealing of her pain, or worse, of what he was doing to her.

"You see, if I go, and that turns out to be wrong, I would have to live with knowing I was too damned rational, even as we're probably being now, talking over this table like friends. I would know I'd gone against any instinct in me. But if I stay, there might be something just as wrong. I don't want to be here anymore. It's not right for me, for my own life. So I'd be making my life over for him, purely for my son, against the grain of my own, and that might be wrong, worse for him than anything."

Ikbal had folded her arms again, staring thoughtfully at Nancy's fingers, and he recognized that old backing off. She stood, brought back the coffee, some cups, and sat down again.

She pushed the cream and sugar toward him and in a quiet voice said, "I'm sorry for that. Oh, not sorry of what I've done, but sorry that it's so hard for you. I'm not sure I know what good it is to tell me all this, though."

Nancy glanced at Carey for the first time. "I want some facts at least. I think you can give me that much."

"Such as?"

"If Carey stays, will he live with you? Will you support him?"

"For a while."

"You can afford that?"

"For a while."

"Because I will not want to have anything to do with it if he lives with you, you understand. Not that there's much I could do in the way of money. But not while he's with you."

"You needn't have said that."

"All right. The other thing is purely professional. You have led him to believe he's good enough to make it in your world. How do I know that's right? What proof do I have?"

"There would be no reason for me..."

"Reason." Nancy's face flushed. "Don't talk to me about reason. Under the circumstances, how could I credit you with any sense of reason or objectivity?"

"Very well. I will give you the names of two or three people who were present at Naples. They are well known enough that I believe you could trust their word."

"Fine. Do. I need that."

For the first time they glared at each other. Carey saw that his mother had touched something in Ikbal that angered her more than any of the other things, her sense of professional pride. He could not stand it anymore. He was beginning to feel as if he were not there at all.

"What good is all this? I'm staying, don't you understand?" As if he sensed some final way in which this went beyond both of them he added, "No matter what either of you do or say."

They looked at him. Ikbal smiled faintly.

"I think, Mrs. Mitchell, that your son is telling us both to go to hell."

"No, I'm not. I just don't see any use in this. I don't want it."

He stood, walked to the kitchen door.

"Carey." Nancy stood also.

"No. You go ahead and talk. The two of you. I'll be home later."

"Let him go," Ikbal said quietly.

He left them there, Nancy still looking after him and Ikbal watching as if curious to see what he would do. He let himself out and walked aimlessly for a while until he came to the Campo dei Fiori where the market was still bustling, and he watched a woman pick out a live chicken from the crate and haggle for fifteen minutes over the price while the butcher held the bird by the legs with one hand and waved his cleaver at her with the other and the chicken looked about perkily but upside down.

# 3

"I've never had to deal with my lover's mother before," Ikbal said quietly.

But Nancy only heard her peripherally. She was still looking at the door, half expecting Carey to come back as he sometimes did when he was a child with that hangdog look he would wear when a dramatic gesture failed. Once he had set out to run away, slamming the door after some statement about never coming back. But ten minutes later the door had pushed open with a slap against the wall and he had trudged in. He had not wanted to miss the ball game on the radio.

She blinked. No. He was much beyond all that now. This walking out had been no overacted gesture but the right thing to do.

"I wonder," she said out loud, as if talking to the wall. "I suppose sometimes it is better to be more secretive."

"Excuse me?" Ikbal was sitting at the table, one hand turning a spoon over and over slowly.

"Oh, it's just that I've tried to be absolutely open about everything with him. That's why I wanted him to be here. But perhaps that's not right. Maybe I should have come alone."

"At least this gives *him* the choice, doesn't it?"

"Yes. But sometimes I wonder if I give him all the choices because I can make none."

Ikbal shook her head. "You are making them for your own life, and trying not to make them all for him. I don't think there is anything else to do."

They looked at each other for a long time. Nancy started to say something but instead simply kept her eyes on Ikbal's.

Nothing in the room moved, even the two of them seemed to have stopped breathing.

"More coffee?" Ikbal said, and as if they both acknowledged the absurdity of the words in the context they smiled.

"I can't help it. Without Carey here, I feel a little foolish."

"Don't. I'm glad you came. Although I'll admit I've dreaded it. I haven't been able to imagine what I would say. So far it has been easier than I expected."

Nancy resented those words. Something in her wanted it to be hard; the woman she had imagined Ikbal to be and the woman in herself she had raised to confront that imagined being were still shaking fists at each other, but they seemed like pale gestures, fading ghosts of some floating drama.

"I can see why Carey cares for you so much," Nancy said.

"And I can see how much he has taken from you."

Ikbal rose and brought back two glasses. "Perhaps some wine," and not waiting for Nancy to reply, she brought out a bottle and began working on the cork. When she sat again, it was in the chair at the side of the table, closer to Nancy. She lifted her glass.

"Please, if you won't take this flippantly, let us drink to Carey."

Nancy paused. Was she being mocked? But there was certainly nothing in the clear, dark eyes of that woman to indicate it, so she lifted her glass, nudged it with a gentle clink against Ikbal's, and drank. Suddenly she felt some sense of wonder beyond the immediate situation and those tugging emotions that still swayed her in every direction even as she looked at the woman's long delicate fingers.

"Lord, Lord," and she shook her head slowly, "how strange it all is. I would never, never have imagined this, drinking to my son with his lover. Or most of the things that happened to me in the past few years."

She was embarrassed. What was she blurting out? But the sense of wonder persisted for a moment longer, and in that space she felt the other woman's hand on hers, looked down and turned hers over to clasp it. Again they looked at each other, and suddenly, without the least warning, Nancy saw her free hand lifting the glass to toss its contents directly in Ikbal's face. She flinched, blinked, but her hand did not let go. If anything it held on more tightly.

"What have I done?"

But Ikbal, eyes closed, was holding on tightly still. She shook her head a few times, opened her eyes, let go, and began wiping at her face. Nancy stood, went to the sink where she found a cloth and returned with it, and as she wiped the table she noticed her own hands were trembling, and her voice began speaking rapidly, whirling, "Never, I mean I've never done anything like that before, it just happened, I never even wanted to, thought I would, my hand just seemed to..." and she stopped, leaned on the rag on the table, eyes closed, aware that the other woman was still sitting there watching, and her hand was on Nancy's arm again, firmly.

"No. It's too complicated. Words can't do all this."

"He's all I've got. Or at least I used to think so. You see, the thing is, I don't think that anymore. I am beginning to see how I have so much I did not know about. But I can't just let him go, let him walk out a door, or let some woman I don't really know..." She held still, looking at Ikbal who, her hair wet at the fringes where the wine had splashed, eyes blinking, looked very young, younger than Carey, a girl almost, and when she stood, Nancy lurched forward and held onto the wisp of a body and Ikbal's arms were tight as ropes around her, hands riding up and down her back.

When they sat again, Nancy kept hold of Ikbal's hand and poured herself another glass of wine.

"I promise to drink this one," and she did quickly and with great thirst, pouring herself another. She sat back. "I hope that is over now."

Ikbal nodded. "So. You are going home."

"Yes."

"I can understand that too. Some day I will go home. But not for a while."

"I don't know," and Nancy watched Ikbal rise, go to the sink and rinse off her face with her hands, shaking them afterward like a cat, "how so many of you do it. Being exiles. The other day I met an Irish poet at an embassy party. He has never been back to Ireland since he left twenty years ago. But all he writes about is Ireland."

She sat again. "About him, I don't know. Or others like him. Some people make a kind of living from their absence, or at least it gives them something fixed to long for, to be absorbed in. Others have no choice. There are many of us like that. For us, we try not to think of it. But that, in its own way, is a little like thinking of it."

"I'm sorry."

Ikbal shrugged. "Nothing to be sorry for. But I have been

so long away that going back will be almost going to a new place."

"That's part of what worries me. I can see it. In a few years, staying here, I would know less and less about what is there, would more and more have an unreal place in my mind to refer to, dream of. My parents would die, the places would change, all the things I know to touch and feel I would have to remake, out of memory." She paused, surprised at how coherent it was all becoming.

"Your parents are old?"

"Getting so." A letter had come yesterday from her mother. Was that why she mentioned them now? Her mother seemed much the same, except some slight shift was there, a tone that Nancy could not identify and yet intrigued her, something her mother had made up her mind about but was not telling, perhaps did not herself know. It seemed also that Pop was doing some walking, with help, and across the bottom in a firm but scraggly hand he had scrawled, "Hi, doll: Hurry home."

"But the thing is the disconnection. Or how can I put it—all my life up to now I felt I was not finding much for myself. Would you understand? With your music, fame, a profession. I did not believe I could do anything but work my will on my husband, raise this child who needs me less and less."

Nancy waved her hand impatiently. "But every day it becomes more unreal. I am making new nets and tangles, a 'new' past, but shallow, half my life cut off and sealed away, back there," and her arm flung out as if gesturing at a country just beyond the window. "I have no illusions. I will go back to a place that will try to make me what I was, parents who will not understand, an ex-husband who will become Carey's father again, no matter how far away he is, but those are my real nets, something to struggle with. Here I can only go around in circles, acting out again and again the things I need to work out in time. Exiled—" but hearing herself making a speech she began to mistrust by the weight of its abstraction, she added, "I think," and began to laugh. When she stopped she had to brush at her eyes. "Perhaps," she said, "I'm quite cracked."

But after they had talked for hours and Ikbal had strolled with her along the bank of the Tiber, the lowering sun still bright and warm on their faces, and after they had parted, having kissed each other on the cheek, Nancy could not help feeling she had lost something, an anger at the least, a right to that anger at most. Was it simply impossible to hate someone once you knew her? But that was not so, because she had talked long and hard with Roberta Wise and surely she hated that woman the more she met her. There was nothing left but to admit that Carey knew what he was doing, as much as anyone could.

He was playing hooky more frequently, but not wandering around the city. He would stay home and practice or read or sit in the sun on the balcony. Nancy knew but did not press him. If she woke in the morning and Carey was still lounging around the living room in bare feet and pajamas, she did not tell him to hurry or he would miss the bus. They would talk and she would go to work, giving him a kiss, a careful look before she went.

One morning he woke to the phone ringing and knew he had slept late and she had not even bothered to wake him.

*"Pronto?"*

There was a crackling silence, then Mladen's voice.

"Carey?"

"Yes."

Another pause. "I wanted to say goodbye."

"What?"

"We're leaving. For Yugoslavia. My mother and I."

"Can't I see you? I'll catch the bus. I'll be there in a half hour."

"They're waiting for me now."

Carey's hand ached with gripping the receiver so tightly. He could think of nothing that would overcome the distance of that voice, no body to touch.

"Mladen," he said finally, giving him his name as if that could grapple him for a moment.

"Will you write?" the voice said.

"Yes."

Mladen had to spell his address slowly, the words incomprehensible to Carey, not even forming into sounds for him on the page.

"And you?" Mladen said.

"Maybe I'll stay."

He heard someone calling Mladen's name.

"Goodbye, Carey."

He tried to speak, but his throat was lumped and he must have been barely audible. The line clicked. A whoosh of dead space filled the phone. Carey said, "Mladen" into it once, loudly, and then hung up, frightened by the sound of his own voice being smothered. He sat on the couch for a long time, and when Nancy came home he told her. They tried to talk about it, but there was not much to say.

She took a deep breath. "I'll tell you what I've decided. I'm going to go. Home. To the States. One of the lawyers is going back and he can get me a job with his firm in Philadelphia. But I'm also going back to school. To law school."

She had never mentioned that before. "Why? You want to be a lawyer?"

She smiled. "Why not? I'd like to try, anyway. I know something about it, after all, and they tell me I'm good at it."

But that did not really interest him. "When?"

"When what?"

"When do you want to leave?"

"Soon. About three weeks. I want to travel north on the way, see Paris, London."

He waited, understanding she was about to do something and had not counted him in.

"I'd like you to come with me. But I'm going to do something that might be foolish. I'm going to leave it up to you."

He started to speak but she held up her hand.

"Don't answer me now, please. I've gone this far, and I'm not sure I'm ready for the next step if you say you're staying. But anyway, I want you to think for a while. I want you to make up your own mind and tell me when you know for sure."

For the first time he did not know what he wanted, had not expected this isolation, nothing to push against.

"All right," he said, and she leaned forward suddenly, took his head in both her hands to kiss him on the forehead and hold his face against her cheek.

As if to put everything away, they walked downtown and met Alberto and went to the movies together.

Carey was not surprised when Mrs. Wise called him into her office. She sat him down and went "right to the point." But she always did that. She prided herself on her "frankness." Only a few weeks of school were left, but she wanted to be sure he missed no more classes, if he wanted to pass. He listened to her, not too politely. He could see past her, out the window to that hummocked field where they played softball, doing their best to miss the scattered piles of sheep dung after the flocks had come through. Finally she stopped. He could tell she had asked a question.

"Are you listening to me, Carey?"

"No, ma'am."

She frowned. She was looking tired again. The school was not doing well financially, and when the parents had taken control of it, starting with the firing of Mr. Anderson, they had set loose an endless process. They could never agree among themselves. Nancy had told him that, and also that Mr. Brewster was pulling out his backing. He and a group of parents were going to start another school, for Americans only.

"I said, if you can't promise me to be here regularly, I'll have to take it up with your mother. You're already in severe difficulty in my class."

He looked at her directly. Something black moved distantly behind her head, the shepherd's dog, but with his eyes unfocused, Carey thought it looked like a lurking bat and he could not help smiling, thinking what she might do if she knew a bat was tangled in her hair.

"Why is that so funny?"

"I guess it's not. No. I can't promise."

"Then I'll have to talk to your mother."

"She won't care."

"Excuse me?"

"Neither of us do."

Her mouth opened, closed. Suddenly she sat back in her chair, still straight-backed but not staring at him. She reached to turn the pencil slowly on her desk. "It's an awful waste, really. You probably won't get any credit for the year at all."

"I don't care."

"I see you don't. But you may some day."

He shrugged.

"It's been a hard year for you, hasn't it, Carey?"

He saw she meant that kindly, but he did not answer.

"You know we're sorry about Mladen."

"Why? It wasn't your fault."

"No, but I mean..."

"I know what you mean."

There was a knock.

"Come in?"

The count's face peered in the crack. "Ah. Occupied."

"Only a moment."

The door closed again.

"Are you sorry about Ian?"

She blinked. "Of course not. Not for what we had to do. But I'm glad you brought that up. You know, Carey, that what he suffers from is a serious illness. But he has made his choices. We're more worried about you."

"You needn't be."

She leaned forward now, and her face for the first time since he had known her was not composed.

"Please. I'm serious. We can help you, you know. We have a psychiatrist through the medical services at the embassy. I think you should go talk to him."

"Thanks. No."

She shook her head, anguished. "Oh, if I were your mother, I wouldn't let you just drift like this." She sighed.

He made up his mind about those last few weeks. He stood and went to the door.

"Goodbye, Mrs. Wise."

She sighed again and muttered something like, "Hopeless."

He brushed by Count Cortese, who was standing very straight in the hallway, his hands clasped in front of him, almost as if he were manacled, and went to his locker downstairs to get his raincoat and the old overshoes he had left there most of the winter. He walked out the front door, pausing once to look back from the driveway. The villa still appeared the same, scrawny hedges around its base not concealing the ill-fitting way it rose abruptly out of the field, still a villa someone wished for but did not know how to place once he had it. The bees were humming madly in the shrubs near him and he heard a jangle of the bellwether somewhere near the rim of the ravine. He started walking back to town.

He was not even halfway when the count pulled over, the door opposite him swung open, and Carey climbed in. Cortese was looking at him a little mischievously.

"Going home?"

Carey grinned. "Yes."

"I also."

"I'm not coming back."

The count laughed, a quiet jiggling of his shoulders. "I also."

"What?"

"Yes. I told her I have finished."

Carey could not help laughing too. They were quiet most

of the way as if they had said all there was to say, and Carey did not feel uncomfortable. Cortese let him off at Piazza Venezia.

"So," and the traffic rumbled around them but he seemed unhurried. "Perhaps you will read Books Ten, Eleven, Twelve sometime yourself."

"I hope so."

But with gravity he said, "He is fine, Virgil," and Carey said quickly, "Yes. Thank you for that."

Carey put out his hand, the count shook it, smiled, said, "I look forward to your concert. And also, *buon viaggio*," and Carey stepped out onto the pavement. The door closed, a hand waved once, and the car wedged back into the traffic.

Carey woke one morning in great happiness because he had figured out a way both to stay and go. Everyone he knew had gone to live with him in a huge house without window panes. It was beside the ocean, and when he sat on the bare floor of the topmost room he could hear all their voices talking quietly under him in different rooms, and down by the water a little boy was rolling the Bocca della Verità that had shrunk, light as a sand dollar. When he woke he knew that all this had been accomplished by a magical speech, but he could not recall the words.

"I want to stay to dinner," he told Ikbal when he came in.

She nodded, and while he played the piano she went to the phone to break some engagement. He was working hard on a late sonata by Beethoven, Opus 110, and had only just begun to master the quiet arpeggios of the first movement, feathering down and up, but now also the fugue was making sense to him, becoming merged with the rest instead of some separate and difficult tangle, and he felt its gathering speed, the final flight into a glimmer of harmony. Standing behind him, she put her hands on both his cheeks.

"Yes," she said, "yes."

They went out into the late afternoon to buy food, and it was like the earliest days when they first knew each other; she was happy, bantering with the vendors, and they bought too much but everything they saw suddenly seemed good to them. They had filled the bottle with wine and were passing back through the square when a barking dog made a wild chase for a cat, all the cat's hair on end, and both animals slammed into the front strut on a three-legged fruit stand. It collapsed and the pyramid of apples, oranges, pears, soft melons from Africa, tumbled, rolled, while the vendor stood in the middle of it and waved his arms in fierce lamentations, and they were in the middle of all the spilled fruit and could not get out without stepping on some of it. The bottoms of their shoes were slippery with juices, even their ankles wet, and suddenly they ran laughing, up the stairs of her apartment, chasing each other, wet shoes in their hands, and when they were inside she put the basket on the kitchen table and he caught her, and they took their clothes off quickly. For the first time Carey lifted her, legs curled over his arms and head tucked to his neck, and he was surprised how light she was. He carried her onto the bed.

They had dozed for a while and it was dark. She rose and cooked and he lay there naked, thinking about her. She brought the food on a tray and they both decided the light was too strong so she set two candles on the floor, one on each side of the bed. They ate, both of them naked, and sometimes he would hold up his fork with food and she would lean forward to eat it, and they did not bother with glasses for the wine. Soon they put the food on the floor and made love again, very quietly and for a long time, and from time to time she would say his name and he would answer her and through his mind the music of the Beethoven played as if carried on his blood or hers.

They lay side by side on their backs watching the shadows from the two candles flutter back and forth against each other on the ceiling. He said quietly, "She left it up to me."

"I thought she would." Her hand tightened and relaxed on his fingers.

"I have to make up my mind."

She turned her head, kissed his shoulder.

"Do you care? Which I do?"

She did not answer at first. "I will always care."

"I mean, does it make a difference to you?"

"Don't be unfair, Carey. You have to make up your own mind. That's what has been given to you now."

"I will. I don't mean to have you do it. But I think you can say how you feel."

"Then I'll tell the truth. I don't know."

He was not quite expecting that.

"Whether you stay or go won't have much to do with you as a pianist. You have that, or you will, no matter what."

"I thank you for that."

She turned slightly as if to see whether his face in that dim light was being sarcastic.

"I mean it."

She nodded.

"But what will I do to you if I stay?"

"We would see," she said slowly.

He waited for more but she held still. Hovering high over his own thoughts, wondering whether he would ever know for certain if he was right, he decided that he wanted to give her something, share some freedom they both should have. He looked into that tenuously, then jumped.

"I'm leaving."

She turned, the whole length of her body pressed against his side.

"Why am I?" He was rushed by both relief and sadness.

Her fingers moved absentmindedly on his chest. "It's odd, isn't it? I would have expected it to be the other way."

"How?"

"I to be leaving you."

"I'm sorry..." But her hand was gently pressed over his mouth.

"I don't mean you should feel sorry. But I usually am the one who leaves. It's been that way ever since Piero. A kind of vengeance, I guess. I will get very close, and then put an end to it. Abruptly. Like death."

They turned their faces to each other, only a breath away.

"But I could never do that to you, Carey, even when I tried." She was quiet for a moment. "What do you think you will do when you are back there?"

He closed his eyes, trying to imagine Philadelphia, a new home somewhere. The only thing that was clear was his piano sitting in storage. "I might go to Curtis. My teacher used to say I could probably get in." But he did not want to think that far ahead. Then, as clearly as if he were looking at a photograph, he saw Frank's face, and he said quietly, "First, though, I'll go to see my father." He turned his face back to her. "I want to stay all night."

She nodded, and he went to the phone, called Nancy and told her where he was and that he would be back in the morning. She did not argue. They hardly slept that night, did not even talk much. The candles burned down, guttered out, and they kept touching each other, holding on, or her hand would play over his closed eyes, his nose, his lips. He touched her tears once during the night. They slept at dawn.

He thought everything was fine as he started down the stairs. He had made the right decision and felt good about it, maybe even a little noble. The sun was out and he walked along the Tiber on his way to the bus, and suddenly he was having trouble seeing clearly so he stopped and leaned on the wall as though he were looking down at the water. He would see her again before they left, but something was over, forever. He could not cry, but he certainly did not feel noble, or right, or wrong. Only empty, and waiting.

When he reached home, Nancy had not gone to work yet. She let him in, as if she were waiting for him. They had some coffee together, and he was very tired. She was about to go out the door when he called to her.

"Yes?"

"I'm coming with you."

She blinked, looked at his face hard, and smiled slightly. "Thank you."

He was glad that was all she said. She walked out and pulled the door shut gently as if afraid of waking someone.

# 4

The town tiered above them as they stood on the station platform, and Alberto, reluctant to be there at all, was trying not to show how weary, even indolent, he felt looking at the steps up to the first level of streets, the small square with its savagely pruned plane trees, and he was burdened by knowing how the town rose even beyond the summit of the old Temple of Fortune. Nancy, more energetic and open in these last days than she had ever been, tugged at his arm, steered them through the bright early morning sunshine already drying whatever dampness was left in the morning shadows.

"Come on," she said, as they started up the stairs, "first I want to be certain we find some postcards and that I remember to send them. I have so many people to warn that I'm coming home."

He let her hand ride nervously over his arm, walked slowly up the stairs, as if stunned by the thought of another jumble of ruins and churches and crumbling walls to explain to her endless curiosity, another walk from a station to the top of a town and back, but this one with the gray lassitude of knowing it could be the last. Nancy and Carey were leaving so soon, and there was no way to prevent it. As solid and impenetrable as this heaped town, that fact squatted in front of him, could not be seen through or around. They passed under the plane trees, skirted the beggar by the kiosk. Was it simply that he sensed her life rushing now far ahead of him, as if these present moments were something she was beyond and he swirled in the eddies of her wake? His own life bobbed and spun. What life?

"...was my neighbor for only a little while," she was saying. "But Anna was very kind and I promised to send her a card while I was in Italy."

"Then you are just in time, aren't you?"

But even a tone of irony eluded her now. She said with simple happiness, "Yes. Just in time."

She stopped at the café across from the square, and he took their coffee to a table while she chose some postcards, then joined him to write, asking him the date and if he knew where the nearest tobacconist was, for stamps. She set out for it, and he watched her walk down the street, dark glasses neatly stuck into her hair, those full, somewhat plush hips swaying under the flowered print of a short cotton skirt, and bare, sandaled feet moving her away, away over the freshly watered pavement. La Primavera, he thought, that long-faced image, sad-eyed in its flowers, and then he was embarrassed at the maudlin association. She was no Botticelli at this moment, but an American maenad on her way as they always were—destination not too clearly known, but in motion. Botticelli's woman, he had long ago admitted, was merely the recurring fantasy image for any Italian male, frozen as she was somewhere between mother and lover, an unobtainable but fleshy ikon.

"Ancora un caffé," he barked at the waiter, and watched her begin to idle back, licking the stamps and thumbing them onto the cards, staring into the windows as she moved and halted, oblivious of the way the street sweeper paused to stare, the baker came to his door to lean. She had gained weight slightly during the year, but it was only an increase in sensuality, the slight rise of belly under that tight midriff, the flesh of bare arms already tan. He looked away. Why was it never possible to enjoy without wanting to possess? He heard the metallic clatter of the mailbox, then she was beside him, his fresh coffee was delivered, and she said, "What a lovely little town. They were very friendly," and he agreed and told her how the ancient Romans used the place, Praeneste, as they did so many of the hill towns near Rome, as a cool retreat, and he tried to help her imagine the chilled marble floors, the open, shaded courtyards taking the breezes not to be found on the flat plains below.

"We could go to Greece," he continued. "You've never been there. For a few weeks. Alone. Carey would wait here. You might feel differently, then."

The sun was on their table now and she put on her dark glasses, not looking at him as he spoke so rapidly.

— 299 —

"Tell me about the temple. The town. Before we start walking."

"Paros is a lovely island. You must go by boat and it comes only every few days."

She did glance at him, but he could not see her eyes clearly. "Please."

He put out his hand, touched a straying wisp of hair that straggled at her neck, and then sat back.

"You must not confuse Fors Fortuna with Fortuna, the Primigenia, firstborn daughter. The former, after all, is what we call fortune, or Dame Chance. The latter is more dignified, essential—Fate or Desinty."

He watched her stare vaguely out over the square. When he let the mockery go, spoke in his natural voice, she put out her hand as if to thank him and held his on the tabletop.

"Sulla built it, huge, eighty acres they say, on terraces up the slope, covered by a whole town in the Middle Ages. The bombing brought it back to sight. Her images, you'll see them here and there, are rudder and cornucopia, direction and plenty—or their opposites, I guess, implied."

"And they worshipped her. Here."

"Importantly, here."

"A woman, of course."

He nodded. "First Daughter." He put some money down on the table. "The people did not want to go. They wanted to rebuild their homes. There was much bitterness. But archeology won. Or perhaps Fortuna, again."

They stood, he adjusted his jacket across his shoulders, and they walked along, gradually twisting up toward the bare terraces.

"Oh, and of course you mustn't forget Palestrina. The great composer. So you have rubble, and priests reading the guts, and oracles, and also music rising out of it all."

"The usual jumble," she said.

He wanted to smile, but again a great weariness struck him. They had this kind of banter down so well now, could use it to contain happiness or conceal some argument. What difference did it really make? If she stayed or left. He jerked his hand back. She stared. He pretended to be slapping at a fly on his shoulder. But for a moment a rage had shaken him. The walls of battered houses gave way, they stepped out on the wide terrace as if walking over a huge roof, and in the bright sun they stood dazed, looking over the green ocean of the hazy plain.

"'*Com'é bella la Roma nella primavera,*'" he began to sing, and as if she did not catch anything satirical in his clear baritone voice, she leaned her head on his shoulder.

They walked about in half-excavated chambers, viewed the mostly unsorted artifacts in an unfinished museum while a guard hovered nearby, then came out again onto the final terrace. Above the last scattered houses and a shrine, the hillside rose in a jumble of rocks, green patches, yellow walls.

"Come on," she said, "I'm not hungry yet."

Again she took his arm, guiding them on beyond the last paving stones onto a worn path curving up into the fields.

"There should be sheep," she said, and he did not have to answer because far to the right they heard a leaden clatter of a bell randomly carried on the breeze, saw at the next turn the distant scattered dots of white. The path narrowed and she walked ahead now. He could not take his eyes from her swaying hips, the slight crease of buttocks as her skirt pressed in. He did not even have the energy to ask where she was going, why, what purpose there could be in this aimless trudge. Her feet moved so deftly through rocks and clumps of turf. Ahead were three walls of a roofless hut, and the side of the hill rose abruptly to some small road.

"San Vito is up that road," he said as they paused in the broken cusp of walls.

She stood in the doorway, staring out over the even wider prospect.

"Is that Rome?" She pointed.

He stared at her lifted arm, the contour of breast beneath it, her dress gathered high on her thigh now as she held one foot up on the stoop, and he put both hands on her hips, stood close behind and rode them up her waist to cup her breasts.

"*Si. Roma.*" She put her head back, her cheek salty to his lips.

"Please, Alberto, don't."

But he would not let her pull away. His hand wandered up under the canopy of her dress, touched the hot skin of her inner thighs. She tried to move away more insistently. He turned her to him roughly, one hand twisting back an arm and her glasses fell away with a clatter on the rocks. Her eyes were puzzled. He put his mouth harshly over hers, thrust in his tongue. She winced and when he drew back to breathe she said, "Please, my arm. You're hurting me."

For one moment the thought was so clear and strongly seen that he was certain it was done—she lay heaped in the corner of this decayed house, on that clutter of fallen stone, her clothes torn, her bare legs spread, crotch naked. She was not breathing or speaking and he stooped over her like some huge bird, taking her again and again with raw, rigid flesh.

"I'm sorry," he murmured, letting go of the arm. She rubbed the wrist, still standing close.

"I understand," and she touched his cheek; but shocked, terrified for a moment, he recoiled until he saw by her expression that she had not understood at all.

Something as solid as a heavy footfall struck the grass nearby. They turned their heads, held still. Again, but this time it was on the rock wall to their side, and a small clatter of old plaster fell. Something seemed to be dropping on them. Alberto looked straight up into a blue sky. This time the sound was at his feet, he felt a rock bounce in sharp pain against his shin, looked up again and saw them on the road above, two boys, one of them with his arm already swinging back, and when he flung it out, a dark object arced into the sky, plummeted at them and struck beyond the doorway.

Alberto yelled, shook his fist, and as if being seen were enough to frighten them, the two figures dipped out of sight behind the rim of the horizon.

She was staring up, face pale, one hand ready to shield herself.

"Why were they doing that?"

But he only took her hand, started urging her along the path. "Come, quickly."

"But my glasses," and yet she made no effort to go back. They were almost running.

At the first turn in a path, they stopped. She was out of breath. They looked back up the hill, could see nothing but the dazzling contrasts of grass and stone and sky. But he was glad she was frightened. They walked slowly all the way down, talking about how they could have been injured, how the boys must have been very young and did not understand what could have happened, and all the time when his voice trembled he was thankful for the excuse he had to be upset. But the hand that had twisted her arm would not stop shaking.

As if the incident of the morning had cut them off from everyone else, they became silent, and he could see she was uneasy. They ate in a fine restaurant where the service was excellent, the terrace with its cool arcade of vines a perfect image of what they should expect, and yet they both were listless and did not hesitate to walk slowly back down to the train station when they had finished. Only on the train did she relax again, twisting to look back at the hill, the white scars of the newly released temple. Halfway to Rome she put her hand on his and for a while she held on so tightly that he thought she would say something, but her face was turned to the window and when he said quietly, not wanting to include the other passengers in their conversation, "What is it?" her head merely shook twice, slowly.

They walked out through the concourse, past the beggars and whores and sellers of Parker pens, and when they were nearly to the taxis she turned and put a hand on his chest. As if by reflex he reached up and held onto her elbow.

"Alberto. I am going to say goodbye."

"What?"

"It has to be sometime this week. I want it to be now. I want it to be quick. Over."

Her face was pale and she stared past his head in an absorbed manner. He tried to laugh.

"Come, come, Nancy. This is too sudden. We should relax. Have a nice evening together. Say goodbye in a better way."

She shook her head. "I don't want all the rituals. I don't want to have to know it's coming and think about it and then lie somewhere with you and weep and all that."

"You want?" He was short, a thickset man with a face disfigured by a folded scar running aslant from forehead to neck. He held out a large watch of gold so bright that no one could mistake it for the real thing.

"Beat it," Alberto snapped, and the man turned with a shrug. He tried to smile again, holding his hand now over hers on his chest, but that flick of irritation had released anger in him that he could not curb. "Please, Nancy, not like this."

She only put her arms tightly around his neck, her face against his cheek, and her voice was saying, "Goodbye, Alberto, goodbye, goodbye." He tried to hold onto her, to think of something to say, but could not bear the thought of this scene being enacted where people were waiting for taxis, their faces turned toward them with blank curiosity.

"*Signori, un taxi?*" the driver was saying impatiently at their side. Nancy spun and ducked into the car through the door the man held open. He slammed it and walked around to the driver's seat. Alberto hesitated, hands behind his back.

The window was open. He stared at her, knowing his face had assumed its most ironic pose.

"Nancy, how silly."

But she was leaning with one hand on the seat, her face to him, mouth slightly open. He put his hands on the door.

"Where to?" the driver was saying.

"I will call," he said.

"No, no, no," and her head shook wildly, hair swinging as if in a frenzied dance.

"Well, then," and he heard his own voice assume its clear, even tone, "Goodbye, Mrs. Mitchell. And do have a good trip."

"Piazza San Pancrazio," her voice was saying, Alberto stood, her face looked puzzled, and then he was staring at the back of a green-and-black car that moved quickly out into the traffic, and nothing moved in the rear window at all.

He looked around him quickly. No one was paying attention. A tug on his sleeve made him whirl and at waist level a cupped hand was held out, beyond it the brown, pleading face of a gypsy brat. The child's whining voice, the overacted and nasal plaint like some Arab chant nagged at Alberto. His hand drew back, he saw the boy duck, silenced, but instead of swinging he turned on his heels and strode out, nudging two men who were waiting at the bus stop.

He would go to her apartment. He would call that evening. Surely he could dissuade her. All evening he wandered nervously from park to park, seeing very little around him. He would buy tickets for the trip to Greece. Would present them to her. She would accept. Later, finding himself on the Quirinale, he stood by the rearing horses of Castor and Pollux, watching the sun go down. This was absurd. Why should he plead? He was profoundly indifferent anyway. He stood with his hands clasped behind his back, almost mimicking the two guards at the entrance to the palace behind him. "I am profoundly indifferent," he murmured half out loud, letting the words roll and tumble in his own tongue. The sun dropped out of sight. He was suddenly very tired. A few cars squealed by on the cobblestones.

He walked quickly down the steps and toward the Corso. First he would call Assunta. He stopped at a bar, dialed the number. But it had only rung twice when it was cut off and an officious voice announced that the number had been disconnected, the party was no longer there.

"Why?" he said abruptly. "What do you mean?" She had lived there ever since they had come to Rome.

But the operator had hung up. He held on to the buzzing receiver. The wall was floating away from him, the receiver with its cord was the only thing attaching him to another object. He smacked it back on its hook.

Outside he began to walk rapidly in the drection of the apartment, but near the Corso he stopped. He was certain she would not be there, or Giorgio or Teresa, and something told him the factual certainty of unlit windows, names no longer on the door, would be too much. Down the narrow slit of the street he could see the quick glint and flash of traffic, hear its gathering rumble. Already people were lining up at the door of the movie house beside him. He was hungry. Nancy would not be at work the next day. She had cleaned out her desk Friday.

The line had reached him. A stout bald man with his wife was standing beside Alberto.

"Is it any good?" Alberto asked.

"Eh?"

"The movie. Is it good?"

The man turned down his mouth, held out his hands. "*Be'*. It's Toto and Fabrizio. It has to be."

"My cousin saw it," the woman said, smiling effusively, and her husband raised his eyes slightly to Alberto as if to say, Women, they always say more than they need to. "She said it was very, very diverting. An excellently funny scene where they are in this boat together..."

"*Ahi,* Isabella. You don't need to tell him the whole thing." She threw up a hand. "I was only explaining."

They had started to move forward.

"You're most persuasive," Alberto said suavely. "I'll join you."

"Please," and the little man half turned as if to show he was willing to talk more. "You are from Rome?"

"No. From Verona."

"Ah. Visiting?"

"I am a cultural expert. At an embassy."

The round face showed immediate respect, and the man's wife looked admiringly at Alberto.

"A diplomat?" she said.

"A diplomat." Alberto nodded gravely.

Nancy had driven no farther than the Esedra when she realized she did not want to go home, not quite yet. Carey would probably be there and her mind was too jumbled.

"I'll get off here," she said, leaning forward and touching the man's shoulder.

He pulled over and turned to her sullenly, but she gave him a large tip and he smiled, touching the rim of his battered cap.

She walked around the edge of the circle, past the Baths, the heavy brick façade of Santa Maria degli Angeli. How like Alberto to hide his true emotions at the end, to become so stiff and formal. That hurt, and for a moment she swallowed hard as she strolled up the street, past the Grand Hotel's entrance. But she had been right. The quicker the better. She had wondered all day if she would have the courage to do it. Parting could have dragged on all week, and she needed now to concentrate on getting them packed up, away. Even the thought of that, of sitting in a train compartment, only herself and Carey again at last, their luggage racked above them, on their way north—Florence, Venice, Paris—made her pause, catch her breath, want to laugh.

She needed to sit down. She passed the Acqua Felice, crossed the street and walked into Santa Maria della Vittoria. One more look at this grotesquerie, she thought. She found a pew where she could see the altarpiece clearly, the leering angel with his poised dart, Saint Teresa languidly spreading under her tumbled vestments, eyes lidded, lips spread, her hand drooping and swollen with desire.

How strange Alberto had been in Palestrina and in that ruin high on the hill. He was so passionate, so unpredictable. At least on the surface. Because underneath all that, he was like Frank in some ways, and in the last few weeks she had been often confused, seeing their faces, gestures of their hands, superimposed—until three nights ago she had understood that her mind was trying to put them together, or at least something in her wanted the comparison to be consciously made. Puzzling, because what could be more different than a somewhat unsuccessful director from Columbus, Ohio, and a suave and mercurial Italian from Torino. But that shifting surface only concealed a strong, even devious, self-consciousness; somewhere far inside, plots and conspiracies were being planned, but unknown to the man himself in many ways, disguises within disguises that she was certain kept Frank and Alberto as hidden from themselves as from her.

Patterns. She felt no temptation to kneel this time. How fleshy, sensuous, polished marble could seem when touched by a Bernini, how dead and cold the other statues were. And anyway, the question was not just how similar the men had been, but what was it in her that needed those characteristics, sought them out. Was it truly as Frank said, her own patterned needs looking again and again for the same man in different costumes? But having seen that, would she ever quite so unsuspectingly reach for such a person again? She doubted that. "Oh, Alberto, you remind me of Frank when you do that." She had said that so often recently. And today, looking at him in the piazza waiting for her to come back from buying stamps, she had felt a clear aversion to the way he sat, face staring forward into the bright sun, not looking at her directly but surely seeing her every motion. Peripheral vision. They saw on every side of them, but what they saw was always other people looking at themselves. Had Frank or Alberto ever really seen *her?*

Then, feeling herself flush as if she were exposed to a view more public than any eyes outside herself, she wondered why she had not wanted to be seen, unless she had feared, even more than either of them, that there was nothing there to be seen. She sat back, closed her eyes, but still saw angel and saint poised, an eternally languid anticipation. Alberto must have sensed she had made up her mind about that day, have wanted her the same way she had wanted him; one last time, there in the grass and stones, and even now she imagined her body spread to him again, his short, quick breaths. Those children, the rocks. They could have been killed. But how unreal it was. She would not remember Alberto as he had been in those *pensioni,* naked and passionate, but as it was this last day, wanting each other, clothed and unsatisfied. Or was the truth simply that they had always been that way, even when their naked flesh had touched; so much kept back, kept back. That was no way to live.

An old woman in the pew nearby snapped open her purse, wiped her mouth with a lace handkerchief and returned to prayer. Nancy looked at Saint Teresa again and thought of that glowering, hooded figure in the piazza far below them, Giordano Bruno in his field of flowers buzzing with messengers from the countryside. She had been reading a small collection from his work that Ian had given her. He seemed such a dour figure in the statue, but his words offered an ecstatic view, all things pulsing and radiant with a God, the world as God's body; and on the other hand here was this woman, straining, lying so eagerly and seeming so sensuous, yet there was a painful asceticism in such a willed joy.

She looked at her hands. The light fell on them and spilled over onto the marble floor. Fullness. It was always there. She probably would not understand much of this past year, and there was no way to force the moments she most loved, when things seemed clear. Being ready for them was the only thing, and no matter how the saints went about it, that must have been what many of them had been trying to do also. A light would break out quietly. Radiance. Her hands holding something simple and unexpected. *Kyrie Eleison. Christe Eleison.*

Nancy knelt. None of the prayers she knew seemed right, so she said her name and then Carey's, and when she stood, slightly dizzy from rising too suddenly, she had to close her eyes for a moment, her own blood humming in her ears.

# 5

The concert hall was a large room in the same building as
the British library, and it was full of people. Carey and Ian
had never discussed the audience, and when Ian or Ikbal had
called them "friends" or "patrons" Carey had thought of a
small number of people. But when he stood by the crack in
the door, watching them gather, he realized Ian had many
"friends," and those friends had friends, and people knew
about this man and his voice. He recognized faces from some
of the smaller concerts he and Nancy had attended, and he
picked out the ones he knew—Ikbal and his mother and even
Pierre with Manuel. The count came in and sat down with
Ikbal. Ian was quietly warming up his voice in the room
behind him.

"Don't make yourself nervous," he said, and then he continued slow scales. He was pale, nervously frowning as if his
eyes hurt him.

The room was almost full. People arriving in the back
paused to find space. But Carey could not stop looking at the
audience he knew—the count with the usual childlike shy-
ness in his face, listening and smiling as Ikbal told him something in an animated way, hands shaping in air a circular
object she must have been describing, Pierre so large and
aware of his size as he hunched in his chair, legs drawn
tightly together, but by the very act of trying to become
smaller accentuating his burliness, and then Ikbal again,
finished talking, her hands fluttering vaguely as if trying to
find some place to settle, and his rush of love for her seemed
to have nowhere to go. He was leaving in three days, and
when he looked at Nancy, sheathed in a pale satin dress,
long arms bare, he could not help remembering what she had

said about having her own life ahead of her, and he wondered what that would mean. Her eyes were looking around quickly from place to place, her hands twisted in her lap—nervous again. For him.

"We're on."

Ian was standing beside him, the white-winged collar, the formal cutaway jacket with its tails making him lean and statuesque. He handed Carey the music, smiled, said, *"Merde,"* and they walked out to that moment of silence, then applause, and they bowed and arranged themselves.

The windows were open on to the courtyard. Already the room was very warm, a sultry evening that needed to break in storms, but from time to time a breeze circled in. Carey did not look at anyone. He tried to cut the whole room down to just Ian and himself. They began.

At some point he became detached enough to sense the difference between what they were describing, a cold and barren landscape through which that hopelessly lovelorn wanderer sings his way, and the late May, Roman night. But it was not amusing. As he sang, Ian was making that landscape, singing as if the man were himself, and they went into it, past crows and weathervanes and ice toward the blind organ-grinder, and Carey had the uncanny sense of both following Ian's voice and making that voice rise deep out of himself, through his fingers and the sounding strings. The brief silences between the songs did not interrupt, were merely rests of a different rhythm, until the silence itself worked its way up and into the songs, into the final tenuous and halting questions.

They were applauding. Ian bowed, Carey stumbled slightly against him as they left, and they stood for a moment without speaking before coming out again, and two times more, until they could tell the applause was pattering off. They looked at each other, and Ian was holding his hands tightly together because they were trembling, his face and hair soaked with sweat. That was when Carey noticed how hot he was himself. Ian held out both of his hands and, taking Carey's as if they were going to swing in a circle he said, "Thank you." The audience started coming in and they all said how fine it was, but Carey had trouble saying the polite phrases for a while because he could not forget the way Ian sang that last song, the strange, hushed intensity of those vacant questions.

There was a reception given by the library and he had to talk in Italian to a number of kind people. He was so tired he could hardly stand, but luckily each conversation lasted only a few minutes, and the next one was always the same. When it was finally time to go, he looked for Ian but Ikbal said he had left early, pleading exhaustion, so he and Nancy and Ikbal walked out together. They stood awkwardly on the sidewalk near the four fountains, looking down the long barrel toward the Piazza Quirinale and out the other spokes to the obelisks dimly lit, feeling perfectly centered on an empty stage, and Ikbal took both Carey's hands and kissed him. She said she wanted to walk, even though already there were a few smatterings of rain. He thought of going with her, but he wanted to be alone.

For a long time Carey could not sleep. He lay listening to the storm gather somewhere distantly, muttering toward clearer bursts of thunder, heard the apartment grow quiet, the air outside hushed, and even the slight drizzle paused. Everything was waiting, suspended. He felt as if he could not breathe. And then the air exploded, rain began falling in solid waves, and lightning broke again and again over the things of his room—piano, bench, desk, his own white and naked feet. None of it seemed familiar. He had always liked thunderstorms, the way they would bunch up the air and make him feel tight enough to scream, and then burst and clear up everything. But he felt nothing this time. He closed his eyes and counted the interval between the light on his lids and the thunder. He slept, but restlessly, and as he did, he struggled as if there were something very important for him to pay attention to.

He turned and saw a letter pinned against the wall, only the light was so dim that he could not read the handwriting, and what words he could make out were like Yugoslavian mixtures of consonants. He took it to the window that turned into a door with a long flight of stairs, so he went down hoping to find some light in the room below, but the only things there were piles of old newspapers and he did not want to see them. Outside it had begun to snow and flakes dusted his eyes. Under the frozen surface of the pond he crossed, wherever the black ice was swept clean by the wind, Constantine's face stared up at him, wide-eyed and indifferent, but always in the same position no matter how far he walked, and sometimes it was Frank's face and he was sitting hunched against a wall, hands folded in his lap.

"Dad," he called, but his voice would not come out of his throat. The ice was cracked as if struck by a wrench. The face was Ian's, eyes wide, mouth drawn down, and he was pressing his hands flat against the glass as if he were running out of air.

Carey sat up in bed, soaked with sweat. The storm was over and a clean, cool breeze was on his back. He had to hurry. He dressed, paused in the hallway and let himself out quietly. Three o'clock, no buses were running, so he walked fast down the hill, through the Trastevere with its few straggling drunks, over the Tiber as sluggish and dulled as ever, and as he heard it sluffing beneath him he was not certain whether he was dreaming or awake. He began to run, despite the pain in his side. For the moment of knocking he felt foolish, knowing he could never explain if he was wrong, but when the door opened immediately and Ian was standing there in his bathrobe, his glasses on, hair disheveled, Carey knew he was right to go.

"Carey?" he said slowly.

"Are you all right?"

He did not answer and took off his glasses, rubbing at his eyes. Carey stepped in.

"I was worried. I shouldn't have come, I thought..." and he saw a folded raincoat and revolver lying on it, barrel pointing blankly at the stuffed back of the chair.

Ian closed the door, put an arm around Carey's shoulders and they walked together into the living room where the piano hunched darkly and one small lamp by a chair cast its yellowish circle over pale-green upholstery.

"What did you think?"

Carey stopped. "I thought you might kill yourself. That gun."

Ian cocked his head to one side. A smile flicked over his face and then he was expressionless. He nodded.

"Sit down."

Carey went to a chair, his legs weak, and Ian pulled up the piano bench to sit near him.

"I'm glad you came."

"But was I right?"

"I've thought of it often enough lately. It wouldn't be hard."

"Don't."

"I won't. I don't think I have the courage."

"But you don't need to kill yourself," and then Carey used those words—how things would change, how much everyone needed him—hearing how lame they sounded, and when he was done Ian said quietly, "You know all that doesn't make much difference when you feel at an end, don't you?"

"But I don't want you to. Doesn't it matter that I care, others do? Isn't there something to be done?"

Ian shook his head. "If you mean suicide, it isn't a matter of words or actions of others, is it? Even your caring simply wouldn't be enough."

"But it should be."

He shook his head again.

"I *want* it to be."

"Why? Nobody can be that much to anyone else."

"Wasn't Pierre to you?"

He opened the hand that was resting on the arm of Carey's chair and looked at it.

"There's the illusion at the first pain of break-up that the person is everything, but then you see what's worse, that actually he was nothing, a beautiful vessel you could pour your need to love into. If you could."

"You did."

He looked at Carey, his lips mocking, eyebrows lifted.

"Did I?" And he looked at his hand again. "No, Carey. I'll tell you something I think I understand. All this time I've thought I needed to be loved, and that I was weak maybe, certainly lonely, very absorptive, someone who took, took, took—a form of greed—and that my problem was I couldn't get enough love. So someone like Pierre seemed perfect to me, that big-hearted, generous, mothering creature. But I was wrong."

He shifted slightly, ran a hand through his hair. "What I have is a hunger, not to be loved, but to love. To give. To open all those closed rooms in me and let someone in, taking that risk once and for all. But I can't. Something holds me back. Some fear. Maybe just of being left. But because I can't, I *am* left."

His voice trembled slightly. Carey could not quite follow it all. The words were clear, but they were so exaggerated, as if he had worked it all out too precisely.

"But I thought you just said that was impossible, that no one could mean that much to anyone."

"That doesn't rid me of the need, does it? It is impossible. That's the point."

Carey shook his head. "But if it's impossible, and you can't stop wanting it..."

"Exactly."

Carey stood up. "That's not right. It's all muddled."

"Why?"

"I don't know. But you make it sound so cold. As if it didn't make any difference. Any of it. And you're wrong."

Ian stood too. "Carey, I'm sorry. I don't know if the things I say are right or wrong. I tend to be absolute, I guess."

Carey was not going to settle for that. He would go and nothing would be changed. He could see the chair lumped in the hallway, imagined the gun still lying there.

"Why?"

Ian smiled crookedly, a frozen mask. "Why not? Absolute stand toward an absolute world, it's tit for tat."

Carey hit him, a flat slap hard across the face, his anger dimming everything to black. "You are not to kill yourself, you are not to kill yourself," and when Ian tried to hold on to him, Carey put his fists against the man's chest and hid his face in them and Ian kept saying his name until he calmed.

"It's all right, it's all right," he murmured, and he sat Carey down on the couch. He stood, his back turned, and stared out the opened window. "I'll tell you the truth about this evening. That gun was not intended for me. I had just come back myself when you arrived. Tonight I tried to kill Pierre."

Carey held still. "You shot him?"

"No. I could have. I found them sitting in Piazza Navona. They were side by side on a bench, staring into the fountain, Manuel's arm around Pierre as he always does when he is drunk. But not unless he is. I knew them from far away, and with the water falling, the little group of people nearby with their guitarist, there was enough noise so that they did not hear me, even when I was right behind them. I had the gun in my coat pocket, I held it only a foot away from the back of Pierre's head. Then I thought, No, I will kill Manuel. But when I was about to pull the trigger, Pierre stirred, they had been absolutely still until then as if asleep, and said, 'I think I had too many clams, I feel ill,' and Manuel clucked and patted him on the shoulder, and I aimed at Pierre again because the sound of his voice, so relaxed, so accustomed to finding sympathy by such childish complaints, absolutely enraged me," and Ian leaned now, both hands on the sill, his voice trembling. He took a deep breath, spoke calmly again.

"He burped. Coarse, his usual uninhibited self. Patted his gut, said, 'Ah that's better.' I imagined it, the bullet smashing into the back of his head, Manuel turning, a shot for him. The whole mess. But it was so like Pierre, you know. Eating too much. Complaining as if it were the clams' fault. I started laughing, they leapt up, and oh, it was even funnier the way Manuel's gesture mocked that lifted arm of the statue, shielding himself against some imaginary blow from above. I just walked away. I never fired a shot."

He was silent. Carey had followed it all vividly, was relieved to know nothing had been done, but something else was seeping in that made a complete separation between himself and the man who was now staring at him with kind and gentle eyes.

"You must be very weary," Ian said, and he went to get some pillows and blanket which he piled on the couch beside Carey. He looked down at him.

"And now it is my turn. Are you sure *you* will be all right?"

For a long time Carey did not answer. He thought about the last few weeks, about how everything had begun to seem broken and ended, how at times there was some terrible grayness just beyond everything.

"So that's what it's like," he said finally.

"What?"

"To want to die. To not care."

Ian waited, but Carey had nothing more to say. He would think about all this, and one day, maybe soon, he would make Frank talk to him. They would have a lot to talk about.

Ian helped him spread out the blankets and then he went to the other room. Carey lay in the dark becoming more and more sleepy. But for one moment he woke fully. The problem was that he would never really understand because he could not do it. Whether it was killing himself, or someone else. He tried to decide whether that was good or bad, but slipped off into drowsiness. Later he woke again, certain that Ian was bending over him laughing, a gun in his hand, but the room was empty, until he woke finally to a day of full sunshine and Ian was looking at him from the doorway. This time Carey laughed at the way Ian's hair stood out in tufts, his eyes slightly frowning because he could not find his glasses.

"You look like an ostrich," Carey said.

They went together to the café near his apartment and had some coffee and pastries, and Ian came with him as far as the bus stop.

"You will write me?" Ian asked.

— 315 —

"I'll try."

"I'll be here. For a long time."

After he climbed into the bus, Carey tried to see him, but he had left the corner.

They herded their dolly full of bags through the huge barn of the terminal. It was a windy day, grit blowing up into their faces, scraps of paper suddenly lifting like shreds off the pavement. The train was already in its quay and they hurried along until finding an empty compartment, then worked their way in, stashed their bags, paid the stout and groaning porter, and sat down panting. Nancy made her usual frantic search through purse and pockets to make sure the passports were there, and then she calmed down. But Carey sensed she was looking for someone ever since they had entered the station and she kept glancing out the window.

"There," she said and pointed.

A tapping at the window. Ikbal was standing on tiptoes, her face peering up.

"Go on, Carey. Quickly."

He left the compartment, went through the corridor and down to the platform. For a moment they stood there, apart, and then they held each other, and Carey did not mind that a woman was beside them with a little girl looking up at one of the windows and talking to some man leaning out. He held on blindly and she said his name in his ear. A whistle. She let go of him, pushed him toward the train. He stood on the first step, one hand on the rail, one still holding hers. She moved back, her mouth slightly open. The wind gusted and a newspaper blew up against her legs, clinging against them. The train began to move. He leaned out. "Ikbal, Ikbal," he called, she stared at him, and the little girl as if she found the name wonderfully funny, jumped up and down, holding her mother's hand and echoing, "Ikbal, Ikbal," in a shrill voice.

He paused in the corridor to put his face in the breeze from an open window before he went in and sat down. They watched the city slowly decay into scruffy fields, some ruins, a road with freshly whitewashed markers.

At Civitavecchia a broad face peered at them from the doorway. Two children scrambled in, a boy and a girl, she in pinafore, he in tight shorts that showed his thick, already mannish knees, and their mother wedged in, her hips and billowing breasts so abundant that she had to squeeze painfully as she entered. But she laughed, a gap-toothed spread, pushed with a fist against her breasts as if punching everything back in place, and deposited herself in the space for two people. She spoke constantly to her children to be good, to pull down the dress, not to touch the lady's magazine, and gradually Carey accepted the invasion. The blankness, the unceasing wince of pain began to subside. Next to him the woman, panting even as she sat still, folded her hands on the small jut that was her lap.

*"Ma che bel giorno,"* she said in his ear, and for a while they talked and she satisfied her totally open curiosity about their nationality, destination, relationship, ages.

Carey dozed, in spite of her mountainous stirrings, the voices of the children like distant large birds.

He woke suddenly with the sun full on his lap, his hands open as if cupping it. Nancy was sleeping, and the woman was reaching in a bag on the other side of her, crinkling it, while her children sat on the edges of their seats. Through half-opened eyes Carey watched her hands, also flooded with light, in spite of their pudginess deftly peel back the skin of an orange, the juice and bright pulp flecked with blood-red catching the light as if she held the sun itself. She was breaking off sections, leaning forward to give them to her children.

*"Buon appetito,"* Carey said.

She turned smiling. *"Ah. Grazie. Altrettano."*

Lifting her hand with a bright crescent of fruit in it she said, *"Vuole?"*

Carey smiled, opened his mouth. She popped it in, laughed in a great heave while her children bounced with excited shrieks, and held up another. Nancy, half awake, began to smile, the woman said, *"Guarda, guarda,"* and fed Carey again. The juice broke over his tongue, he swallowed, and asked for more.

## ABOUT THE AUTHOR

T. Alan Broughton's first novel, *A Family Gathering*, was published in 1977. He is also an accomplished poet whose most recent volume, *Far From Home*, appeared last year. Mr. Broughton lives in Burlington, Vermont.

# NEW FROM FAWCETT CREST